THE
STARS
INSIDE
US

KRISTY GARDNER

THE STARS INSIDE US

KRISTY GARDNER

CITY OWL
PRESS

THE STARS INSIDE US
The Broken Stars, Book 3

CITY OWL PRESS
www.cityowlpress.com

Cover Design by MiblArt. All stock photos licensed appropriately.

Edited by Danielle DeVor.

For information on subsidiary rights, please contact the publisher at info@cityowlpress.com.

Print Edition ISBN: 978-1-64898-480-8

Digital Edition ISBN: 978-1-64898-481-5

Printed in the United States of America

PRAISE FOR KRISTY GARDNER

"Heartbreaking, beautiful, terrifying, and hopeful. The journey is one of several twists, ups, and downs that kept me captivated from the first page. The world is so immersive that there were moments I forgot I was reading at all. *The Stars Inside Us* is the perfect finale to a riveting series." — *Madison Lawson, author of The Registration*

"An incendiary end to the series, *The Stars Inside Us* takes readers deeper into the bowels of a post-apocalyptic world ravaged by an alien invasion where the only way to survive is together. For fans of twisty dystopian queer fiction." — *Sarina Dahlan, author of The Four Cities series*

"Visceral, creepy, and disturbing. Dark horror fans will love this startling debut." — *Chana Porter, author of The Seep*

"High passion, high stakes, and otherworldly romance! Kristy Gardner delivers sultry sci-fi and a journey of self-acceptance with *The Darkest Stars.*" — *J. Dianne Dotson, author of The Shadow Galaxy*

"*The Stars in Their Eyes* is a juicily twisted path through what it means to be human, what it means to be alien, and, above all, when our world is lost, what it means to find home in each other." — *Ann Fraistat, author of What We Harvest*

"*The Darkest Stars* is that rare smooth sequel that gives you just enough resolution to leave you even more desperate for the next installment. Readers will be on the edge of their seat as they run along after Calay's struggles through danger, deception, and darkness." — *Ciel Pierlot, author of Bluebird*

"A gripping tale of survival. *The Stars in their Eyes* shows us the dark, violent side of humanity, but also the promise—however out of reach it may seem—of something brighter." — *N.C. Scrimgeour, author of The Waystations Series*

"A pacy, visceral and action-packed romp through a vividly depicted broken future. *Resident Evil* meets *War of the Worlds* in this compelling debut." — *Kate Murray, author of We Who Hunt The Hollow*

"Heartbreaking and heartwarming, this book has great chaos and all the feels. It's sci-fi and adventure and romance and a must-read!" — *K.C. Harper, author of Marked For Grace*

"A harrowing journey of self-reliance and acceptance–while kicking some serious ass. *The Darkest Stars* proves even the most damaged people can heal and do incredible things." — *Heather Chambers, author of Earth Sucks*

For those who (eventually) choose their own ending.
Light 'em up.

AUTHOR'S NOTE

At the gentle request of some readers, I have included content warnings for this book, and others, on my website. If you are someone who prefers to know what they're getting themselves into (protect your mental health), please scan the QR code below or visit KristyGardner.com/Books.

CHAPTER ONE

THE NOISE in the cafeteria was almost loud enough to drown out the screaming in Calay's mind.

She gripped the aluminum tray with white knuckles, surveying the expansive room for the first time. Long rows of plastic tables formed the dining area. Resistance members hunched over their own trays, shoveling nondescript globs of leafy green vegetables and some kind of thick paste into their hungry maws. She squinted, cataloguing each bobbing head, one by one. Men. Everywhere she looked. The room was heaving with them. She shuddered. Slivers of grey light peered through rectangular windows lining the concrete walls. The scraping of spoons on metal reverberated through her mind, aggravating the headache she hadn't been able to shake since she'd arrived. Every atom in her cells vibrated, reminding her—not for the first time—she shouldn't be here. They hadn't stopped reminding her since she made the decision to take the first step down off that ledge, toward the compound.

As she'd knelt in the snow, her arms raised high above her head while they'd shoved the barrels of their guns into her ribs, she knew convincing them to fight together was going to be the hardest thing she'd ever had to do. Harder than living without her parents. Harder than existing without Tess. And definitely harder than escaping an alien starship millions of lightyears away, leaving Jacob for dead, along with everyone else she'd ever loved.

She thought she'd prepared herself for the challenges ahead.

She couldn't have been more wrong.

It'd been six weeks since she'd crash-landed back on Earth and walked through the front door of the Resistance. Well, walked was an overstatement. It was more like they'd dragged her through it by the skin of her neck.

Calay pulled her stiffening shoulders back at the memory.

Six weeks since they locked her in a four-by-four cement room with steel-grated floors. Five weeks since they strapped her to a gurney, flipped her upside down, tried to force their version of the truth out of her. Four weeks since she told them to go fuck themselves and drove her point home with an elbow to one guard's nose and another's groin. Three weeks since she resolved to fix the damage she'd done. Two weeks since they finally took the zap-straps off her wrists. One since they promised she'd be released into the general population.

And they'd made good on their word.

Here she was, free to roam as she so chose. Only now, as she chewed on the truth of what she'd gotten herself into, she wasn't so sure she was ready to swallow it.

Calay lurched forward at a sudden jolt to her left side. Her tray angled sharply. Half of the beige contents slopped on her Resistance standard-issue black boots. She threw one hand up against the cold wall, steadied herself. She didn't know how things worked here, but she knew she'd have to be tough in this place. Not let anyone push her around. Even though she was a woman. *Because* she was a woman. She turned to give her assailant a piece of her mind and gasped, her breath catching in her throat as she sized up the person who'd shoved her. He was a beast of a man. He towered over Calay's 5'4" frame. He had to be at least a foot and a half taller than she was. Probably more. Wider, too. His thick neck bulged at what looked like seams. *No, scars.* They traveled up his throat, over his right cheek and eyelid, and across his bald head before disappearing under army-green fatigues. His grey eyes—the one he still had left—tore through Calay's bravado. She shrank under his gaze. The last thing she wanted to do was get pulverized before she'd even begun her mission. In front of everyone.

More bees with honey.

She tried to apologize, to make amends for whatever slight she may have caused by simply being at the wrong place at the wrong time, but no sound made its way past her lips. A menacing growl rumbled past his. It hovered between them before he mumbled something about new recruits and plodded toward the nearest table. Several Resistance members scattered out of his way as he forced himself down between them. His attention turned to the people in front of him, Calay allowed herself to breathe again.

That was close.

She chanced a glance back. The line for food was getting longer, the number of free seats, fewer. The energy, unruly. She shuddered and forced her shaking legs forward, aiming for a spot in the exact opposite side of the room.

Calay set her tray on the table, felt a foldable plastic chair bend under her weight as she sat down, and tried to make herself invisible. Difficult, given she seemed to be the only woman.

She pushed around what was left of her breakfast, realizing she wasn't the only one who'd noticed that fact. She peeked from behind her lashes to catch them watching her, only to look away when she'd meet their gazes.

It was a familiar feeling. When she'd been forced here against her will by Guy all those months ago, she'd experienced the same thing. Only this time, no one had attacked her. Yet. Calay gripped her spoon, shivered. Guy was dead. For good, this time. She'd watched Tess execute him at point blank range. She could still picture the Rorschach shapes of his blood on the cavern floor. Still, something about him lived on in her mind, pooled like oil. The way his rank breath clung to her skin, the feel of his rough fingers against her belly.

She dropped her spoon and clasped her hands beneath the table, as if she could clamp her memory shut. Seal it forever. It could have been worse, she reminded herself; he could have raped her. She was grateful that hadn't been the case. Still, the threat was there.

Here.

Everywhere.

Since the Change.

Before it.

It'd been a while since Calay had felt this way. She'd forgotten how afraid she'd been, and for how long. How safe she'd felt in Jacob's company. His presence insulated her from it. Not that she needed him to protect her, but he'd been a safe place to land.

Until he wasn't.

Finding out he'd lied to her, betrayed her, manipulated her. They might have had a special connection, but Calay would never really know how much of that was real and how much was fabricated.

It didn't matter. The truth was all that mattered now. That, and the mission.

Calay pried her hands apart. Her heart ached. She traced her thumb across the thin dark outline of a heart she'd carved into her right wrist after they'd uncuffed her. She'd slipped a pen off the table after she signed her life away to them. Or at least, her loyalty. Late that night, she'd taken the pen apart. Using the ink and a thin piece of barbed wire she'd found in the yard on one of her escorted outings, she'd given herself the tattoo. A memento to remind her of the promise she'd made to herself. To Tess. It wasn't the lockets she and Tess shared, which Calay had tossed off the side of the Loft before going with Jacob to Téras, but it was the next closest thing. Something to remember their love by. Something to remind her to keep fighting when the going got tough.

Like now.

It wasn't fair. None of it was. Calay was going to see to it that women, gays, and theys had a safe space here. Hybrids, too. But first, she had to get these men to listen. She wasn't sure how she was going to do that, but she needed to do it soon. Locked away, she'd heard the guards whispering about increased attacks by the Others. Evidently they'd abandoned the pods, taken up their true form. A vision of Ash, half-transformed in the starship, lurked at the back of Calay's mind.

The Resistance didn't know what forced the change. Calay did. It was her.

Jacob had warned her they'd come for her. That they could sense her heat signature, and now that she'd destroyed their ship and killed Elora, their leader, they'd hunt her down. Her heat signature might be invisible to humans, but it was like a honing beacon for the Others.

Calay knew she didn't have much time. If she really was going to lead the Resistance—and humanity—to victory, she was going to need her strength.

She picked up her spoon and shoveled greens into her mouth. She grimaced at their bitterness. Though she had to admit it wasn't the worst, and at least it, for once, wasn't green beans. She took another bite.

"This seat taken?"

Calay dragged her eyes up a pair of dark pants, grey T-shirt, and dark journeyman jacket. They settled on Adam's clean shaven, well-chiseled face. Before Calay could answer, he tossed a heavy book on the table and slipped his tall frame into the chair opposite her.

"Do I get a choice?" Calay tilted her head.

"Not really. Last I checked, you're still on probation." Adam raised his eyebrows, settling.

"So what's this then? A performance review?"

"Something like that."

"Hm." Calay nodded, poked at her food some more. She eyed the book. The cover showed a drawing of a wild plant with thick thorns and dark berries. She reached forward, ran her fingers along the cracked spine. She flipped through the pages. Inside were sketches of other flora, notes in the yellowed margins about seasonality and companion planting. "You like reading?"

"I like eating." Adam smiled, scooped a spoonful of paste into his mouth. "This is how we're going to do that."

"We're going to eat books?"

"Ha-ha. Did you just make a joke, Calay?"

"I have my moments."

"You'll have more of them soon if you behave yourself this time. I know it's only been a few hours, but how's it going so far?" Adam's wide green eyes grew soft as he trained them on her. "Settling in?"

"Oh, you know." She placed the book back on the table. "Aside from being bullied by ogres, and aliens trying to kill us, and the only woman in a sea of men who can't keep their eyes to themselves, it's all hunky-dory."

Adam blinked through a curtain of dark lashes. "You aren't the only woman."

"The only one I can see."

"Then you aren't looking hard enough. What about her?" Adam pointed his spork over Calay's shoulder.

She turned, scanned the bustling crowd. It parted and her eyes grew wide when her gaze settled on the group perched just two tables over.

Adam was right. There was another woman.

Warm caramel skin, short dark hair styled into a fauxhawk of ringlets, strong cheekbones. Calay watched as the woman's shoulders shifted beneath an old, faded grey T-shirt, her hips curved beneath fitted blue denim jeans. She moved with a confidence Calay had never felt, a grace she couldn't name. The woman's lips turned upward, her smile reaching her wide, charcoal eyes. Calay couldn't look away. She was striking.

"Earth to Calay?" Adam's voice broke through her thoughts. "Now who's staring?"

Calay's cheeks flushed. He was right a second time. She'd just been wishing she could disappear under the weight of others' gazes, and she'd just done the same to someone else.

"She's not the only one," Adam continued, dragging a wide hand through his dark, floppy hair. "There's more."

"Why are there so few of us though? So many men?" Calay cleared her throat and turned back to him. "It doesn't make any sense."

"I'll admit the...leadership...under Smith was, how do I say this?"

"Sexist and misogynistic as fuck?"

Adam cleared his throat. "Problematic."

Calay grunted.

"We had rules and most of the time, the rules worked."

"Most of the time isn't good enough."

"Which is why I'm working to change things."

"Right." Calay shook her head and dropped her eyes to her tray.

Once Calay recovered from being waterboarded, Adam had explained what happened to Smith. He'd suffered serious injuries from Max's attack after Calay escaped the compound all those months ago. He would have recovered from them too, had they not become infected. He'd later died and in his place, Adam stepped up to lead the Resistance. To bring about change. To fight the Others. Calay was lucky he did. If Smith was still around, she wasn't so sure he would have let her go free. Or even live. After some serious word gymnastics, Adam did. She'd never say it to his face, but Calay knew the only reason she was still alive was because he'd believed her when she told him she wanted to help them. Adam understood the value of working together. Or at least, the complexities of it. And that had been Calay's Hail Mary.

"I know you don't believe it, but I told you the first time you were here, this is a good place. It's safe. You're right about it not being safe enough, though. We're working to bring more women in. Make it more equal. Safety in numbers, right? So that's one problem solved. There's not much I can do about the aliens, but we can see about that ogre."

Calay seized her opportunity. "I appreciate that, Adam. I really do. I know we didn't end things on the best of terms last time, and I'm grateful for everything you've done for me."

"Stronger together." He nodded.

Calay angled herself across the table. "That's exactly my point. We need to collaborate to fight the Others."

"We are."

"We need to do more."

"We're working on it."

"Not fast enough."

Adam frowned, lowered his spork. "How many times do we have to go through this, Calay? There's a process. Not to mention trust. Show me you can do things the right way. You'll see they work."

Calay's brows matched his furrow. She pushed her tray aside, leaned closer. "There is no right way, Adam. That's what I've been saying. We do things your way and people—these people—die."

"Not to be dramatic or anything," Adam muttered as he scraped the last of the food off his tray.

"Call it whatever you want, but you know I'm right. That's why you let me out after I—"

"Shh," Adam hissed. He glanced around, tossed a glare at Calay. He took a deep breath. When he continued, she could barely hear his voice above the hum of the cafeteria. "As far as anyone in this place is concerned, that was a Council decision. No one will ask; it's standard procedure. But I swear to God, Calay, no one can find out I ushered you through the system."

"Why not?" Calay was practically climbing over the table. She lowered her voice. "I mean, they're going to find out eventually. The Council will, anyhow."

"They'll find out when I know what the hell I'm going to do with you. I don't mean to be rude, but in the meantime, keep your head down and your mouth shut. You're right, I know we have to do more. The Others' attacks are getting worse. But now is not the time. Not yet. Calay, please. I took a huge risk and already sacrificed my convictions for you once. Don't make me regret it."

An unsettling anger rose in Calay's stomach. She clenched her teeth. The chair groaned as she leaned back in the seat. "Or you'll what? Lock me back up? Torture me again? You talk about trust—how am I supposed to trust you after that?"

"You know I'd never give that order. It's not okay to treat people that way. I stopped it as soon as I found out what was going on. I'm sorry it happened to you." Adam huffed, pushed his tray away. It clanged against Calay's. Calay watched a smile dance behind his eyes. "Though would you blame me? You did smash a computer over my head."

"You were going to shoot me." Calay raised an eyebrow and grinned back.

Despite Adam's unyielding morals, she'd come to like the guy. He was friendly from the beginning, albeit cagey with the details. He'd protected her from Guy, offered her friendship when she had no one else to turn to. He'd done nothing but try to help her until she'd forced his hand. It seemed like a lifetime ago that she'd broke into the records room and uncovered the Resistance propaganda, not to mention the truth about who—or what—Jacob was. It was one of the things Adam was trying to fix. Calay understood change happened slowly. And that was okay. As long as it did, in fact, happen.

"Guess we'll have to work on learning how to trust each other, then." Adam shrugged. "No one's clean anymore."

He wasn't wrong. The idea of good and evil, right and wrong—they were just that now: ideas. The fact of the matter was everyone had done something to survive. To get here. And if they hadn't, they'd been lucky. Sooner or later that luck was going to run out and in a way, Calay was grateful hers ran empty when it did. Everything she'd gone through had made her into the woman—the fighter—she was today. It was because of that that Tess's legacy would live on.

"I guess no one gets to be the good guy." Calay reached for her tray. She prodded the congealing mash. "I'm sorry I tried to electrocute you with an iMac."

"That thing was heavy."

"Yeah, why were the monitors so old anyhow?"

"It's not like we could have just walked into our local Genius Bar and picked out a top-of-the-line model. We needed something that was reliable, sturdy." Adam winked.

"I'm just saying there had to be better options around than that brick."

Adam crossed his arms over his chest. "Beggars can't be choosers."

Calay smirked and abandoned the spork upright in the leftovers. "You're just chock full of wisdoms today, aren't you?"

"Not just today." Adam's gaze fluttered to the far end of the room. Some freckled-faced kid was waving him over, his eyes wide like a deer in headlights. Adam rose, snapped up both their trays. "Finished?"

"Yeah, thanks." She watched as he made his way across the room and dumped them in a bin before following the young man around the corner and out of sight. Not quite ready to brave the walk past the endless rows of tables still overflowing with male bodies, she turned her attention back to her own and noticed Adam had left his book behind. She picked it up, flipped through the pages.

The smell of the musty paper reminded her of Jacob. He'd shoved his nose inside a book every night at the Loft, waiting for her to return from her self-imposed exile.

How many lifetimes ago had that been? It felt like a billion.

She knew nothing would bring him back from the inferno she'd left him to die in. Though someone had made it. She couldn't help but hope, despite everything he'd done to her, that it'd been him. Not that she ever wanted to see him again, she just didn't want him to burn to a crisp in the vast emptiness of deep space. He deserved better than that.

And yet, she'd left him behind.

Calay sighed, tucked the book underneath her arm, and pushed her chair in as she forced herself to stand. She figured she could sit there and lament the dreams she'd lost, letting the disappointment thrum in her heart, or she could make herself useful and learn how to forage for wild dandelion until Adam finally came around to her way of thinking.

She turned to quietly make her exit, but the curly fauxhawk woman's gaze locked Calay in place. And she wasn't alone. The two men she was sitting with just about tore Calay in half with the force of their stares.

The smaller one with the olive skin and black-rimmed glasses squinted at her, pressed his pouty, upturned lips into a thin line. The bigger one was more worrying, and not just because of his classic Hollywood good looks. Calay braved eye contact and the dark grey sweatshirt he wore bulged across his biceps. His nostrils flared. She watched his jaw twitch beneath a long, heavy beard as the smaller one whispered something in his ear.

Calay held her arms close and balled her fists, hoping they couldn't see the shake she felt. She didn't know what the hell their problem was, and she didn't want to find out. She may have been done with running from her fears, but that didn't make her stupid.

This wasn't a fight she could win.

She shuffled forward, averted her gaze, and hoped it would be enough to skirt by without incident. To her dismay, she practically felt the air ripple when the big one pressed himself up and away from the table. From the corner of her eye, Calay could see he'd begun making his way toward her, moving slowly between errant chairs and flowing bodies.

She tried to slow her breathing when something glinted in his hand against the overhead lighting.

Then, the lights went out.

The chatter in the room, too.

Calay halted. She forced her one free hand into a fist, raised the book in the other. It wasn't exactly her weapon of choice, but if push came to stab, she figured its ample page count could do some damage.

Despite it being mid-day, even the light outside seemed to fade to black.

She peered through the shadows, strained to hear the tell-tale shuffle of someone sneaking up from behind. Or rushing from the side.

The only sound was that of her heart against her chest.

She couldn't see more than a foot in front of her. There was nothing but darkness. The outline of bodies. But which one was his? She scanned the shadows for movement. It was as if the entire room and everyone in it froze, but how could that be? A vision of a million Eloras stacked one behind the other fluttered through her mind. This wasn't the starship. She wasn't trapped in that basement. Hell, she wasn't trapped here either. She could move any time. Still, the vast emptiness of the dark held her in place.

Calay could feel the scream rising in her throat, but before it could pass her lips, an alarm blared and the whole room went red.

CHAPTER TWO

It took a beat for Calay's eyes to adjust to the crimson floodlights.

The bodies around her rose in unison and made for the exit like their lives depended on it, overturning chairs and the last of their meals in their haste. Their shouts were barely audible above the alarm.

Calay's heart lurched into her throat. Her eyes grew wide at the realization the big guy with the shiny thing in his hand seemed to absorb into the crowd. She craned her neck behind, to the sides. Fought to see through the glowing darkness. One profile in the mass was no different from the next. A shadow here, a silhouette there. She braced herself for a pair of thick hands around her neck or a sharp jab against one of her internal organs. Waiting for the attack was almost worse than the act itself. That was the worst part of the last five years. The unknown. It sank into her bones and made them ache for a past lined with fluffy bedsheets and bottles of red wine. Kisses. The safe embrace of Tess's arms around her. Uncertainty clawed at her breath, billowed in the chaos.

Then, the entire crowd rushed past her.

She felt herself being jostled in one direction, then the other. She stumbled, clung to a nearby table to keep from being overwhelmed by the tide of bodies, and hung on for dear life.

She fought to wrangle her thoughts beneath the wailing high-pitched squeal of the alarm. This didn't make sense; it was a quiet place. The Resistance had taken every precaution to remain undetected by the Others. Silent. This though—this was the very opposite of silent.

The throng thinned, and finally Calay could make out individuals. The man with the weapon seemed to be gone. A small group, shrouded in red light and what she could see were the standard-issue Resistance uniforms, was huddled nearby. She gathered her courage and tugged on the sleeve of one of the smaller members. A close-set pair of fearful eyes turned to meet hers.

"What's going on?" She strained to be heard over the alarm.

The young officer blinked at her, looked her up and down. The six others didn't even turn their heads in her direction. He faced back to the group.

Rude.

"Hey!" Emboldened by his indifference, Calay braved a hand around his bicep. She steeled her voice and tried again. "What's going on?"

This time, their blank stares turned her way.

Her hand dropped from the officer's arm. Finally able to see in the harsh red light, Calay took a breath to size them up. Young, fresh-faced, all in perfectly pressed uniforms with a shine to their boots. One of them was visibly shaking. Another swiped at a tear before it reached his chin; his gaze darted to his comrades, as if hoping they hadn't noticed.

They peered back at Calay. The contempt on their faces grew palpable, but no one moved. They were probably as new as she was. Hell, if you counted the time she'd spent here before, she likely pulled rank on them.

She swallowed, pulled her shoulders back. The one closest to her—the one she'd grabbed—looked back at the others, shrugged.

Calay cleared her throat. "I deserve to know."

"One got inside," the youngest finally yelled, leaning close to Calay. He smelled like fresh laundry and cigarettes. Like home.

"One what?" Calay's blood was already running cold. She had an idea where this was going, and she didn't like it.

"An alien." The recruit pulled away, trained his gaze on Calay.

If she didn't know better, she'd think he was looking to her for reassurance. Or refusal. To tell them none of this was actually happening. That it had all been a bad dream they'd wake from any day now. She couldn't fault him for it; she'd thought the same thing herself many, many times. But she didn't have time for that kind of self-pity anymore. None of them did.

Just when the pressure had eased in her chest, it spiked again. "What? Are you sure?"

"That's what the alarm is for."

Understanding dawned on Calay. Of course. The Resistance was careful to be quiet because it was how they went undetected. But the blaring alarm, the death-lights, the shouting. All of this—they wouldn't risk being found unless they already had been.

"How?" she pressed.

"The Faceless have been helpin' them."

"Yes ma'am." The teary-eyed one stepped forward, shaking arms clenched at his sides. "We've seen it. From a distance, mind you. Our commander wouldn't let us get too close, and if I'm bein' honest with you, we sure didn't want to. But what Teddy says is true. The aliens and the Faceless, they're workin' together."

"The Faceless?" Calay tried to keep the impatience out of her voice. Getting answers around this place was like pulling teeth—painful and tedious.

"What don't you get about Faceless?" the shaking recruit spat. "They don't have faces, okay? Just those rotting blank masks. It's sick."

Dread crawled down Calay's back and pooled at the base of her spine. Her breath grew short. 'The Faceless'—that's what they called them. Those creepy, gruesome things she'd fled from in the theater. Black holes where their mouths and eyes should be, bulging black veins underneath translucent skin that seemed to writhe with each heaving breath. Their bald, bulbous heads. She shivered at the memory of them peering down at her through the hole in the stage.

She'd told herself zombies weren't real, that there had to be an explanation. At least, a better one than the undead. It appeared she'd lied.

Calay swallowed the lump forming in her throat. "What are they, exactly?"

Teddy shook his head. "We don't know, but we're supposed to stop them."

Calay blinked at the seven soldiers. She watched as one shifted their weight from one foot to the other, another was gnawing on their already non-existent fingernails. She didn't know how she suddenly went from prey to parent, but this could be the chance she'd hoped she'd get. The one Adam didn't want her to have. Not yet, anyhow. She wanted to gain his trust, do things by the rules. But she wasn't exactly breaking them by simply trying to keep up. At least, that would be her defense if she needed one. These kids needed a leader, and if Tess were here, that's exactly what she would have done: lead.

"What are we waiting for then?" Calay hoped she sounded more dauntless than desperate.

In confirmation, the seven nodded at her and loped out of the cafeteria. *That was too easy*. She gripped Adam's book between her fingers and took off after them. She allowed herself to hope convincing the rest of the Resistance members would be as simple. As she caught up with their strides, the alarm cut out.

"Finally." One of the recruits exhaled.

Calay wasn't entirely sure she agreed. The repetitious sound of their boots on the slick tiled floor wasn't much better. She tried to focus on the dangers to come, rather than those in her past, but she couldn't stop picturing the army of Eloras marching through the hallways of the starship. *One nightmare at a time*. Calay focused on the echo of voices ahead. She charged forward, took the lead, ignored the burning in her thighs. The sooner they got where they had to be, the sooner she'd be able to carry on Tess's work and bring an end to all this. Besides, if what these kids were saying was true about the Faceless helping the Others, they had even less time to waste than she'd thought. The idea of these monsters helping each other to eradicate the human race was almost more than Calay could conceive. So, she didn't. Instead, she ran, increasing the distance between herself and the boys on her tail.

She was done with running away from the danger. Now, she ran toward it.

The voices grew louder, the light brighter. She rounded a corner and Calay came face to face with the barrel of a gun. Several, in fact.

"Get down!" a deep voice bellowed.

Calay hit the deck. The impact knocked the wind clean out of her lungs. She gasped, coughed, fought to breathe.

Until she heard the horrific, awful screech behind her.

She writhed, flung her head in the opposite direction. There was no missing it in the dim lighting of the hallway.

Through a cloud of dark brown dust, at the other end of the corridor was an Other in full form. It's grey, raw-looking swollen body teetered on pin-sharp malformed limbs, its joints sharp as knives. Patches of short, wire-thick hair jutted out in every direction between pustules and spines, the hump on its back grazed the ceiling with each undulating, foul breath. *Gods*. It was one thing to see the Others in a galaxy far removed from her own, but here, on Earth, within the Resistance walls, was another thing entirely. One Calay wanted nothing to do with.

Through the haze, the creature's cracked lips seemed to smile.

If it was possible, she would have sworn her heart stopped in that moment.

It jumpstarted when Adam lunged from the hallway. His eyes wild, clothes disheveled. He raised a machete above his head and hollered an ungodly sound.

Calay choked back a scream. She watched Adam swipe at the beast and miss. He tried again. The alien gracefully sidestepped Adam's advances, moving in long fluid movements like a ballerina.

A retch crawled up Calay's throat. There was something wrong about how intelligently it moved on those pointed limbs, how beautifully.

Then the beast charged. It ripped the large blade from Adam's grasp and flung it to the other side of the hallway with ease.

Calay had to do something.

She leapt from the floor and grabbed Adam. They fell backward, crashing to the ground just as one of the alien's long talons sliced through the air. It missed Adam's waist by less than an inch. If Calay had moved a moment later, Adam's insides would have painted the walls.

The alien released another shriek.

They had nowhere to go.

A barrage of bullets sung over their heads, the flash of machine gun muzzles marred Calay's vision. Her body urged her to run, to hide, be smaller. She grit her teeth, pinned herself against the wall, Adam beside her, and screamed. Or at least, she tried. No sound came out. Instead, she gagged on a horrible, putrid stench that filled her nostrils.

The alien grew closer. One foot. A meter. It was nearly on top of them.

The Resistance continued to launch a full-scale assault at the other end of the hallway, which was proving ineffectual at best.

Black phlegm erupted from a mouth filled with rows and rows of serrated teeth. It seared through the fabric of Calay's favorite sweater. The tattoo on her wrist burned. She gripped the mark between two fingers, shocked to find she was still holding Adam's stupid book. Maybe it was the only thing she had to hold onto in that moment. The dream of building something new, something real. A do-over they all deserved simply because they were human and alive. A utopian future she'd never see. Her gaze darted to Adam. He was pressed against her, eyeing the machete that was irretrievably out of reach. She clenched her eyes, braced herself, hugged the book to her chest.

Bullets continued to soar overhead while she tried to ignore the nagging voice deep within her mind that told her she'd fucked up. Somehow she'd managed to survive an expedition to another galaxy, brought down an alien starship, and got her butt back to Earth, and then the first day she was left to her own devices, she'd met the same end she was determined to avoid in space. *Stupid stupid stupid.* She'd come so far. There was so much she had left to do. She pressed her lips together, her eyes sealed shut. Regret flooded her almost more than the fear.

The shooting stopped.

A loud *thunk* shook the wall she was pressed against.

The silence was absolute.

Calay pried open one eye. She peered behind a curtain of tears to find the Térasian's enormous, stinking body slumped on the floor not more than a foot away. She pulled her knees in to increase the distance. As if that would make a difference if it lunged back to life. She released a shaky breath, grateful to be alive. She frowned, not quite sure how that was possible.

"You're okay." A voice commanded from above. It was more a statement than a question.

Calay willed herself to turn her head from the monster and looked up to find a woman with brilliant, full red lips squinting at her. Her long, impossibly straight dark hair flowed forward like a waterfall when she leaned down and offered Calay a hand. Calay blinked, swallowed, and allowed herself to be pulled to her feet.

"Really should look before you leap, almost got your tits shot clean off ya." The woman nodded to the book Calay still had clutched to her chest. The woman wasn't wrong. In the center of the front cover was a jagged hole the width of Calay's index finger.

"Holy shit," Calay whispered through clenched teeth. She turned the book over in her hands, thumbed the edge of the bullet still lodged between the pages.

"Everything else still in one piece?" The woman gave Calay a once over, spun her around.

Calay nodded. "I think so."

"Be more careful next time, yeah?"

"Yes, of course." A mix of relief and embarrassment settled in Calay's stomach. "I guess I was just in a hurry to help."

"I'm not saying don't do what ya can." The woman dug through the layers of a wrap-around skirt twisted over a pair of black fitted cargo pants and pulled out a handkerchief. She handed it to Calay, her crimson lips twisted into a frown. "Look. Then leap."

"Got it." Calay allowed the corners of her mouth to turn up, accepted the swatch of dark fabric. She dabbed at the tar-like ooze on her sweater.

Satisfied, the woman turned to Adam. "You okay, boss?"

Adam winced and wiped the beads of sweat from his forehead. "I am now."

"Up you get, then." The woman reached for Adam. Calay helped, taking one of his hands in hers. Together, they pulled him to stand. The woman frowned at both of them. "That was a close one."

"Too close," Adam agreed, running his hands over his body as though to make sure he really was still in one piece.

The woman shifted her weight to one hip, she raised her brows. "Look, then what?"

"Then leap." Adam nodded a little too fervently, his pupils dilated.

She eyed him closely, then nodded and turned back to what Calay saw was a strong formation of Resistance members. They were lined up the width of the hallway, poised and ready to shoot. Calay blanched. The woman wasn't kidding—Calay had nearly taken a chest full of lead when she'd come around that corner. She was lucky the book saved her and even luckier she'd arrived when she did. Half a second later and the book wouldn't have stopped all those bullets.

"Hey!" Calay called after the woman as she sashayed away. "I'm Calay."

"Salem." The woman replied over her shoulder.

Well, that was one friend. Or at least, one non-enemy. And she wasn't a dude. Calay exhaled, wrapped her arms around herself. She tried to avoid looking too closely at the alien. Some of the new recruits she'd arrived with were prodding it with their guns. She gazed around for the man from the cafeteria. Wherever he was, it wasn't here.

Calay was safe. For now.

She turned to Adam. "She does have kind of a point, you know."

Adam shook his shoulders loose, released a slow exhaled. "What's that?"

"My default setting is pretty much impulsive, but you? You're supposed to be better than that." Calay winked.

Adam's smile was weak. "Noted."

Calay saw his hands were shaking, his legs too. His nervous system was probably still processing how close he'd come to a very untimely and very painful end. He wasn't the only one. She was contemplating returning to her room for a much-needed recharge when Adam braced her elbow.

He pulled her close, not quite into an embrace, and said in a low voice, "Thank you, Calay. For saving me."

"You would have done the same for me. Hell, you tried to. That was some pretty epic shit, running out of the hallway like that, weapon raised, like a bat out of Hell."

"No, you're right. I should know better than that. People expect better. I wouldn't be here if you hadn't moved so quicky."

Calay pulled back, brought her gaze to his. "Me either."

"I guess we're even then."

"Does this mean you trust me now?" Calay tried to keep her tone light.

Adam straightened. "It's a start." He turned then, his strides were long, his gaze fixed on his people. "Is everyone alright?"

Calay stood to the side. She watched as the others visibly relaxed to see their leader, alive and effectively unhurt. At least on the outside. She couldn't say the toll all of this would take on his mental health. What might appear in his dreams when all was still and dark. In the harsh light of the hallway though, their shoulders eased; they released the tension on their weapons. Some of them even gave Adam a god-honest smile. They seemed to like him, they trusted him. His presence was a comfort. The compound was a completely different environment than what Calay'd first experienced. He'd managed to do something in his short time in charge that Tess hadn't. He'd made this place better. Calay had to give him credit—his way worked.

Until now.

The Others weren't playing games anymore. They'd come out of the relative safety of their pods and forced their way into ours. They were coming for her.

If she didn't stop them—if she and Adam didn't work together—the Others would kill them all.

"Everyone's alive, if that's what you mean." One of the men with guns shouldered his.

"I see one of theirs isn't. That's good news. Thank you, Ryland." Adam eased around the creature on the floor. He retrieved the machete and planted himself amongst the soldiers, his free hand resting on his hip. "What else?"

"A few were injured trying to contain the animal. They've already been taken to the infirmary." A tall man in a black bomber jacket came forward. His silky brown hair bounced with each step. He ran a hand over the five o'clock shadow on his chiseled chin before continuing, released a deep sigh. He narrowed his deep blue eyes. "Again."

Adam's gaze drew dark, but he didn't look away. "Holden will take good care of them."

Calay made a mental note of the new name. Holden was probably their resident doctor. Someone she'd need to rely on, if not now, then later. When she took control of the group.

The tall man met Adam's gaze with full force. "But what about the next time?"

Adam firmed his stance. "We don't know there will be a next time."

"Of course we do." The tall man stepped closer, resting his hand on Adam's chest with a familiarity Calay was surprised to find herself yearning for. She watched the man's hand linger a moment longer than necessary. He pressed harder. Both men's eyes softened. This wasn't the way a soldier treated a commanding officer. There was something more between these two. Something close. "This is the sixth attack in as many days."

"There's been an increase, I know. We knew this was coming though. We're prepared." Adam's voice wavered.

"Are we?" The man's voice softened in response.

"You don't have faith in me?"

"Adam, it's getting worse. This is the first time they've made it inside."

"And it'll be the last. I'll make sure it's at the top of the Council's agenda tonight." Adam placed his hand over the other man's but turned his attention to the group at large. "The important thing now is we re-secure the perimeter. Fix the fence. Fortify the doors. Add more guards to the towers, and if we need it, more around the yard, too."

"I've already got people on it." Salem nodded.

"Of course you do. Good work, Salem. The rest of you, partner together to clean up and get this thing to the lab. I'm going to check on those receiving treatment for their injuries, make sure they have everything they need." Adam turned to leave as the others happily got to their assigned tasks.

Calay blocked his path and crossed her arms over her chest.

"I think you've seen enough excitement for one day." Adam exhaled.

Calay turned her chin up. "I can help,"

"Not right now you can't. Look, if it weren't for you, I'd be dead right now. I'm glad you're here, but—"

"Are you?" Calay narrowed her eyes at him.

"Of course, yes." His gaze dropped to her hand. "Is that my book?

"Oh, yeah." She lifted it, ran her hand over the jacket once more before she handed it to him. She hadn't realized after all that had happened, she was still holding onto it. "You left it in the lunch hall. I was going to read it, see if I could help find some food. I was going to give it back to you after."

"You keep it." Adam handed it back to her.

Calay blinked. "Are you sure?"

"By the looks of things, you need it more than I do." Adam grinned as he poked the bullet hole.

"Sorry about that."

"It's okay, I'm glad you're safe. Maybe we can look at it like an exchange of information."

"How so?"

"My plant knowledge for your alien expertise. In processing you said you saw these things on, what did you say the planet was called—Téras?"

Calay nodded. He'd gotten it only partly right because she'd told him only part of the truth. Before they released her into the general population she'd told him nearly everything she'd been through over the last several months. With the exception of one tiny insignificant detail of course—she was half alien herself. Oh, and someone had followed her back from deep space. Oh, and the whole heat signatures thing. Yes, other than that, he pretty much knew everything.

Tess had always told her to keep her lies as close to the truth—and her heart—as possible. Made it easier not to confuse them. With red flags like that, Calay was surprised she didn't see the truth about Tess's nature earlier.

"Well, they said it was Téras. It turned out the Others colonized the planet, used its resources. Then destroyed it when they were finished. But yes, I saw them, and what they can do. I'm also familiar with what they can't do. Adam—look at its hands."

"What's your point?" Adam didn't look at the creature. He kept his gaze honed on Calay's. Neither of them wanted to turn away from the promise in front of them. Or the threat.

"They're fine needle points. They don't have anything to grip or turn with. They aren't supposed to be able to open doors."

"We have things under control, Calay."

"No you don't." Calay surprised herself with the resolve she felt. Something had shifted inside her since returning to Earth. Something important.

"Yes, we do." Adam pulled Calay toward the hallway, dropped his voice to a whisper. "I'm going to need you to keep your cool right now, okay?"

"Keep my cool? I just about got my head shot off. And bit off. So did you. Are you kidding me? Cool is the last thing I feel right now."

"It isn't about how you feel. These people need us to stay calm. They depend on me. They'll depend on you too if we play our cards right, but that kind of trust takes time."

"That's exactly my point. We have to keep them safe. We can't do that like this." Calay thrust her arm at the tarp that now covered the alien. Her temper was rising, and so was her voice. "Adam, how did it get inside?"

The remaining soldiers in the hallway turned then. Calay could feel their eyes on her, questioning. This was for the best. She'd dared to ask the question no one else had brought to Adam. There were murmurings, sure. The young recruits who'd led her here had told her as much. But if Calay was going to save anyone, she needed facts, not theories.

"Adam?" she pressed.

Adam ran a hand over his mouth, closed his eyes, sighed.

"Adam, don't." The tall man whispered.

"It's time, Callum." Adam shook his head, turned to the now-silent crowd. "The rumors you've heard are true. The Faceless have been helping the Others get past our defenses. If we want to keep this place safe, we need to step up our security. We'll all have a part to play in that."

"I'll patrol." The words rushed out of Calay's mouth before she decided to say them. Her hand flew to her lips, but it was too late. There was no taking them back now.

"To be fair, you did almost just die. Are you sure you're up for it?" Salem frowned.

"Please," a soldier scoffed.

Adam raised his hands. "I think what Ryland's trying to say is we'll talk about who belongs where. We don't have to make any snap decisions."

"I think we do." Calay fought to keep her voice from rising. "You— Callum was it? —you said there's been six attacks in six days. I know I'm the new girl who just got herself shot at and almost eaten alive, but like Adam said, we all have to do our parts. We have to rally immediately."

"Why the increase in attacks now though?" Salem pouted. Calay was beginning to think she wasn't actually glowering, that was just her face.

Adam pulled his shoulders back, visibly uncomfortable with not having the answers his people needed. "We don't know for sure. Before now the orbital ships didn't know where we were. The moat, fence, and cover overhead were enough to keep us concealed. It seems that's no longer the case."

"Why not?" one of the newer recruits asked, a tremor in his voice. Calay couldn't help but wonder if he regretted his life choices. If he would have chosen differently, if he'd known how quickly his role was going to escalate from searching abandoned cars for supplies to hand-to-hand combat with alien beings that would always have the tactical advantage. Would she? She found herself shaking her head; she knew it was coming to this. She'd chosen her path when she'd committed to continuing Tess's work. This was humanity's chance. It was Calay's.

Everything she'd been through brought her right here. To this place. This moment. And she was going to make the most of it. She just had to play the hand she was dealt—and play it right.

Calay sucked a breath between her teeth. "I know."

Everyone turned expectantly to her.

"Calay," Adam cautioned.

She ignored him. This was something she had to do.

"The fact that the Others and the Faceless have been helping each other isn't the only thing Adam hasn't told you."

'It's not just Adam, it's the whole Council. We vote as a group." Callum offered.

Adam threw a frown in Callum's direction. He shrugged in response.

Calay smirked. "Great. Okay, so that's not the only thing they've been keeping from you. There's something else."

"Calay, please. Don't." Adam's gaze grew heavy.

Calay stiffened under it. She wanted his trust, but she wanted to do right by Tess—and humanity—more. The cause was what mattered now.

She mouthed the words 'I'm sorry' and then continued. "They've also been keeping me a secret."

Ryland coughed, his weight shifting back on his heels. "And who exactly are you?"

This was it.

Now or never.

Once Calay opened her big fat mouth, there was no going back.

They may not have known who she was, but she was willing to bite nails they'd know her dead girlfriend. It wasn't the classy move. It was, however, the one that would gain her influence. And right now, that was exactly what Calay needed.

"Tess—your previous leader—was my girlfriend. And I killed her."

CHAPTER THREE

AFTER THE GUNFIRE and Calay's confession, the silence bloating the hallway nearly suffocated her where she stood.

She watched as the Resistance members' scornful faces turned blank, then, confused. Their gazes darted between Calay and each other, everyone looking to the person beside them to elaborate. Salem even seemed to lose what little color she had as she swallowed the words Calay shoved between them.

Calay shifted her weight from one foot to the other, reminded herself to breathe. She just had to give them—and herself—a moment.

"She's lying." Ryland's scratchy voice was the first to break the quiet. Despite his accusation, Calay could have hugged him. As if sensing her thoughts, his thin lips snarled, he crossed his arms over his broad chest.

Calay mirrored his movement, then thought better of it, dropping her arms by her sides. If—and it was a big if—this was going to work, she had to remain open. Approachable. Believable.

"Tess is on reconnaissance. She's scouting a new base. A second location." Ryland's fingers wrapped around the sling on his shoulder. Calay's brows furrowed. She couldn't tell if he was drawing attention to the gun on purpose or if it was an unconscious thing—an emotional support thing. Was it possible he really thought Tess was still alive?

"What? No, she's not. I..." Calay's gaze floated to Adam, whose lips were pressed firmly together beneath his large palm. He glanced down, refused to make eye contact with her. With anybody, she noticed.

Ryland strode forward, his thick hands balled into fists. "You came here to infiltrate us. To spread confusion. Disloyalty. What are you, some kind of spy?"

"What? No. I'm here to help. I—I killed Tess. Months ago. I buried her." The aching hollow in Calay's chest gaped wider.

"Bullshit, liar."

"I'm not a liar!" Calay felt the falsity of the words coming out of her mouth as she said them, so her voice rose to match his. Her temper, too.

"Then you're a murderer," he accused between clenched teeth.

"Both of you, stop it." Callum's gentle voice cut through Calay's panic. He positioned himself between her and Ryland, placed one hand on each of their shoulders. Ice cold defiance seared through Calay, but the firm warmth of Callum's grasp pinned her where she stood. Smoothed out the hard edges, reduced her anger to a simmer.

"Adam?" Salem's head tilted in their direction, but her gaze was firmly planted on Adam's now heaving chest. He took several deep breaths before he let his arms fall to his sides and met their desperate stares, starting with Calay's.

Her stomach plunged at what she saw.

Oh, shit.

While it was true Adam was keeping Calay's previous visit under wraps, it hadn't occurred to her the Council wouldn't have told their people what had happened to their Dear Leader. This definitely put a wrench in her original plan. The whole point of announcing her relationship with Tess was to leverage her credibility. But if they were only just now finding out Tess was dead, her confession was just that—a confession. To a crime. A big one. Some would say the biggest. And as Adam so diligently reminded her, they had rules. Rules she'd broken.

She had to fix this.

"Let me explain—" she started.

"You've said enough for today." Adam sighed. There was no venom in his voice, just regret. It nearly broke Calay's heart. She had a mission, but she didn't want to accomplish it at anyone else's expense if she didn't have to. Especially Adam's. They'd all lost enough. "Calay's telling the truth. I found Tess myself on a supply run to the Alpine Checkpoint. She's gone."

"What happened to her?" Ryland gaped.

"We found Guy. I'll spare you the details, but it wasn't pretty."

Salem groaned. "No real loss there."

Adam forced himself to continue, speaking slowly as if each word were a betrayal in and of itself. "It was clear there'd been a struggle. Tables overturned. Papers everywhere. At first we thought Guy had attacked her and that she'd gotten the upper hand. Maybe escaped. But that's when we found the grave. We didn't have to dig far to find her body."

Listening to Adam's version of events caused bile to rise in the back of Calay's throat. She hated that Tess didn't get the burial she deserved. Calay wanted to scream the ground on the mountain was too hard, the weather too harsh. That she and Jacob had to get out of there before the Resistance's forces found them, save themselves. That she didn't know then what she knew now about Tess's mission. The truth behind what the Others aimed to do to humanity. To Earth. That she was so fucking sorry she thought she might just die. Instead, she gagged, swallowed. Fought to keep herself upright under the weight of their glares.

Salem took a long, slow inhale and held it. "Did you know at the time who killed her?"

Adam's eyes grew glassy. He didn't swipe away the tears. "No, I swear we didn't. After we found her grave, we revised our original theory. Maybe she'd killed Guy, but then who killed her? We combed the mountain. Searched nearby for days. We came up with nothing."

"How do we know she's telling the truth? That she's the one who did it?" Ryland glowered.

"Her version of the event lines up with what we found at the mountain. If she wasn't there, she couldn't have known all those details." Callum's shoulders lifted. It wasn't quite a shrug, not quite a slump. If Calay had to guess, he'd carried the secret of Tess's death as much as Adam. It was further evidence of something between them.

Something special. Calay noted it, filed it away for later. Even if it wasn't useful, it gave her hope.

"Callum, how could you know and not tell me?" Salem slouched, her eyes glistened with tears.

Calay gaped. She'd been terrified last time she was here, and she'd missed so much. It would seem Tess meant something to these people. People Calay had never even known existed. Tess had kept that from her. This place, too. Or maybe Calay had just been too naive to see it. Her chest ached with the thought. She'd do so many things differently if she had the chance. But she didn't.

This was it.

She shook her head. It didn't matter how she felt right now. These people had just lost someone they cared about. And she'd been the one to take her away from them.

Callum opened his mouth to reply, closed it. His head hung, he nodded.

"Don't blame Callum." Adam eased his arm around Callum's waist. "He kept quiet because I asked him to. This is on me."

"No, this is my fault." Calay pulled herself forward. She turned to the group. "I did what I had to do at the time. It was her or me. I regret every moment that led to that one, and every moment since."

"Lock her up." Ryland snarled, his eyes darkened. "Put her on trial."

"It's more complicated than that Ryland, but I assure you everything is being handled in accordance with the Council's governance." Adam drew his lips taught.

Calay was willing to bet her life that wasn't true, but this was neither the time nor the place to call bullshit. There seemed to be more to Adam than she'd first thought. This guy wasn't just the lap-happy-puppy-dog she'd imagined him to be. There was something darker underneath. Something that needed to be in control.

"She has to be held accountable," Ryland pressed.

"She will be. Leave it to us."

Salem sniffled. "Tess was our leader."

"She was the love of my life." Calay's voice cracked as she forced the words past her quivering lips. What Elora had said was true—she'd murdered Tess in cold blood for doing the very thing Calay was doing now. She didn't know how to come to terms with that. She only knew she had to do something. Anything. Tears swelled behind her eyes. She blinked them back. "This whole thing is a mistake. All of it. I promise you—I'll make it right."

"Hold on a sec." Callum cleared his throat and ran his hands along the front of his jacket as if looking for something. Or fidgeting. He leaned deeper into Adam's embrace. A source of strength, Calay thought. "I don't see what this has to do with the increased attacks. Why would your relationship with Tess have anything to do with the Others?"

This was the tricky part. Calay knew it was coming. She couldn't give them the full truth, so she bent it. Hell, she outright snapped it into a billion tiny pieces and rearranged them to create a new narrative. A new story. One the Resistance could believe—one that didn't get her killed where she so awkwardly stood. She released a deep exhale and repeated the lie she'd told Adam days earlier.

"I've seen the schematics. The maps. After Tess...passed...the Others found me on that mountain. They followed me from a distance for weeks. I think they tracked me here."

"The Others shoot on sight. Why didn't they just blast you?" Salem wiped her tears away, pulled herself taller.

"I don't know. I didn't exactly stick around to ask questions. I hid in an old factory for weeks. Tried to figure out my next steps. Every time I left for supplies or food, I could feel them. They were watching."

Salem raised her chin. "And you led them here? Right to us."

"I waited for as long as I could." Calay fought to keep the tremble out of her lie. Her legs, too. "I thought I'd shaken the tail. When I surrendered to you that morning, I believed I was alone."

"How did you find us in the first place?" Ryland's fingers were turning white where they gripped the strap. "We're pretty remote. Must have been some luck coming up on our compound. Especially in this weather. It's a bloody blizzard. Has been for weeks. How'd you survive all the way out here?"

"Before the Change, Tess and I used to spend a lot of time hiking around here. When I saw the maps at the cave, I recognized the trails. I hadn't been this far out but I knew from other hikers there was a cabin nearby. I stayed there." Calay swallowed. She knew this was where her story got dicey. Her biggest risk of getting tripped up because anyone could have been to the cabin in the days leading up to her arrival and found it empty. Her heart swelled at the memory of the time she'd spent there with Jacob. The feel of his hands around her waist. His mouth on her mouth. Their hearts pressed together as their bodies collapsed with passion on the hardwood floor. Within his embrace was the first time she'd felt safe since Tess had disappeared. Calay shuddered, knowing she'd never feel that way again. "I didn't know exactly where this place was. So I'd search during the day and sleep there at night. I finally found you one afternoon. I gave myself the evening to think things over. Came back the next morning. And here I am."

The snarl never left Ryland's lips. His eyes were cold. "Convenient."

"It makes sense to me," Salem finally exhaled. Calay offered her the echo of a smile.

"It made sense to us too." Adam released Callum and strode forward, his eyes clearer. "Believe me, there is due process and we have processed Calay. She's one of us now."

"We need all the help we can get," Callum nodded.

Ryland released a huff between pursed lips but said nothing more.

"I know it'll take time for you all to trust me." Calay tucked her hair behind her ears, recalling her earlier conversations with Adam. "The reason I finally came here was because we *do* need all the help we can get. Like Callum said, six attacks in as many days. The Others and the Faceless are going to keep coming. We have to work together if we're going to win this war."

"What makes you think we can beat them now? You were Tess's girlfriend, so what?" Ryland leaned against the nearest wall.

"I know things." Calay gestured toward the tarp on the floor. "I was able to learn a lot about them while they followed me."

"Like what?"

"Lots of things. We can use that knowledge to our advantage. They think they know us, but they only know one version of us."

"What version is that?"

"The scared version."

A terrible grin flashed across Ryland's face and then disappeared almost as quickly as it appeared. "But we are scared."

Several soldiers nodded in agreement.

"We're also brave." Calay levelled her gaze at them, held each one for a long, deep breath. She let the silence billow in the air. "Right?"

Now they nodded in agreement with *her*.

Ryland cocked his head. "Little good that's done us."

"Look, we have a duty to loyalty. To humanity. To each other." Adrenaline coursed through Calay's veins. She pulled on the threads she'd rehearsed alone in her cell. She'd had weeks to practice this. To fine tune it. To recall the propaganda she'd found the first time she was here. She didn't need to harvest a detailed plan. She just needed to plant the seeds. To sprout the idea of a revolution and continue Tess's work. They'd figure the rest out later. "The Others underestimate us."

"They're stronger than us." Salem flipped her long dark hair over her shoulder. "A hell of a lot stronger."

"Sure, at first. They had the element of surprise. After that, fear and firepower. Now? Now it's our turn." Calay paused for dramatic effect. She was met with the gentle sound of rustling.

She watched as one pair of hands rose above the crowd, their palms rubbing together in support. Then, another.

She grinned, *yes*.

It wasn't quite cheers and clapping, but it was a start.

Emboldened, Calay thrust her hands open, pleading. "Through chaos, we will bring order! We use that to fight them."

"But what about the Faceless?" Ryland pushed himself off the wall, stepped forward. "They're new."

Calay's breath quickened. "Which means they're inexperienced. Not as coordinated. We take them out, too. I hate to say it, but it's Us vs. Them, and *they* are on our home turf. This is *our* planet. We have numbers. Strategy. We survive together."

Several other pairs of hands rose above their heads, their palms pressed together. The soft sound of swishing flowed through the hallway. Calay smiled as Salem brought her hands together. Callum too. She noticed Ryland had yet to be won over as she watched him cross his arms over his chest again.

Give him time. Give them all time.

As the group of soldiers pressed forward, their excitement growing, someone called out for more, another wanted specifics. Calay didn't have those yet, so she raised her own hands in solidarity. She'd just brought her palms together when Adam stepped through the blooming bodies, his expression grim.

"This is excellent. I love seeing us come together like this." Adam cleared his throat, his voice dropped. "But like I said, we aren't making any decisions this minute. We'll figure this out, but for now, Calay, I think it's best you return to your room. We don't know what else might be out there right now, and we have to be cautious. I'll come to you when we know it's safe. Okay? Everyone else, you have jobs to do." Adam gestured to the alien still sprawled on the ground, underneath the tarp.

Calay had almost forgot about it. She didn't want to stop now. Not when she was just getting some support. But she knew she had to work within the system if she was going to make change.

This was just the beginning.

HOURS PASSED SINCE CALAY RETURNED TO HER ROOM ON Adam's direction, evidenced by the hunger pangs in her belly. She'd barely eaten breakfast that morning and now the light was already fading. She didn't want to press her luck any more than she already had. Adam asked her to wait here. So she waited. She knew he wasn't being honest with her; he was definitely hiding something. She had to admit, if she wanted them to trust her, she was going to have to extend the same courtesy. That, and she was going to have to show she could, in fact, actually be trusted. That she could play nice with others. Follow directions. Whatever it took to save herself. And humanity.

She thrummed her fingers against the metal frame of the single bed, tapped her feet against the wall. She slowly heel-toed her legs skyward. Her head hung off the side, boots discarded on the concrete floor nearby. The sink in the corner dripped an endless series of pings as water leaked from the faucet. From down here, the view outside the small, rectangular window embedded in the far wall wasn't much. Grey oblivion, darker clouds. There wasn't much to keep her occupied while she waited, so she imagined what the world might look like once they actually defeated the Others. She'd done a good job of convincing everyone else it could be done, she almost believed it herself. Like it was more than a dream. That it was actually possible.

In her new world, women and self-identified women would finally be safe. Hybrids, too. They may have been part alien but they were also part human. Everyone would have safety of person and right to personhood simply because they existed. They'd live in harmony where people would be valued more than profits. They'd develop agriculture and no person would ever go hungry again. Careers wouldn't be mandatory, but contribution would; everyone would give what nourished them, and vice versa. Tess would still be alive and the two of them would live happily ever after in their own little cottage by the sea. Okay, now she knew she was being ridiculous. That, or hunger was driving her mad. She had to admit, even to herself, alone in this box of a room, a reunion was impossible. But what about the rest of it? Was it just a flight of fancy? Or could she—or the Resistance—really turn this war around and reclaim their planet? Fix the ecosystem? Build anew?

They had to. For all their sakes.

The sound of a gentle knock on the door pulled Calay from her reverie. She swung her legs up and over her head, and stood. The blood threaded down through her limbs. It was a welcome feeling. One that reminded her she was here. Alive. Ready to fight. She steadied herself on the wall, took a long slow breath in.

Another knock.

"Coming!" She un-bunched her sweater, ran her hands over her dark jeans, and unlatched the door. It swung open to what was quickly becoming Adam's default grimace. "What's up your butt?"

"You. You are what's up my butt, Calay. May I come in?" He hovered, as if ready to charge through the door, but hesitated at the precipice. Trying to give her the benefit of consent, she figured. She waved her hand and stepped aside. He strode forward, came to an abrupt stop at the other side of the room. "They put you up in one of the smaller suites, I see."

"Better than the cell they put me in last time. At least now the lock's on the inside." Calay shrugged. She tried to keep her voice even, but the reminder of the dungeon she'd escaped from before—the memory of Smith, and Guy, and the feeling she'd never see Jacob or Tess again—was too much. She cleared her throat. "I've been here for hours, you know. I haven't even had lunch. Or dinner for that matter."

"You didn't miss much."

"I missed everything. I'm starving."

"Well, let's get this over with and you can make it to the cafe in time in time for scraps."

"Lucky me." Calay blinked. "Get what over with?"

Adam parked himself on the corner of the bed, only to stand again half a moment later.

"Adam, get what over with?"

"You did some serious damage today, Calay." Adam ran a hand across his face. "I trusted you, God knows why, to keep your mouth shut and do as I say. I want to keep you safe. I need to protect them—they're my people. And you jeopardized that with your little speech."

"I rallied them, Adam." Calay shook her head, thrust her hands on her hips. "They need someone to lead them. Someone strong."

"Someone like you?"

"Yes, exactly. Someone like me."

"You're a liar, Calay. A murderer. A fugitive now. How can we trust you? Why did you really come back here?"

"I told you why. I want to save us. I want to survive. We aren't going to do that alone." She took a deep breath, steadied her shaking hands. "Do you think one of them will turn me in for what I did to Tess?"

"I don't know. Maybe? I don't think so." Adam shoved his hands into the pockets of his dark pants. He pulled them out again. Exhaled. "But people talk. Honestly, the Council doesn't know who you are and I intended to keep it that way. Do you have any idea how difficult that will be when the truth about you and Tess gets out in gen pop?"

Calay edged the corner of the bedpost with her toe as she tried to calm the emotions knotting themselves in her stomach. A pang of guilt riddled inside her bones. Nothing about this was fair. Between being forced to murder the woman she loved, leaving the man she couldn't quite love, and every other moment of terror that was etched into her mind, she was here. She'd survived. Was ready to fight. Adam didn't get it. All she wanted to accomplish. How they needed to get there. Here he was lecturing her about morals when he didn't even know half the truth of what she'd done. Who she was. *What* she was. How was she supposed to trust him in a war when she couldn't even trust him with the truth?

"Excuse me for surviving." Calay hugged herself. "Do you even remember what it's like out there?"

"Of course I do." Adam's tone softened. "But you aren't out there anymore. You're in here. And if the Council finds out you were not only a prisoner *in here* before, but you murdered our leader in cold fucking blood, not to mention the responsibility you hold for Smith's—our top commander's—death, I can't protect you. They will vote to kill you, Calay."

"You think I don't know that? I'm well aware of my situation. Speaking of killing, what the fuck was that out there anyhow, Adam? They didn't even know Tess was dead."

"I...." The color drained from his face, his jaw hung slack. His eyes glazed over, lost somewhere in a memory, probably. Maybe one where he found Guy with his balls shot off and Tess covered by a few inches of dirt and loose rock.

Calay steadied herself on the wall. "I'm just saying for someone who is such an advocate for following the rules, you sure seem to break a lot of them. You pride yourself on doing what's right and following procedure, but from where I stand, you're making your own up as you go along."

Adam flinched. "I wanted to keep this place secure. You have no idea how unstable it is. You saw how vocal some of those soldiers are.

Ryland's angry, but harmless. Not everyone is, Calay. There are those who would cause problems if they thought the leader was dead. Do you remember what it was like after the invasion?"

"Which part?" Visions of Calay's neighbors evaporating into red mist scratched at her mind. The sound of glass breaking and women screaming. The smell of burnt flesh and raw sewage in the streets. The feeling of her apartment building crashing down on top of her. "I'll never forget."

"Exactly. It was utter chaos. Violence. Rioting. Looting. As soon as people didn't feel cared for and protected—as soon as there wasn't somebody in charge—everything fell apart. I can't let that happen here."

"It doesn't have to happen here. That's my whole point. They have you, Adam. And me. They have us. I meant what I said. We need to work together if we're going to survive the Others. But it isn't just them anymore. It's the Faceless—that's a horrible name by the way. Earth, too. There's something fundamentally wrong with the weather. Their presence here has shifted something. They're like a disease. An infection. A fungus. If we get rid of them, things could go back to normal."

"You think I haven't thought of that? But how?"

"Those people out there—they're waiting for someone to lead them into battle. We have a whole army of people itching to take their anger, their fear, their frustrations out on the beings who did this to us. They just need to be given the resources and the chance."

Adam shook his head and sank down onto the corner of the mattress. "I don't know what that would look like."

Calay resisted the urge to collapse next to him. Instead, she plodded to the window. The view wasn't much better from there than it was from her bed. A thick blanket of snow covered the ground as far as she could see. It clung to the branches of spruce trees in the distance and atop the barbed wire that ran the length of the fence line. The clouds grew darker, the sun settled against the horizon. As she pressed her nose against the freezing glass, she let the cold seep into her skin. A brutal but beautiful reminder that another day was almost over. That this era was coming to an end. She shivered but didn't pull away from the cold. She let it sink deep inside her. The surrender, the torture, the events of the last five years—she could make them all mean something. She was sure of it.

"I'm sorry I spilled the tea about Tess." Her breath fogged the glass with each syllable.

"I'm not against working together." Calay watched Adam's reflection lean forward, resting his forearms on his knees. "But I need you to trust I know what I'm doing. After the Others shadowed you for so long, you might know more about them, but I've been here longer than you. I know this place. These people."

"You're right. We have to trust each other." Calay cast her eyes over the darkening horizon. She couldn't bring herself to look at the earnestness on Adam's face. She still suspected he was hiding something, but he seemed genuine now. She didn't want to rock the boat more than she already had, or risk giving up the full truth she'd worked so hard to protect—that she'd gone to the Others' galaxy, someone had followed her back, and was one of them herself. If she could keep her mouth shut while they waterboarded her, she should be able to keep one measly lie (or three) to herself. "I'll do better. I'll keep a low profile until you think we're good and ready."

"Good." Adam stood. "Now get ready."

"Huh?" She spun to face him.

"Lace up." He reached for the blue scarf folded at the end of her bed and tossed it in her direction. "I've got something to show you."

CHAPTER FOUR

B Y T H E T I M E she and Adam burst through an unmarked door, braved the darkness of the yard, then into another nondescript building, the frigid wind worked its way through Calay's bones. As her eyes adjusted to the light, she pulled the scarf tighter around her neck and shivered, but not for the cold. This wasn't just any building—it was *the* building.

She'd been here before. Five months ago, to be exact.

"This is…"

"Yes." Adam glanced back over his shoulder. "If you could try to not assault anyone with a piece of late-century technology, it'd be appreciated."

Calay pulled back as if she'd been slapped. "Don't try to shoot me and we won't have a problem."

"It's not you I'm worried about," Adam mumbled, turning his attention ahead.

Calay was tempted to ask what he meant by that, but she suspected she was about to find out. She followed Adam deeper into the maze of hallways, and it took every ounce of strength she had to keep moving forward.

She'd never forget the bright overhead lighting, the sterile tile floor, the deathly silent emptiness. Emotion swelled in her stomach. It was one thing to remember what she'd found here the first time, it was another entirely to sift through the memories, reliving the pain and horror of uncovering what she'd believed to be the Resistance's true mission. The truth about Jacob. It was what led her to flee and escape, and discover the truth about herself—that she was half Other. Half alien.

This place had changed everything.

As the fear built in her chest and her legs urged her to turn and run the other way, she tried to keep her wits about her. Adam couldn't possibly know what she was. She'd passed their tests with flying colors thanks to her half humanness—her father's biology. As far as Adam was concerned, Calay'd only broke the rules, snuck into a room, and read documents she was never meant to see—information on the Resistance and their operations. She was sure if he knew she was an alien, she wouldn't be walking these blindingly bright hallways.

She'd be dead.

When she decided to surrender herself to the Resistance, it hadn't occurred to her she'd end up back here. In this building. It was the one place she was determined to avoid. She'd been so preoccupied trying to keep her jacket done up and not slip in the ever-growing blanket of snow and ice outside, she hadn't noticed where they were headed. And here she was, whether she liked it or not. Now she was simply going to have to suck it up and do what needed to be done.

She didn't know where they were headed, but it didn't matter. Tess was her compass now, her true north. As long as nothing got in the way of that, Calay had to believe they'd succeed. There wasn't any other option.

Adam stopped suddenly and Calay sucked in a breath as she walked smack into the back of his journeyman jacket. Her cheeks flushed red when he turned, a grin curved from his lips to his wide, green eyes. He ran a hand through his floppy dark hair and cleared his throat. He really was classically handsome.

Calay grinned back, relieved this time they weren't trying to kill each other; they were on the same team. Or at least the same side. She followed his gaze to a thick plastic sheet hanging from two metal hooks attached to the ceiling, and the grin slid off both their faces.

On the other side of that plastic was the room where she'd found Jacob strapped to a table. The room where she'd believed she'd killed him, murdered Guy, then fled. She'd been wrong on both counts.

"Okay, here's the thing." Adam drummed his fingers against the nearest wall and exhaled. "I'm taking a big risk by bringing you here."

"You can trust me." Calay tried to ignore the pounding of her heart. "I mean it, Adam."

"I believe you do." Adam narrowed his eyes and nodded, then disappeared through the plastic.

Calay didn't know what was on the other side of that sheet, but she needed to find out. She'd been so afraid last time she was here, so small and confused. This was her chance for redemption. To face her fears. Her mistakes. She just had to take three steps forward.

The plastic parted and she forced her legs to walk.

The smell hit her before anything else. A putrid stench like rotting meat with an underlying sweet aroma filled her nose. Her hand flew up to her face, her eyes watered, she tried not to gag.

"Breathe through your mouth," Adam called from somewhere to the right.

Calay turned and gasped.

An Other's bulbous body was cut wide open atop two gurneys strapped together, its spindly, thorned legs slack and draping on the floor. Beside it, a stark white human-shaped thing, naked and bald as the day they must have been born. Cavernous, black circles existed where its eyes and mouth should be. No nose. A faceless mask.

Through the stench, Calay gagged. "Oh my god, is that…?"

"The alien we shot earlier? Yes. And that's the Faceless who we suspect helped it get inside the building. One of the soldiers was able to shoot it before it got away." Adam crossed his arms, puffed his chest. "Come over, it's safe."

Calay paled. She wasn't so sure about that, and she wasn't convinced Adam was either. She'd personally seen the damage these things could sustain and keep on coming. Hell, one had ripped its own leg off to bust down the door of her cabin aboard the Térasian starship. Still, if the smell was anything to go by, Adam was probably right.

"Bucket's against the wall if you need it," a person with olive skin and short dark hair mumbled over the rim of a ridiculously large mug. They took a sip, gentle wafts of steam rose in the air. Some kind of tea, perhaps.

"I'm okay," Calay mumbled.

"Suit yourself." They raised an eyebrow.

Calay watched the person haul themselves from the edge of the stool they were perched and lean over the bodies. If Calay had done that, the scent would have knocked her unconscious. She suspected they'd grown used to it, but how someone ever got accustomed to the smell of death —alien death—she didn't know. The muscles in their forearms tensed beneath the rolled-up sleeves of their fitted button-down shirt as they reached for the glasses in their breast pocket. They peered closer before thrusting their gaze to Calay.

She started, tried not to jump. Their round blue eyes almost seemed to pierce through her. As if they could peel back her skin and see inside. There was something oddly familiar about them, but Calay couldn't place it. Though if they'd met before, surely she'd remember that stare.

Adam rested against the empty, neighboring gurney. "This is Holden, our resident doctor, mortician, and scientist. Kind of a jack-of-all-trades when it comes to biology and keeping us all alive. They can be a little intense, but we like 'em. Holden, this is Calay. The new—"

"I know who she is," Holden interrupted.

Calay swallowed under the weight of their gaze, which was still trained on her. She shoved her hands in the pockets of her jeans, pulled her shoulders back, and met their stare. She watched the way shadows clung to their high cheekbones, the pouty curve of their lips that made them look like they were smiling even when they weren't.

A small grin curled at the side of Holden's mouth. "I've heard a lot about you, Calay. Nice to meet you. Officially."

She wasn't sure what they meant by that, if they meant anything at all. Was she being paranoid? Maybe being back in this building—this room—really was getting to her.

Calay tried to shake it off, focus on what her purpose was in being here now. "Nice to meet you too."

"You'd be a little intense too if you spent your days cutting open dead bodies. Live ones, sometimes, too," Holden muttered under their breath, finally turned their attention to Adam after glancing at the antique watch strapped to their wrist. "What are you two doing here? Isn't curfew in a few minutes?"

"We won't stay long." Adam waved Calay closer. She inched forward, eventually coming to stand by his side. "I wanted Calay to see what you were doing here. To get a better understanding of how they work."

"To what end?" Holden's eyes narrowed before disappearing behind the lip of the cup as they took another sip.

"She came to us from the outside. She was followed for months, and they didn't vaporize her. She's got intimate knowledge about their pods and how they coordinate. Whatever information she has is valuable."

Holden's expression held irritatingly neutral. "I'm sure it is."

"I was hoping you two could talk, maybe come up with something we can use to fight them."

Holden swirled their mug as if they didn't have a care in the world. "Hmph."

Calay's pulse quickened at their apathy. "You got a problem with that?"

"A problem?" Holden blinked.

"I came here to help." Calay blinked back, straining to keep her voice even.

"Did you, now?"

"Yes, of course I did!"

"Because from what I hear, you broke out of your cell, snuck into our administration room, tried to kill our darling Adam here, tracked and murdered our captain, and then several months later, showed up in the middle of a blizzard claiming to be on our side. Like we wouldn't remember everything that happened before. Does that sound very helpful to you?"

"Holden—" Adam started.

"No!" Tears sprung in Calay's eyes, and this time, it wasn't from the smell. "Look, I made mistakes, okay? I've apologized for them. I don't know how many more ways I can say it, but I fucked up. A lot. And I live with that every single day. I risked my life coming here to make things right."

Holden's brows furrowed, they eased their way toward Calay. "And what does 'right' look like to you, exactly?"

Calay fought to hold her stance. To not cower under Holden's blue stare. "Don't you want to stop the Others?"

Holden grinned from behind the safety of their large cup.

Calay bristled.

She didn't know what this person's problem was, but she'd be happy to fix it for them with a fist across that smug mouth of theirs. She was just starting to make inroads with Adam, and she wasn't about to let them take that away from her.

"I want to stop them more than you know." Something softened in Holden's face. Calay watched the flicker of a shadow pass over it. Then, just as quickly, it was gone.

"Then we have to work together." Calay almost rolled her eyes. She was starting to sound like a broken record even to herself.

"You sure about this?" Holden sighed, turned to Adam.

"No, but I'm not sure about much these days," Adam admitted. "Just see what you two can come up with."

"Alright." Holden set the mug down and took a deep breath. "We don't have much time before you both have to be back in your bunks, but we can go over a couple things. Give you something to mull over when you can't sleep tonight."

"Dark," Calay muttered.

A shadow passed in the depths of Holden's eyes. "You have no idea."

"Tell her about the mutations," Adam adjusted his lean, as if the mere mention of mutations made him squirm—whatever mutations were.

"Are you going to let me do this?" Holden peered over their glasses. Adam nodded, adequately rebuked, pretended to zip his lips shut. "Appreciate it. Adam's right though, I'd be remiss if we didn't start with those. We have one of each right now, it's a good place to begin."

Calay was about to ask what the mutations were but Holden didn't give her the chance. Barely pausing for a breath, they continued.

"A few weeks ago, we caught our first Faceless. Some of the soldiers trapped it in the forest, shot it, killed it, brought it back here. We dissected it and several others since then. They're fast, but they aren't hard to catch. They tend to come straight to us. Well, for us."

"For us." Calay whispered, a shudder rolling down her back.

"Yes, for us." Adam nodded, but barely. "They don't seem to have fear or an instinct to survive. Just one to kill."

"That can't be right." Calay wrapped her arms tighter around herself. "They're living things. Every living thing wants to survive."

"Living things also tend to be fairly territorial. If we look to the wild —lions, wolves, orcas—all hunters, all highly protective of their territory. If the Faceless see this planet as theirs, they'll fight to the death to claim it." Adam gestured toward the gurneys as he made his point.

"This is our theory, anyhow." Holden cleared their throat. "We've used it to our advantage to capture them and learn about them."

Calay narrowed her eyes and her curiosity, keen to find out if their information matched what she already knew. "What have you learned?"

"Based on what we've been able to gather, the Faceless and the Others are the same creature."

Calay's arms dropped to her side, her mouth gaped. "Are you saying the Faceless are a mutation of the Others?"

Holden nodded while pulling the two stretchers together, placing the creatures side by side as if to compare them. "Yes, exactly."

"That's too fast." Calay's gaze flickered between Adam and Holden. "That's impossible. Biology needs years, decades—millennia—to mutate."

"You're correct, in a way." Holden waved Calay closer. "That's true for living things on Earth. We don't know a single thing about how alien biology works,. Not on a cellular level, anyhow. We don't know what it needs to mutate. Or how long."

Calay shuffled alongside Holden, forced herself to look up close and personal. Their shapes were so different, so terrible. "What brought you to this theory? Where's your proof?"

Holden picked up something shiny. It glinted under the florescent lighting.

A scalpel, Calay realized. Her eyes widened in disbelief as she watched them twirl it between two fingers, stepping deliberately to the Faceless's corpse. Bile rose in her throat. She'd never been good with blood. Or dead bodies, for that matter. There was a reason she'd hidden in their camp for four years while Tess had been the one to fall into the role of the protector. It was the same thing that had driven them apart—Calay further inside herself, and Tess, into the arms of the Resistance.

Calay knew the parts they'd played in the early days didn't matter anymore. None of it did. If she was going to put an end to the Others and save humanity, she was going to have to grow a spine. Or at least, a stronger stomach.

She steeled herself as Holden brought the knife down to the almost translucent skin of the Faceless, the blade disappearing into its chest. Their hand steady and their gaze focused on the task at hand, they slid the knife down below its belly before carving a T at the top and bottom of the incision.

There was something unsettling about how human, and yet, how inhuman, the body looked. There was no blood, no spillage of organs as Calay expected there might be. She glanced to Adam who looked as if he was even more disturbed than she was.

Holden set the scalpel gingerly on a nearby metal tray which housed several other glistening instruments.

Calay tried not to picture Jacob strapped to a gurney just like this one, only vertical. In this very same room. Deep slashes across his skin, his eyes soft behind a cloud of sedation. His chest exploding as she shot him at almost point-blank range.

Calay clenched her eyes, forced the image from her mind, just in time to watch Holden slip their hand inside the Faceless's body. She winced when a loud crackling sound broke the silence and Holden expertly pulled one flap back, then the other. The flesh parted and hung heavy off the side of the table.

Calay pressed her lips together and inched closer to the flayed Faceless. She peered into the cavity. Inside, long, black threads knotted themselves around even blacker lumps of flesh. Organs, probably. But they weren't where any human organs would be.

Calay lunged for the garbage can and threw up nothing but the very little remnants of her breakfast from earlier that day. Right, she hadn't eaten that afternoon. Maybe it was for the best. When she was finished, she wiped the side of her mouth on the sleeve of her sweater and stood to find both Adam and Holden staring at her.

"You alright?" Adam frowned, pale.

"She's fine." Holden turned their attention back to their work.

"Yeah, good, thanks for caring." Calay eased back to Adam's side.

"If you compare the two," Holden began as if she hadn't just thrown up her guts in front of them. Then again, they chopped up dead bodies and dug around them for fun. Or, maybe they were just doing what they had to. Like her. "The inside of the Faceless is almost identical to the inside of the Other. The organ placement is different and the strands— or veins? —are denser in the Other. Their outsides are shaped differently so I suppose it makes sense their insides wouldn't be quite the same."

Adam shook his head, covered his mouth with his hand. "The thing I don't get, is out of all the shapes they could have taken, why humanoid?"

"I think I know." Calay stiffened. Something shifted for her in that moment. A light bulb clicked on. If she could just shine the light on the truth pacing the edges of her mind.

"Please, enlighten us." Holden stepped back from the gurney and waited.

Elora had told Calay a lot about the replicas. They embodied human form to gain the trust of hybrids. Posing as her mother, they were almost able to recruit Calay to their side, use her to enact their final act of war: human extinction. Calay fought to find the words to tell these two that without telling them she was an alien herself. Try as she might to fix her mistakes, it would all be for not if she couldn't somehow distance herself from the Others. They were one and the same, but the Resistance couldn't know that. Not now. Maybe not ever. Still, she had to keep as close to the truth as possible. That's what Tess would have done.

Calay took a deep breath. "I don't think they're so much mutations as they are mistakes."

"Come again?" Holden leaned forward and pressed their glasses up their nose.

"I met someone before I came here. He claimed to be an Other." Calay levelled her gaze at Adam who nodded so subtly, if she blinked, she would have missed it. She swallowed, knowing he understood she was talking about Jacob. "He looked human. Would have convinced me too, if I hadn't found out the truth in your admin room."

That whisper of a grin curled at Holden's lips. "The truth you stole."

"Yeah, well if I didn't steal it we wouldn't be having this conversation now, would we?"

"Yes yes, everything happens for a reason." Holden shrugged.

Calay bristled. "It does!"

"Please." Adam righted himself and cleared his throat. "Continue, Calay."

"He looked human, but he was still alien, inside, right? We know water is toxic to them, and Earth is mostly water. We're in the pacific northwest, for fuck's sake. We live in a rain forest. But like you've said Holden, we don't know how their biology works on a cellular level. What if water doesn't actually kill them? At least not at first. What if it just mangles them?"

"What are you saying?" Holden's voice dropped in volume. They nodded their head, their shoulders relaxed. They might have been a giant pain in the ass, but Calay could tell they were smart. They had gleaned information about these monsters. Their interest, if not their approval, reassured Calay she was onto something and that gave her the confidence to continue.

"I think the Faceless are the Others, trapped in human form."

Silence followed as Calay's words settled between them. Neither Adam or Holden moved. They barely breathed. Calay paced between the two gurneys, waiting for someone to say something. Anything. A moment passed. Then another. She wondered if she'd gone too far. Shared too much. Finally, she came to a stop at the head of the tables.

Calay turned, unable to bear it any longer, and exhaled. "Well?"

"Is that possible?" Adam shuddered.

"If you'd asked me five years ago if aliens would ever invade Earth, destroy life as we knew it, and kill everyone we ever loved, I would have said you'd watched too many science fiction movies. Now look where we are." Holden shrugged. "I suppose anything's possible."

The truth nestled in Calay's stomach. The more she said it, the surer she was. "Doesn't that make more sense than a mutation? Evolution doesn't work that fast, but errors happen in nature all the time. Come on you guys—"

"Not a guy." Holden raised their hand.

"You're right, I know. I'm sorry. You *two*—" Calay paused, glanced to Holden who nodded in approval. "Mutation takes too long. The Others haven't been here for enough time to really consider that a viable possibility. But what if the Faceless are just an aberration in a process we already exists?"

Holden disposed of their mug in the nearby sink. "She might be onto something,"

Good, maybe they were getting somewhere after all.

"Look outside, too." Calay pointed toward the plastic sheeting. "The weather is doing some pretty crazy shit because of them. Doesn't it make sense that if they have an effect on our environment, the environment might have an effect on them too?"

"I have to admit." Adam peered at Calay from the top of his brow. "I like the idea that they're more alien than human."

"They might look humanoid, but make no mistake, they're monsters, inside and out." Holden pushed their glasses further up their nose before folding them into their pocket. They sniffed, nodded. "Okay, so let's play with Calay's theory that they're just a horrible mistake. Something the Others hadn't accounted for when they came to a planet that was made up almost entirely of water."

"That would explain the same biological composition inside their bodies. They're effectively the same creature," Adam concurred.

"They have the same activity in their brains too." Holden turned to Adam but their blue eyes never leaving the dissected Other on the gurney. "Even in death."

Holden kept talking, but Calay missed the rest of what they said. Her thoughts suddenly went blank. Something about their statement wasn't right. She wandered across the room, away from the conversation, stared up at the paneled ceiling. She let her vision grow spotted while she stared into the overhead lights.

A ghost of an idea lurked in the darkness of her mind. A thread. She pulled on it. One fistful, then another. Until she held it clear as day in the front of her brain.

A cold wave of panic crept up her spine and nestled between her shoulder blades.

"Wait, what?" She interrupted, blinking the fuzzy dark spots out of her eyes.

Adam slid his hands in his pockets, already bracing himself for the cold outside. "I said we can get some rest, come back fresh tomorrow."

"No, before that. Holden said something about brain activity."

"That was ages ago." Holden smirked. "But yes, the circuitry in their brains is identical."

"But they're dead when you dissect them, aren't they?"

"Sure, that's the crazy thing. For all biological processes we understand, they're dead. No heartbeat. No blood flow. No functioning organs or bodily movements that we can tell. But..." Holden sprung to the Other, it's form equally lifeless and flayed as its Faceless counterpart. Holden slid their fingers along a thin line that ran the length of its cranium, peeled back the skin. It made the same crackling sound as the Faceless chest did when Holden had opened it.

This time, and Calay wasn't sure how, she kept the contents of her stomach in check. That is, until the room lit up in gold light. Then, it plummeted.

Gazing into the glow, something behind Holden's eyes came alive. "Their brains, if this is the brain, it's tough to tell because there's no identifiable organ here—just a bunch of loose elastic bands—is still online."

Calay stilled her movements, as if that could contain the panic rushing through her body. Holden was right. Several strands, not unlike the ones in their chests, were flashing brilliant gold. One tiny lightning strike after the other.

A gentle but persistent buzzing rattled inside Calay's mind. She recalled what Jacob had told her, time and time again. The way he'd found her, and how they communicated. Suddenly Calay understood why the attacks on the Resistance compound had increased. It wasn't just because she was there, as she'd thought earlier. It was because the Resistance had tortured and dismembered not just one, but several of their family members. The flashing gold lights were a beacon, leading the Others right to the compound. They knew exactly where to go to recover their bodies. And exact revenge.

The vibration in Calay's brain grew louder. It flooded her thoughts, her limbs, the very air between them. Adam and Holden didn't seem to notice. It was as though it was coming from inside Calay. The Other's brain activity—it must be where the heat signatures are, she realized. The Hivemind. For the first time ever, she could feel it. It was everywhere. And if she could feel it, the Others could too. The Resistance may have killed their bodies, but their ability to communicate with each other was still alive. It wasn't some abstract concept. It was something real. Something tangible. Something right fucking here. Exposed.

Calay's blood ran cold.

If these monsters really were like other animals—territorial, hungry, defensive—they weren't going to stop until they killed every last person there.

CHAPTER FIVE

CALAY'S VISION SWAM, the room grew dark. She could feel the ground swaying beneath her.

Nope, not the ground.

That was her. All her.

She reached for the gurney but stopped herself a moment before her fingers brushed the Térasian's bulging flesh. Instead, she grounded herself with a clammy hand on Adam's sleeve. He peered down at her, his strong brows knitting together with concern.

"Calay, are you alright?" Adam's voice sounded far away. As though he was speaking to her from a long, deep tunnel.

She focused on his words, tried to make sense of them. No, of course she was not okay. She was the exact opposite of okay.

"She looks a little green." Holden's voice inched its way inside Calay's ears. She was distantly aware of them sliding the already puke-filled garbage can closer.

"Do you want to sit down?" Adam reached for the stool while gripping her forearm. He guided her as she sunk onto the edge. "Holden, why don't you get her some tea?"

Calay shook her head. She didn't want to sit down. She didn't want tea. She wanted to run. As far away from this place—and these people—

as possible. She'd assumed it was all her fault the attacks on the compound had increased. That was something she could handle. Guilt was an emotion she'd grown familiar with. Cozy, even. Ash and Jacob's warnings echoed in her mind. They'd promised the Others would come for her. They'd search and find her. Destroy her. When she'd fled from the remnants of Téras and Galaxy 3C303, that was what she was prepared to fight. One at a time, until humanity prevailed.

This was something else entirely. Calay wasn't ready for it.

A trickle of sweat crawled down her back, she shivered. The idea that the Resistance were keeping the Others online, sending a direct beacon to their species elsewhere in the universe, was more than unnerving.

It was downright terrifying.

Calay didn't know how the Others' biology worked, and even with all their science and Mad Hatter experiments, Holden admitted the Resistance wasn't sure either. Calay was certain of one thing though: through the hive mind, their bodies were relaying every single thing humans had done to them: cut them open, dismembered them, tortured them.

On the starship, she'd seen with her very own eyes the way they protected their own. The lengths they'd go to ensure their survival— they'd destroyed planet after planet, civilization after civilization. Humanity didn't know what they were about to unleash.

Not like Calay did.

If the Resistance brought the full weight of the Others down on them now, no one was safe anymore. Not behind these thick, concrete walls. Not within the confines and reinforcements of the Loft. Not on Earth.

Not anywhere.

It wouldn't be a few rogue aliens trying to get to Calay. It would be the entirety of their species coming for this place. For them. For her.

A coldness curled up her spine at the realization that running wouldn't do a damn thing for any of them. The Others were coming. The Faceless, too. They were going to have to stand and fight until one side or the other or both was properly slaughtered and dead. It was what Tess would have wanted. And the only choice Calay had.

"Drink this, it'll help." Holden offered Calay a porcelain cup with small red roses on the side. She absently peered over the lip. It was filled with a dark green liquid. "It's nothing fancy, just some mint tea. It'll help soothe your stomach."

It occurred to Calay this was the first kindness Holden had extended to her since they'd met. Maybe they weren't so bad after all. She blinked at the loose leaves settled at the bottom of the cup, letting resolve slowly circle her mind. She peered between Holden and Adam, both of them staring at her. Waiting. For what, she wasn't sure. To accept the cup. To explain herself. To die. She sighed deeply, pushed the relentless buzzing from her mind.

They had no idea what they'd done.

She needed to warn them, without giving herself away in the process. They still didn't know about her journey to deep space and she intended to keep it that way for as long as possible.

"No, thank you Holden." Calay swallowed, pushed herself to stand. The black dots cleared from her vision, the room righted itself. "Adam, I need to talk to you."

"I think you need to take a moment." Adam's hands hung in the space between them, ready to catch her should her legs betray her again. "I'm pretty sure you just about passed out, Calay. Let's all just take a deep breath and relax. Maybe we should go get you something to eat. You said you were hungry, right?"

It was true. She was bloody starving. But food wasn't what was on Calay's mind right now. Surviving was.

"After." She nodded. "I have to talk to you. Now."

"Okay," Adam sighed, shrugged. "So talk."

Calay shook her head. "Not here. Alone."

"Hey now. Why can't I listen?" Holden frowned and raised the tea cup they'd intended for Calay to their lips.

"Holden's right, I trust them. Anything you have to say you can say right here."

That wasn't true. Though the sincerity in Adam's face almost brought Calay to her knees. He assumed he knew all her secrets. He probably figured she'd already outed her relationship status with their dearly departed leader and the fact that she'd dispatched her, so whatever was about to come out of Calay's mouth couldn't be that bad. He was wrong.

"I need you to trust me when I say I can't." Calay pressed her lips together.

"Calay—"

"Adam, please."

She watched Adam's gaze float to Holden's. Holden took another gulp from the mug, closed their eyes, nodded. Adam gave them one sharp nod in return and turned to Calay.

"Have it your way."

A COLD SNAP OF WINTER AIR ALMOST STOLE THE BREATH from Calay's lungs when she and Adam exited the building. She pulled the scarf up over her head, secured it around her neck.

"Do we have to talk all the way out here? There are perfectly good, and might I add warm, offices inside." Adam pulled a pair of old leather gloves over his wide hands. He shoved them in his jacket pockets for good measure.

"I can't risk being overheard." Calay peered over her shoulder, watching the heavy utility door latch behind them.

"Everything's on record now."

Calay blinked up at him from behind the snowflakes settling on her lashes. The corners of her mouth turned down and she averted her gaze to the footprints they'd left in the snow.

Adam sighed for the umpteenth time since she'd met him, pulling her attention to his concerned face.

"Calay, what aren't you telling me?"

Calay mirrored his sigh; this wasn't going to be easy. "I know we just finished talking about trust."

"Do you? Because it feels like you're about to betray mine."

"I'm sorry." Calay's words were barely above a whisper. Her pulse too.

Adam pulled his shoulders back. "This is why you didn't want to talk inside. You didn't want Holden to hear what you're about to say because I don't know what you're about to say."

Adam wasn't dumb, he was a clever guy. It never took him long to put the puzzle pieces together. Calay had to give him that. She almost envied his naivety. His innocence. His ability to trust. Almost.

If only she wasn't about to destroy it. Again.

Calay nodded.

"I seriously don't know why I let you out of that cell." Adam kicked the snow off his boots, bunched his shoulders up to his ears. "Out with it then. It's freezing out here."

Calay forced herself to hold Adam's gaze. "You have to take the Other offline."

"Excuse me?"

"The activity happening in its mind. We have to stop it. Now."

"Why would we do that?"

"It's important."

"Calay, why?"

"It just is, alright."

"Okay, let's assume that it is. But is it as important as learning more about the Others? Seriously Calay, I thought you of all people would want to understand them. Figure out how they work. Maybe there's a key in their biology that could lead to our victory. Our chance to fight them will be stronger if we know how they tick."

Calay's tone turned cutting, "We won't have that chance if we don't turn it off now."

"Turn it off?" Adam blinked, half grinning. "I know it looked like electricity, but's not exactly like it's plugged in. Besides, it's dead."

A realization dawned on Calay. The memory of Elora's body engulfed in flames assaulted her memory. She didn't want to think about it. Couldn't. She knew that thing wasn't her mother, but that fact didn't lessen the pain of watching someone who looked just like her burn alive. The smell of her charred flesh embedded itself in Calay's cells. It was something Calay would never forget. It was also why she torched their starship. Nothing seemed to stop the Others but total annihilation.

"Holden has to destroy the brain," she said through clenched teeth, her eyes pleading.

"Do you hear yourself? You've read too many apocalypse books."

Panic was rising in Calay faster than her tempter. The words poured out of her before she could sensor them. "I mean it. Smash it. Set it on fire. Weight it down and throw it in the ocean. Get rid of any physical remains of its body. The Faceless, too. Get them out of here."

Adam frowned. "That's not happening, Calay."

"Adam—"

"Look, I'm doing the best I can to work with you, but unless you give me a valid reason—the real reason—why we should stop our research, this conversation is over." Adam turned to go back inside.

This was it. Whether Calay liked it or not, she was going to have to come clean. At least, a little.

"Okay," she yelled into the night sky. Her breath pooled in the brisk air. "Look, I just... I didn't tell you this before because I didn't think it mattered. But it turns out it really, really does."

Adam tapped his boot on the frozen ground in response.

"The reason we have to get rid of the body—"

"Destroy the brain, I think were your exact words."

"Yes, the reason we have to destroy the brain and get rid of the body is because those gold wires in its brain are emitting a signal."

Adam tilted his head. "What kind of signal?"

"It's a beacon." Calay wrapped her arms around herself. It did little to keep out the truth or the cold. "They call it a heat signature. Every alien has one."

Understanding dawned on Adam's face. "That's why there's been an increase in attacks. It's leading them to us."

"I haven't even told you the worst part yet." Calay cringed.

Adam levelled his gaze, his voice low. "Go on."

Calay was sure Adam was listening, the real question was, would he believe her? Could he believe her? After she'd kept this from him, she wouldn't blame him if he didn't. Still, she had to continue. Even if it meant he never believed her again.

"The whole time that thing has been here, it's been communicating with Them. Relaying information—what Holden's done to it, what we've said. Everything. Which means anything you and Holden have discussed within range of its hearing—"

"—It's told the Others," Adam finished.

"Yes. As long as it's online, it's communicating."

"Are you sure?" Adam narrowed his eyes at her. He pulled his hands from his pockets and crossed his arms over his chest. Calay wasn't sure if he was keeping the cold out, or the truth.

So much for not giving myself away.

"I saw it myself."

"When they followed you?"

"No, not when they followed me." Calay shrunk under Adam's gaze. She knew what she was about to say would sound insane. It could cause her a world of pain, but not nearly as much hurt as it would if she didn't say anything. "When they took me to their home galaxy."

What little warmth Adam had left drained from his cheeks. "What?"

"Before I surrendered myself to the Resistance, I was aboard their ship."

"That's impossible."

"I swear to you, Adam."

"How?"

"Do you remember the Other I was here with last time? Jacob?"

For the second time, Adam nodded so subtly Calay almost missed it.

"He brought me with him to what he told me was their home planet, Téras. It turned out it wasn't a planet at all. Not since before I arrived with him. They'd invaded it, used up the resources, and then they destroyed it."

"You're saying an alien abducted you and took you away on his spaceship?"

Now it was Calay's turn to nod slowly, as if she might break.

"Why would he do that? And if you say to perform tests on you, so help me, Calay…"

"No, well, kind of, actually." She grasped at details, things she could share that wouldn't spill her darkest secrets. The ones that could actually get her killed for simply existing. "They wanted to understand people better. Not so much through physical testing, but mental. They hate us, Adam. They want to break us. Eradicate us. Extinct us."

"And what? After they gained a better understanding they just let you go?"

"Not exactly, no. I escaped. I got into one of their pods and it brought me back here." Calay took a deep inhale, ignored the tears that sprung behind her eyes. She skipped the fact that she got into the pod through use of the hive mind and that she was able to pilot one because she was herself, Other. "When I came to, I was outside the compound. I knew they'd be coming for me. So…"

"So you decided to hide here." Adam's lips curled into a sneer.

"Not hide, no. I chose to come here to fight them. Together. I meant it when I told you I know details about them. Things that will help us! They might have brought me to Téras to use me, but I used them too."

"Well this makes a lot more fucking sense why they didn't blast you away out there. Before, you said when they followed you, you evaded them before you came here. Was that even true?"

"Absolutely." Despite the cold, a gentle warmth flushed to Calay's cheeks. This was why she skirted as the truth as much as possible. It made it easier to remain indignant when someone called you a liar, which, she hoped made her story more believable. "But that happened before Jacob took me away."

"You lied to me, Calay."

"I didn't lie, I just omitted a few details." Calay almost rolled her eyes at that one. It was the understatement of the century. Even now, she was still hiding things. But it was either that, or they'd do what Tess had tried. They'd kill her along with the rest of the Others. Maybe they were right to do so. But Calay—and hybrids like her—were human, too. They deserved a chance to survive just like anybody else. If they could end this war, the Others' plans would die with them, including the replica program. And hybrids would no longer pose a threat to humanity, they'd just be different.

Adam grunted, his face fell. "A lie of omission is still a lie."

It took everything Calay had not to recoil. Adam's words stung. Hadn't she told Jacob the exact same thing a few weeks ago? Held him accountable for his omissions? His lies? She'd left him to die on a burning ship for them.

"I think we're getting a little off topic here." Calay shifted her weight and changed the subject. "As long as we allow that alien to maintain hive mind activity, we're making ourselves a bigger target."

"If we kill it, we'll be safe?" Something akin to hope flashed behind Adam's gaze.

Calay half-shrugged. "I'm saying if we kill it we don't have to worry about it healing itself and coming back to kill us. I know you know about their ability to repair. I read all about it in that records room when I was here last time. From what I saw in space, the damage of keeping the hive mind intact is already done. They know where we are. They know what we've done. The only thing we can do now is prepare for the assault."

"Fuck!" Adam's voice echoed across the snow-covered yard and through the nearby forest. He thrust his hands on his hips, glared at her. "What else?"

"What else what?"

"What else are you keeping from me?"

"Nothing, I swear Adam." Calay knew if anything else came to light, this promise might be her last. So, she offered him one final morsel of truth. It was the most she could give him and keep herself alive long enough to carry out Tess's mission. To save humanity. She exhaled heavily before she continued. "Just one small thing, actually. At least one of them followed me back to Earth."

"You mean back here." Adam ran a gloved hand over his rage filled face.

"Maybe. When I crawled out of the pod, there was another one nearby, but it was empty."

"All this protection. All our efforts to remain unseen. The lengths we've gone to so they wouldn't see or hear us." Adam shook his head. "They worked for years. Then you show up and bring one of them straight to our door."

"Whoever it was took off before I saw them. I don't know if they saw me. They might not have." Calay's voice cracked. "I think if they did, they would have killed me on the spot."

"You think? Or you know?"

She had no idea.

Silence crept into the space between them. It lasted a moment. An eternity. It was all Calay could do to keep from running inside and smashing the Other's skull herself. She wrapped her arms tighter around her waist to keep herself in place. She wanted to ease Adam's fears, to give him something to hold onto. She'd lost everything, but she still had Tess. Or at least, the memory of her. Calay clung to it like a life raft. Tess did a terrible thing, trying to murder her, but Calay understood now.

Like Adam said, no one was clean anymore. Everyone was just doing what they needed to, to survive. She hoped he understood that, too.

"Go."

"You want me to leave?" Calay blanched. She didn't blame him. Not entirely.

"What? No. Go. Find some dinner, Calay. Sleep. I don't fucking care what you do." Adam wrenched the heavy door open and was already several long strides inside before the rest of his words found their way past his lips. Alone and adrift outside, Calay only barely caught the tail end of them. "Right now, all I care about is getting that thing the hell out of here."

CHAPTER SIX

THE SNOW CRUNCHED under Calay's boots as she shifted her weight from one foot to the other. She knew she should go after Adam. Make sure he and Holden did what needed to be done. She just couldn't bring herself to go back in that building and face those deformed, mutilated corpses again. Words couldn't describe the terror they stirred inside her. Though if she was being honest with herself, it wasn't just them she wanted to avoid. It was the anger in Adam's eyes. The judgement she was sure would be in Holden's when they found out she'd lied. They'd only just met and if first impressions were anything to go by, Calay should have, for all accounts, not given a shit about what Holden thought. They'd been rude, intense, even a bit hostile. But she understood first impressions were mostly garbage. Facades that were meant to hide something deeper. Like fear.

Calay knew that game better than anyone.

If she never saw another alien in her life, it would be too soon. She'd do just about anything to avoid it. To never have to stare into the abyss of the grotesque aberrations of the Faceless. But that dream that was a long way from coming true.

They were coming, and there was nothing she could do about it.

A loud screech sounded in the distance, echoing through the night, a stark reminder of that fact.

Calay braced herself, shivering in the cold, and peered through the dark. The forest swelled in the night like an inky wave, the tops of the trees swaying in the brisk air.

The horrible noise sounded again. Further, this time, if she had to guess. *Good.* The Resistance still had some time. How much, Calay didn't know. All she knew was she needed to fix things with Adam. She needed him to trust her. Work with her. Otherwise, she was already dead.

They all were.

Calay shifted her gaze to the fences. Someone had patched the hole the Faceless had torn in it earlier that day. It was a lattice of metal and zap straps. Coils of barbed wire lined the perimeter. Yards of camouflage mesh layered between buildings. Instinctively, her eyes focused beyond the netting, searching the sky for something. What? She could not name it.

There were no stars peeking through the canvas tonight. Just a sliver of moon under a layer of midnight blue clouds. Fat, chunky flakes settled on her eyelashes. She blinked them away, sighed. Maybe Adam was right. Calay should have been more forthcoming. At least then he would have known what he was getting himself into when he allowed her to stay. She put everyone at risk by coming here. But the danger she packed with her was not nearly as much as he'd unfurled when he sanctioned experiments on the Others.

The difference was she knew better.

She pulled the scarf tighter around her head and tucked the fringe ends inside her jacket. She swiped at any stray hairs that dared to escape. The wind calmed as she plodded across the yard, back toward the main building. If she didn't get back soon, she'd miss dinner and it would be a full twenty-four hours between meals.

A glimmer caught her attention out of the corner of her eye. She turned. It was the moat. Last time she was here, she'd almost drowned in it trying to escape. She wondered if this time it would do anything at all to protect her. Protect them. All their defenses were Band-Aid solutions. Temporary measures that had worked when the Others stuck to the skies in their pods. They'd never even known the Resistance was here. But now, that had changed. The Others were braving Earth's atmosphere and the inherent dangers that came with it. Calay wondered how much longer they could maintain their safety here. Anywhere, really. And whether they'd ever get to feel safe again.

She inhaled a deep breath. Then exhaled. Tried to calm the noise of thoughts rattling around in her mind. Suddenly there was water in front of her. She'd somehow approached the moat. She hadn't even realized she'd crossed the yard. She shuffled onto the dock, inching her way across the slippery wood. She pressed her toes against the edge. Let the lip of her boots hang over the side. A thin layer of ice formed on the water's surface. It twinkled in the sparse moonlight.

She'd do everything she could to protect her last remaining secret. Lies had already damaged her rapport with Adam and the Resistance, but she needed to safeguard the one that remained. With her life. Literally. If they were to find out she was half-alien, she'd never do what she came here to do. Save them. Humanity. Herself. This was her one chance and she wasn't about to give that up just because it didn't align with Adam's moral code.

Rules were meant to be broken. People weren't.

Calay would have to be more careful from now on. With her secrets. With Adam's trust. With their lives. A war was coming, and they were going to need their collective strength.

She searched past the fences, into the wilderness beyond. Between snowbanks, a grassy knoll rolled out into the darkness like a red carpet. An invitation for the Others. A wall of trees sprouted at its edge. A fortress. It didn't matter whether it would shield them from the impending attack or simply make it easier for their enemies to hide. Something was out there. Something bigger than Calay. Something worse. She squinted through the shadows, a ripple of fear shuddered through her—she was afraid of what she might find, yet unable to look away.

"What's out there?" she whispered.

The Others.

The Faceless.

Jacob...?

Calay's heart hitched. An image of the second pod, discarded like a child's toy, floated through her mind. It couldn't be him, could it? An ache bloomed deep within her chest. In a way she couldn't help but hope he'd survived, somehow made it to safety. Though she had to acknowledge that if that was true, it was only a matter of time before he found her again. Like he always did.

Which meant it was only a matter of time before she had to kill him.

As much as it pained Calay, Tess's mission was her mission now. Tess had been right all along, and Calay was determined to do right by her. Make up for her wrongs. And that meant putting an end to the Others.

Every. Last. One.

The truth was, Calay still didn't know who'd followed her back to Earth. Or why they were waiting to reveal themselves. She closed her eyes, opened her thoughts and tried to connect with the hive mind, to feel their presence. All she received back was an inky void. She didn't know if she'd somehow used up her ability to connect with the hive mind as she'd returned to Earth, or if they simply cut her off. If that was even a thing.

Probably for the best.

She had no doubt the Others were evil. That aligning herself with them in any way was a betrayal of Earth. Of humankind. Still, she couldn't help but feel a sense of emptiness and longing in the hive's absence.

She'd caught a glimpse of it inside earlier. When Holden had revealed the Other's firing synapses, the buzzing almost brought Calay to her knees. If the sheer panic hadn't gotten to her first, maybe it would have. It had been too long since she'd felt anything close to the innate connection the Others had. The one she'd experienced on the starship. It wasn't until it was gone that she realized how much it had filled her with a feeling of wholeness. Completion. Whether she liked it or not, it was—the Others were—a part of her.

When Calay opened her eyes again, the clouds had swallowed the moon. Long shadows crept across the boardwalk, shrouding the water in a cloak of darkness. Everything stilled. Even the snow had stopped falling.

It was time to go inside.

Tomorrow was another day. After a bit of rest, some time to cool down, and disposing of those hideous alien bodies, she'd approach Adam and start strategizing about how to save everyone, together.

Calay took a step away from the edge when a hand closed around the back of her neck.

A sharp searing pain erupted from her shoulder.

She opened her mouth to scream but her voice was cut short by the impact of her chest slamming into the wooden platform. She gasped for air, tried to suck in giant mouthfuls. None of it seemed to reach her lungs.

Whoever was attacking her shoved their boney knee into the center of her back. Blood pooled under her. She reached up to feel the hilt of a knife sticking out of her shoulder blade.

She'd been stabbed.

Her eyes rolled back in her head. She struggled against their weight, but it only made the pain worse.

She changed tactics. She stilled. Forced herself to go limp. To surrender. Whoever it was couldn't mean to kill her, could they? Out in the open like this? Where anyone could find them? She just had to wait them out. Thankfully, oxygen was now trickling down her throat, she was able to breathe. Barely.

She winced as warm breath curled around her ear.

"I know what you are," the attacker whispered.

"I don't know what you're talking about." Calay sputtered between short breaths.

"Of course you do. You're not going to get away this time."

"What are you talking about?" Terror rippled across Calay's exposed skin, creeping into her bones. Did whoever this was know her final secret?

"There's nowhere you can run I can't find you again," they growled.

The breath grew hotter against Calay's skin with each syllable, burning their way into her soul. She wanted to scream, to fight. It was all she could do to force the next words out of her throat.

"Please, you don't have to do this," Calay squeaked. She could barely see—let alone speak—through the fear and the growing heat in her shoulder.

"I'm only finishing what I started."

"What?"

"I told Tess we never should have left you alone in that warehouse. We should have done it right the first time."

Dread flooded Calay. This person was one of the men from that first morning all those months ago. When she'd woken up, bloodied and without Tess. He'd left her for dead and only returned to dispose of her broken body. He'd looked her in the eye—chased her off the edge of that roof.

"Wait," she pleaded.

The man tensed, but that only caused his weight to grow sharper. "I'm sorry."

Calay wracked her brain on how to buy herself time. She needed another moment. Maybe two. Just to catch her breath and regain some of her strength.

She wouldn't get it.

The next thing she knew her face was in the icy water. She gagged on the cold liquid. It overwhelmed her senses. It filled her ears, her mouth. Her nose. It was everywhere. She tried to push herself up on the dock, but the heaviness of his hand on the back of her head held her there, despite her flailing.

Then it was on her back. He'd straddled her, she realized in horror. She wasn't getting out of this.

The night muffled, the trees rippled and merged.

He shoved her deeper. Her arms were now submerged. The wooden planks of the boardwalk dug into her hips. Calay thrashed. She punched, and clawed, and kicked, for everything it was worth. It turned out, not much. She knew surrendering would only get her so far. In this case, the bottom of a very cold, very dark body of water.

Calay was going to have to fight.

A raw, blood-curdling scream wrenched itself from her throat. She twisted one way, then the other. The arm pinning her beneath the surface didn't budge. Every second under water was another closer to death. She tried to think of anything other than the piercing cold. It pricked every inch of her skin. Her lungs. Her mind. There had to be something she could do to free herself.

In a brief moment of clarity, she realized whoever was holding her had to be leaning pretty far over to keep her in place; half her body was submerged. She swung her hands up and around, above her head. The tips of her fingers reached into the frigid night air. She couldn't hold the position for long though, her arms ached with the effort. She tried again. Grasped at anything she could. Her palms grazed something soft. Fabric. The darkness closed in around her. She dug her fingers in, grabbed hold with the last ounce of strength she had, and dug her boots into the dock.

Then, Calay dove.

The solid grip on the back of her head eased with a loud splash. Relief rolled through her. Her attacker hadn't been expecting *that*.

Calay kicked at the water, pushed herself to the surface. With each stroke, her arm thundered with pain. Higher still. She reminded herself she'd been through worse. Only a few more inches. Three. Two. One.

She swallowed the cold night air in thirsty gulps. When she reached for the dock, she was yanked backward.

Something had ahold of her ankle.

She kicked furiously, clawed at the wood. A ragged scream tore through her throat, crying for help. If she could just get herself up and out of the water, she'd run for the nearest building. Someone had to hear her yell.

It wouldn't matter though because suddenly she was under water again. Despite her efforts, she was sinking. They weren't letting go. She refused to believe whoever was down there with her was willing to die in this grave. But why wouldn't they? Tess had been willing to give her life up for her cause. Jacob, too. And Ash. Elora. Even her father had died for his convictions. It seemed every choice was a life-or-death one now.

Calay glanced down, her lungs on fire. She couldn't even see the face of the person gripping her ankle. Just a dark silhouette against a darker backdrop. Calay had been here before. In the depths of this moat. She'd been ready to give up then. To let the darkness swallow her whole. She wasn't ready this time.

She kicked. She flailed. It was no use.

She wouldn't get to make amends; Tess's work would remain unfulfilled. Adam might even think she'd left after their fight. Everyone would die. And soon.

No, this was wrong.

She peered up, into the nothingness above. Only, there wasn't nothingness. There was the outline of a face.

Calay would have gasped if she had any oxygen left. She'd know that face anywhere.

Tess's almond brown eyes shone down at her. She giggled, the dimples in her honey-colored cheeks winked at Calay. Her long, curly dark hair spread in all directions, floating like a life raft in the dark water. The murky depths of the moat faded away. Tess's smile seemed to radiate light in all directions.

So this is death.

A warmth spread through Calay's chest as she reached for her dead lover. Tess reached back. Their fingers intertwined and palms kissed. Their hands fit together. They'd always fit together.

Then the light faded. Darkness returned. The cold, too. Any respite Calay thought she might find in sleep recoiled with the sting of near-freezing water.

Her heart pounded against her chest. She was rising.

Her head breached the surface. Her shoulders too. She felt herself being pulled onto the dock. Someone was calling her name. She tried to focus, to bring some awareness back into her body. Everything hurt.

It was all that ever was. All that ever would be.

She clawed at the deck, peered over the edge.

No.

She searched for her one true love. The woman whose life she foolishly stole. The one she'd never get back.

No, no, no.

Tears sprang to her eyes, freezing on her cheeks before they could fall.

There was nothing but darkness. Shards of ice littered the surface where she'd been pulled under. Where she'd dragged whoever had attacked her down with her.

Someone wrapped a blanket around her shivering shoulders. She heard the sound of yelling; someone was calling for help. Calay peeled her gaze from the water. She searched the shoreline, the yard. Her attacker was gone. And with them, Tess, too.

Calay slumped backward, coming to rest within the gentle arms of someone she refused to look at. Instead, she closed her eyes. Tried to hang onto the vision of Tess's smile. Her laugh. The feel of their hands pressed together.

Calay thought she heard a woman's voice tell her everything was going to be okay.

Only, it wasn't.

WHEN SHE CAME TO, CALAY WAS DRY, WARM, AND TUCKED into her own bed. Covered in blankets. Lots of them. For a moment she allowed herself to imagine everything that happened had just been a terrible dream, but the sharp ache radiating from her shoulder betrayed that fiction.

A gentle beeping sounded through the room.

Calay gazed down to find herself dressed in over-sized, military green sweats, warm compresses tucked on either side of her torso.

"Where are my clothes?" Calay's voice was scratchy, her throat raw.

"You're awake," a voice said.

Calay blinked and rubbed the sleep away from her eyes to find Holden perched on a stool at the end of her bed, one leg draped over the other,. They were peering at her over their black-rimmed glasses.

They stood, smoothed the creases in their pants, and made their way over to the sink in the far corner. It was covered with a sheet of thin metal. On top were a variety of medical supplies—bandages, some kind of cream, a needle and thread. There was also, of course, Holden's signature giant mug of steaming tea. They reached over it and picked up something Calay couldn't quite see.

Calay tapped her throat with her bandaged fingers. "It hurts."

"It should after what you've been through."

"What happened?"

"You tell me." Holden approached Calay's side, shook whatever it was they had in their hand. "Open up."

A thermometer. Calay opened her mouth, her jaw ached with the effort. She wasn't sure if it was from the cold or if she'd hit it in the struggle. Holden placed the mercury-filled stem under her tongue. They pressed their glasses up as they waited.

In a few moments, Holden nodded. "You'll live, but barely. Well?"

"I'm not sure." Calay cleared her throat, pushed herself to sit. She winced with the effort. Holden set the thermometer aside, moved to prop an extra pillow behind her before checking the intravenous needle sticking out of her arm.

Holden's ice blue eyes glanced at her from over their black rimmed glasses. "Try."

"I was out in the yard." Calay took a slow breath. "Someone attacked me from behind. I think they stabbed me."

"You bet your ass they stabbed you. Took twelve stitches to close the wound. You're lucky, though."

Calay eased against the pillows. "How's that?"

"Another couple inches to the right and they would have punctured your lung."

"Yeah, real lucky."

"Seriously." Holden pulled their stool to the side of the bed before tossing another blanket across Calay's legs. Their intense blue gaze found hers and held it. "Who did this to you?"

"I don't know." Calay shook her head. She closed her eyes only to see that cold, dark, endless water. She opened them again. "I didn't get a good look at them."

"Calay, they almost killed you."

As if she didn't already know that. But Calay had no fight left in her this evening. Her shoulders slumped. "What do you care? You hate me."

"I don't hate you." Holden blinked at her.

"Seriously? You have a funny way of showing you like someone."

"I didn't say I like you."

"Oh." Calay folded her arms across her chest. This was the weirdest bedside manner she'd ever seen. She didn't want to be alone, but she wasn't sure she wanted Holden's company either.

"I like facts. I trust reason. " Holden said. "You know what I don't trust? Hubris. Lack of order. You've thrown this place into chaos."

"I can respect that." Calay painfully swallowed. "I haven't been here long. I know it takes time to build trust. I haven't exactly been doing my part in that."

"I don't just mean about the last few days." Holden took a sip out of the mug, hesitated, then handed it to her. "It's got local honey in it. It'll help with your throat."

"What do you mean, then?" Calay accepted their offer, held the rim up to her lips. She let the warm liquid ease the jagged edges. It burned. But in a good way. She closed her eyes, nodded her thanks.

"I know what you are."

That was the second time Calay had heard those words tonight. The memory of a rough hand on the back of her neck flashed through her mind. She could almost feel the air being knocked from her lungs all over again. She froze, the cup an inch from her lips. Her gaze darted toward the door. It wouldn't take her long to heal, given her ability to regenerate, but she knew it would take more than a few hours. In her state, with her injuries, if she needed to break out of this room right now, would she make it if she had to?

"You..." she rasped.

"Me what?"

"The person who attacked me said those same exact words earlier."

"I didn't attack you, Calay." Holden shook their head, their curved mouth almost smiled.

"Can you prove that?" She bristled, pressed herself against the pillows as if that would increase the distance between them.

"I can, actually. I was with Adam until Briar came running into the lab like a bat out of Hell, hysterically shouting you needed help. We'd just finished incinerating the...evidence."

They meant the bodies. Adam had done it. Destroyed them, thank gods. And thank Briar, whoever she was. Calay made a mental note to thank her later.

Calay tensed. Holden knew, then. Everything she'd told Adam. No wonder they looked at her like she was dirt. But that still didn't explain what they meant when they said they knew what she was.

"Thank you," she whispered.

"Oh you're so welcome." Holden rolled their eyes but smiled. For the first time, they actually smiled. Calay allowed her body to relax. Just a little. The amusement fell from Holden's face as they continued. "About the 'heat signatures' thing. We never would have known that. Thanks for the tip. I had my theories about how they were finding us, but..."

"What theories?"

"After seeing the way their brains lit up, I figured it was like light— every single thing on this planet emits light. The question of whether we see it or not depends on whether the wavelengths are within range of human eyesight."

Calay frowned. "Are you saying there's some light we can't see?"

"Exactly. There's lots of different kinds of light people can't see. Radio, infrared, ultraviolet, X-ray, gamma ray. We need special machines to see them. It stands to reason if a species evolved outside our world— our galaxy—they'd be able to see different kinds of light. Maybe even communicate through it."

"You think that's what heat signatures are?"

"I wasn't sure, but when you said 'heat signature,' it got me thinking. The temperature of an object defines the wavelength of light emitted. There's more to it than that, and if you make it through tonight I might bore you with the details over coffee sometime. But what if it's a heat signature because the temperature of their biology is something completely unmeasurable by our tools? At the very least, it's unique."

"That's why destroying their remains is the only thing that silences them." Calay leaned forward, spilling half the mug's contents. "Because you literally change their biological composition, which changes the light they emit."

Holden took the mug from Calay's hands and raised their eyebrows while lifting it to their lips. "Yes."

"I think you're onto something, Holden." Calay nodded, following. She wasn't sure she understood the science behind Holden's theory, but maybe she didn't need to. Their explanation made sense. It also explained how the hive mind worked—something she couldn't talk about without revealing she herself was an alien.

Holden's mouth twisted up on one side. "I think I'm onto something else too, and we have to talk about the elephant in the room, so to speak."

"What elephant?"

Holden cleared their throat. "Did I say elephant? Maybe I should have said alien."

Calay's mouth dropped open. So much for not revealing herself.

"How did you know?" Tears welled behind her eyes. Her heartbeat thundered in her ears. She focused on her breathing and forming actual words.

This could be the end of everything. The end of her.

Holden got up and methodically placed the mug on the metal tray before returning to Calay's bedside. "If I tell you, you have to promise not to freak out, okay?"

Calay nodded. She wasn't sure she could promise any such thing. But for all their sakes, including her own, she'd try.

"We've met before. Twice."

Calay squinted, looking closer at Holden's features as though trying to place them. "We have?"

"Yes. The first time you wouldn't have been aware, though. You were asleep." Holden scratched the back of their head, dropped their gaze to the floor. They smoothed the creases out of their shirt before continuing. "The second time you were more conscious. I replay that moment over and over in my mind. I still can't believe you jumped from that building."

"You were part of the group Tess sent for me." The sense of dread Calay had grown so familiar with washed over her. "To kill me."

Holden's gaze grew dark. They crossed their legs and folded their hands in their lap. "I was neither thrilled, nor proud, about it."

"And you were there that day. In the warehouse. That's why your eyes look so familiar. I've met you before. You were one of the ones who chased me across the roof."

"Let the record show I never agreed with Tess's methods." Holden pulled themselves taller. "At the time, we didn't see another way. I was afraid, Calay, but that doesn't excuse my actions. I would do things so differently now that I know the truth."

"When I met you earlier in the lab, I felt something familiar. Like déjà vu. Like I'd met you before. But I...I couldn't figure it out."

"It's one of the reasons I've been cold with you. I guess I feel bad."

"You should feel bad!"

"Yes, I should. I'm sorry. All Tess told us was that you were an alien and that we had to do what we did. She was our leader, and we trusted her. I trusted her. Hurting you was one of the first experiments we conducted on the Others. Tess was right about a lot of things, but she was wrong about what we did to you. I didn't know then that you were also human. I didn't even know that was possible. I would have never..."

"Yeah, well." Calay leaned back, her heart falling with her expression. "It turns out Tess had a way of twisting the truth."

"Indeed. So you understand?"

Calay didn't want to admit it, but she did understand. Everyone was just doing what they thought they had to in order to survive. How many times would she forgive those who wronged her? There had to be a point where lines crossed could not be forgiven. It was hard to imagine where that might be.

A shiver ran down Calay's spine despite the heating pads and blankets and pillows. That line was crossed when the Others invaded Earth and began systematically killing everyone she'd ever loved. That was the enemy now.

Calay rested her hand on Holden's. Their gazes met. The sincerity behind their eyes was almost heartbreaking.

"We're good, Holden." Calay pulled her lips tight and nodded.

The shadow behind Holden's gaze lifted. "You sure?"

"Honestly, it's kind of nice to have someone to share my secret with."

"I'm honored to carry your burden. It's the least I can do after... everything." Holden's shoulders visibly relaxed.

"Thank you." Calay leaned back against the ocean of pillows. "Ugh, this day couldn't possibly get any worse."

Holden exhaled. "Don't count your chickens."

"What else?"

"You said the person who attacked you said they knew what you were. I think I know who did it."

"What—who?"

"Ezra."

"Who the fuck's Ezra?"

"The other guy who was at the warehouse. He's the only one who would know what you are—the only one with a proper motive to kill you."

"What motive would that be?"

"He's a true believer. To him, any alien is the enemy. I think you can see where I'm going with this."

"That would include me."

"Precisely."

"So let's go find out." Calay swung a leg over the side of the bed. Her vision swam with the motion. Her stomach spun. "Whoa."

"Easy. Lay back." Holden helped Calay back into bed. "Besides, we don't have proof. Only suspicions."

"How do we get proof?"

"We'll figure that out in the morning, after you've gotten some sleep. Your body needs rest to heal."

Calay was about to tell Holden he had no idea how quickly her body repaired itself. That in a matter of days she'd be as good as new. On second thought, they knew that. Intimately.

"You promise?"

"I promise. I won't let anything happen to you. We'll have someone stationed outside your door all night. You can lock it from the inside too, right?"

"Yes," she mumbled.

"I'll meet you at the Atrium for breakfast, okay?"

Calay nodded as exhaustion washed over her. The Otherness in her might repair her body faster than average, but the human part of her needed sleep. She was vaguely aware of Holden gathering their mug before they made their way to the door.

"Wait." Calay forced the words through a growing haze. "What's the Atrium?"

"Walk one hundred fifty paces due south when you exit this building. You have to see it to believe it."

CHAPTER SEVEN

HOLDEN WAS nothing if not accurate. Calay was pleasantly surprised to find the Atrium was exactly one hundred fifty paces from the main building. She was unable to stop the damning thoughts rolling through her brain, so she'd counted each one until she came to a vast dome of green and blue glass that rose from the cement like a beacon. How she— or the Others—hadn't spotted the structure before was a mystery to her. Compared to the low-rise, sprawling concrete buildings within the fence line, this one should have stuck out like a sore thumb. Or in her case, a sore shoulder. And ribs. Not to mention the two-inch bump on the back of her head. Instead, it almost dissolved into the background, the roof reflecting the atmosphere above. Like magic.

She winced while she balanced her breakfast tray in one arm and pulled one of two heavy fire doors open. Despite her origin story, she was grateful it wouldn't take too long for her to heal. A few days maybe, a week at most. The blue scarf she'd fastened around her neck whipped her cheeks in the crisp morning breeze. She stepped through and the door swung shut with a loud click, shuddering against her back. She stumbled and swallowed a pained yelp as the tray nearly toppled. Calay barely noticed. She was busy gawking at the scene in front of her.

Tiered slate platforms rose on either side, circling the wide perimeter. They spiraled upward, one after the other. She counted eight total, rising like mountains. Between each level was a padding of verdant greenery. Ferns and tumbling vines billowed beneath a lush canopy of Douglas firs and Arbutus trees—their craggy, dark red bark had always been a West Coast favorite of Calay's. She allowed a tight smile to creep across her lips. They reminded her of campouts with her dad and summer adventures with Tess. Before the Change. At the tree's base, mounds of sculpted sandstone and dark rock peeked between layers of moss and pinecones. Sunlight winked through the top of the dome, setting the room in a golden glow. From in here, Calay could almost forget it was unseasonably winter outside.

She dropped her gaze back to the center of the room and noticed each platform was bustling with small collectives of Resistance members, smiling and rapt in whispered conversations.

The gentle sound of plucked strings reached Calay. She could hardly believe her ears. It was music. Actual music. When was the last time she'd heard something so sweet?

Her shoulders relaxed; she released the death grip on her tray. This was nothing like the tense atmosphere of the cafeteria.

This was much better.

Holden may have been right about the distance to the atrium, but Calay decided he'd deliberately undersold it.

Out of the corner of her eye she noticed a woman waving her over. She had short, dark curls with the sides of her head shaved, a warm caramel complexion, and a smile that stunned Calay where she stood.

She swallowed, a stirring of nerves and delight rose in her stomach. It was the woman from the cafeteria. The one that had been sitting with who she now knew to be Holden and the big guy who'd disappeared.

Across from the woman was Salem—the soldier who'd pulled Calay to her feet after she'd almost took a bullet when the Other breached the compound. She had her legs folded underneath her, a rich blue instrument cushioned in her lap. This must be where the harmonic sound was coming from.

Calay hurried to them, grateful for a soft place to land.

She climbed the platforms, slowly making her way to the third level where the two women were perched. She tried to ignore the pang in her shoulder with each lunge. As she reached them she realized she hadn't thought of anything to say. She wasn't sure why, but she wanted to make a good first impression. Her mind suddenly went blank. Thankfully, Salem beat Calay to the punch.

"Hey." Salem nodded at the open space beside them. "Sit."

"Hi," Calay mustered.

"Hi." The woman cleared her throat. "Would you like to sit with us?"

"Oh, yeah." Calay remained standing, their words hanging awkwardly between them. She glanced at the woman whose charcoal eyes peered up at her from behind a curtain of long lashes.

Salem snickered, turned her attention back to the instrument. Her fingers delicately strummed the chords. It was a wistful song, slow and a little tinny. Calay's fingers gripped her tray, her mouth turned dry.

The woman Calay couldn't stop looking at pushed herself to her feet, held out her hand. "I'm Briar."

The name rang a bell in Calay's mind. She'd heard it before, but where?

"Calay."

"Oh, I know."

"You do?" Calay's stomach fell. She didn't know what people were saying about her, but given the events of the last forty-eight hours, she didn't think it could be anything good.

"Sure." Briar grinned, her eyes soft. "I was the one who found you last night."

Calay's mouth dropped open. Right, Holden had said Briar came running into the lab calling for help the night before. Calay caught a groan of embarrassment before it passed her lips, wanting to disappear. She should have remembered that.

Instead, she said, "Oh, yeah, sorry."

"Nothing to be sorry about. You were nearly unconscious and kind of dying." Briar's smile faded from her mouth. "I'm glad you pulled through. It's nice to meet you."

Calay let her lips curl upward. "Nice to meet you too."

"Properly."

Briar still had her arm outstretched.

Get it together.

Calay took Briar's hand in hers and shook it with a little more enthusiasm than intended. She closed her eyes and when she opened them again...

Briar beamed.

"Now that that's out of the way, are you two going to sit down and eat or are you going to keep standing there like idiots?" Salem grinned.

Calay nodded, famished, and sank to the deck.

"That's a beautiful song. I don't know the last time I heard someone play guitar."

"Not a guitar. Mandolin," Salem replied without looking up. "And thank you."

"I'm surprised they let you play music. Aren't we supposed to be super-secret quiet around here?"

"They let me get away with it if I promise not to get anyone killed." Salem smirked.

"She's being modest." Briar leaned back, as if she didn't have a care in the world. "She's really very good and puts on a hell of a show when she gets the chance."

"It's good for morale." Salem shrugged.

"It's good for you, too," Briar said. "You know Salem was going to be famous, before?"

"Actually?" Calay raised her brows.

"I'd recorded an album," Salem conceded.

Briar nudged Salem, a playfulness in her voice. "Recorded an album. Please, she also signed with a major label and was scheduled to start touring. Nationally."

"That's amazing." Calay titled her head. "Would I know any of your songs?"

"Maybe." The whisper of a smile tugged at Salem's full red lips, her eyes twinkled.

If Calay had to guess, she was lost in a memory. Of a different time. A different place. A different life.

"You would have known all of them." Briar unleashed a full-watt smile. She gathered a chunk of Salem's impossibly long hair in her hand, pulling it away from the instrument and tucked it behind her shoulder.

Calay narrowed her eyes, gazing between the two women. They seemed close and for some reason, that troubled her. She wasn't sure if she was envious of their friendship or jealous of the fact that Salem so easily garnered Briar's attention. Either way, she caught herself wanting to find out. She shoved a spoonful of grits in her mouth. A moan escaped her throat before she could stop it.

Salem smirked. "That good, huh?"

"It's been a while since I've eaten." Calay's cheeks flushed even as she swallowed another spoonful. "Things got a little out of control yesterday."

"Here, have the rest of mine." Briar set her roti on Calay's tray.

"Oh, no, I couldn't." Even now, even here, Calay knew food was a scarce resource. She began to hand it back, but Briar placed her hand on hers.

"Please, take it."

"That's your breakfast."

"Never was much of a breakfast person." Briar leaned close. Her curls smelled like roses and nutmeg.

"Thank you," Calay whispered.

"You're welcome," Briar whispered back before easing back against the upper terrace.

It took everything Calay had to stay where she was and not fold Briar into her arms. Thankfully, her stomach was making most of her decisions this morning. She tore off a piece of the bread and dipped it in the porridge. Calay shoved it in her mouth and moaned again. The other two laughed.

"You!" a voice thundered.

Calay turned to see the towering man from the cafeteria stomping toward them, his face twisted into a miasma of rage beneath his dirty-blonde beard. The hate behind his blue eyes was homed directly on Calay. She slid her tray away and scrambled backward before he lifted her by the neck of her sweater, his breath hot against her cheek. He shoved her against the next step, the ledge dug into the small of her back.

"Hey!" Briar was on her feet almost just as fast.

"Don't!" Salem was quick to follow.

"Don't what?" the man growled over his shoulder. "I haven't done a thing."

That wasn't entirely true. Calay struggled to get her feet underneath her, felt a dampness beneath her shirt. He'd torn her stitches.

"What the hell!" she yelped in equal parts fear and anger.

"That's exactly what I was thinking," the man snarled. "In what Hell do you think you have a right to be here?"

"I don't know what you're talking about. I don't even know you!" Though Calay was sure she was about to find out. She hadn't gotten a good look at her assailant last night, and Holden suspected it had been the other soldier from the warehouse. Ezra, they'd called him. Could that man and this man—the one from the cafeteria—be one and the same?

"Ezra, stop it." Briar shouldered herself between them, pulled on his arm.

His grip didn't budge.

A chill wound its way into Calay's chest.

Oh good, worst fears confirmed then.

This was the guy. The one who'd assaulted her. Stabbed her. Tried to drown her. Assuming Holden was right, of course. Their assumptions could be wrong, but she suspected they weren't.

Everything in her wanted to break free from his grasp and run. But that wasn't going to do her—or the Resistance—any favors. If she was going to carry on Tess's work, she had to make this a safe place for all of them. Her plans would never come to fruition if she couldn't actually get her boots on the ground and do the leg work. Right now, they hovered a good inch off the floor. And that meant she needed proof of what he'd done. Something irrefutable. Adam was a stickler for protocol, after all. The rules. A confession would work. In front of everyone.

"Is that why you tried to have me killed last night?" Calay went straight for the jugular. She wasn't wasting any time—she had to get him to admit what he'd done before she lost her nerve.

"Ezra." Briar's eyes grew wide. "You didn't. Did you?"

"Admit it, you coward," Calay pressed.

A burst of anger flashed through Ezra's eyes and his knuckles tightened around her shirt. He pressed his lips together. If she had to guess, he likely didn't trust the words that would come out of his mouth right now. *Good, he shouldn't.* She stuffed the panic threatening to overtake her and continued.

"You fucked up last night. Couldn't hack it. Now you're back to finish the job. But guess what? You failed then just like you'll fail now."

Calay meant it. She hadn't come this far, or survived this much, to let Ezra take this away from her. Tears filled her eyes. She blinked them away and was surprised to see they were in his too. His arm shook under the weight of Briar's hand. The stares of everyone in the Atrium. Calay glanced past his shoulder to find at some point, they'd all turned to watch.

"She has to go," Ezra said, voice low. He released the hold he had on Calay's shirt.

Calay gaped as Salem pried him backward and Briar blocked him from view entirely. They were putting distance between the two of them. Protecting Calay. As always, she appreciated the sentiment, but she'd escaped death by Ezra's hands twice already. If she succeeded today, it'd be a third. She didn't need protection. She needed backup. Support. Even if she had to rally it herself.

"Wait." Calay straightened her sweater, cleared her throat. "I'm not going anywhere. You're the one who has to go."

"What did you just say?" Ezra bristled and pushed back against Salem's hand on his chest.

"I said get out."

"Who the fuck do you think you are?" Ezra's fitted sweatshirt pulled tight across his chest as he flexed and balled his hands into fists.

"There are rules here, Ezra." Calay channeled Adam's words. She'd heard them enough. "Protocols. And you've broken them. You need to go. Now."

"You're joking." He scoffed.

"You're the joke."

"Watch your mouth—"

Calay levelled her gaze, raised her voice. "I think you'd better watch yours and do as your told. Before we're forced to make you."

Several people were already nodding. Some definitely weren't, though, and were gathering behind Ezra. This could get ugly. Calay realized she may have overshot her landing. She hoped she hadn't made a terrible mistake.

Before she had the chance to question herself further, Ezra launched forward.

Calay sucked in a shallow breath as she watched Salem be knocked to the side, into the greenery on the level below. Her mandolin clanged, bouncing down one tier to another, all the way to the floor.

Briar's hands shot out to slow Ezra, but he flung her aside as if she hadn't even been there.

Shit, this was not how this was supposed to go.

Ezra was only a few feet away now.

Calay braced herself for impact.

"Ezra, stop!" Holden's ordinarily reserved voice boomed through the space.

Much to Calay's surprise, Ezra actually stopped. She assumed Holden was so well mannered, their demeanor calm, that when they spoke up, people listened.

"As much as it pains me to say it," Holden paused as they made their way up the platforms. They pulled Salem from the bushes and helped pick twigs out of her hair before they continued. "Calay's right. We have rules. They're the only things that separate us from the animals. You can't just go around attacking people."

"But she's one—"

"—One of us now. And she will be treated with the same rights and freedoms as anyone else in the Resistance." Holden's stare bore into Ezra. Their pouty curved lips that normally looked like they were smiling were turned downward, their shoulders pulled back. They turned their severe glare toward Calay. Her shoulders sank inward.

"Which means she will keep her voice down, and if she has a problem with another member, she'll elevate it to the Council instead of antagonizing the problem. Isn't that right, Calay?"

"He tried to kill me," Calay muttered, but nodded her acquiescence.

"Prove it," Ezra hissed.

Holden rested a gentle hand on Ezra's shoulder. "She doesn't have to, brother."

"Calay." Briar slid between Calay and Ezra. "Do you want to get out of here?"

Did she? A big part of Calay just wanted to escape. To put as much distance between herself and her would-be murderer as possible. She would have, before. She squinted at Ezra. There was so much she wanted to say, but none of it would help her achieve her mission. After all she'd seen—the systemic execution of her neighbors, the abandonment by her parents, the betrayal by the one woman who was supposed to love her the most, and the clusterfuck that was her expedition to Téras—Calay was done with running.

"No." Calay softened as she looked to Briar. "I'm going to finish my damn breakfast. He should go."

"Alright then." Holden nodded. "Ezra, go."

Ezra's nostrils flared. "Seriously? You're making me leave?"

"Not the compound."

"Not yet," Calay growled.

"Just…" Holden's frown turned toward Calay before they continued. "Go cool off."

"This is bullshit!" Ezra roared.

"This is the last time I'll say it, Ezra. You know better. Keep your voice down. The last thing we need is to call more attention to ourselves. Especially in here."

Ezra shoved his hands in his pockets, his eyes pleaded. "Holden."

"Don't make me bring this to Adam." Holden shook their head.

Calay held her breath, waited. A shiver of guilt ran down her spine. Holden was right, of course. This wasn't about them right now. Fights and outbursts wouldn't help their cause, and they needed as much unity as they could wrangle. Ezra may have tried to kill her, but at this point, who hadn't? She watched him ball his fists at his sides before he huffed and stormed down the steps and out the door.

She almost exhaled in relief but froze as Holden directed their furious gaze to her. "And you."

"I didn't do anything." Calay threw her hands up.

"It's true, Holden. She's innocent." Briar said.

"She's not that innocent." Holden raised a single eyebrow. "Calay..."

"I know, I'm sorry. It won't happen again."

"It better not." Holden held her gaze for a beat before carefully folding their legs underneath them. "Show's over folks."

The people remaining in the dome turned back to their groups, some filtered out after Ezra.

That was close. Too close. Ezra could have exposed Calay. The truth of who—what—she was. She sank down beside Holden, watching Briar help Salem examine her mandolin at the center of the room. A light twang strummed through the air—the sound a vestige of what once was the promise of a better future. Now that the immediate danger had passed, Calay finally allowed herself to breathe. She'd meant it when she promised Holden it wouldn't happen again. She couldn't afford that risk. She'd just started building a real foundation in this place. Making real friends. In her darkest moments, even if her life didn't matter, these people did. Earth did. And she was going to do everything she could to help them survive.

Calay chewed her bottom lip. "Holden, thank you. I—"

"I might not be here next time, Calay."

"There won't be a next time."

"Good, because if there is, I won't be able to protect you." Holden pushed their glasses up, something that was starting to seem more like a personality tick than an actual necessity. "Your secret's safe with me. I can't say the same for Ezra."

"He hates everything I am. What if he tells people what I am?"

"He was upset. I know you won't believe it, but Ezra's actually pretty well liked around here. If he says something now, he'll have to explain how he knows. He probably didn't think about that before he came at you this morning, but he will now. It's why he attacked you when you were alone last night. I know him, better than most. He won't risk his reputation by admitting what he did to you."

Calay stiffened, the reality of her situation settling in her gut. "First chance he gets, he's going to try to kill me again."

"I'll handle it."

"When?"

"Today. After breakfast." Holden pulled their tray alongside their perfectly ironed olive-green cargo pants, each pocket buttoned and clasped.

Calay caught herself wondering how they got them so wrinkle free. So tidy. Her clothes, everything about her really, was a wild mess, perpetually ruffled. She smoothed the flyaways in her hair, the bunches in her sweater. If only combing through the mess of life was so easy.

Briar and Salem settled beside them. Salem's full attention was on the mandolin; two of the strings were broken.

"I'm sorry about your instrument," Calay offered and meant it. Salem looked like she might cry. It was the first time her hard outer shell seemed to give way to something softer. "I really am."

Salem nodded in reply, plucked at the remaining strings.

"You're bleeding." Briar's warm hand cupped Calay's elbow, gently leaning her forward. Right, the stitches. Calay had been so consumed with the Ezra situation, she'd forgotten about the raging pain in her shoulder. "Holden—"

"She'll live." Holden swallowed a mouthful of green beans and gestured at Calay. "After breakfast."

"Well if the doctor thinks it can wait, it can wait." Calay reached forward, plucked a bean off his plate, and popped it into her mouth, but not before Holden playfully smacked the top of her hand with their spork. She grimaced—both from the slap and the fact that even here, green beans persisted. "Ew."

Everyone laughed. It'd been so long since Calay heard that sound. Despite the threats knocking at their door, the four of them conversed easily. Their smiles reached their eyes. She could tell they trusted each other, and she was beginning to believe she might be able to trust them, too. Everything from her past screamed to never do that again, but for the first time in as long as she could remember, she didn't want to run. Given her mission and the events of the last forty-eight hours, Calay didn't exactly feel at ease, but surrounded by new friends, a flutter of hope rose in her chest.

The worst was yet to come, but at least she wouldn't have to face it alone.

The sound of boots scurrying pulled Calay's attention away.

Resistance members were jumping to their feet and, one handful at a time, fleeing out the back door. It wasn't the mass exodus of people that had stampeded out of the cafeteria only two days ago when the Other had broken into the compound, but something about this was disconcerting in a different way.

"Something's happening." Calay pushed herself to her feet and made her way toward the door wafting in the brisk morning air.

She peered around the corner. The rising sun brought little warmth to the cold blue sky outside the Atrium. Ribbons of snow drifted across the yard. A trail of footprints disappeared behind the building. Wherever everyone had gone, it was to one place. Calay wasn't sure she wanted to find out where that was.

"See anything?" Briar's voice floated across the room.

"Just a bunch of footprints." Calay pointed. "What's back that way?"

She turned to the sound of someone's steps crunching in the snow in the opposite direction. It was the soldier from the cafeteria. The weepy one. He didn't look like he was faring much better now. He dragged his feet as if they weighed a ton, out of breath, and by the looks of things, out of options. Calay didn't judge—she felt his pain, she was just better at shouldering it.

"Hey!" She waved him over, vaguely aware of the others approaching from behind. Whatever was happening had their attention now, too. "What's going on?"

The young soldier took a moment to catch their breath. A moment too long, if anyone asked Calay.

"Well?" Holden barked from behind.

"There was another attack."

"Oh no." Salem's voice cracked, but she'd already set her mandolin aside and was in the process of securing her hair at the base of her neck.

"What do you mean? We didn't hear an alarm." Calay frowned. Her gaze floated to Briar, who shrugged. It seemed her new friends didn't know any more than she did. "What kind of attack?"

The soldier wobbled on their feet. "They caught a live one."

"A live what, exactly?" she pressed.

"An alien."

Calay watched what little color was left in the kid's cheeks drain in the frigid gold light.

Given the events of the night before, Calay couldn't make rational sense out of why the Resistance would take another alien into custody.

"Why would they catch one?" she asked.

"Why haven't they killed the thing?" Salem said.

"It's in disguise."

It took everything Calay had not to shake the answer out of him. "What does that mean?"

"Human. It looks human."

Holden frowned, confusion clouding their blue eyes. They were as dumbfounded as Calay. "We haven't seen them take human form for a while. They haven't needed to since the Faceless showed up."

Calay tried to keep her face neutral, her voice even. She failed. "What does it look like?"

A memory of the second pod flashed through her mind. If someone had actually followed her back from Téras, maybe this was the moment she'd find out who.

"I don't know, but they say he's a big one."

Calay's stomach dropped, her mouth went dry.

She could hardly believe it.

The soldier had said "he."

CHAPTER EIGHT

CALAY'S HEARTBEAT pounded against her chest almost as hard as her feet on the snow-packed concrete. The group rushed beyond the Atrium and into a courtyard at the back of the compound. The young soldier who'd led them there disappeared into the crowd as she slid to a stop just inside towering, makeshift sheet metal doors, gawking.

Curved concrete rose well above their heads, culminating in rows of razor-sharp barbed wire. Exposed black brick peeked from behind the walls. Snow piled on thick metal grates lining the edges.

Calay had never been back here before, didn't even know it existed. This place had more secrets than Holden or Adam were willing to admit. Maybe more horrors, too. It chilled her to the bone to realize her initial impressions of the compound weren't right, but they weren't entirely wrong either. Something about this place felt wrong.

She turned her gaze to the rising sea of Resistance members. The morning when the Other had broken into the main building, people had scattered, many fled to the relative safety of their rooms. This morning was different. It seemed everyone had gathered to feast their eyes on the alien who looked human.

Calay frowned, pushed up onto her toes, uneasy. She couldn't see a damn thing from back here. Nothing except the danger they were all in.

They wouldn't be there if they knew how quickly the Others could shape shift. She was intimately—painfully—familiar with what the Others were capable of. They might look human, but they were far from it. Whoever the Resistance had caught might be allowing their own capture, but Calay had watched Ash transform on Téras. Elora, too. And if this alien decided to do the same, everyone here was already dead.

Calay shivered. "What is this place?"

Holden's eyes shifted to hers but their lips remained tight. Whatever it was, they weren't saying. *Fine, be that way.* Calay huffed, probably didn't want to know anyway. Not when she had more pressing concerns. Like finding out who they were holding up there.

"Can you see anything?" Briar leapt in place, what good may it do her.

Salem clasped her hands together. "Just the backs of too many heads."

"Come on." Calay didn't know if it was impulse or intent, but her legs were already moving, pressing her way between the throng of bodies. She thought she heard Holden tell her to wait, but the whispers floating through the air and consistent rush of blood in Calay's ears drowned out their voice. She had to get to the front of the crowd.

A hand clamped down on her good shoulder.

Calay spun to find Briar's charcoal eyes trained on hers. Behind her, Salem held Briar's other hand, and behind her, Holden—forming a train behind Calay. Briar's chin dipped, reassuring Calay she should continue. Calay nodded back, almost smiled. They were there. With her.

The group parted when she turned, easing one foot closer. Then another. One person at a time, people's eyes turned to her, fell on her every move. She became painfully aware of how few people she knew here, and even how fewer she could trust. How alien this all was. How alien *she* was. She didn't belong in this place. Not yet. Neither did whoever they'd captured. She'd hoped against her better judgement that Jacob had somehow made it. Prayed to a god she no longer believed in that Ash hadn't. Then there were the incubators housing millions of aliens intent on destroying her home planet.

No big deal.

She'd spent weeks fearing who'd followed her back from deep space and what the ramifications might be. How she might handle them. Now she was about to find out.

Her progress through the crowd felt painfully slow. And yet, far too fast. Calay shouldered her way past the last group. The tattoo on her wrist stung with an energy she didn't understand. Her heart leapt. Then her stomach dropped.

There he was.

"Oh Jesus." Holden gasped.

"Oh Jacob." Calay's hand flew to her mouth. The words escaped her lips before she had the chance to stop them.

Briar flinched. "You know him?"

"I..." Calay shook her head. She could feel their gazes on her. Waiting for an explanation. She tried to come up with one. None came.

On some level, she never really thought she'd see Jacob again. Didn't want to, she told herself. But looking at him now, she didn't quite believe the half-truths she was telling herself.

She couldn't help herself and she drank him in, eagerly. His dark curls were damp and hung in thick ringlets from the crown of his head. He was still in the dark button-down shirt he'd been wearing when she'd last left him, the one that was a little too tight across his shoulders. Only now it was marred by soot and streaked with dirt. His suspenders hung around the waist of his black jeans by their gold rings. The heavy duster jacket he'd relied on to keep him out of the harsh winter elements, gone. Four Resistance soldiers flanked him, two on either side, gripping his shaking arms with each of theirs.

Something broke in Calay in that moment.

After everything they'd been through together, after everything had gone down, she'd thought she lost him. She'd been terrified that she'd killed him; terrified she hadn't. And somehow, here Jacob was. Alive. Which, if Calay was being honest with herself, scared her even more. He'd lied to her. Manipulated her. Betrayed her. From the beginning, his mission had never been hers. So she'd done what she needed to in order to survive. Now, as she faced down the barrel of saving her species or saving his, she knew they could never coexist.

A wave of guilt washed over Calay. Her breathing shallowed. It felt almost as if her heart halted in her chest. This must have been how Tess had felt. When she'd realized what Calay was and decided to kill her.

A low moan vibrated from somewhere deep within Jacob's chest; it echoed through the crisp morning air. Calay blinked away a wall of tears to find his ice blue gaze was trained on hers.

She stilled.

He swayed.

Calay could feel the familiar heat of his gaze, but was he seeing her? His eyes had a disconcerting hazy quality to them. His pouty lips hung slack. Then he dropped from the soldier's grips and slumped to the ground.

No, not like this.

Before she could stop herself, Calay rushed forward. No one else stopped her, either. They gaped while she heaved herself up and onto the platform, ignoring the jolt of pain in her shoulder. Her ribs. Her soul. Jacob was Other, which meant he couldn't survive if humanity was going to. Calay grimaced as she reached him—these were probably the exact thoughts that ran through Tess's mind as they'd attacked Calay, breaking her bone by bone.

Calay hadn't deserved that, and Jacob didn't deserve this. Whatever this was.

"Stop!" Calay dropped to her knees, pulled the scarf from her throat. She draped it over him, pulled his head into her lap. She dried his hair as best she could. He was shaking, his shirt damp and clinging to his hard chest. She dabbed at it. There was little she could do out here. In the snow. The cold. The crowd. She ignored all of them and pulled his face into her hands. "Jacob. It's me."

He moaned again.

"Hey," she whispered through her tears. She swiped at them, furious. Afraid. Desperate. "Jacob. Look at me. Right here. I'm right here."

"Calay."

"Yes, it's me. Can you hear me?"

Jacob coughed.

"Jacob, I need you to open your eyes."

She waited for what felt like an eternity. He didn't reply. Didn't move.

"Jacob!"

Maybe it was for the best, she told herself. He didn't deserve to die like a dog in the street, but this way, she wouldn't have to put him down herself. At least his suffering was short.

"I'm sorry." She released a shaky exhale, but her breath was cut short by the feeling of a warm hand sliding across her lower back. Jacob's wide arms wrapped around her, pulling her down, tight against him. She could barely breathe. His chest rose against hers. He clung to her, like a life raft. "I'm so sorry."

"You don't have to be sorry, Calay." His voice was rough against her ear. "I'm the one who's sorry."

"You should be." Calay pulled out of their embrace, watched the freckles across his nose wink at her. His lips curled up in a smile that didn't quite reach his glazed eyes.

Calay adored this face. She hated it, too. He'd put her through so much, but if it wasn't for him, she would never be where she was now. At the Resistance. Ready to fight. To survive. To right the wrongs Calay had made. In a lot of ways, she was closer to Tess than she'd ever been. Even if Tess wasn't there. But he was, and for the moment, Calay was grateful.

She shook her head. "What am I going to do with you?"

"Anything you want," Jacob growled and raised an eyebrow. He pushed himself to sit.

Heat flushed to Calay's cheeks. Now was not the time. It never would be again. A ripple of fear crept up her spine. Jacob should know that. He was well aware of how things had ended between them—painfully. The man in front of her looked like Jacob, but how could Calay know if this was Jacob at all? What if it was just another replica, like Elora, her mother?

Bile rose in the back of Calay's throat. The sound of guns cocking forced her to swallow it. Calay's gaze darted to the soldiers surrounding them. Their guns—a mixture of automatic and semi-automatic weapons —were raised and pointed squarely at her and Jacob's heads. Whatever

Calay's fear about clones were, were going to have to wait. For now, she was going to have to trust him at his word if she was going to get out of this alive.

"How do we know he's an alien?" Calay heard herself ask.

"We caught him trying to cut a hole in the fence," one of the soldiers volunteered. Calay only now recognized him from the other morning in the hallway—Ryland. "Just like the Faceless. We did the tests. The water one. The light behind his eyes. He failed."

Calay couldn't argue with that. She'd seen the stars behind her own eyes. Followed them all the way to Galaxy 3C303 and back again. They led right here, in the end. It seemed Jacob had done the very same thing. Maybe they weren't so different after all.

"Calay?" Briar moved forward, pulling Calay's attention to the front of the crowd. She had her hands wrung in front of her, her eyes wide.

Salem tapped her foot, impatient. "What the hell is going on?"

Calay wish she knew. *Just for once, god damn it.* It seemed like the moment she got her feet underneath her, something knocked them back out again.

She steadied herself, sucked in a long breath, and raised her arms above her head. She nodded at Jacob to do the same. She noticed his arms weren't shaking as badly now. His breath steadier. Calay couldn't help but wonder how much of his fragility had been an act.

"What are you doing here anyway?" she muttered underneath her breath so Ryland and the other soldiers couldn't hear her.

"Looking for you." He peered at her sideways. "But you already know that, don't you?"

"Suspected it." Calay swallowed.

Holden pushed their way through the group. "Everyone just needs to calm down."

"The hell we do!" someone from the crowd yelled.

"Traitor!" someone else shouted. Calay thought it sounded like Ezra, but couldn't spot him. To be fair, it could have been any one of the people here.

Calay clenched her eyes shut, shook her head. "I'm not a traitor."

Just very, very confused.

One of the soldiers pressed the barrel of their rifle into her back. She raised her arms higher. Jacob had put her in a tenuous position by coming here. Assuming he was indeed who he said he was. Mind you, that was before she'd panicked and rushed to his side. Now she had to deal with the cumulative consequences.

"Lower your weapons." Holden turned to where Calay stood next to Jacob. Their tone conveyed calm reassurance, but their posture said otherwise. Holden's shoulders were clenched, their brows pinched, their arms outstretched in front of them taught as the wire that lined the fence. Calay was aware Holden knew damn well what she was. They'd been willing to protect her secret—to protect her—and she'd been careless with their trust. She hadn't thought this through. Jacob may have compromised her circumstances here, but she'd just put her new friend in a very uncomfortable one, too. And now they were risking their safety by standing up for her.

"Holden, I've got this," Calay tried.

"I really don't think you do." Holden maintained their position between the crowd and Calay. "It's protocol everyone receives fair treatment. We don't know what Calay went through before she got here. For all we know, this alien tricked her as he was trying to trick us. So lower your damn weapons."

One by one, the soldiers turned their guns to the ground, but none returned them to their holsters. Calay exhaled, glanced at Ryland, who half-shrugged but wouldn't meet her gaze. She didn't know a lot, but she was sure of one thing: one quick movement from either she or Jacob and both of them probably wouldn't be walking out of there. It didn't matter that Ryland had been one of the soldiers who had saved her before; Calay was under no false pretenses about his eagerness to pull the trigger. She'd seen him in action. He wouldn't hesitate to put Jacob —an Other—down if he needed to, whether she was in the way or not.

Holden lowered their arms. "That's better. Now, everyone take a long deep breath. I'm sure Calay has a perfectly reasonable justification for what just happened."

Calay eased some of her weight back onto her heels. "I can explain."

Movement out of the corner of her gaze pulled her focus to the very back of the space. She scanned the blur of bodies staring up at her and found Adam positioned among them.

She'd promised him no more lies. That she'd do what she was told. Fall in line. He folded his arms over his chest. He shook his head, his shoulders turned inward. She couldn't tell if he was disappointed she'd already let him down, or afraid. But she couldn't be honest with him until she was honest with herself. She forced herself to meet his gaze and realized she wasn't just done with running, she was done with secrets, too.

"Don't," Adam mouthed. Maybe he said it out loud, Calay couldn't be sure. He was too far away. Always had been. Adam had a lot of good ideas, but Calay had to admit that's all they were. He wanted to protect this place. To keep all of them safe. But she'd learned you couldn't protect people with ideas. You couldn't save them with theories. You needed strength. Tess had told her that. Calay hadn't believed it. Not at first. And it ended up costing her everything—her parents, her home, the great love of her life. Everything that had made being alive mean something. She'd be damned if it took away the meaning she found here now.

"I'm sorry." Calay mouthed back in response.

It seemed all she'd done since she'd arrived at the compound was apologize. To Jacob. To Adam. To herself. She had a lot to make up for, and though she couldn't be sure, she hoped coming clean was going to be the path to make amends. Her atonement. Their salvation.

"I'm sure by now you've heard the rumors that your previous leader —Tess—is dead, that I was her girlfriend, and that I killed her." A handful of gasps floated through the air, but as Calay suspected, word traveled fast around here. "But that was only half the truth."

"What are you doing?" Jacob whispered.

"The only thing I can do to save your dumb ass. To save all of us." she said in a hushed tone before she turned her attention back to the crowd. "There's something else I need to tell all of you."

Calay's gaze flicked to Adam. He steeled his jaw as he stared up at her, his green eyes dark and narrow. He was not the only one watching with bated breath, however. Holden looked up, frowning. Salem wore her signature scowl. Briar listened intently, giving away nothing. Calay's heart lurched. She was risking everything with what she was about to say, but she was risking it if she kept quiet, too. Dozens—if not hundreds—of faces gawked up at her. Waiting. Their features blurred as she scanned them, one pair of eyes after another until they disappeared into the crowd bulging out the door at the back. That's where all of this began. Her unraveling. She lamented her decision, as she did many over the last five years, to force her way to the front. She should have stayed back there. Where she was. *Faceless*. Maybe then none of this would be happening. Though deep in the corners of her heart, she knew that was a fiction. Another wish that would never come true. She was meant for this. If not fated by the stars, then her biology. She was Self and Other. And it was that fact that was going to save them. Provided it didn't kill her first.

Calay fortified her resolve.

"The other day I spoke about what we need to do to save this place so we all have a chance to survive. We have to trust each other. Work together. The truth is, we can't do this alone. We need allies. And that means accepting people who we might see as different from ourselves." Calay paused, closed her eyes, and gathered her courage. When she opened them again, she said the words she hoped she'd never have to say out loud. "The thing I didn't tell you was the reason I had to kill Tess was because she was trying to kill me. And she was trying to kill me because I'm Other, too."

CHAPTER NINE

GOOSEBUMPS RIPPLED along Calay's arms as the energy hovering in the air shifted from concerned to undeniably hostile. The eruption from the crowd nearly sent her on her ass. She stumbled backward at the sudden explosion of voices, the rush of bodies. If Jacob hadn't been there to catch her, she would have tumbled right off the back of the podium. She was falling, and then, she wasn't. He enveloped her in his embrace, though the warmth of his arms did little to muffle the shouts of confusion and fear, demanding an explanation. Calay clutched to him in return, her guard lowered. The feel of his heartbeat thundered against her palm when he tightened his hold around her.

"You okay?" Jacob asked.

"Not even a little bit." Calay muttered while she righted herself. She'd just unleashed a fury of hellfire, and while she'd known what she was about to do, she wasn't prepared for the swiftness or intensity of the crowd's wrath. She held Jacob's gaze, not wanting to turn away.

His ice blue eyes bore into her, and he nodded in understanding.

In that one look, he acknowledged her fear in a way the people before them never would. It awoke something in Calay—something foreign and fierce. It kindled a heat which surged through her limbs like wildfire. She and Jacob may have had that in common—the inability to exist in the place they were from—but that's all they had. He was no longer her lover. Nor was he the man she'd befriended, or the alien she'd trusted. She eased away from the familiarity of him—and his signature scent of leather and cinnamon—and her heart ached a little. For what they'd had. What they could have been. What they'd never be, ever again. Her lips parted, as if to explain, but when she turned her attention from him to the crowd, she gasped.

At some point, Adam had pushed his way to the front. His arms were stretched wide, as though they could hold back the torrent of bodies crushing forward. Salem and Briar were by Adam's side. Salem drew a pistol, Briar, her fists. Holden, surprisingly, had positioned themself to the side, blocking the stairs.

Calay wasn't sure who they were actually protecting—Adam or her. If she had to guess, it would have to be the former. She strained to hear the shouts coming from Adam, but it was impossible amidst the voices of the crowd. They pulsed like a beast's gasping breath, fighting to free itself from a too-tiny cage. Her new friends wouldn't be able to hold them for long.

Calay didn't think it was possible for her heart to shatter any more than it already had, but in that moment, it did.

She'd only just found this place. These people. They hadn't had much time together, but there was something special here. She was sure of it. For the first time in as long as she could remember, she'd started to feel like she might actually belong. She might find a home. And she'd risked it all because she had a stupid conscience. Maybe some secrets really were best kept secret after all.

"Stop!" she shouted. They didn't stop. The horde pressed forward. Calay resisted the flash of a memory—the army of Elora's, converging on her in the starship. She reminded herself that was a different time. A different place. A different fucking galaxy. This was here. Now. And her friends needed her.

"They're not stopping," Jacob muttered.

"They can't hear me." Calay's voice cracked.

Jacob turned to the soldiers. "You going to do something?"

The soldiers on the platform still had their weapons by their sides.

Calay expected to turn and find their barrels pointed at her, but instead, they stared in awe at the tide of people trying to reach them. Two leapt off the back and disappeared into the throng. Only Ryland and a young woman remained, both eyes wide, their mouths slack.

"Evidently not." Calay rolled her eyes.

Jacob wrapped one of his strong hands around Calay's arm. "We have to run, Calay."

"No."

"If we don't get out of here, they'll kill us."

"I'm sick of running, Jacob. All I've done for the last five years is run from the Others. From other people. And look where it got me."

"There's no shame in running. It's kept you alive."

"No, it's kept me afraid. Alone. I lost my family because I ran. I lost Tess, too. Running's what brought you here and put us in this position in the first place." Calay pulled her shoulders back, sucked in a breath. She tried not to let the pain that fluttered across Jacob's face cause her resolve to waver. She tugged her arm out of his grasp. "I'm not running anymore."

Panic thrummed in Calay's veins. Adam, Salem, Briar, and Holden were being milled against the platform. She winced, imagining her dreams—Tess's dreams—being crushed along with them. She'd made this mess. She was going to have to clean it up. Somehow.

A darkness bubbled behind Jacob's eyes. "They're going to rip us apart."

Desperate, Calay scanned the arena for something—anything—that would stop the stampede and save her friends. Then she saw it. "Not if I can help it."

She was only going to have one shot at this, so she committed; decided to make it count. Calay twisted and lunged. She reached for Ryland's firearm which hung loose against his leg. Her fingers wrapped around the shaft, the metal cold and hard against her fingers. His grip tightened, but he was too late. She pulled hard and down and wrenched it out of his grasp. It clattered to the platform. Her gaze flew to Ryland, who didn't waste a moment before pouncing for it. Calay was faster. She grunted, thrust her sore shoulder into his ribs, and hip checked him right off the side of the platform. She didn't bother to see if he was alright. Instead, she grasped the gun. It took both hands for her to swing it up as she aimed into the crisp morning sky, finally fading from cotton-candy pink to a soft blue.

Calay checked the safety and pulled the trigger.

An explosion of pops boomed across the yard. She watched the mob cower, their hands flung over their heads. Some froze. A few at the rear fled back the way they'd come.

Now Calay had their attention.

"Nicely done." Jacob cleared his throat.

Calay stepped forward, angled herself in front of him. A shiver of warmth radiated across her skin when he rested a hand on her lower back.

His breath sent shivers across her skin when he whispered, "Now what?"

She wasn't sure. She hadn't gotten that far. All she knew was that she had to talk some sense into these people.

"Like I said, I can explain." She trained the gun on the first row of people in front of her. They flinched, her finger remained steady. "But first, you all need to calm the fuck down. Back up! That's it, nice and easy."

Adam slumped against the platform when the pressure relaxed, his clothes rumpled and his dark hair matted and damp. Briar and Holden guided him to the floor where he was able to catch his breath. He turned his head to Calay, his mouth pressed into a thin line. He didn't bother to swipe away the sweat beading across his top lip and trickling across his temples. They were going to have words later, Calay could tell. But first, she was going to save all their lives.

"Explain then," Salem muttered out the corner of her mouth, her gun still pointed.

"There's nothing to explain." Ezra appeared at the side of the crowd. His hair disheveled, his eyes red. "She's one of them. She's admitted it herself."

"I am one of them." Calay nodded. "But I'm human, too."

"What?" Adam's voice rasped.

"How is that possible?" Briar looked to Calay, her normally bright eyes were narrow slits, the side of her mouth turned down. A pang of disappointment whittled its way into Calay's heart. They were all looking at her like she wasn't from this planet—and in a way, she wasn't. But there was something particular about the way Briar was staring at Calay that made her want to disappear. Like she wasn't even human.

Ezra scoffed, his rage palpable. "It's not."

"Yes it is." Calay's arms were shaking, though she wasn't sure if it was from holding the weapon or the truth. She let the barrel fall, just a little. It didn't help. "My mother came from the same place as the Others. A place called Galaxy 3C303. A planet called Téras. Through a freak electrical storm, she was teleported here and got stranded. Eventually she met my father and they made a life for themselves."

"Your dad and an alien hooked up? That's...something," Salem snarled, but her gaze wasn't unkind.

"That's me." Calay shrugged like it was the most normal thing in the world. She'd resisted the Others, fought them for so long that she hadn't realized she'd accepted that part of herself. As she said the words though, she saw the truth as clearly as she saw the people in front of her. Adam had said no one was clean anymore, that they'd all done what they needed to in order to survive. Something stilled inside Calay, a newfound confidence bloomed. She was Self and Other; light and dark; good and evil. It wasn't even a question of whether she liked it or not— it just was. She cleared her throat. "I didn't know this until after the invasion. Recently, actually."

"How'd you find out?" Briar asked. "How do you know it's even true?"

Calay's gaze fluttered to Jacob. He may have helped her, saved her more times than she could count. He was proof there was good in them. Still, she was going to leave him out of this as much as possible. He was her past, this was her future.

"Your tests, actually. I passed some of them, but the stars in my eyes were undeniable proof. I'm not entirely human." Calay continued despite a series of hushed whispers hastening across the crowd. "I *am* human, though. I was raised here, on Earth. We can use my duality to fight the Others. Defeat them."

"Like you tried to defeat that one?" Ezra pointed violently past Calay to Jacob. "Looks to me like you two get along pretty well."

"Jacob came here because of me. He means you no harm."

"What about the other ones? With the legs and the teeth?" Salem stiffened, understanding settling across her sharp features. "Are they here because of you, too?"

"They might be," Calay admitted.

A voice, "Then let's get rid of her!"

Another, "Kill them both!"

Still another, "Kill them all!"

"I'm on your side." Calay's confidence cracked. She willed herself to hold steady.

"How can we be sure of that?" Holden pushed themselves to stand. They levelled their gaze at Calay. She swallowed. Trust was difficult to gain and so easily broken. The last thing she needed was to fracture this group even further, or to implicate Holden or Adam. They'd known some of her secrets and protected her, despite the risk to themselves.

Calay crouched, set the gun on the ground, and measured her next words very carefully while she raised her hands.

"I wouldn't be here if it wasn't for you all. I owe you my life, and if that's what it costs to repay your kindness, I'll gladly pay it. But not here, not like this. Don't you see? We can use my unique position to target and trap the Others."

Briar's shoulders lifted. "How?"

"They communicate through something called the hive mind. If I focus, I can access it. We can signal to them that I'm here. They've been looking for me, it'll be like offering me up on a big fat plate. They'll come running."

"Why can't we just throw you out? Let them come to you out there?" Ezra claimed a step forward. His stare raked Calay, his mouth curling as though he might lash out and attack again at any moment.

"Ezra has a point. Why risk our lives?" Adam finally spoke.

The simple question jarred Calay, pulled her closer to the truth. She couldn't blame them for questioning her allegiances. Her loyalty. Their words heralded the simple fact that she was an outsider. Always had been. She did not belong. But that didn't mean she couldn't.

"Because I can't do it alone, and neither can you. No one can. We need to pool our resources."

Adam raised his eyebrows. "What resources would those be exactly?"

"My...natural talents. And your artillery." Calay licked her chapped lips. "Without both, we'll never win. It's why they've beat us so far. Why we're struggling. But together, we can do this."

A heavy silence settled between them, and Calay nearly choked on it while the Resistance considered her words.

"I believe her," Holden finally said. They made their way up the steps to stand beside Calay, took her hand in theirs, squeezed. A scattered sound of snapping fingers reached the platform. Not everyone was with her, but some were. It was a start. Holden continued, "She's right. We haven't been able to defeat the Others. This could be the solution we've been looking for."

"And if she's wrong?" Adam rose, grim. He turned to face Calay.

"I'm not." Calay steadied her gaze on his. One moment stretched into two, then, an eternity.

This was it, Calay realized. Her final chance to rally the troops, as it were. If she failed now, she'd hang along with Jacob and what was left of humanity. Sure, there were other hybrids out there. Maybe they'd figure out how to win this battle. Maybe not.

"It's settled then." Adam leaned on Briar to climb beside Calay on the platform. "Calay stays while we figure out how to finish this. We're stronger together."

"What about that one?" Salem tipped her gun toward Jacob.

Calay's pulse quickened. "We have to keep him alive." Jacob stiffened against Calay. The hand he was still resting on the small of her back tightened around her waist. Despite her best efforts, a shaky exhale escaped her throat. She pushed down the urge to fold into him and focused her words. "Because I'm human, I have trouble connecting to the hive mind sometimes. He might come in handy."

"Fine, for now, but we're locking him up." Adam gestured to Ryland and the woman soldier, who'd since crumpled against the nearest wall. "Get him to a cell. Everyone here will respect that and keep their distance until the Council reviews all of this and comes to a final decision."

"That's fair." Calay couldn't agree more—both for their sake and her heart's. She peeled Jacob's hand away, perhaps for the last time.

"Do I get a say in all this?" Jacob gaped, his arms falling to his sides.

Calay shook her head. "Nope."

"We're going to hold that thing? Here?" Ezra rushed the stage. After his earlier attacks, it took everything in Calay to hold her position. She steeled her legs and her resolve. She wouldn't be intimidated by this school-yard bully. She had bigger things to worry about. Like defeating an entire alien species and reclaiming their planet.

"Every person is allotted the same rights as every other Resistance citizen." Adam rested a hand on Ezra's shoulder as he tried to reason with him.

Ezra thrust an arm in Jacob's direction, "He's not a person."

"He's a living being in our care. Is your respect for life so limited, Ezra? Is that what inspired your actions last night?" Holden shifted their weight and peer over their glasses, Ezra's mouth fell open, his lips parted as if to protest. Holden didn't give him the chance. "I know what you did. And if you want to keep it between us, you'll do as you're bloody well told."

The moment Holden finished speaking, Ezra glowered at Calay. Her blood boiled, her skin crawled. She imagined his did, too. She shook her head and turned her attention to Jacob.

He embodied everything that was wrong in the world, and yet, everything that was right, too. It didn't matter which way she sliced it, he was dangerous. Ezra—like Tess—wasn't wrong: The Others had to go. But Ezra's hostility toward Jacob was misplaced. His anger misdirected. His words were an insidious thorn that threatened to derail everything Calay was trying to do.

She cursed herself for not staying hidden. For giving Ezra yet another reason to come after her. She forced herself to meet his gaze.

His eyes drilled into hers, the hate unadulterated. Unfiltered. Unflinching.

"I don't trust you." Ezra huffed, crossing his arms across his chest.

Calay laughed, a hollow sound—she could hardly blame him, but rage bloomed in her veins. Blood rushed in her ears. How many times had she told herself trust was a luxury she couldn't afford? Yet she knew that without trust, they'd never win the war that was quite literally knocking down their doors—never mind rebuild the world. She'd said it once and she'd probably say it a hundred more times—they had to work together if they were going to survive this. Ezra didn't get it. Not yet, anyhow. She was grateful some of them seemed to. Still, there was something to be said for caution. She refused to blindly put her confidence in the Resistance. There was too much that had to change. Too much damage that needed to be repaired. Calay hoped that by the time this was all over, they could begin that process. Until then, she'd take every step necessary to protect herself and the people she was very quickly beginning to care deeply about.

"Yeah, well. That makes two of us."

CHAPTER TEN

SALEM and the other remaining soldiers monitored the disbanding crowd while Holden and Adam escorted Jacob to the cell block on the other side of the compound. The one Calay had found herself locked inside the last time she was here. Before she knew what she or Jacob were. It seemed so much simpler then. Humans bad, aliens worse. The idea of trusting others was as mythical as life on other planets—except that one had proven to be true. The world was ripped inside out when the Others invaded. As it turned out, trusting other people was an inevitability Calay would also have to accept. She could only hope that when it was all over, it wouldn't be as painful as the last five years had been.

As Resistance members whispered among themselves, she quietly fell behind until she was the only one remaining in the yard. She wandered past the Atrium, back toward the moat. She crossed the bridge, careful not to slip on the icy wooden planks or look too closely at the surface that had frozen back over, or the memories it conjured of the other night. She eased herself out the front gate. It was against the rules to leave the sanctuary of the fences. To risk one's own wellbeing or that of others. But then again, Calay had pretty much shattered every regulation the Resistance had thrown at her, and she was still there. She imagined there wasn't much Adam could say at this point. Besides, Calay needed a moment. To get some air. To clear her head. And to figure out what the hell she'd just committed herself to doing.

She wasn't sure if it was confidence or hubris, but she'd just promised the Resistance she could save humanity. Like, out loud. People were relying on her to pull through. People she cared about. Entire governments hadn't been able to stop the Others, what made Calay think she could? The truth was, she didn't know exactly *how* they'd do it, but she was sure of one thing—they'd better.

Calay sought solitude. The snow crunched underneath her feet, her breath pooled in the air. She made her way toward the forest's edge. Something rippling above caught Calay's eye. She peered up through the dense branches to find a structure, held aloft by beams secured in place by braces made of pine and metal. The Resistance's signature camouflage netting wrapped around what looked like a large box. As she looked closer, she noticed several smaller planks of wood were nailed into the trunk, painted to match the crackled bark. It was a lookout bunker.

Calay hadn't realized the Resistance had posts way out here. She'd assumed—wrongfully—that they would keep their members safe within the confines of the perimeter. This was good; they were more willing to take risks than she'd initially thought. This bode well for Calay. For what they'd have to do.

Her fingers clawed at the rungs and she climbed the makeshift ladder, one step at a time.

She crested the top and found herself squeezing through a small hole in the bottom of the box, just wide enough for her shoulders. The inside was barely bigger than the chamber she was starting to consider home, just large enough for a couple people and a stack of wool blankets in the corner.

Three sides were fully enclosed with tiny peepholes meticulously carved into the panels. The fourth was open to the woods, save for a support beam that ran the length of the structure. Calay grabbed a handful of blankets and shook them free of the dust and pine needles that clung to their rough fibers. She wrapped them around herself and settled, using the beam to ease herself onto the floor. She let her legs hang over the side, peering into the ever-lightening forest.

Snow gripped evergreen branches. Pine cones littered the woodland floor. A hint of frost clung to fallen logs and the ferns that dared to billow from them. Sunlight peeked between the canopy, settling on Calay's cheeks. It brought little warmth, but even the simple fact that the sun still rose every morning, and the moon each night, brought her an ounce of comfort. This weather was wrong. The planet was struggling. But it was still there. Unlike Téras.

An image of Earth floated through Calay's mind—cracked, shattered, with fire at its center. Boulders drifted out into the darkness of space. The topography of the continents, unrecognizable. Gone.

Calay refused to allow that to be Earth's fate. She was going to stop the Others, she just didn't know how.

As if in response, a high-pitched shriek splintered through the air and stabbed at Calay's thoughts, followed by the familiar clicking and whirring of an alien pod in the distance. A stark reminder of the threats to her species. To her. She rested her forehead on the railing, closed her eyes, and finally let the tears fall.

They were almost out of time.

"You have room for one more?"

Calay started, sniffed. She swiped the tears from her eyes and peered around the trunk to see Briar's glowing smile aimed directly at her. She was balancing a silver carafe in one hand, two speckled camping mugs in the other. Calay's pulse quickened at the sight of her. While she couldn't name why, she didn't want Briar to see her pain, to know the fear that pooled in her heart. As if Calay could hide the fact that she was endangering them all.

Calay sniffed and leaned further against the railing. "What are you doing here?"

Briar squinted. "I was going to ask you the same question."

Calay shrugged. "I just needed a minute."

"I imagine you would." Briar nodded in response. "Is that minute up?"

"Huh?"

"I came with supplies." Briar grinned and tipped the carafe. Steam tickled the air. "It's warm."

"Why didn't you say so sooner?" Calay grinned back and tilted her head, an invite.

The upturn of her lips melted from her face when Briar disappeared from view, replaced by the nervous flutter of her heart against her chest. It increased in volume with every one of Briar's steps up the ladder. Something about Briar got underneath Calay's skin. She couldn't quite put her finger on what it was, or why, and that was troublesome. In the best possible way.

Briar nestled in beside Calay on the sun-drenched ledge. Calay tried not to look too closely at the graceful way Briar folded herself onto the floor, or the confidence with which she poured from the container. Calay was sure if the roles had been reversed, she would have spilled it and made a big mess. Like she seemed to do with everything else.

"I can't feel my fingers." Calay rubbed her hands together before cupping them in her lap.

Briar lifted a metal mug brimming with near-boiling liquid. "Maybe this will help."

"What is it?" Calay clamped her stiff fingers around the mug. The heat warmed her palms. Not that she really needed it now; the proximity to Briar brought a flush to her cheeks and gentle warmth through her limbs. The steam kissed her eyelashes, danced across her cheeks. She hoped it might disguise some of blushing that had yet to fade.

"A bunch of different kinds of mint. Some chamomile. It's my own special blend."

"You make your own tea?" Calay took a sip. The liquid oozed down her throat, coating it in a bloom of warmth. It tasted floral and herbaceous. The tension in her shoulders relaxed, her nerves settled. "It's sweet."

"That's my secret ingredient." Briar winked.

"What is it?" Calay peered over the rim of the mug, her eyes narrowed, shifting to Briar.

"Nothing sinister." Briar laughed, amusement danced in her eyes. "I'll tell you if you promise not to share it with anyone else."

Calay frowned. "I'm not sure I'm someone you want to trust with promises."

"Then I'll just have to take my chances." Briar smiled. "It's honey."

"Where did you get honey?" A memory flashed in Calay's mind from the starship. The Others had granted her every wish, satiated her every craving—honey and peanut butter sandwiches. BBQ chicken and cheese pizza. A mother. They'd blinded her to the truth by giving her everything she'd missed from before the Change.

That was then, she reminded herself. *This was now.* She was safe with Briar.

Well, mostly safe.

Briar swallowed from her own mug. She closed her eyes and exhaled before continuing. "I have a bee colony. It's nothing fancy, but I'd love to show you one day. Assuming they haven't frozen to death."

Calay's breath shallowed. "A hive body."

"That's right, but I guess you know something about hives, don't you?"

Calay shuddered, averted her eyes beyond the tree line. She took another drink to hide the pout forming on her lips. She knew she was going to have to clean up the mess she'd made earlier, she just didn't think it'd be so soon.

"Hey." Briar nudged Calay with her shoulder. "You had your reasons for keeping all that to yourself. I don't know what they were, but you don't have to explain yourself to me or to anyone. It doesn't matter what we did before. It only matters what we do now."

A surge of hope flooded Calay. She wanted to believe that was true. It was why she was there, after all. The reason she'd risked her own life. Why she'd fought for Jacob's. She had to believe there was something better for them, and she was going to do everything in her power to make that happen.

"I did what I had to."

"To survive."

"Yes." Calay turned to Briar. Met her gaze. "To survive."

"I get it." Briar smiled.

It lit a candle in the darkness of Calay's heart. This close, she noticed Briar's charcoal eyes contained flecks of blue in them, too. They splattered across her irises like stars. Calay found herself wanting to count them, one by one. Chart a path toward Briar's soul. Instead, she cleared her throat and took another drink, almost draining her cup.

Calay drummed her fingers against the heat of the cup. "Why are you being so nice to me?"

"Why wouldn't I be?" Briar blinked.

"The way you were looking at me earlier. When all that went down in the plaza. I thought you hated me."

"I was listening. Trying to make sense of what was happening, that's all." Briar's brow furrowed, her hands tightened around her mug. Her face darkened. "Why would I hate you?

"I'm one of them."

"So?"

"So?" Calay gaped, furious with the Others as much as herself. "Look what they did to our planet. To people! I hate them for what they've done, and I hate that they're inside of me."

"And you think I'd hate you for that, too?"

"I don't know. Maybe? This place..." Calay searched for the words buried in her heart. She'd thought them enough times, but giving them a voice seemed like it was kind of a big deal. Dangerous, even. "It has a way of being unkind."

"You mean the compound?"

"Sure, the compound. Earth. Humanity. All of it. The love of my life tried to kill me for what I am, and I don't blame her. The Others tried to use me and then exterminate me. Even the people I've thought were my friends betrayed me. It's been a very long time since someone was nice to me for no reason." Calay gnawed on her bottom lip.

Briar cast her gaze cast toward the snowy, pine-needled ground below. "I know what it's like to not be accepted for who or what you are."

"You do?"

"Of course. All gays do." Briar's gaze caught Calay's, a fire burned behind them. "There was someone, once. I loved her with everything inside me. I thought I'd die if we were ever separated."

"What happened?"

"The world—what was left of it—forced us apart. She went one way, I went another."

A terrible stillness settled in Calay's heart. She knew that story all too well. "Do you think you'll find each other again?"

Briar shook her head, sighed.

"I'm sorry." Calay whispered, emotion lodged in her throat.

"So am I. My point is that even after all this, after society was destroyed and I lost her, I didn't die." A rosiness rushed to Briar's cheeks, her voice dropped. "Even though society as we knew it is gone, I'm still fighting to be seen and loved. It isn't easy to feel like you don't belong. Or to yearn for something so badly and be too afraid to reach for it."

A frenzy of emotions thundered through Calay. She wanted to hug Briar. To run from her. She was giving voice to the very things Calay was too afraid to admit out loud. Hell, she was afraid to even think them. It was terrifying, and exhilarating, and horrible. Mostly, it was wonderful.

"That's how I've felt my whole life," Calay managed.

Briar rested against the beam and cocked her head. "But that's not how you feel now, is it? You were brave up there this morning. You were vulnerable. You didn't wait for someone to give you permission. It was badass. You spoke your truth and asked for what you wanted."

"What I want comes at a cost."

"And you'll pay it. There's a price for our decisions. We don't always get to choose what the cost is, but we do get to decide how we respond to it."

Briar was right, of course. Threats were everywhere. Consequences, too. The Others were coming. The Faceless. For all Calay knew, the Resistance was planning her demise that very moment. She didn't know what the hell was up with the weather. She couldn't control any of them, but she did have agency over one thing—herself.

"Thank you." Calay fumbled with her empty mug, her hands. Gods, why was she so awkward? "I needed that."

"I'm always here if you need a good swift kick in the ass." Briar laughed. "While we're on the subject of secrets though, I have one of my own to confess."

"Oh?" Calay stiffened, she'd had enough secrets to last a lifetime.

"This morning, when you took my flatbread, I told you I wasn't much of a breakfast person." Briar cleared her throat. "I lied. It's actually my favorite meal of the day. I just wanted a reason to talk to you."

Calay blinked. "You wanted a reason to talk to me?"

"I haven't been able to keep my eyes off you since you walked into the cafeteria."

Butterflies. They fluttered around Calay's stomach before departing up her chest and burrowing in her veins. Her mind went blank. Her words, too. She and Briar gazed at each other, neither one of them speaking. Calay's heart pounded so hard, she was sure Briar could hear it. She searched her face for a sign of malice or ill intent, but she saw none. Instead, she noticed Briar's chest rising and falling in an uneven rhythm, not unlike her own.

This time she fumbled for a response. Something. Anything.

"Me neither," she managed to say between breaths.

The scent of pine needles wafted up to them on the breeze. Mixed with the honey, it aroused a heady aroma and kindled something deep inside Calay. Longing. Want. Desire.

She hadn't felt this way for a long time. Not since she'd first met Tess. Calay thought perhaps the all-consuming love she'd almost allowed herself to feel with Jacob or the self-sabotaging passion she'd succumbed to with Ash were necessary, but impulsive. Fleeting moments driven purely by her desperation to at once exist, and not. In a way they both erased who Calay was deep down—her mind and heart—while giving her the space to be in her body. Away from her thoughts. Her fears. Her true self.

The spark that radiated between Calay and Briar now was different. It inspired something purer. And not because it would obliterate Calay, but it held the ripe possibility of making her whole.

As though in response to her thoughts, Briar raised an eyebrow. "How are those fingers doing?"

Calay swallowed. "Better, thank you."

"You sure?" Briar reached forward and tugged the empty mug free from Calay's grasp but didn't let go of her hand.

Calay watched as Briar set the cups aside, shifted her weight. She swung back to face Calay. Briar looked at her with such clarity in her eyes, an earnestness and openness Calay didn't think people possessed anymore. It wasn't innocence though; it was wiser than that. More tragic. Then the shadows behind Briar's eyes grew darker. Her gaze dipped, sliding down the arch of Calay's lashes, resting on her lips.

Calay's mouth went dry, her pulse quickened.

Briar leaned closer until the curls of her faux-hawk grazed Calay's cheek. Calay breathed in the smell of Briar's hair—roses and nutmeg, just as she remembered. Her mind swam, the butterflies in her stomach did somersaults. Backflips, even. Everything besides them—the danger, the cold, the relentless fear—disappeared.

Briar gently lifted Calay's hand between them. She laced their fingers together, clasped them to her cheek.

Then Briar turned and brought the back of Calay's hand to her parted lips and kissed it.

Her lips were full and warm, competing against the crisp morning air on Calay's skin. A low moan crept from deep within Briar's throat as her gentle kiss became more hungry. Her mouth hovered over one knuckle, then the next, pausing just long enough to churn a longing inside Calay. Just when she thought she couldn't take the wait any longer, Briar brought her lips—the soft caress of her tongue, the edges of her teeth—to Calay's skin.

Blood rushed through Calay's ears, drained from her mind, and pooled between her legs. She sucked in a mouthful of air. The scent of Briar and the woolen blankets. She ached to wrap herself and Briar inside them, press their mouths together. To taste her. Swallow her whole. Yet she held herself perfectly still, afraid to lose this moment. To break it. Whatever it was.

When Briar pulled her mouth from Calay's hand, Calay reached for Briar's cheek, allowed her fingers to trace the shaved sides of Briar's hair. Calay rested it there, traced the back of her neck, hung on tight.

Their eyes met, their foreheads, too. They closed their eyes while their breathing steadied.

"I'm not going anywhere," Briar whispered.

Calay inhaled, desperately wanting to hold onto this moment. "Me neither."

"You better not." Briar ran her tongue over her bottom lip, exhaled. Calay resisted the urge to kiss her. "So what are we going to do in the meantime?"

"I have no idea." Calay grinned. Just a little. She pulled herself upright, gazed beyond, toward the forest. Tall trees groaned in the breeze, the sound of screeches echoed in the distance. Humanity might have been out of time, but people could still have each other. That had to count for something. "I do know one thing though."

"Oh, yeah?" Briar opened the carafe, emptied the remaining tea into their mugs and handed one to Calay. They shuffled closer together, wrapped themselves tighter between the blankets. "Do tell."

"The Resistance was winning before. At least, that's what they told me. They were on the right track, but Tess missed a vital component to their success."

"What's that?"

"Me."

CHAPTER ELEVEN

WHEN ADAM FETCHED Calay out of bed at the crack of dawn two days later, he brought a fur-lined parka and a shovel. He thrust them in her general direction, said little. Calay fumbled to lace her boots and get the coat on before he'd already turned and made his way out the door. His usual friendly demeanor replaced with a hard shell, a coldness that before today, she'd assumed he wasn't capable of. Now, as he pulled back a large tile on the floor, revealing a dark hole that led to who knew where, she couldn't help but wonder what she'd gotten herself into this time. Maybe she'd pushed him over the edge in the courtyard. Broken him. Did he intend to break her in return?

Calay peered over the threshold of the abyss. The light from the hallway did little to illuminate the inky blackness below. The iron ladder welded just underneath the floor seemed to disappear into nothingness.

An unsettling nausea rolled in Calay's stomach. "You're not going to leave me down there, are you?"

Adam merely tilted his head, shrugged.

Calay pressed her lips into a hard line and nodded. Adam was clearly upset, but she couldn't imagine him locking her inside. Could she? A lot had happened in the last week she didn't think was possible: she'd outed herself to the Resistance, Jacob had survived the starship, Ezra the would-be murderer roamed free, and then there was the whole Briar thing. Whatever that was. They hadn't seen each other since the afternoon in the treehouse. Calay had been lying low, avoiding the general population for fear of what they might do to her. Ezra still wanted her dead, and she had no idea who fell under his purview. The Resistance was not what it had first seemed, and Calay noted it would do her well to remember maybe Adam wasn't either.

She knelt down and eased herself onto the ladder. Her shoulders dipped into the darkness.

Adam cleared his throat." You're going to die."

Calay dug her nails into the metal, wished he'd continued giving her the silent treatment. "That's comforting."

"We all are, unless something changes." His brows drew together at the center. "I hope you realize that."

"I'm well aware."

"Good. Now keep climbing. I have a lot to do today, and I don't want to waste it down there with you."

"Gee, thanks," Calay mumbled. She continued down the ladder. She took each step with care, but her knees buckled when her feet came to an unexpected and abrupt stop on hard pavement. She winced, steadied herself. Evidently, she'd reached the bottom. A shiver rolled up her spine—both the cold and the unknown making themselves real in her bones. "I can't see a thing down here."

"Watch your head." Adam was descending after her, quickly. He really didn't waste any time.

Calay shifted her weight and shuffled out of the way but was reluctant to sink into the shadows beyond the wavering light of the opening. She held her arms close to her body, narrowed her eyes as she tried to peer beyond. There was a wet chill to the air, a heaviness she didn't want to breathe. It smelled damp with rot and something foul. Like a rat—or something—had died down there. She clamped her eyes shut, hoped it was nothing bigger. Adam's boots scuffed the floor, and when Calay opened her eyes, she found him holding a long black flashlight toward her. "Take this."

She wrapped her fingers around the long black barrel. "What are we doing?"

Adam switched his own flashlight on, the beam carving a sharp line through the darkness. "I have something to show you."

"It's not my grave, is it?" Calay swallowed a hard lump in her throat.

Adam shrugged a backpack up on his shoulders and plodded ahead down the tunnel. "Not yet."

Calay gazed longingly back up the ladder to the light, braced herself against the chill. What she wouldn't give to be back in her bed, snuggled and cozy. But that wasn't the plan for this morning, and if Calay's suspicions were right, it wasn't going to be the plan again for a very long time.

She zipped the coat Adam had been gracious enough to give her all the way to her chin, tightened the drawstrings in the hood, and ran to catch up with him.

They walked in silence for what felt like the better part of forever. Adam's ominous warning clung to Calay like tar. He'd said it as if she didn't know the kind of danger they were in. As if she hadn't measured it—carefully. Despite the incessant trepidation running through her mind, she'd taken her time deciding what to do next. Maybe it didn't seem like it to him, but for the first time in her life she was taking calculated risks. Not just impulsive ones. She was daring herself to not only trust others, but herself. It was the only good choice she had.

"Are we there yet?" she dared to whisper.

"Yep."

The sound of metal grinding on metal squealed through the tunnel, and then blinding white light assaulted Calay's vision. She grimaced and shielded her eyes against the glare, but the sound of snow crunching ahead pulled her gaze forward. Her feet, too. Her eyes acclimatized, and she was surprised to find they were outside the fence. Far outside it, deep within the forest. She peeked behind them at a metal grate on the ground, a layer of ferns blanketing the top.

"You have a secret tunnel?" She gaped.

"We have a secret tunnel."

"We? So, you're not mad at me?"

"Oh, I'm mad alright. But that's not going to keep us alive." Adam spun to face Calay, his features tight. "I'm done fighting with you, Calay. I'd be done working with you, too, if I thought we'd make it through this without you. Holden makes it difficult to argue that we can."

Well, that was a surprise. Calay wrapped her arms around herself. "Holden stood up for me?"

"Against their better, judgement, if you ask me. But yes, they see something in you. Something I don't. You lie. You keep secrets. You've gone against me at every turn. I can't trust you."

A pang of guilt riddled through Calay, she pushed it down. "Just because you have a different way of doing things doesn't mean my way is wrong."

"We've done it my way since you ki—" Adam took a long, slow, deep breath. The redness in his cheeks flared. "Since Tess died. It's kept us alive so far."

"You've been in charge for what? A hot minute?" A surge of emotion rippled through Calay. Adam may have not finished his sentence, but she knew exactly what he was about to say. It hit a little too close to home. "Last I checked, you were basically keeping aliens hooked up to life support so you could do experiments on them. You were drawing the Others straight to you. You need me, Adam. I care about this place, too. These people. I'm fighting for them. It's the whole reason why I'm even here. Do you think I like the looks people give me? You think I don't know what they think? That they're judging me? In the week that I've been free, someone's tried to kill me. Twice. And I'm still fucking here. You can trust me."

"No, I can't, but I have to." Adam sighed; his shoulders sagged. "I have to or we're all going to die. Much sooner than later."

Calay wanted to push back. To convince him of her worth. To make him happy about it. But that wasn't the goal. Sure, she wanted to make friends. To feel comfortable. To belong. But all that could come after. Assuming there even was an after.

"Great." Calay exhaled, shoved her hands on her hips. "So what are we doing out here then?"

"We need a plan to present to the Council."

"You keep talking about this so-called Council. I haven't seen any evidence they actually exist."

Adam's tone was even, but the tension in his shoulders betrayed his façade. "You haven't had clearance."

"And now that you know I'm one of those aliens you hate so much, I do?" Calay scoffed.

"Now that we know you have special abilities that could help us, I was hoping we could pool our resources. We'll start with this. Once we have a solid plan, you can come to a Council meeting to present it. Like you said, we're going to have to work together if we're going to beat the Others."

Calay wanted to move things along faster, skip the bureaucracy. Adam had proven he'd let the rules slide if he had no other choice, but unless Calay could convince him that was in fact their current situation, she'd have to do things his way whether she liked it or not.

"That's fair." She nodded.

"I'm glad you agree. At least now we're on the same team." Adam glanced into the forest, his eyes searching. Seemingly satisfied they were alone, he continued. "Do you think you can use your telepathy to call them here?"

"I guess, but I'm not very good at it. I don't know if it's the human in me, but I felt it much more strongly on the starship. When I was closer to them."

"Hm, that does present a problem. Is that something you can work on?"

"Not without signaling to them where I am. What are you going to do when they get here?"

"I haven't gotten that far."

"Could we funnel them down this tunnel? Shoot them as they come through?"

Adam shook his head. "Not enough fire power. Hasn't been for a long while."

"When I was here the first time, I was told the Resistance was winning. Was that true? How were you doing it then?"

Adam blinked. "Who told you that?"

Calay bristled at the memories this conversation was bringing up. She persevered. "Smith. The guy who seemed to be running this place while Tess was at the mountain."

"Ah, Smith. Right, well, Smith said a lot of things."

"Was he lying?"

"Not exactly." Adam shook his head. "We managed to take down some pods, but we never had the power to make a real difference. Smith believed we were on our way to something bigger though. I guess he was right." Adam levelled his gaze at Calay. "We do need you, Calay."

"I'll do everything I can to stop them." She strode away from the tree line, stopping only when she reached the outside of the perimeter fence. Adam followed. Calay wrapped her fingers around the frozen chain-link, pressed her fingers into the snow, and waited for it to melt under the fleeting warmth of her hands. She squinted at the long coils of barbed wire extended above them, the low-rise buildings on the other side. Exhaled. She pulled her shoulders back. She knew what she was about to say wasn't going to go over well, but it was the only chance they had. "But we're going to need Jacob, too."

Adam nearly laughed. "Not possible."

"It has to be, Adam. The abilities I have? His are stronger than mine. More connected. If I can't reach them, he will. And you can bet your ass they'll come then."

"I understand you like to break the rules—"

Calay spun to face Adam. "Fuck the rules. The rules are already shattered. You're working with one alien, why not two?"

"What if he betrays us?"

Calay steeled her gaze. "He won't."

"How can you be so certain?"

She swallowed before shoving her hands in the pockets of the over-sized jacket. She was going to have to say it. To another person. She could barely stomach the thought—and disappointment—herself. But she meant her silent promise to Tess. She was going to do everything she needed to do. Even if it meant twisting something beautiful into something ugly. That was the way of the world now.

"Because he loves me."

Adam's eyes grew wide, he threw his hands in the air. "We're banking our survival on *that*?"

"We don't have anything else." Calay shrugged, her heart torn in two. Half for the world as it was, the other half for the future. A gaping chasm between them. Her tone softened, she continued, "I get it, okay? We're in an impossible situation, and I helped put us here. But Adam, we're out of time. The choices we're making now will determine the fate of the Resistance. Of humanity. Rules will only get us so far, and I didn't come all this way to lose. We may need to rewrite a few to win."

Speechless, Adam's mouth fell open before he closed it again. He ran his hand over his face, his lips pressed into a thin line before he stalked back toward the tunnel's opening. Calay watched shadows fall on his back as he made his way underneath the sprawling canopy of ice-covered pine.

She felt the weight he carried. The burden of it all. She wanted to tell him he wasn't alone. To share it with him. But she had enough to bear on her own.

Her gaze drifted past Adam's silhouette, into the dim forest beyond. Mounds of snow carpeted the ground, disappearing under bushels of ferns. Ivy crept between the trees, spiraling around their trunks and disappearing among the leaves still clinging to their branches.

To life.

A morning fog had risen, it cloaked the landscape like ghosts.

The hairs rose on the back of Calay's neck. Her heart fluttered in her chest. She knew this sensation. It was the feeling of being watched.

She looked closer, peering into the dense greenery. Saw no one. She pulled the fur lined hood closer around her neck. The Others were out there. The Faceless, too. The end wasn't just nigh, it was smashing down their front door, hungry to swallow them whole. So many of their people had already died, how many more would have to before this was all over?

"Calay?"

Calay started at Adam's voice, a shiver ran across her skin and deep into her soul. She turned to Adam. A slice of rising sunlight cut across his sharp features, sparkling in the green of his eyes.

"Yeah?"

"Do you really think we can do this?"

She looked back toward the trees, the unknown beyond, searching for an answer. She knew what Tess would say, what she would do. Calay intended to honor that, but she wasn't a fortune teller and she didn't possess magic powers. Her journey to Téras had proven she was capable of manipulating some of the environmental adaptations of the Others, but she wasn't exactly confident in her abilities to wield them. She was human, after all. Raised on Earth. She was only beginning to understand what that meant for her. Whether Calay liked it or not, if she was going to make good on her promises to Adam and his people—now her people —she was going to have to depend on the very person she wanted nothing to do with anymore: Jacob.

She stalked forward until she stood toe to toe with Adam.

"I do." She peered up at him, her resolve hardening as their gazes met. She wanted to believe it.

She had to.

The sound of their footfalls echoed through the tunnel as they made their way back inside the compound in silence, both consumed by their own fears. Calay chanced a glance behind her. Adam had latched the door tight. Not even a sliver of light made its way past the seal. She knew the door was well hidden amongst the foliage, that it was unlikely anyone—or anything—would find it without already knowing it was there. Still, she couldn't shake the feeling of someone watching them. Then again, cold dark spaces had a way of etching their way into one's mind, nestling in the dark corners until ready to spring forward and snatch them.

She exhaled, grateful when her toes reached the spotlight peeking down from the opening in the floor.

She forced her stiff, frozen muscles to climb the ladder, inching her way back into the lab. After the nightmares she'd experienced in this building, she didn't think she'd ever be grateful to be back here. Yet the gentle warmth was a welcome reprieve from the harsh early morning air. Calay wasn't sure which she found more chilling—the brisk temperatures or the cold hard truth that she was going to have to make some difficult decisions in the coming days.

They entered the main building. The clang of the fire door closing jarred Calay from her thoughts.

"Do you think you can have some ideas put together about how to defeat the Others by tonight?" Adam turned to Calay. She frowned at the ground, which was still stained black from where they'd shot and killed the alien only a few days ago. She could still hear the violent gnawing of its jaws, the clickety-clackety of its jagged, pointed legs on the hard floor. "Calay?"

"Sure, yes." She pulled her attention to Adam, nodding. "I can do that. Why tonight?"

"The Council is calling a meeting. I'd like to present them with something tangible then."

"No time like the present."

"No time *but* the present." Adam's words chipped away at the crater in Calay's heart. She knew what he was saying was true, of course. Hell, she'd said it herself not long ago. Still, hearing it from someone else made it even more true. Undeniable. Unavoidable. "This stays between us until then, right?"

"Right," she whispered.

"Right?" Adam's voice hardened.

Calay forced her shoulders back, held herself taller. "Right."

Adam nodded a final time, glanced at his watch, and left Calay to make her way back to her bunk on her own. She didn't mind. She needed space to think about the secret he'd just made her promise to keep. God, she was sick of secrets. Thankfully, the soft, warm sheets of her bed were calling. She was unlikely to sleep, given the fact that she needed to come up with a plan to save the whole fucking world in the next eight hours, but it didn't mean she couldn't be cozy while she did it.

Calay stuffed her hands in her pockets. She turned the corner and came to a quick stop when she ran straight into Briar.

Calay gasped, her pulse quickened.

Briar's surprised laugh carried through the corridor; her dark eyes danced with amusement. Calay found herself wanting to hear more.

They hadn't seen each other in two days and Calay, despite the challenges ahead, was stunned to realize she'd legitimately missed Briar. A gentle warmth flooded her chest as the two women's eyes met. It took everything Calay had not to reach out and hug her.

Briar beat her to it when she pulled Calay close. Wrapped her strong arms around Calay's puffy jacket. Squeezed. Then released her way too fast.

Calay tried to slow her breathing and get herself together before she said something stupid.

"Hey," Calay said. *Good start.*

"Hey," Briar replied, her normally deep voice light and breathy.

A moment passed. Then another. A warm rosiness swelled in Calay's cheeks. She knew she should say something else, that it was her turn, but nothing came to mind. She didn't know what it was about Briar that stole her words away, but she liked it.

"Hey," someone else said from beyond Briar's radiance.

Calay turned to find Salem waiting awkwardly behind them. She stood beside a tall man with chiseled features and hair Calay found herself jealous of. He shifted his weight on hiking boots that had seen better days, the ridge on his nose crinkling as he grinned.

"Callum," Calay remembered. He'd been there when the alien had invaded the compound. He was the one who'd comforted Adam. "Right?"

"Good memory." He zipped his bomber jacket over a denim button-down shirt that hung open over a loose t-shirt.

"Thanks. What are you all doing up this early?"

Briar grinned. "Us? What are you doing? We're usually the only ones who are crazy enough to be up at this time."

Calay felt compelled to share the details about her meeting with Adam. She wanted to connect with these people. Give them more reasons to trust her. But if she did that, she might lose Adam's. There was a reason he'd come to her before anyone else was awake. She remembered his warning—to keep their conversation between them. She stuffed the urge down.

"Couldn't sleep." Calay shrugged. It wasn't exactly a lie. "Figured I'd stretch my legs."

"I do that sometimes, too." Briar's lips drew downward. "Helps clear the cobwebs."

"Exactly."

Salem hiked a backpack on her shoulders, impatient. She and Callum shuffled past before disappearing outside. If Calay didn't know better, she would have thought the two of them were snickering.

"You two gonna stand there all day?" Salem called back before the door shut, not bothering to look back.

"Coming!" Briar fingered the drawstring on Calay's hood. "You're already dressed. You should come."

"You didn't say where you're going."

Calay had shit to do. Plans to scheme. Worlds to save. Yet her curiosity was peaked. She and Briar had only met a few days ago, but when Briar looked at her, Calay felt something she hadn't in a very long time. There was something about Briar that was beginning to feel comfortable. Like home. As if they'd known each other for much longer.

Briar raised her eyebrows. A wicked grin spread across her full lips. "Well?"

"Is it dangerous?" Calay tried to keep the shake out of her voice.

"A little, but I'll keep you safe." Briar winked as she tugged on the drawstring, leading Calay toward the door.

CHAPTER TWELVE

THE OTHER TWO had the engine running by the time Calay and Briar slipped outside the main fence and approached the truck. They were hunched in the back seat, huddled underneath a dark wool blanket. A thick layer of frost on the windshield was already starting to thaw. A discomfort settled in Calay's chest when she saw the way Callum and Salem peered at her through the glass, their eyes narrow, slick grins pasted on their mouths. Like they knew something she didn't.

Briar jogged ahead, opened the passenger-side door, and waited. Her eyes caught Calay's, and the space between them thickened with an energy Calay couldn't place. Something abundant and lush—something warm. Under the weight of Callum and Salem's stares, she resisted the urge to sink into it, and instead hoisted herself up on the metal running board and into the cab.

She forced herself to turn her gaze from Briar, who was making her way around the other side, and turned to the others.

"What?" She frowned.

"What, what?" Salem grinned.

"You're staring. Like, a lot." Calay smoothed the parka that was now bunched against the seat.

Salem blinked innocently. "Are we?"

"It's just…" Callum cleared his throat, ran a hand over his five o'clock shadow. "You shouldn't be here."

"Oh." Calay tried to keep a straight face despite the twinge of nonbelonging vibrating through her chest.

"In the truck, I mean." Callum clarified. "With us. You shouldn't be leaving the compound right now."

"We won't be long." Briar smiled, easing the pain in Calay's heart.

Callum leaned forward, resting his hands on the front seats. "Adam doesn't want her going anywhere. She isn't cleared."

"Well Adam isn't here right now, is he?" Briar settled, secured her seatbelt.

Calay watched closely, entranced by the ridges in Briar's knuckles, the scar on her thumb. She ached to kiss it. To do to Briar what she'd done to her in the treehouse.

As Briar adjusted the rearview mirror with her free hand, she spied Calay's gaze, raised an eyebrow, and grinned.

Calay inched her hand across the seat. Briar did too. They stopped only when the tips of their fingers looped around the other's. A rush of warmth flooded Calay, her breath shortened. She wanted more. It took everything she had not to reach over and wrap Briar in her arms.

"I don't want to get anyone in trouble," Calay said as she squeezed Briar's hand.

Briar squeezed back. "No one will get in trouble."

"Don't make promises you can't keep, Briar." Callum's brow furrowed. "I have to hear enough drama about this place when Adam stomps home every night. He's been in a mood lately, not that I blame him. Seriously, if he comes down on us, I'm blaming everything on you two."

"What? Why me?" Salem puckered her bright red lips.

Callum gestured to Briar before he tucked himself back under the blanket. "Because she's your friend."

"Only because she lets me borrow her Walkman." Salem reached over the seat and playfully punched Briar in the shoulder.

"You're lucky you're cute." Briar blew her a kiss.

"You're welcome." Salem rolled her eyes.

"You're fucking welcome." Briar laughed.

A familiar yearning tugged on Calay's insides. She watched in awe at the ease in which these three joked. The friendship between them. Almost as if nothing had ever happened.

She sighed, hoping she'd have that one day, too.

The corner of Briar's lips turned up, and she thrust the vehicle into Drive. They peeled across the frozen field—the one Calay had barely escaped from only a few months ago.

Calay gazed out the window, remembering the fear that had almost swallowed her whole. It had been so different then. Long reeds of grass, the air heavy with the heat of summer, the Resistance chasing her down like a wild animal. The only thing that had stopped them and given her the chance she needed to get away was Max. He'd saved her in more ways than she could count. Her heart ached, fearful of what had become of him. He wasn't just a dog. Not to her. He was family. Her pack. And she'd left him behind to return to Téras with Jacob. Calay shook her head, her jaw hardened. She'd told herself he'd survived without her before, he could do it again. That had been a mistake. Another thing to make up for if she ever got the chance. She added it to the laundry list she'd compiled in her mind. In the meantime, she'd do her best not to make any new ones.

She glanced in the side mirror, caught Callum watching her, his mouth drawn into a tight line. He didn't look away when she made eye contact. Didn't even flinch. As she stared back, she tried to imagine what he saw when he looked at her. A liar. A traitor. A monster. She could only guess what Adam told him behind closed doors. She didn't need to know, and frankly, didn't want to. The echo of the group's camaraderie lingered in her mind. Yes, she wanted to make friends. To find people she could connect with and belong to, but she had to remember that wasn't why she'd come back. She was there to do a job. To make things right. But that didn't mean it didn't sting when she wasn't included.

"Seriously, is there something on my face?" Calay huffed, feigning impatience to mask her yearning and disappointment.

Callum shrugged, turned his attention out the window.

"Nah." Briar squeezed Calay's hand again, tossed her a comforting smile. "He just likes what he sees. So do I."

Calay tucked the compliment inside her heart and a silence fell over the truck as they made their way beyond the tree line.

It didn't take long for the dirt to give way to pavement, and then for pavement to give way to gravel.

The truck roared over the rocks, leaving a cloud of snow and dust behind them. The road snaked along a snow-packed hillside, frozen waterfalls clung to the cliffs. Calay gripped the holy-shit handle, peering out the side window at the chasm of snow-topped evergreens below. When they first left the compound, they'd been surrounded by them. A forest of giants. But now, as they climbed, the trees grew smaller, Calay thought almost comically so. You know, if she wasn't so worried about sliding off the edge of the mountain.

She chanced a glance at Briar, whose gaze was trained ahead. She almost asked where they were going again, but on second thought, sealed her lips shut—Briar's focus was on the ice-covered road, and Calay intended to keep it there. Behind her, Salem had propped herself on Callum's shoulder, her eyes shut. Callum looked bored. Calay wished she could feel that relaxed.

She turned her attention forward just in time to feel the ground start to shake.

"What's that?" She started. It reminded her too much of the morning of the Change. The day her apartment collapsed; her life.

Briar's eyes narrowed as she continued driving. "Probably just a tremor."

Calay didn't like the sound of that any better. "Do you mean an earthquake?"

"Just a little one." Briar nodded. "We're on a fault line. They've been happening more frequ—"

Before Briar could finish her sentence, the shaking grew. The rumbling, too.

Briar released Calay's death grip, squared both hands on the steering wheel. She slowed the truck to a stop.

"What's going on?" Salem sat up, rubbed her fists against her groggy eyes.

No one answered her. They waited. Calay sucked in a deep breath, her lungs felt like they might burst. Her fingers dug into the bar on the door, of which she hadn't yet let go.

"We can't stay here," Callum hissed.

"Let's just give it a minute, it'll pass," Briar said.

Calay wasn't so confident. The tops of the trees outside her window heaved back and forth, as if rocking to slow, deep, horrible melody. The ground swayed, as if breathing.

A wave of nausea passed through Calay, though she wasn't sure if it was from fear or motion. It wasn't normal for the ground to move. She didn't like it. She clenched her eyes, wishing she'd heeded Callum's warnings and stayed at the compound. She imagined they all did. If they had, they wouldn't be here now. She'd be safe, tucked between the sheets of her bed, wondering how she was going to save the world. Now there was nowhere she could go. Nowhere she could run. She was trapped.

Just when Calay thought she couldn't take it anymore, the rocking slowed. The trees righted themselves. Everything stilled.

Calay exhaled, she allowed her breathing to return to normal.

"See? We're fine." Despite her words, Briar's voice trembled, her hands too. Calay dared to reach across the seat and placed one of her own on Briar's denim-clad thigh. She noticed Briar's legs were also shaking.

"You did the right thing," Calay said.

Tears welled behind Briar's eyes. "If anything happened to any one of you... I didn't know what else to do."

"Hey, there wasn't anything else to do. You couldn't have known. We're alright, right?" Calay hadn't seen this side of Briar. The one that protected the people she loved. The one that cried. Briar had been there for Calay when she needed it, the least Calay could do was return the favor. She patted Briar's leg, gently squeezed. She turned her attention to the back seat. Salem's fists were balled at her sides. Callum was taking measured breaths, his eyes trained on the floor. Everyone seemed to be in one piece. "You two okay?"

"Define okay." Salem frowned while exhaling through a twisted grin.

Salem's sarcasm was beginning to grow on Calay. She almost laughed, and she might have if it weren't for the deep rumble that suddenly filled the interior of the truck. The reverberations traveled through the tires, up into the cab, and buried themselves in Calay's core. It sounded like a freight train was about to come through the front window.

Then the rocks started falling. Little ones at first. Pebbles and dust.

Calay gaped at the others, who had turned ashen, their eyes wide. They looked how Calay felt—completely petrified.

Beyond the driver's side window, sheets of ice sheared off the cliff faces above, splintering into sharp fragments all around them.

The rocks got bigger. Fist size, if Calay ventured a guess. They pinged off the hood, rattled in the truck bed, dented the roof. If one came through the window... Calay couldn't stomach the thought. She wouldn't.

Then the boulders started. They tumbled behind the truck, several bouncing off the road into the deep ravine below. Others blocked the group's way off the mountain.

"Shit." She braced herself against the seat as she peered out the back window. Salem tucked herself against the door, threw her arms over her head. Calay turned forward—the view wasn't much better. Big fucking rocks scattered the roadway.

"We have to go." Calay turned to Briar, who was staring straight ahead, her fingers clamped around the steering wheel.

"We aren't going to make it," Briar whispered.

"We will if we're fast. There's still a path."

"This is my fault."

"Today is not the day we die."

Briar shook her head, her eyes wide. "I shouldn't have brought us here."

"Briar, listen to me! Look at me!" Calay grasped Briar's hand in hers, slid across the bench until their legs were pressed together. Briar turned and met Calay's gaze. "This is not your fault, and we're going to keep it that way, okay?"

"Okay." Briar nodded.

The truck was jolting so hard, Calay had trouble getting the words past her lips. The sound of falling rocks and shuddering earth was relentless. She forced the sound from her mind and continued, "We're going to get through this. Together, right?"

"Right." Briar blinked, swiped at the tears that dared to escape her eyes, sniffed. "Yes."

"We're going to be crushed." Callum yelled to be heard through the roar.

"Now drive." Calay slid back to her side of the cab, fastened her seatbelt with resolve. "While we still can."

"Fuck, okay," Briar hissed. "Everyone buckled up?

"We are now." The sound of Salem's seatbelt clicked into place.

Calay gripped the strap of hers with both hands, terror flowed freely up and down her nerves like fire. "Drive!" she commanded through clenched teeth.

Briar slammed on the gas. The truck careened forward just as a boulder the size of the vehicle slammed into the spot where they'd been parked. The road disappeared under its weight, crumbling into a mist of rocks and snow until there was nothing left. Calay gasped, shocked by how close they'd come. If they'd waited a moment longer, they would be gone along with it.

As if they had never existed.

She wasn't ready to for that. Not anymore.

Instead, she leaned forward and braved the view out the windshield, spotting for Briar as rocks threatened to knock them off the mountain.

Briar responded to Calay's cues, almost like a third arm, as if they were one.

The truck staggered around one fallen rock after another. A loud screech echoed across the canyon as the side of the truck collided with one, leaving behind a long red line of paint. Calay's heart thumped in her throat when Briar over-corrected, skirting the ledge of the cliff before pulling it back center. Calay thought she heard Salem scream, but couldn't be sure. She didn't dare look back. Briar was depending on her as much as they were all relying on Briar. A shiver ran down Calay's spine. Despite her pep talk, she hadn't realized how much they really would need to work together to get out of this alive.

As if it wasn't enough the Others wanted them dead, now it seemed the planet was closing in on them, too.

Calay's stomach lurched as the truck fishtailed, near miss after near miss, until the road started to descend into the valley.

They made their way back amongst the trees, the earthquake calmed. The rumbling quieted. Calay wasn't entirely sure how, but it seemed they'd escaped the worst of it.

Briar followed what was left of the road around a hair-pin curve and brought them to a stop deep between two mountains.

Nobody spoke. They didn't move. They barely breathed.

Sunlight cut through the windshield, casting the interior of the truck in a bright amber glow. Eventually, Calay curled her fists in her lap, forced herself to take a long, slow, deep inhale. They'd made it. Barely.

They were alive. And they were together. That had to count for something.

Briar killed the silence when she cut the engine. "Well, we're here."

Calay sighed with relief. "I was just thinking the exact same thing,"

"No, she means we're *here*," Callum muttered. He opened the back door and exited the vehicle.

"Lucky us." Salem followed him.

Calay watched them stumble across the snow between blocks of land marked into large squares, cordoned off by rope and makeshift fences. Within each one were rows of plants, carefully spaced. In the far corner, several colorful wooden crates were stacked on top of each other. Bee hives, by the looks of it. Calay realized this must be where Briar harvested her honey.

Calay finally released her grip on the seatbelt. "What are they talking about—*here?*"

Exhaustion washed over Briar's face. "The farm. It's where we were going this morning. I was hoping to show this place to you, though for a second there I didn't think I'd get the chance. Now I'm not sure how we're going to get home." Briar pointed beyond the plots. A rough dirt path disappeared into the darkness of the forest. "There's a road on the other side of those trees. I think it leads back the way we came. Bit longer though. Adam will definitely notice that we've gone."

Calay shook her head. "You mean that I've gone."

"That is what I mean, yes." Briar unclipped her seatbelt.

"I'll handle Adam."

"You going to handle Callum, too? He's normally pretty sweet, but he's going to be a right pain in the ass to ride back with now."

"At least he's *alive* to ride back with. Adam'll be grateful for that."

"You're probably right."

Calay pointed in the direction Briar was still trained on. "You're sure that road leads back to the compound?" Knowing the danger they were up against, and after hearing the sounds in the forest the other morning, the idea of getting lost in there wasn't exactly appealing.

"Nope. But we'll find out together, won't we?" Briar exhaled before she pocketed the keys and slipped out the driver-side door.

Something lightened in Calay in that moment. She wasn't sure whether it was relief they weren't dead or Briar's promise that she wasn't alone, but she was willing to find out. Calay hopped out of the truck and met Briar, who was waiting for her to catch up.

They moved to meet the others, their arms grazing as they shuffled through the snirt. Even between the layers of fabric of their coats, Calay felt an energetic pull to Briar each time they touched—two magnets, drawn together. She knew the connection she felt was beyond reason, beyond explanation. After all she'd been through—the deceit and betrayal—she hoped it was genuine. That she hadn't manufactured the feeling in her broken heart. That she wasn't being tricked again.

She peered at Briar out of the corner of her eye. Briar seemed so strong. So sure. Except for when she didn't. The moments between alien invaders and crumbling mountains appeared to shake Briar as much as it did Calay. In a way, it was a comfort. It meant Briar was real. Human, hopefully.

Gods, when did everything get so complicated?

They stopped a few paces from where the other two were hunched over plants, checking the underside of leaves and hilling up mounds of thick, dark soil.

"What is this place?" Calay asked.

"That sludge you eat for breakfast every morning?" Salem grunted, heaving several fallen rocks out of the garden. "Bon appetite."

"We grow our own food?"

"We did." Callum flicked his hair back with a toss of his head, only for it to fall back into his eyes a moment later. His gloves were covered in wet dirt. "Until this happened."

"The change in weather." Calay tucked her hands into her pockets.

Callum exhaled as he gazed across the snow-blanketed valley. "We had full crops for a long time. We were able to feed everybody. We have to ration it now. The Pacific Northwest has some of the most fertile land in the world, but because of the snow, the only thing that'll grow are hardy vegetables, and even they're struggling."

Briar pointed at the different rows. "Kale, Brussels sprouts, potatoes, some squash."

"Breakfast sludge." Salem squatted, continuing to clear debris from the garden.

Briar shook her head. "If the earthquakes keep happening, we won't have that either."

"Adam's working on a solution. He's figuring out how to turn the Atrium into a greenhouse." Callum coughed, stalked to the next plot. "We've been successful with a few seedlings, but nothing's grown enough to feed people. Not yet, anyhow."

A coldness ran through Calay. The hairs rose on the back of her neck. Rage flowed through her veins, warming her cheeks. If people weren't killing each other to survive, they were literally starving to death.

"This is because of the Others." Calay fumed.

"Come again?" Briar turned.

Calay's resolve grew. "The change in the environment. It's their fault."

"What makes you think that?"

"You know how we were talking about hives the other day?" Calay swallowed and looked toward the bee boxes. "I got a first-hand look at how they work when the Others brought me to their most recent home planet, Téras. In Galaxy 3C303."

"You've actually been there?" Salem sidled up beside them, Callum too. They gaped, waiting for her to continue.

"Briefly." Calay nodded.

Horrific images of melting skin and hordes of Elora replicas clutched at her mind. The sound of her feet on metal staircases, the smell of burning flesh. Her focus grew hazy as the memories threatened to tear her apart even now. Despite the chill in the air, she could almost feel the heat from the fire when she'd torched the starship. The fear that she'd never make it home. She had, though, hadn't she? She was here. On a very broken Earth. She could feel it beneath the soles of her boots, hard and unyielding. Like the truth bomb she was about to drop.

"It was something they said while I was there. They want us to think the environmental collapse is because there aren't enough humans left to balance the ecosystem. I think that's a distraction, though. Like magic. It's meant to trick us into looking one way, while they use slight of hand in the other."

"Come again?" Callum narrowed his eyes.

Salem pursed her lips. "Keep going."

Calay knew she was onto something. If she could just come up with the right way to say it. She trudged through the snow to the bee boxes, Listened to their buzzing. The gentle hum was unsettling. It was also the answer.

She pointed. "The change in the weather is less about the fact that there aren't enough humans and more that we're competing with an invasive species."

Briar's eyes widened in understanding. "Like bees."

"Exactly."

"We're competing with bees?" Skepticism dripped from Salem's voice.

"In a way, yes," Calay said.

"Bees are instrumental to environmental balance." Briar lifted the top off one of the boxes. She carefully removed one of the panels, holding it up in the crisp morning light for the others to see. "Look closely. They're pollinators. They support the growth of trees, flowers, fruit. Our entire food system is dependent on them."

Calay watched with fascination at the way Briar expertly handled the hive. The bees seemed to know Briar. To trust her. Like she was one of them.

"Exactly. Without bees, we have no food, we die. It's possible because there are so few humans left in the world, our planet could be out of balance, but it existed millennia without us just fine. I think it's much more likely things are collapsing because it can't support the imbalance of the Others."

Briar sighed. "Like bees struggled to survive when there were too many of us."

"So people are the bees in this analogy?" Salem pushed herself to stand, abandoning her rock-clearing effort.

A fire roared inside Calay. They were getting it. "Yes. The bees are a community. Instrumental to life on this planet."

Salem crossed her arms. "That would make the Others, us."

Calay pulled her shoulders tight. "More than you know."

"I think we know just fine thanks to your performance the other day." Callum gave himself a wide birth around the open hive. "Why would the environment collapse because of the Others though?"

"I don't know how," Calay admitted. "It could be the transmissions through the hive mind, a vibration or some chemical emission their ships give off. We didn't get a chance to find out before everything fell apart."

Salem pouted. "So how do we find out? For sure?"

"I have no idea. I don't know if we do. I just know we have to stop them."

"We have to work together." Briar replaced the frame and the lid before taking Calay's icy hand in hers.

Calay's heart leapt, so did her hope. This was what they needed. What Adam had been missing all this time. Tess, too. Their success against the Others wasn't dependent on a few authority figures governing from some powerful, unseen council. It was on the ground level. With the people. They just had to come to a mutual understanding. A reason to pool their differences and build something stronger. A movement.

"Exactly. The Others tried to convince me humans were the problem. But my experience of them has been if they say run one way, you definitely turn and run the other."

"People won't have the energy to run in any direction if we can't feed them." Salem crossed her arms over her chest.

"Then we better harvest what we can," Calay said.

"Yes, Calay's right," Callum agreed. "If her theory is correct about the Others and what's happening to the planet, the tremors and the storms won't stop. The road up top is already washed out. All we have left is the long road along the bottom. We don't know what might happen between now and...whenever. We might not be able to access the valley again."

"See?" Calay gave him a half smile. "It's a good thing you brought me. Extra hands."

A grumble vibrated from behind Callum's pursed lips. "I'm just starting to like you, don't push it."

"If we harvest everything, that'll be it. We won't be able to plant again until the ground thaws." Salem's voice took on a troubling undertone.

"*If* the ground thaws." Callum's brow furrowed, his shoulders sagged. "Adam is going to have a fit."

"Forget Adam's fit. If we run out of food for everyone before..." Salem didn't finish her sentence. She didn't have to. They all knew where this was headed if things didn't go according to plan.

Callum ran his hand over his jaw, huffed. "I don't know if we'll be able to scavenge enough to eat in the cities."

"People will panic," Salem added.

"People are already panicking." Calay forced her tone to remain even, despite the flare of irritation curling inside her. It wasn't directed at Salem, it was for the Others and the corner they'd backed humanity into. "They've lost too much. We all have. Callum has a point. The environment isn't going to improve, and the attacks on the compound are going to get worse. Unless we do something, and soon."

"So it's settled then?" Briar adjusted her weight from one hip to the other. "We're going to pull everything up. The vegetables, the bees. Bring it back with us?"

Calay waited. Silence hung between them, thick with anticipation. With fear. Something shifted between them. Calay could feel it in the air as they peered at each other. They were about to cross a line. A boundary they might never come back from.

"Well, we're going to be out here longer than we thought. We better move before the Others find us." Callum was already making his way across the field. "I'll get the storage bags out of the truck."

"This'll be fun," Salem muttered and followed in Callum's footprints.

Calay watched them go, her hand wrapped in Briar's, and prayed to a god she no longer believed in that she hadn't just sentenced her new friends to their deaths.

CHAPTER THIRTEEN

By MID-AFTERNOON, the sky was a searing blue, devoid of the usual overcast Calay had come to expect. The chill in the air all but dissipated. It wasn't warm, but it wasn't glaringly cold either. If she could force the memory of the Others and fears of the Faceless from her mind, the day was actually almost enjoyable.

Almost.

She knelt in the snow, her knees frozen and sore, and plucked a handful of small potatoes from a mound of compact dirt. She tossed them into the harvest bag Callum had unceremoniously thrust her direction when he'd returned from the truck. He'd done it without a word and without looking back as he made his way to the others. Part of Calay resented his forwardness, his audacity. She'd never done well with authority, and his unsaid demand for her to get to work put her on edge. A bigger part of her savored the satisfaction that rippled through her when she watched him do the same to Salem and Briar.

She was one of them now. A member of the Resistance. For better or for worse.

Several hours passed. Calay was relieved to find they'd cleared most of the garden, harvesting the vegetables that were ripe or not too rotten to glean. Between them they had nearly eight bags bulging with winter veg—it wasn't a lot, but it was something. More than they'd have if the road to the valley became impassible. Or worse, if they couldn't leave the compound.

She plunged her hands deeper into the soil, buried them up to her wrists as if she could bury her fears of what was inevitably going to come. Eventually. For all of them.

Something nudged Calay's boot. She turned and gasped to find a dark silhouette blocking the sun. A halo of golden light sprang from the center of whoever had pulled her from her reverie. Calay shielded her eyes from the brightness, though it did little to numb the radiance of light bouncing off the snow.

"You want to get out of here?" Briar's voice was like warm honey. It melted across Calay's skin, thawing the deepest parts of her.

Calay squinted. "Are we done? Did we get everything?"

"The other two will finish up. I had one more thing I wanted to show you before those two haul us out of here, possibly for good." Briar reached her hand toward Calay. Despite the shadow covering Briar's face, Calay could hear her smile. Maybe she just imagined it. Either way, she wanted nothing more than to join Briar—wherever she was going. "So?"

"Absolutely." Calay surprised herself with the resolution in her voice. She took Briar's hand and allowed herself to be pulled to her feet.

She followed Briar down the center line of the garden, between the plots, and approached the forest. The smell of pine needles was overwhelming as they tramped across them, avoiding muddy puddles, under the cover of the trees. Sunlight lurked at their rear, giving way to more shadows and denser brush.

The path here was less trodden. Wilder.

Stray brambles crept across their path, logs, too. Calay found herself glancing over her shoulder, searching. Her sense of danger pressed firm against her thirst to keep up with Briar. A twinge of fear rose in Calay's throat. She swallowed it as she threw her leg over a fallen tree limb that was wider than her thigh. The bark was hard, rough, and uneven beneath her palms. She heaved herself over the other side, grunting.

"Where are we going?" She chanced a glance back the way they'd come.

Darkness lingered at the path's edges, and her thoughts. She could still see the opening to the field, but for all it mattered, it could be a hundred feet or a hundred thousand. They didn't have weapons or a way to protect themselves. They didn't even have numbers. A thrill rushed through Calay at the acknowledgement that she was with Briar. Alone. Just the two of them. She couldn't discern if the feeling was excitement or dread. Either way, if something decided to attack them now, they'd be in very real trouble.

"We're almost there." Briar hitched a cloth bag higher on her shoulder.

"We're almost where?"

It was only then that Calay noticed the sickle-like knife strapped to Briar's belt. The crescent shaped curve of the blade tugged at Calay's mind, her heart. She risked taking her eyes off the untamed trail and lifted the edge of her coat to reveal the half-moon tattoo on her wrist. The reason she was there. She reminded herself it wasn't because something about Briar pulled her like a moth to a flame, or because she needed a safe place to call home, though both of those things felt like light at the end of a very long, very dark tunnel. She was there because of Tess. Tess had always been her reason, and she couldn't help but wonder if Tess always would be. Calay intended to make things right. To fix the mistakes they'd both made.

She peered up when the sound of Briar's footsteps halted. Briar turned, the corners of her full lips curled, the gleam in her dark eyes on fire. Unlike everything else in this world, she had an openness about her, a candor. It inspired an honesty in Calay, a longing to be vulnerable instead of guarded. To be seen instead of hidden.

Briar tilted her head as if to say 'this way,' her gaze trained on Calay's until the two were side by side. Calay thought Briar looked radiant and was feeling almost brave enough to tell her so when Briar spun on her heel and trudged beyond the trail, stopping at the base of a Douglas fir with a trunk wider than Calay was tall.

Calay pulled the sleeves of her parka over her hands, resolving that when all this was over, the battle won, this would be it. She'd leave the past—and Tess—where it belonged: behind her. There was too much riding on the future. The most important of which was literally right in front of her.

"Here." Briar unclipped the varnished beech handle of the knife and spun it between her fingers while Calay caught up.

"Okay, we're here. Wherever here is." Calay grinned despite herself. "What exactly are we doing here?"

"I wanted to show you something, in case we can't come back."

"What did you want to show me?"

"This." Briar smiled, crouching down beside the tree and pulling Calay's arm to follow. Here, the snow gave way to soil, the ground littered with pine cones and soft, brown needles. Calay was delighted to find it was softer than the trail, bouncing under the weight of their boots. Roots forged their way between tufts of lichen and moss. She steadied herself, laughing at Briar's enthusiasm. Calay found it infectious, and it dulled the edges of her nerves.

Briar nodded. "Look."

Calay peered closer and noticed something she hadn't before. Among the greenery were pockets of brilliant orange. They practically shimmered among the shadows, sprouting from the ground in tiny crests.

"Mushrooms?" She gaped.

"Not just any mushrooms. Golden chanterelles."

"Are they special?"

"Yes, and more importantly, edible."

With a confident grace Calay was becoming more and more in awe of, Briar levelled the blade of her knife along the base of one of the mushrooms, sawing through the stem in one smooth motion. She plucked it from the ground and held it out to Calay. Calay pinched the delicate stem, a shiver of warmth trailed up her arm when her fingers touched Briar's. A strange feeling came over Calay as she peered closer at the mushroom, examining the tender, wavy cap and fine ridges on its underside. It smelled of fresh apricot and ripe earth.

Calay turned the delicate mushroom over in her palm. "It's beautiful."

"So are you."

Calay's gaze flicked to Briar's. She opened her mouth, but no words came. She closed it again.

Briar laughed, taking the mushroom back from Calay, and tucked it into the bag that hung from her shoulder.

"I'll let you in on a little secret." Briar continued harvesting caps, one at a time, as she spoke. "I've been hoarding these for myself."

"Salem and Callum don't know?"

"Nope. I sneak into the kitchen when everyone else is asleep. It only takes a couple of minutes to cook them. I top them with whatever herbs and fat we have. A drizzle of honey of course. They make the most amazing midnight snack."

"You do love your honey." Calay took a surprising amount of pleasure in knowing that about Briar. Like it signaled a closeness between them. An intimacy.

"What can I say? I have a sweet tooth." Briar blinked at Calay from behind the curtain of her long lashes. "Maybe that's why I like you so much."

"I'm not sweet." Calay scoffed.

"Yes you are, but you're sharp too." Briar paused. "I love that about you."

"You're delusional. You sure you haven't picked the wrong mushrooms by accident?" Calay teased, brushing Briar's shoulder with her own. Not wanting to pull away, she settled against the tree trunk, their shoulders resting against one another.

"I wish." Briar laughed, turned her attention back to the task of clearing the patch of any remaining mushrooms. "I guess all this is gonna change now. Like it always does."

"What do you mean 'like it always does'?"

"Just things from before."

Briar's words tugged at a truth that was all too familiar. Still, Calay didn't want Briar to stop talking. She wanted to hear more.

"Things like what?" she asked, hoping she wasn't crossing some invisible boundary. That she hadn't misread their connection. A moment of uncertainty fluttered through Calay when Briar pulled her lips tight and didn't say anything. Branches high above creaked in a passing breeze, the leaves clinging to their branches rustled. Calay waited, the tension building between them. Or maybe it was just between her heart and mind. The former pulling her in one direction, the latter in another. She began to regret her foolhardy assumptions and then, thankfully, Briar spoke.

"My family, I guess."

"Tell me about them?"

"How much time do you have?"

"How much does any of us have?"

"Good point." Briar released a shaky exhale. "After everything happened, my parents were really protective of me and my two younger sisters. They wanted us to have a proper childhood. As much as we could, anyhow. Even when it all changed, we still had dinner together every night. Mom took on most of the responsibility for teaching us survival skills, she was a great hunter. She's the one who taught me to forage. Dad made sure we had the supplies we needed and negotiated with other groups when he had to. It didn't always go well, but they tried to shield us from the worst of it."

Calay steeled herself, knowing all too well happy endings were for fairytales. She swallowed. "What happened?"

"We were together for the first couple years before I messed up. It was my job to look out for my sisters when my parents weren't there. I let Jada—she was the youngest—go to the well to get water on her own. I shouldn't have." Briar's eyes darkened, her strong shoulders sagged. She tucked the knife back into its sheath. Her voice cracked. "When she didn't come back, Halle and I went looking for her."

"You don't have to say it."

"I haven't told anyone this. It's good to talk about it."

Calay nodded, silent.

"When we found her, she was already dead. We knew it wasn't a pod because there was a body. Which meant it had to be people. Who would do that? Who would kill a ten-year-old girl?"

A shiver ran down Calay's spine. She didn't have to answer Briar's question, because of course, they both knew the harsh truth about humanity. The Others did a lot of horrible things to people, but people did a lot of horrible things to each other, all on their own. The reality was the Change did one of two things—brought out the best in people, or the worst.

Calay's eyes teared over. "I hate that that happened to you."

"It wasn't over. It was my fault, obviously, but my parents blamed themselves for not protecting us. Somehow, despite all that collective pain, we managed to hang onto each other for a few more months before everything fell apart." Briar sighed, her shoulders trembled. "We tried to stay together after Jada, no more solo trips. Late one night, a group ambushed us while we were on a supply run and we were separated. I don't know if they were the same people who did the thing to my sister or different ones. A bunch of men cornered me behind a gas station. All I could picture was Jada's torn clothing, her little body lifeless in the leaves. I panicked, and I ran."

"It… What happened to her…" Calay choked on the words. "It wasn't your fault."

"I can still hear the yelling and the gunshots and my sister screaming for me. I never saw Halle or my parents again. I searched, Calay. I looked for weeks, but I didn't find anything. I just miss them so much."

Calay didn't know how to tell Briar she knew how that felt, and yet, not. Calay's family had been torn apart under the pressure of her Otherness. She could never miss them the way Briar missed her own. Yet she understood the weight of not only losing someone you love, but being responsible for it, too. Calay wouldn't wish that on her worst enemy, and it broke her fragile heart to see Briar struggling with the very same thing. Calay'd do anything to carry that for Briar. To relieve her burden. That inexplicable, unmeasurable pain.

At a loss for words, Calay leaned over and wrapped her arms around Briar. "I am so sorry."

"Sometimes I think they're still out there, you know?" Briar sniffled into Calay's shoulder and returned her embrace. "Maybe they escaped and they're out there, searching for me. Maybe we'll find each other again."

"You will." Calay hugged her tighter to conceal her doubt. "You will."

"Maybe so." Briar pulled out of Calay's arms, wiped away her tears. She exhaled, a shudder passing over her face. "But it doesn't matter. Not if our plans don't work. We'll all be dead within the next few months anyhow."

An understanding blossomed in Calay. She wasn't the only one making up for past mistakes. This was why Briar was so protective of her friends. Why she panicked when they were in danger and felt their fear so deeply. Briar's grief tore at Calay, but Calay took a small comfort in knowing they'd made their decision to fight for what was right. Beyond that, they had no way to control what was happening to the planet. Each other. Or themselves. The best they could hope for was that by defeating the Others, they might regain some balance. Restore some normalcy. Rebuild, slowly.

"We're going to do it. For them." Calay trained her gaze on Briar's.

"Yes, for them. And for us."

A warmth tightened around Calay's chest. "For *us?*"

"You and me." Briar nodded.

"Don't say anything you can't back up," Calay said, her voice barely above a whisper. She couldn't take any more broken promises, more false truths.

A glint nestled in Briar's eyes. She leaned forward and zipped Calay's coat higher. Briar's hands wrapped around the fir trim of Calay's hood, pulled their faces together, stopping only when they were an inch apart.

Calay, trembling, forced herself to breathe. Her lips parted.

Briar's charcoal eyes shifted to them, deep as the night sky. The speckles of blue in her irises mirrored the stars behind Calay's.

"I never do," Briar whispered, her breath warm against Calay's lips.

Briar bent then, pressed her mouth to hers with an aching

tenderness Calay felt in her soul. She inhaled Briar deeply, her warm scent of roses and nutmeg between them, the fur lining of their hoods tickling her nose. One of Briar's hands wove around the back of Calay's head, bunching in her hair. Briar gripped the roots and tugged, while the other encircled Calay's waist. Calay's arms wound tight around Briar's neck.

They held each other closely, Calay's back pressed firm against the rough bark of the tree. Her hood fell back, there was nothing between them at all as their kiss deepened.

Briar's lips pressed down harder, forcing Calay's open. Her breath slipped into Calay's mouth. Her tongue, too. Calay met her edge, ran her lips along the ridges of Briar's teeth. Hungry for more. Calay's breathing quickened, her pulse. Their tongues intertwined, and a heat radiated from the deepest part of Calay, pooling between her thighs, all the way down to her toes.

Just when she thought she might combust, Briar pulled back.

"Wow," Calay gasped between breaths. "We waited far too long to do that."

A darkness settled in Briar's eyes, the corner of one side of her mouth curled upward. Calay's eyes widened, and her heart thumped against her chest. Briar leaned close. Her lips grazed Calay's before retreating across her cheek, over the curve of her jawline, to the tender spot behind her ear.

"I'm not finished," Briar growled.

Briar's lips pressed down, a shiver rippled through Calay. A yearning. A need.

Calay let Briar unzip their coats as they sank onto the spongy ground beneath the tree. They pressed their bodies together. Wanting to be closer. Craving it.

Briar's kisses traveled from Calay's ear, to her throat, to the hollow between her collarbones. A low aching groan echoed between them—Calay wasn't sure who made the sound—as Briar nestled herself between Calay's thighs.

Desire wound itself like a coil between her legs, ready to spring at any moment. She didn't know how she could be so turned on with so many clothes still between them.

She liked it.

Calay arched her hips under Briar's weight. She slid her hand underneath Briar's jacket, her fingers tucking beneath the hem of her shirt. Briar's skin was warm, despite the chill in the air.

Briar gasped. "Cold hands!"

"Warm them up for me?" Calay sheepishly giggled.

Briar grinned, brought them to her lips, kissed each finger, before sliding the length of each finger in her mouth.

Calay couldn't take it any longer. She needed to feel Briar. Touch her. Taste her.

Calay wrapped her arms around Briar's waist and rolled Briar onto her back. Their winter coats sheltered them against the worst parts of the cold, folding around them like a fort. Their eyes met for the briefest moment. Then Calay brought her lips to Briar's neck, her hands slipped inside the front of Briar's shirt. Briar rose to Calay's touch. The way they fit together —it was like breathing. Natural and effortless. Calay knew this wasn't an impulse she was going to regret later. Not like before, with others.

This was special.

Calay's kisses trailed to Briar's stomach, the mounds of her breasts. Calay thought her skin tasted just like the honey she loved so much.

Their soft bodies pressed together, Briar's fingers traced Calay's back, over the roundness of her belly, grazed the inseam of her jeans.

Unable to hold the floodgates back any longer, Calay was ready to tear both their clothes off when someone cleared their throat.

"Sorry to interrupt." Salem's voice floated toward them from beyond the shelter of their coats. "We're ready to go."

Calay cringed, shrinking into the pile of coats. "Oh shit."

"This is awkward." Briar laughed, her cheeks flushed. "Um, we'll be right there."

Salem chuckled. "Cool."

The declining sound of crunching snow signaled Calay and Briar were alone once again.

"Time to go, I guess." Calay's lips were puffy and raw. She didn't mind. The only thing she wished happened differently was...nothing. She blinked, taken aback. Unlike the impulsive, starved flings with Jacob, or the dangerous one with Ash, Calay didn't regret this for one second. Not for a single moment. Somehow, she knew she never would.

Briar smiled, running the tips of her fingertips along Calay's back. "I guess so."

Calay and Briar laughed as they pushed themselves to sit. They straightened their clothes, secured their jackets. They took turns plucking stray twigs and pine needles from each other's hair.

"I don't want to go."

"Me neither."

"But I guess we have to."

"I guess we do."

The loud and sudden screech of a Faceless echoed through the air.

Calay's adrenaline spiked, her gaze darted to the woods. Briar's did too. They waited. Watching for movement, listening for the telltale rustle of leaves or snapping of large branches. Any sign of attack. When it didn't come, Calay allowed herself to breathe again.

She shook her head, lifted the bag full of mushrooms. Briar shouldered it and they made their way out the same direction from which they'd come.

Calay knew it didn't matter what she or Briar wanted. What mattered was getting their friends back to the compound safely and doing what they needed to do to survive. Everything else could come after.

The air lightened and the sun sparkled as Calay and Briar left the shadows of the forest. Despite the renewed daylight, a hollowness followed Calay across the field toward the truck, haunting her steps. It took her a moment to place the feeling, but when she did, it all but shattered her heart. After their hard work that morning, all the food the Resistance had for the foreseeable future was piled in the back of the pickup truck. She frowned, watching Salem and Callum secure each bundle around the beehives, every single organism irreplaceable.

What was once a thriving—albeit limited—living food cache was now a graveyard. Wooden sticks marked the places where crops had been planted. The future, too. They'd worked so hard to nurture something that would never be realized. In the farm's place, empty dirt and overturned mounds of snow.

Calay realized if they didn't succeed this time, there was nothing left for any of them here.

It was a wasteland.

CHAPTER FOURTEEN

DREAD HUNG in the air the whole way back to the compound.

It haunted Calay, thick and cloying, pooling in the darkest corners of her being. As they weaved between the mountains on the low road—the longer road—that ran the length of the valley, the seconds ticked by, one on top of the other, until they built an impossible maze inside her mind. She wracked her thoughts, trying to figure out what it was that gnawed at her so.

In any other scenario, today would have been considered a win. The people she cared about were relatively safe, and they had a truck bed loaded with fresh food. She peered at Briar, who clearly still hadn't relaxed from the harrowing drive there, her hands firm at ten and two, her gaze forward. They were together. Yet despite the warmth pumping through the heaters, blowing hot air against Calay's knees and across her cheeks, a chill gripped her and refused to let go.

By the time the truck rolled into the yard, she'd begun to worry it wasn't necessarily the inescapable threat of the Others that had nestled so deep inside her. It was the fear that after all she'd done to get here, it wouldn't be enough.

She wouldn't be enough.

She'd fought for so long just to survive. To keep breathing another day. To exist. She'd kept her distance, and she'd thought she'd done the right thing—that by being alone, she'd lived. It didn't matter whether she was hiding in the forest, sequestering herself at the Loft, or keeping secrets from the people here; in the end, the walls she'd built didn't only keep out the bad, it kept out the good, too.

As she peered out the window, the low-lying buildings of the compound sprawling across the snow-covered concrete, Calay had to admit she'd been wrong. Not just about Tess's motivations or the Resistance's purpose, but about herself. In the deepest shadows of her heart, she had to admit her entire strategy had been a giant miscalculation. It hadn't made anything better; it had only made things worse.

Calay swallowed as the brakes groaned and the truck rolled to an abrupt stop. The Others may have stolen everything from humanity, but people still had one thing that could never be taken away—choice. Calay would always have agency over her decisions. Regret clawed at her insides, knowing she'd made the wrong ones for so long. If she had the opportunity, she'd do everything different. But she couldn't go back in time any more than she could go forward.

All they had was this moment.

That's why she was there now. There were things she had to make right. As she gazed at the others in the cab, their faces grim but determined, she realized she might not be the only one with that purpose. Maybe that was what pulled them together, and what would save them in the end. It wasn't just their desire to survive, it was their need to thrive.

Calay drew her brows together and she released her seatbelt, resolve hardening in her veins.

They would live.

The soft warmth of Briar's fingers on the back of Calay's hand pulled her from her thoughts.

"You okay?" Briar leaned one arm atop the steering wheel, her other rested on Calay's.

"Not at all," Calay admitted. "But we will be."

A gentle smile flickered on Briar's lips before she drew them together and nodded, her voice low. "Yes, we will."

Calay hoped that was true. For her sake. For Tess's. For all of them.

Movement beyond the windshield caught Calay's attention. Adam's long strides were quickly closing the distance between the heavy double doors of the main building and the vehicle.

Briar pulled the key from the ignition. "Here we go."

Calay paled. "I'm sorry if I get you all in trouble."

"I'm not." Briar smirked. "It was worth every second."

"You're worth every second." Calay's cheeks warmed as she slid out the side door, a grin creeping across her mouth. She couldn't believe she'd just said that. Then again, there was so much more she wanted to say. She hoped she'd get the chance to.

They coalesced at the back of the truck where Salem and Callum were already a third of the way unloading the harvest.

"Nice of you two to join us." Salem heaved a bag of potatoes from the back of the bed to Callum, who was lining them up on the ground.

"Yeah well, we have company." Calay pointed.

The group followed her finger to watch Adam approach. With his mouth turned into a scowl and his usually calm eyes wide, Adam didn't just look mad, he looked downright furious. He didn't even bother to fasten his jacket, and the laces on his boots were undone, dragging in the snow.

"Uh-oh," Salem muttered, redirecting her attention to a crate of leafy greens.

"Do you have any idea what time it is?" Adam barked, his voice strained and tight. "Where have you been?"

"We went to the farm, babe." Callum opened his palms, showing he had nothing to hide. "Just like I told you."

"You conveniently neglected to include the fact that Calay was going with you."

"I invited her," Briar offered.

Adam frowned, his gaze shifted to Calay. "She wasn't supposed to leave the compound."

"I just wanted to help," Calay started.

Briar hefted one of the bags of produce into her arms. "Don't be mad at her, Adam. Turns out we needed the extra hands. It's a good thing she came."

"Briar's right." Callum reached forward to help steady Briar's load. "Things didn't go according to plan."

Adam frowned deeper. "What exactly does that mean?"

"There was another earthquake. You didn't feel it here?" Briar said.

"No, I didn't feel a thing."

Callum abandoned the unloading to give Adam his full attention. "That's curious. You should have, we weren't that far away."

Salem perched on the lip of the truck bed. "The planet's doing some weird shit."

"Or the Others are." Calay's brows drew together.

"Whatever it was, it knocked the whole side of the mountain down. The road's a wash," Callum said.

Adam's focus shifted to the bags of produce. He stilled, the rage falling from his face. "Can we fix it?"

"Impossible. We can't go that way anymore." Callum shook his head, ran his hand through his hair. "I've never experienced anything like this one, Adam. You should have seen the rocks that sheared off the side."

Briar set the bag of produce down and hopped into the back of the truck as if to get Salem moving again. "If Calay wasn't with us, I don't know how I would have navigated it. We might not be here if it weren't for her."

The pink in Adam's cheeks drained, his mouth fell open. "Are you okay?"

"We're fine." Callum nodded.

"Farm's gone though." Salem huffed and rose to help Briar slide one of the bee boxes forward.

"Lift with your legs," Briar gently chided. She squatted to lift the other side.

"What do you mean the farm's gone?" Adam shook his head, waited for further explanation.

Calay envied his patience, his restraint. He was clearly seething, but something else was settling in his features. Concern, if Calay had to guess by the way his attention shifted from her to Callum. To all of them. Whatever it was, he handled it better than she would have. That's what made him a good leader, and why people respected his authority. He listened to people, gave them the benefit of the doubt. Maybe there was something she could learn from him after all, she thought.

"We picked everything," Salem said.

Adam's mouth fell open, his hands dropped limp to his sides. "You what?"

Calay didn't think Adam could look more ashen. As the realization of what they'd done crawled across his face, she saw she was wrong.

Briar popped down off the truck and positioned herself to catch the box should it fall. "We weren't sure how much longer we'd be able to get through the valley. We had to harvest what we could, while we could."

"And this is it?" Adam asked.

Salem strained to hand most of the weight to Briar. "This is it."

"Oh my god." Adam exhaled. "Do you have any idea what this means?"

Calay rushed forward to help the other two women. They placed the box on the ground. She brought her gaze in line with Adam's. "We didn't have any other choice."

When Adam's expression didn't change, Callum rested the bag he was shouldering against the tire and wrapped his long arms around him.

"If anything happened to you," Adam started, but his voice caught in his throat. "What are we going to do?"

"We'll figure it out, just like everything else." Callum cupped Adam's face in his hands and kissed his cheek.

"This isn't like everything else."

"I know that."

"Callum—"

"In the years we've been together, I've always come through, haven't I?"

"Yes."

"Then believe the words that are coming out of my mouth. I

promise, okay?" Callum sealed his oath with a kiss. Their foreheads rested together, their arms around each other.

"I do, too," Calay whispered. Something about their exchange tugged on her heart. She felt their eyes turn to her. "I'm sorry, I didn't mean to say that out loud."

"No, it's okay." Callum's voice was softer than it had been earlier. His gaze shifted between her and Adam. "Babe, I know you wanted to keep Calay close, but we really did need her today. If she didn't help, I don't know if we'd even be back yet."

"Would have been back sooner if these two didn't get...distracted." Salem smirked.

Mortified, Calay opened her mouth to protest but her voice died on the wind when Briar laughed.

"That's one word for it." Briar's cheeks flushed.

The radiant sound of her voice carried across the yard, halting any words Calay could have come up with. Before Briar, Calay didn't think such joy existed anymore. Such lightness and beauty. But there it was. There *she* was. Calay would do anything she could to make sure Briar never stopped laughing.

An idea etched at the corners of Calay's thoughts.

It splintered through her mind, rough and sharp. If the Others would do anything to ensure the survival of their species, including burning entire planets to ash, why couldn't she? She'd done horrible things over the last five years; they all had. Like Adam and Briar said—no one was clean anymore. Morality had become skewed and knotted.

The question burrowing itself in her mind wasn't about whether or not what she wanted to do was right or wrong, but whether or not love justified the means? Could she could live with her choice when all of this was finished?

There was no way to tell. Not until she saw it through. Then, and only then, would she know for sure.

"I'm grateful for your contribution, Calay." Adam pulled himself from Callum's embrace, but his hand lingered on Callum's arm. "Thank you for being there when they needed it."

"That's the whole reason I'm here." Calay stepped forward. Between the Others, the Faceless, and the planet's shifting ecosystem, the world seemed more dangerous than ever. She wanted to tell him she'd always be there, but she didn't know if she could keep that promise. "But I have to go now."

"Go where?" Adam blinked.

"There's something that I have to do."

Adam's brows furrowed. "We're supposed to talk about things from now on, remember?"

"I know, Adam. We will, I swear it. I know I've made a lot of promises and haven't kept most of them."

Adam scoffed. "That's putting it lightly."

"You're right. I've lied. A lot. But look, I have an idea, okay? And I just have to take care of this one thing. So I know for sure that it'll work." Calay was already backing toward the buildings. Her heart thundered against her ribs, her legs ached to turn and run. There was no time to waste. "Gather the Council tonight?"

"I don't like this. I'm reluctant to call a meeting without knowing the agenda." Adam's face grew dark. "What are you planning, Calay?"

"I think I have an idea of how we can save this place. How we can save all of us."

"How?" Briar practically whispered.

"You'll see soon enough."

THE CONCRETE HALLWAY WAS AS CALAY REMEMBERED IT: grey, unyielding, cold.

The sound of her footsteps echoed as she made her way further down the corridor. Shadows licked the walls. Doubt clawed at her mind. The last time she was down here she was barefoot, fleeing for her life. She could still feel the surge of panic that drove her ever closer to the truth about who—and what—she was. Everything had changed that night. For better or for worse. Never in her wildest nightmares did she ever think she'd return to this place of her own volition.

It was different now, though, wasn't it? At least this time she had her boots.

The crescent moon tattoo on her wrist tingled as she got closer, like a beacon. He was so close, and yet, so far away.

Her breathing shallowed. She held it. Willed herself to exhale.

There he was.

Jacob sat on the concrete floor, opposite the cell door, blanketed in darkness. His knees pulled to his chest, Calay could barely make out the rise and fall of his shoulders with each breath. She couldn't see his ice-blue eyes, but she could feel them, nonetheless. She always could. They were trained on her like a hungry predator on prey. Like the blue lights snipered on her neighbors the morning of the Change. Like the way he always looked at her—as if she was the entire universe and he wanted to swallow her whole.

A shiver rolled up one side of Calay's spine and down the other. She couldn't tell if it was anticipation or rage. Maybe both. He'd always inspired a surge of competing emotions inside her. If she was being honest with herself, that was probably the biggest reason she'd avoided coming down here before now. It wasn't only because she hated the effect he had on her, it was because she loved it, too.

"Hey," Calay mustered.

"I was beginning to think you'd forgotten they had me locked up down here." Jacob's voice was low, his tone even.

"I didn't forget."

"So you just didn't care."

"I cared." Calay frowned. The resentment in Jacob's voice chipped at her. His words held some truth to them, but it wasn't the full story. Of course she cared. But their history was so much more complicated than simply caring and not caring. Needing and not needing. Loving and not loving. He inspired all of those things inside her and more. He always would. "I care more than you know."

A shadow rose and fell against the darkness. "Could have fooled me."

Calay placed a tentative hand on the bars, then withdrew it—unsure of how to best get Jacob on her side. She wanted to reach for him and make contact. She wanted to run.

"I'm here now, aren't I?"

"Yes, you are." Jacob sighed. She thought she could see the splinter of a smile as his full lips curled upward. "I'm glad."

"I can't see you all the way back there." Calay shifted her weight, squinting through the bars. "Can you come closer please?"

"Don't want to join me?" he teased. "There's a perfectly terrible bed we could destroy together."

Unable to stop her body from reacting to him, Calay's breathing shallowed. There was a time she would have jumped at the chance. She sealed her lips to keep from moaning. Jacob was too easy to fall into, too hard to get out of. Even after everything he'd done, everything he'd put her through, he still turned her knees to jelly.

"No, thank you." She swallowed. "Over here will be fine."

"Only because you declined so nicely."

A rustling sounded from the darkness. A moment passed and felt like an eternity.

Calay braced herself.

Then Jacob appeared from the shadows. Tall, broad, and lean, he looked better than the last time she'd seen him. Better than ever, actually. The cuts and bruises were healed, the smudges of mud cleaned. The freckles around his eyes crinkled as he came closer.

A memory fizzled through Calay's mind of kissing each and every one. She let it go, focused on the pressed linen of his dark button-up shirt. The stretch of his suspenders across his chest. The dark stubble that lined his chiseled jaw and the way his dark curls fell casually into his eyes.

She didn't expect the Resistance would have cleaned him up. It was quite likely they hadn't—this body was, after all, a projection. Hers. It was entirely possible he simply embodied what she wanted to see, and not just physically. He was an expert at reflecting her fears and doubts back to her. Whatever she needed most, he provided. None of it mattered though. Because in the end, it was all a manipulation. One big lie. She didn't know a single true thing about this man—this alien. And that scared the shit out of her.

"Miss me?" Jacob raised an eyebrow.

"I didn't think you'd make it."

"Surprised?"

"In a way. You always seem to find me though."

"I always will."

"No, Jacob." Calay gripped the wrought iron bars in part to keep herself from reaching for him. She forced her stare to meet his. "You won't."

"Wanna bet?" Jacob grinned and wrapped his broad hands around hers. They were heavy, tender, and warm, just as she remembered. He'd felt every curve of her body, every sharp point of her soul. Then he'd tried to mold them into a shape he preferred.

Calay dropped her gaze, swallowed the sob that swelled in the back of her throat. "We have to stop this."

"I think we're just getting started." Jacon's voice melted over Calay's body. "I missed you."

"You don't get it, do you?"

"What are you talking about?"

"Jacob, I made a mistake. A lot of them." Calay released a slow, steady exhale. "From the moment I met you I've told you I can never be with you. Not the way you want me to. You never listen to me. The last time we were together I torched your ship and left you for dead for fuck's sake, and you still don't get it. Why are you even here?"

"Love does crazy things to people."

"No, you've done crazy things to me. You've made me feel insane." Calay pulled her fists from his, clenched them against her legs. She'd salvage what pride remained. She'd lost too much already, and she'd be damned if he'd take that—or what this place meant to her—away. "I've been such a fool. Do you remember the night you came into my camp? Starting that very first night, you toyed with my feelings. Manipulated my emotions. Took advantage of my humanity. It was callous, Jacob. Do you even know what you've done?"

"I'm trying to help you. To save you." The light in Jacob's eyes darkened, the veins in his neck blackened and bulged.

Calay gasped as his arm shot between the bars and wrapped around her throat. She knew if he let himself transform from this human shape into his natural one the bars between them would do little to hold him back.

She reached for something—anything—to get him to let go.

Her hands found the leather straps on his vest, the suspenders. Her fingers clawed at the taught fabric of his sleeves, rolled to the elbow. They tangled in his soft hair. She fought for oxygen while he squeezed for one moment. Another.

Her vision began to swim, and panic flooded through her as her toes lifted from the floor. Then, he released her.

She stumbled backward against the far wall, the impact sending a shudder down her spine. She sank to her knees. Her hand flew to her neck. She gasped for air. As she regained her composure, she blinked beyond the curtain of her hair.

Jacob's extended arm shook violently, his eyes glazed as if in shock.

"The shit was that?" Calay rasped.

"I'm sorry..." Jacob shuddered, seeming to shaking off the daze. His eyes searched the shadowy hallway as if looking for someone who was never there.

Calay coughed. She scurried against the wall, pressed herself against the cool concrete. It did little to relieve the fire burning inside her. "Seriously."

Jacob cleared his throat. "I...I don't know what happened."

"You choked me, Jacob."

"It wasn't me." Jacob said, his tone eerily even.

Calay shuddered against the fear rolling through her, the rage. "Do you think I'm fucking stupid?"

"No, I swear it. Listen, Ash followed me back here. She must have traced my heat signature, knowing I'd come for you."

"Right," Calay spat.

The intensity of Jacob's gaze returned, locking Calay in place. "It's true. Look, I've been having these weird thoughts. I think she's been trying to reach through the hive mind and control me. Each time she tried, I pushed her out of my head. I thought it was just my mind; I had no idea she'd be able to control me physically."

"Oh my god." Calay blanched, covered her mouth with both hands. "Can she hear us right now?"

"No, the hive mind doesn't work that way. But she can sense when we're together. Calay, you have to believe me. I didn't know she could move my body."

"Did she let me go or did you?" Calay pushed the panic down, forced her voice to remain calm. Freaking out wouldn't do her, or the mission, any favors. She needed to keep a clear head.

"That was me. I managed to regain control. I wasn't ready for her, but I am now."

Calay willed her shaking legs to hold her weight as she pushed herself to stand. She leaned against the cold concrete wall, not ready to put herself in arm's length of Jacob.

She took a long inhale. "She's here to kill me."

Jacob grinned, but it fell from his face as the gravity of this new development seemed to worm its way inside him. "Did you doubt she'd try?"

"I kind of hoped she'd burned slowly and painfully to death on the starship."

"Like I was supposed to?" Jacob eased himself against the cot and leaned forward, his strong forearms resting on his knees. His gaze didn't leave Calay. "Look, that's why I surrendered when I did, okay? Ash isn't going to stop until one of you is dead. You're in danger, I couldn't wait."

"I'm in danger now, Jacob. With you here." Calay's mind reeled at the many different ways this fact was now true.

"Not as long as I have a say. I'd do anything for you." Jacob frowned, pulled his shoulders back. "I'm yours, Calay."

"Well, I'm not yours!" she yelled, shook her head in frustration.

It wasn't enough. It would never be enough. Not to ease the ache in Calay's chest, the lump in her throat, the queasiness churning in the pit of her stomach. Jacob had promised her he'd never lie to her, and that was all he'd done. She was finished with the writhing, twisting, emotions which swelled and burned and scorched from within. The emotions he'd put her through. Calay closed her eyes. She could almost imagine what this place would be once she was finished with it. Once she was free of him and they won the war against the Others.

Her nails dug into her palms. She let the sharpness of them push against her emotions.

For the first time in her whole life, Calay saw herself as something more than an extension of someone else. She would not let Jacob's betrayal—or anyone else's—define her. She had herself to think of, and this place. Earth. She had her own dreams to fulfill, and a god damned planet to save.

She looked away from him, not from spite, but to hide her tears.

"I can't live without you." Jacob's voice wavered.

Calay's gaze turned cold. "Then don't."

"What are you saying?"

"You said you'd do anything for me." Calay took a tentative stride forward. "Is that true?"

Jacob rose, pressed himself against the bars of the cell. "Of course it is."

"How do I know that's not another lie? Or that Ash won't make you hurt me again?"

"You don't." A shadow flickered over Jacob's face. He reached for Calay, but she drew back at the last moment. The memory of his hand laced around her throat was far too real. Too soon. His fingers folded into a fist, fell to his side. "But you're just going to have to trust me. I won't let that happen."

This was the one part of her plan she hadn't thought through at all. She didn't much like the idea of taking Jacob at his word—something he'd proven time and time again meant little. Then again, Adam could say the same thing about her. She made a mental note to make it up to him—she didn't wish this uncertainty on anybody.

After a long pause, Calay finally pried the words from the back of her throat. The ones she knew she had no right to ask and would never be able to take back.

"Die for me," she said.

Jacob smirked. "Is that all?"

"I'm serious, Jacob." Calay levelled her gaze at him.

"So am I." Jacob pressed his lips together. His usual light manner replaced by something more ominous. His blue eyes bore into Calay as if they could drill a hole into her very core.

She didn't like the direction this was heading, but she was driving the conversation all the same. She didn't have time for their banter, nor the interest. She took a brief glance down the hallway to make sure no one was listening and then continued.

"How many planets did you destroy before you came to Earth?"

"Don't ask questions you don't want the answers to."

Something dark flashed across Jacob's features. It seemed to ooze through the air between them, hanging just out of view. The harder Calay tried to make sense of it, the more fragmented it became.

"Dozens? Hundreds? Thousands?"

Jacob exhaled, averted his eyes. "Why are you asking me this?"

"I'm just wondering how many species need to be sacrificed so one can live?" Calay narrowed her eyes and braved a step closer. Then another. She knew it was risky; Ash could take control of him again at any moment. She hoped he meant what he said and that Ash wouldn't get the upper hand again. Calay reached for his chin. The stubble pricked her fingers as she turned his gaze to hers. She rubbed her lips together and chose her next words with a great deal of care. "Don't you think it should be the other way around?"

"You think one should die to save the many."

"I'm asking you what you think."

"The answer's nebulous."

"It's pretty fucking clear to me, Jacob. The Others are an invasive species. You've contaminated Earth. And now it—and we—are dying because of you. That isn't right. But you can fix the wrongs. You can make it up to me."

"What are you asking of me, Calay?" Jacob narrowed his gaze. "Specifically?"

"I want you to sacrifice yourself for the greater good." Calay surprised herself hearing Tess's words come out of her mouth. She took a deep breath, tears walled behind her eyes and spilled onto her cheeks. She knew sharing even a few details of her plan with Jacob could be a complete and total disaster. He could thwart it, or leak it to the Others, or even kill her right on the spot. She was done hiding, though. This was her, broken parts and healed parts and everything in between. Besides, her plan was far more likely to be a success if he wasn't constantly getting in the way by trying to save her. This time, it'd be on her terms. "I want you to help me cause chaos to bring order."

"And I have to die for that?"

"It's a start." Calay shuddered, pulled her shoulders back. "But I want you to do so much more than that."

CHAPTER FIFTEEN

CALAY STOOD in front of the Atrium for what felt like a forever. She'd been in the relative safekeeping of the Resistance for less than a month, but it seemed like it took a lifetime to get here. As if everything she'd ever been through was preparing her for this moment. This eventuality. All the pain and loss, the uncertainty and fear—it had drained from one experience to the next until it seeped, thick and heavy. inside her. Ready to ignite.

To strike back.

She wrung her hands together, pacing outside the Atrium in the snow.

If that line of thinking was true, she didn't know why she was hesitating. Maybe it was because it was late, or because her nerves had finally gotten the best of her. Hell, maybe she was just hungry. But on the other side of those doors was the infamous Council—whoever they were.

Adam had gathered them as he'd promised, though his warnings circled around Calay's mind like a shattered record, catching on the tender bits. She shivered as visions of secret societies lurked in her head. Thoughts of blood rituals and cloaked oaths. They made her want to turn and run. Never look back. But the promise she'd made to herself —to Tess's legacy—kept her feet pinned to the frozen concrete.

She may have been afraid of what was to come, but none of it compared to the nightmares she faced in her sleep. The ones she hoped would cease once she eased her conscience and avenged Tess. Then again, she might incur new ones for what she had in store for Jacob.

It was also entirely possible the reluctance she was stewing in was because once she walked into that room, there'd be no turning back. This was it. An unease settled in her stomach. She swallowed. She could do this. She had to. If only she had some kind of sign to tell her she was doing the right thing.

Under the cover of a charcoal night, she peered skyward, hope pooling in tiny puffs with each exhale. She searched the blanket of clouds for a sliver of light. The gentle glow of the moon. A twinkle of stars. Even the floodlights attached to the perimeter fence would have sufficed. She didn't need a lot. Just enough to ease her way into the darkness. Something to tell her she wasn't entirely wrong—again.

Though as she scanned beyond the camouflage netting, the sky was stubbornly empty. The only signs of life were her own. Maybe that's what she should focus on, she thought. What she *needed* to focus on.

Calay took a slow, deep breath, raised her fist, and knocked. Her knuckles stung with the force against the frozen metal. Her breath hitched in her throat while she waited. She glanced behind her, scanning her footprints in the snow. Her eyes traced them back the way she'd come. She could still leave, if she wanted to. Hide in her room or disappear into the forest and make it far, far away from this place. From Jacob.

She sighed, realizing it didn't matter where she went—she could never run from herself. The truth would always be inside her, clawing and nipping to get out until the Others or the Faceless ripped it from her frail human body. She shuddered, steeled her will. That was the very reason she was here, wasn't it? After everything they'd done to the planet, she couldn't run now.

She turned her attention back to the Atrium when the latch thunked in its socket and the heavy metal door creaked open.

The heat inside warmed Calay's tingling cheeks, but it failed to defrost the chill that buried itself in her bones.

Briar slipped through, sealing the door behind her. Her gaze settled on Calay's. The tension in Calay's shoulders eased. Briar's deep brown eyes were all the light Calay needed to find her way.

Calay exhaled. "You."

"You." Briar smiled.

"I didn't know you were on the Council. Why didn't you say anything earlier?"

Briar shrugged. "I'm inconsequential."

A tickle of a grin curled on one side of Calay's mouth. "You willing to die on that hill?"

"Are you willing to die on yours?" Briar raised her eyebrows.

Calay swallowed. "I just might."

"How can we prevent that?"

"Trust me. Vote my way."

"That's why I didn't say anything about being on the Council. I'm an introductory member, I don't get a vote. Adam is letting me sit in tonight though because I told him if he didn't, I'd tell the rest of them exactly how he's been going behind their backs, trying to keep the peace without their knowledge."

Calay shook her head. "I don't want to cause problems for you."

"All we have are problems, Calay." The intensity of Briar's frown deepened. "You claim to have a solution. If I can do anything to help you make your case, I will."

A warmth spilled through Calay's chest. "Thank you."

"Right. They're ready."

"I'm not." Calay half-grinned.

"You will be." Briar nodded. "What are you going to say?"

"What I need to." Calay reached for Briar's hands. Briar gave them easily. Their fingers looped together as if their hands had been cupping their whole lives. "I'm afraid though."

"What could you possibly be afraid of?" Briar teased.

"Oh you know, just...everything."

"Well, there's that."

"No kidding." Calay's heart pounded against her chest. She took a deep breath as butterflies threatened to burst out of her stomach. "Do you trust me?"

"That's usually something someone says before they're about to do something dangerous."

"Maybe I am." Calay gave a meek smile. "So, do you?"

Briar's eyes narrowed, she pressed her lips together as if deep in thought. She tilted her head toward Calay. "I do."

"Then let's get this over with."

The Atrium was as Calay remembered, only now it was awash in golden twinkle lights. They winked at her in the glass dome, reflected back like stars. Tiers of wide platforms rose around the room in almost a full circle. Billowing trees and ferns planted between them, dotted now with lush, white, star-shaped flowers nestled between dark green, arrow-shaped leaves.

Calay blinked, those were new. She couldn't help but hope they were a sign of good things to come. Then again, the Death Lily didn't look too dissimilar. A shiver crawled the length of her spine as she thought it best not to read too much into it. After all, she didn't really believe in signs, did she? She wasn't so sure anymore.

At the center of the platforms, several levels above the main floor, sat the Council.

They spoke in hushed whispers while Calay crossed the room. She counted twenty people. Among them was Adam. He was positioned in the middle of the others, engaged in a conversation with several people Calay didn't recognize. Salem was off to the far side, her characteristic red lips pressed together as she strung a silver mandolin. Holden was there too, sipping on something warm, the steam fogging up their glasses as they browsed a manila folder filled with god-only-knew what information. Calay thought maybe it was the results of their last experiment; she hoped it wasn't about her. She scanned the group, grateful to also recognize Ryland, the soldier who'd been partly responsible for saving her life the first day, and Callum, who was pointing over Holden's shoulder at something in the folder. Behind them, leaning against the next tier and his arms crossed across his chest, was Ezra.

Calay faltered, her steps blunted. *He* was a part of the Council? Adam had told her he was well liked, but she never would have guessed he'd have any real power. Calay couldn't believe her bad luck or that someone so volatile could be a deciding member of the Resistance. He'd wanted her dead and had tried to kill her—three times, by her count. She had no doubt there would be a fourth. She wasn't going to be able to convince them of her plan with him there.

From the far end of the group, Holden peered over their glasses and caught her eye. They nodded encouragingly.

Calay closed her eyes, steadied her breathing. She reminded herself Ezra was just one vote. There were nineteen other voices here. Voices of reason. Of truth, she hoped.

She nodded back, continued until she reached the center of the room.

"You've got this." Briar squeezed Calay's hand and then made her way up the ledges until she reached the Council and nestled in a seat next to Salem.

If Calay was being honest, she wasn't sure she had this. Not yet anyhow. There was too much at stake. Too much riding on what she was about to say. She was just one woman; who was she to save these people? Humanity, for fuck's sake? Her mind spun, her vision blurred.

She reminded herself she wasn't doing this alone.

She had friends here. They were in it together.

A hush fell over the room. All eyes turned to her, sizing her up. Making assumptions. Judging.

"Hello," she said, her voice cracking. She cleared her throat. "Should I just start?"

One of the council members huffed.

"Calay, welcome." Adam stood. "Usually we conduct ourselves more formally than we are tonight, but seeing as you're not a member and don't have authorization to sit in on our proceedings, we're going to forgo them for the time being."

"Okay..." Calay swallowed. Maybe she hadn't been so far off with blood rituals and cloaked oaths.

Adam gestured to the Council members. "We're gathered here tonight to hear your proposal on how we can diffuse the recurrent attacks by the Others and ugh—"

"The Faceless." Holden handed Adam the folder.

Adam traced the page open in front of him, his hand pausing three quarters of the way down. His eyes met Calay's. "Right, the Faceless, as you call them. The Council has agreed that you're in a unique position to offer insight on how we can defeat them and hopefully restore some normalcy to our world."

"Adam's informed us of your...history." The councilor who'd huffed said the word as if it left a bad taste in his mouth. Calay bristled, but she couldn't fault him for it. He blamed the Others as much as she did. The truth was, she'd collaborated with them, albeit unknowingly. "We're willing to hear you out, but only so far as it benefits our community. We won't put our people at risk just to help you."

"I would never ask you to do that," Calay said, her voice small.

"We'll see about that."

Adam shuffled the papers in the folder, glancing around the room. "Before we begin, does anyone here formally oppose Calay offering a solution? As always, all decisions are voted on unanimously to proceed. If you have objection, this is your final chance to share it."

Calay's mouth fell open. She'd thought this was a done deal. That was what she was prepared for. What she'd readied herself to accept. The idea her preparation—her journey—could all be for nothing, at the most pivotal moment, almost stole the breath from her lungs. She couldn't let everything she'd fought for slip through her fingers now. The air hummed with tension. Or maybe it was just her. She gazed at the council members and waited on bated breath. She knew Adam wanted to hear what she had to say, and that Holden and Briar were behind her. She'd only just begun to know Callum and Salem, but after their harrowing morning, she believed they were at least a little on her side. The rest of the council were wild cards. All except one.

She forced herself to make eye contact with Ezra. A sneer marred his face, his blue eyes grew hard. It took everything Calay had not to just let her plan tumble past her lips before he could stop her. With each passing moment, Calay's resolve wavered. He was going to ruin this, she thought. He was going to ruin everything. Then, Ezra simply shrugged his strong shoulders and dropped his gaze.

"Good." Adam exhaled and assumed his seat. "Then you may proceed, Calay."

Calay drew herself up tall and folded her hands in front of her. She sucked in a deep breath. Suddenly, she didn't feel nervous. She felt powerful. She had their attention and they had the means to save them all. She was going to make the best damn use of it she could.

"As you know, the attacks from the Others are increasing, nearly one a day. Sometimes more. This isn't just the case at the compound. It's happening everywhere."

"How do you know that?" someone said.

"I've seen it. Experienced it." Calay felt a wave of apprehension rising in her nerves. She pushed it down. "That, and they've told me first hand."

"What do you mean they've told you?" said someone else.

Ezra coughed. "Because she's one of them."

"Because I'm part of them." Calay's eyes narrowed, but she refused to give Ezra the satisfaction of looking at him. "I never wanted to be, but after I saw the proof that my mother was an alien, I couldn't ignore it. Neither could the Others. They came for me. They lied to me and convinced me humans were the aggressors. That they were only defending themselves. I guess I wanted so badly to believe them, they convinced me. It wasn't until I discovered the truth that their real plans became evident. They confessed. I guess they thought they could control me. Control all of us."

"Calay, look." Callum leaned forward, his arms resting on his knees. "How do you know their confession wasn't another lie?"

"I saw it with my own eyes. There were hundreds of them. Thousands. Millions, maybe. They told me the final phase of their plan is to use hybrids against us. They tried to do it with me, but I found their secrets."

"How?" Adam ran his hand over his mouth.

He could have shut her down. Shut *this* down. But he didn't. Calay nodded, grateful he was still willing to hear her out, even though she hadn't shared all the gory details with him before. She knew how important truth was to him.

"They underestimated me, just like they underestimate all of us. I might be part human, but I'm part Other too, and they didn't count on me being able to harness the energy of the hive mind." Calay shrugged. "I guess they miscalculated."

Salem flipped her hair behind her shoulder, out of the way of the instrument she was still stringing. "And you want us to put our faith in an alien math error?"

Calay faltered. She knew how crazy this sounded. She wouldn't have believed it herself if she hadn't lived it. She had to give the Council credit for at least hearing her out.

She nodded, but barely. "Essentially, yes."

Holden pushed their glasses up the bridge of their nose. "What happened after you found out what their plans really were?"

"I destroyed their ship. I think I killed most of them, but they're still out there. I don't know how many or where, and I don't think it matters. What I do know is they'll project our likeness and then use it against us. By replicating the people we love most, they'll get us to come out of the holes that have kept us safe. If they can convince other hybrids to collaborate with them and round us up, they'll reach us where it hurts us most."

Ryland grunted. "Where's that exactly?"

Calay's eyelids fluttered at the memories of all the Others had done to them. "Our hearts and our homes."

"Our humanity," Briar shared. "We won't stand a chance."

"We have nowhere to hide," Ryland whispered just loud enough for Calay to hear.

Emboldened by Briar's support and Ryland's understanding, Calay shifted forward, her arms wide. "Exactly. They annihilated our cities. Our communities. Our planet. Then they waited, let us take care of who was left. We've all seen people can do some pretty shitty things to each other when we're scared. We were the dominant species on Earth, and now there's so few of us left—partly due to what we've done to ourselves—the Others are basically going house to house, eradicating us like pests to be exterminated."

"You say they want to use hybrids to attack humans. For all we know they're doing exactly that with you now." Ezra pressed himself off the ledge, inching closer toward Calay.

She raised her hands, pressed her lips together. "I understand your concern, and I think what I'm about to propose will help alleviate some of it."

"I don't like it." Ezra spun to the others.

Anger sparked inside Calay, like a match struck her insides and lit it ablaze. "Look around you, Ezra. People are dying! If we wait—or worse, do nothing—we'll all be dead in a month. Once they kill us, they'll use our bodies for fuel to hit the next planet. They'll rape what's left of Earth. Everything we've ever called home will all be ash and space dust by the time they're finished with it. No one will ever know we were here. Our legacy will be gone, as if we never even existed."

"That doesn't sound good." Salem's voice carried a strange mixture of sarcasm and sorrow. For once, her signature smirk was smeared clean off her face.

"This is our extinction era," Calay confirmed.

A numb silence fell upon the room. Hardly anyone breathed, let alone spoke for fear that doing so would bring Calay's ominous prediction into reality that instant. With her heart pounding for too many reasons to count, Calay wished it had all been one long, horrible dream. Something they could escape and forget in the clear, warm light of a spring day. That wasn't the case though. It hadn't been for a long time. The ground was frozen. Their hearts, too. Everything they'd ever known was one stone's throw from shattering into a million tiny pieces.

As the quiet hovered between them, Calay dared to think that maybe in another universe, a parallel one perhaps, none of this was true. That she'd made it all up. In that world, they could forget the terrors that haunted their dreams, their thoughts. Every fucking waking moment.

As if hearing her thoughts, Callum's voice finally gave voice to the question she knew everyone was thinking. "What if you're wrong?"

Calay shook her head. "I'm not."

"Okay, but what if you are?" Callum pressed.

"Then we'll all have a good laugh when the ground thaws and the Others get bored and move on." Calay huffed. "You can lock me up for treason and replant the crops. You'll live."

Holden crossed their arms over their chest. "And if you're right?"

"Then we fight, or we die."

"We've been fighting the Others for years and haven't made a dent," Ryland said.

"That was before you had me."

A series of murmurs rustled from the others, a nod of heads.

"Okay, Ms. Calay." Briar stood. She pulled her shoulders back, her hands brushed aside her faded army jacket and planted on the round of her hips. "What exactly do you propose we do about this shituation?"

Calay gnawed on her bottom lip. This was the moment she'd been waiting for. The moment of truth. The thing that she was hoping would save them all. She gazed at Adam, whose eyes had gone narrow with anticipation or worry, Calay thought. She chewed his warnings over in her mind about protecting the compound and the people inside it.

She shook her head—rules were meant to be broken.

She crossed her fingers and leapt.

"We're going to destroy this place with Them in it."

"What?" Adam blanched. Calay could hear him grinding his teeth across the room. His fingers gripped the ledge he'd skirted to the edge of, turned white.

Callum wound one arm over Adam's shoulders, the other reached across and patted his hand. "Can you elaborate before Adam launches himself into space, Calay?"

"I've given this a lot of thought, and I don't think there's a way we can beat them in open terrain. There's too many of them and too few of us. Especially with the Faceless. They're more agile, they're faster, and infinitely more deadly. We need to get them into an enclosed space and then attack them there."

"We don't have the firepower for that." Holden pulled their glasses off and polished them with the hem of their shirt.

Calay inclined her head. "You're right, we don't. We never did. Bullets are a limited resource, but water isn't. And we have more than enough of that."

"Water's toxic to them." Briar nodded, realization seeming to dawn on her.

"Right," Calay said with renewed vigor as she imagined her plan coming to fruition. "We use the tunnels Adam showed me to funnel them where we want them to go—right here."

"Here?" the snarky Council member said.

"Well, near here. Look at the greenery in this place. It's everywhere. Plants need water and warmth to grow. We'll need both to kill the Others."

Salem finally set the mandolin aside, giving Calay her full attention. "How exactly do you intend to do that?"

Calay grinned. "We have easy access to the outside from two different directions, right? We use both to fill this place with snow. Like, brimming. We trap the Others in here with it. Then we use the generator fuel to blow it up. The snow will melt, the sprinklers will come on. Those who don't burn will essentially drown."

"The water should put out the fire afterward, too. Theoretically, that should protect the surrounding buildings." Holden nodded, understanding.

"I don't know, Calay," Callum countered. "What if the explosion blows up the Atrium itself?"

"It won't. That's why this place exists." Calay pointed skyward. "The glass is fortified, right? It's protected."

Adam frowned. "I can't guarantee it'll withstand an explosion of the size you're talking about."

"Maybe that's okay. If it's big enough to destroy the glass roof, it's big enough to incinerate the Others," Calay said.

Adam gazed across the platforms, a certain forlornness behind his eyes. "This is our home. Why not somewhere else? Away from here?"

Calay didn't fault him. She knew what it was like to lose a home. She sighed, knowing there was no other way but forward. Even if it hurt. "Because we know the compound. It's better to bring a fight onto familiar ground. Home territory, right? Besides, we have everything we need to defeat them right here. Whatever happens after we lock them in won't matter. The point is to herd as many of them as we can into one enclosed space."

"This is insane." Ezra scoffed. "We can't round up every alien in the universe and blow them up. There'll be more."

"Yes, there will be," Calay agreed, "but there'll be less. A lot less."

"People are going to die." Ezra took another threatening step forward.

This time, Calay matched him, closing the gap. Ready to fight. "You didn't seem to care if people died when you tried to kill me the other night."

"Wait, what? Adam's mouth fell open. "Is this true, Ezra?"

Ezra steeled his jaw. "It was time."

"The rules—"

"Fuck your rules, Adam. I was following orders."

Adam blinked. "Whose orders?"

"Tess's."

"Ezra." Adam rose, meeting Ezra's gaze. "Tess isn't here anymore."

"But I am." Calay's voice cracked, urging them to stay on topic. "We can do this. We can save all of us."

"What makes you think they'll come?" Adam turned his glare from Ezra to Calay.

Ezra's face twisted as he took a deep breath. "Or that enough will come to make our risk worth the effort?"

"After what I did to their ship, they're looking for me. I'll connect to the hive mind. Between that and my heat signature, they'll quickly pinpoint my location. Believe me, they'll come."

Briar's head snapped back as if slapped. "Wait, your plan is to use you as bait? No fucking chance."

Calay's breath nearly lodged itself in her throat at the mix of fierce protectiveness and pleading behind Briar's eyes. It radiated in the dim golden light, filling Calay with a tenderness she ached to return, but couldn't. Not now. This—the mission—had to come first. Not because it was something she wanted, but because it was what they all needed.

She paused in the middle of a breath. She stared up at the windows, tracing the curvature of their arch with her gaze. She braced herself for what she was about to say. This was her ace in the hole. The only way her plan would work. She tried to imagine a scenario where something —anything—else would do the job, knowing that after everything, this was the only reasonable option. The only thing that would guarantee their success.

Their survival.

"Not just me," she said.

"What else then?" Briar asked, her voice low.

A loud groan resonated through the Atrium.

An icy breeze cut Calay to the bone almost faster than his stare did. Like always, he'd found her before she'd even turned. The intensity of his gaze felt right—it probably always would, and also very, very wrong, given the circumstances. She wasn't ready for this, but would she ever be?

Calay grimaced and grasped the sleeves of her sweater, turning toward the door that was now ajar.

The others followed.

Jacob, his brow furrowed and his mouth drawn into a thin line, loomed at the precipice.

"Him, too."

CHAPTER SIXTEEN

CALAY THOUGHT she was prepared for the Council's reaction. She was wrong.

The furor of their anger swept across the Atrium and out the double doors, echoing into the cold night well beyond the relative safety of the perimeter fences. Their voices were far louder than she ever could have imagined. It seemed she'd gotten used to the quiet tones in which they carried out conversation—hadn't given them, or their objections, enough credit.

The impact of their outrage damn near bowled her over. Logically, she knew their words couldn't hurt her. Not physically, anyhow. But she also recognized she couldn't avoid them forever.

Afraid to face them, she kept her eyes trained on Jacob. He didn't even flinch. Just raised a serious eyebrow, shrugged a little as if to say, "What did you expect?"

Calay tamped down the voice in the back of her head telling her to flee—the one she'd never questioned before returning to the Resistance. Tried to slow the thudding of her heart. She might not have been safe, but for the moment, she wasn't in mortal danger. Not with Jacob close by.

Involving him in her plans held a two-fold benefit. The first being he was more of a threat to the Resistance than she'd ever be; he was the decidedly the bigger fish in a small pond. The second was that if Ezra tried anything again, she'd have backup. Just in case.

A big part of Calay grieved at the thought of putting Jacob out on a limb like this. He did offer to help her, after all. He'd agreed to her proposal without complaint when she'd told him every gory detail. She'd wondered whether it was a good idea to reveal her full plan, but in the end, she'd done it. Whether she liked it or not, she needed him on her side—even if it meant risking he could betray her. Again. The only way to get him beside her was to tell him the whole truth. Now, as she stared at him under the twinkling lights of the Atrium and the bellowing shouts of the Council members, she couldn't help but wonder how they got here. Two sides of the same coin, with entirely different faces. Suddenly there were two whole galaxies between them. Then again, she supposed there always had been.

Unable to hold Jacob's gaze any longer for fear she'd break down right then and there, Calay finally pivoted on her heel and brought her attention to the Council members.

Their outcries dwindled as she held up her palm, forced herself to look each of them in the eye.

Most of the members she hadn't yet met congregated as a mass—a thick wall Calay feared she'd never penetrate. Between them, she spied Adam. His hand rested hard over his mouth, his knuckles white where they gripped his jaw. The folder containing the secrets Calay feared most was splayed at his feet, papers loose and shuffled across the floor. Callum tensed next to him, his arms rag-dolled at his sides, as if he'd lost his ability to move them. Salem's were crossed over her chest, her red lips pressed together, her expression unyielding. Holden's mouth hung open, their glasses slid forward on their nose.

Then there was Briar.

She seemed frozen in place. Her hands extended in front of her, her knees bent as though ready to spring into action. Only her eyes darted between Calay and Jacob.

Calay couldn't tell if Briar was losing her mind, or Calay was losing her. Calay ached to go to her, take her hands in hers, and explain. Feel the warmth in her eyes. The gentle caress of her lips. She feared she'd broken the connection between them by freeing Jacob and bringing him here. She hoped to God she hadn't.

Ezra shoved his way from the back to the front of the group, his eyes wild with rage. "How the hell did he get out?"

Calay's stomach turned in knots. She hadn't seen him when he attacked her the first two times, but she remembered this look from when he'd come after her in almost this very spot just the other day.

"Aw, that's cute," Jacob growled, his gaze darkened. "Did you honestly think your little cage would stop me if I really wanted to escape?"

"Keep talking and I'll stop you myself," Ezra hissed.

Jacob grinned, crossed his arms over his broad chest. "I'd like to see you try, Sweet Pea."

Ezra scooped forward, his hands rolled into fists, as if to make a break for Jacob.

"Both of you stop it." Calay blinked back into action, shook her head. She only came up to Ezra's chest but she pulled her shoulders back and blocked his path, stopped him cold with a hand against his chest . He stared down at her, the anger in his face twisting his features into something monstrous. Panic leapt from her gut, bloomed through her body. This was getting out of control, and she very much needed to get it back under control—hers, specifically. "I let Jacob out."

Adam exhaled from behind the curtain of his hand. "Why would you do that?"

"Because we need him, Adam." Calay strode across the room and pulled Jacob forward by the sleeve of his jacket. She made sure the door thumped shut behind them. While she doubted inviting aliens to their meetings was decorum, she was beginning to see why the Council held them in secret. "Without him, none of this works."

"Say more about that," Salem whispered.

Calay swallowed while she gathered her strength. "Since I'm part human, I'm not strong enough to connect to the hive mind on my own.

Not on Earth, anyhow. I was stronger on their ship, but it's faded since then. I can feel it, but then I lose the signal."

Holden peered over the edge of their glasses. "He's one of them."

"He's powerful enough." Calay nodded, maintaining her hand around Jacob's sleeve. "He can fortify my connection and signal our location. Between the two of us, the Others won't be able to resist our beacon."

"We can figure out another way." Ryland's fingers flexed as he worried them in front of his chest. "One that doesn't involve collaborating with the enemy."

"Jacob's not our enemy." Calay raised her chin, steeled her jaw. She wasn't so sure about that, but she hoped her tone would convince them otherwise.

"He could leave and tell them our plans at any moment." Ezra sneered.

"I'm not going anywhere." Jacob bristled. He firmed his stance and squared his shoulders. His gaze fell on Calay. "I'm staying. For her."

Ezra moved as if to rush forward, but something invisible—perhaps Adam's hard stare—held him in place. "I should kill you for everything your kind has done to us."

"What my kind has done?" Jacob scoffed. "Have you seen what people do to each other? After what *you* did to Calay, you're lucky you're still breathing right now."

"Listen, motherfu—"

"Ezra! Shut your mouth or I'll shut it for you," Adam roared. He sprang forward and wrapped his fists around the neck of Ezra's bomber jacket. Calay had never seen Adam move so fast. Surprise overwhelmed Ezra's face, washing the anger away. Adam ushered him across the Atrium, shoved him against the wall, pinned him. Calay gasped—she wasn't the only one. Every member of the Council stared as the two fumed at each other, no one spoke. Finally, Adam turned and looked at Calay. His chest rose and fell with heaving breaths. A spark flared behind his green eyes. Calay was pretty sure if flames could have come out of his nose, they would have. "I've had enough of this!"

The energy in the room shifted with anticipation. Fear maybe, too. Of the unknown. The Others. Each other.

"It makes sense, but..." Callum ran his fingers through his hair, he exhaled. He let his hand fall to Adam's shoulder. "What do you think, my love?"

Adam cleared his throat, his green eyes cleared as if just realizing what he'd done. He released Ezra, brushed his palms on his dark cargo pants. "I think it's the best shot we have. Calay's right. I don't agree with her methods, but her plan makes sense."

Jacob smirked. "Holds water."

"And you—you don't belong here." Adam thrust an arm in Jacob's direction, spit flying from his mouth with each syllable. "Don't make the mistake of thinking because you're part of what's happening that you have a say in a goddamn thing."

A callous smile crept across Jacob's mouth. "Of course not."

"Look, I understand you might not like what I've done, or even me, very much at the moment." Calay paused, her gaze flicked to Briar's. Briar had yet to say anything. To move. To breathe, by the looks of it. Still, if Calay could alleviate the concerns of the Council and salvage something that was between her and Briar, she'd bleed herself dry trying to do it. This was her chance. Maybe the only one she'd ever get. "But everything I'm doing is for the good of these people. Even if my actions don't seem like it, the facts don't lie. The Others and the Faceless are coming. We have a plan to stop them and it'll work—as long as we work together."

A wave of murmurs flowed toward Calay from the back of the crowd. They whispered amongst themselves. Calay understood how unusual her request was. How dangerous, too. She was asking people to trust the very beings who were responsible for their near extinction. They'd watched their loved ones die at the hands of the Others. Their cities fell. Their world burned. Now here she was—presenting them with one of their executioners and asking them to forgive and forget. If their positions were reversed, she wasn't so sure she'd be able to do it. Then again, that was the last thing on her mind. She had no intention of letting the Others get away with what they'd done. Not a single one of them. Not even Jacob.

Calay's eyes stung with tears. After the events of tonight, nothing was ever going to be the same again.

"Hey." Calay was surprised to find Jacob at her elbow, his lips against her ear, tilting his head toward the sound of rustling fabric. She wasn't sure how much time had passed. Footsteps echoed through the Atrium as the Council aligned themselves in a single row. They spanned almost the entire curvature of the floor.

"The Council requests you please step forward." Briar laced her fingers behind her back, focused her gaze on the reflective dome. Calay tried to steady the tremor creeping its way up her spine. She failed. Briar's mouth turned up at the corners, her eyes sparkled. "Ms. Calay."

It took everything Calay had not to return Briar's smile. She did as she was asked, feeling as though she was gliding to the center of the room, being pulled by some unknown force. She tipped onto her toes, as if hovering on the edge of a cliff, alone.

Then, everything dropped.

It was like the universe had reached up inside her, grabbed hold of her soul, and pulled. The sensation was strong—blinding and visceral.

Her mouth opened wide in a silent scream. She gasped in deep, heaving breaths. Fought to see through a sea of tears. It whirled inside her, crashed against her skin.

Then, as soon as it began, it stopped.

Calay stumbled forward, fell to one knee.

She steadied herself against the cold floor with her palms. Her vision tunneled, growing black at the edges. She gulped mouthfuls of air, her heart smashed against her ribs.

Footsteps approaching pulled her gaze up. Calay halted Briar's advance with one hand, and Jacob's with her other. She shook her head. Calay didn't know what this was. Whether it was the Others—Ash perhaps—trying to grab hold of her through the hive mind the same way she'd attacked Jacob, if it was a panic attack, or maybe, it was something else. Something she couldn't name.

When the haze lifted, Calay's senses stilled at once.

For a moment she wondered if she imagined the whole thing. She gazed from behind the curtain of her hair to see Briar a few feet away, her hands over her mouth. Jacob's eyes were narrow slits, his full lips pressed into a thin line. The rest of the Council members stared. She didn't know what they saw or how much of what she'd just experienced happened deep inside her, hidden from their wide, prying eyes. It didn't matter. Whatever it was, had passed.

Her legs shaky beneath her, her breathing shallow, Calay willed herself into existence and pushed herself to stand.

She pulled her shoulders back, exhaled. She watched the group exchange glances with each other before they met her gaze as one. "Go ahead."

"We have reviewed your proposal," Holden began, "and have come to a consensus."

"And?" Calay's brow raised.

A breath of hesitation filled the room, then Adam stepped forward with purpose.

"We'll move forward with your plan," he said with a subtle nod of his head. "But only under the condition that Jacob remains in custody until he's absolutely needed."

Jacob seethed. Calay shot him a sharp look and shook her head. Her thumb passed over the tattoo on her wrist. Tess would have locked him up. She would have eaten the damn key if that's what kept him away from her people. But Jacob was right—those bars wouldn't hold him if he transformed. It was better if she kept him close. Well, relatively close.

"We have to work together for this to succeed." Calay forced her face to remain neutral. She didn't want to give either party a reason to doubt her any more than they already did.

"Putting him behind bars is for the protection of everyone here." Adam cupped his hands behind him. It seemed Calay wasn't the only one trying to keep their cards close to their chest.

"Putting him behind bars isn't the answer," Calay said. "I've picked that very same lock with a spork. He's more useful out here. Given what he is, he's got a special advantage, just like I do. You'd be smart to use it."

"We'd be irresponsible, more like it. How do we know he won't kill us in our sleep? That we can trust him?" Ezra pouted like a child scorned.

"If you're going ahead with my plan, you're going to have to sooner or later. Put him to work spotting weak spots in the fence. Have him build up our security."

Something heady pooled in Jacob's eyes. "You're going to need it."

Calay stared at him. *Really* stared at him. His dark curls traced the smooth lines on his forehead. His ice blue eyes shined back from behind a veil of long lashes. His pouty lips were pressed together, any trace of his signature smirk gone. She urged herself to see him as she once had. The man who'd saved her, who'd kissed her, who'd loved her. She'd cared about him. Loved him, in her own way. It dawned on her if she ignored that or forgot it, she'd not only betray him—which she knew was inevitable—but she'd betray herself, too. If she was going to survive this, she had to embrace every aspect of herself. The good, the bad, and the alien. He was a part of her past whether she liked it or not. A part of her. Despite everything he'd done, she couldn't help but wonder if he'd somehow make it through this and be around for her future.

"Fine," Adam muttered. "But keep him on a short leash."

Callum tilted his head. "We'll be watching."

Calay nodded in agreement. A grumble resounded from the group. Calay tried not to notice Briar frown at their decision.

Calay had some explaining to do.

She watched everyone file out of the Atrium through the back door without bothering a glance back at her, dispersing one by one into the night. It was late, and she assumed it was to go back to their bunks to get some much-needed rest. Though for all she knew, they could be reconvening elsewhere. The Resistance were organized. Methodical. There was no way they wouldn't establish some kind of backup protocol —one that didn't include her. She just hoped it stayed in their back pocket.

Holden squeezed Calay's hand as they moved past her. "I hope you're right about all this."

Salem grinned. "Buckle up."

Calay mouthed a thank you to both of them as they made their way out the door.

"You better not fuck this up." Ezra sneered before Ryland herded him after Adam and Callum, who were retreating arm in arm.

Calay closed her eyes, exhaled. She'd done it. Like, actually done it. A warmth spread through her at the thought that Tess would be proud. When Calay opened her eyes, she started to find Briar standing in front of her, silent as their possible impending graves.

"This is it, huh?" Briar stuffed her hands in the pockets of her jacket.

"I'm sorry I didn't tell you about any of this before. I was still figuring it out."

"You didn't want to figure it out with me?" Briar scuffed the toe of her military-style boots against the floor. "I could have helped you. You didn't have to…"

"Didn't have to what?"

"Go to *him*. After everything you've told me, I mean."

"I didn't go to him; this was all me. It was something I had to do on my own." Calay released a shaky exhale. "It's been a long time coming."

Briar nodded. "Hm."

"I can explain everything, if you'll give me the chance." Calay's desperation tinged the edges of her words. She didn't care. For the first time in a long, long moment, her heart was finally open. To hope. To herself. To Briar.

"You'd better." The flecks in Briar's eyes sparkled.

"I promise." Calay held her hand out until her and Briar's fingers touched. She let her hand hover, her breath quicken. She waited.

Finally, Briar reached back and enfolded Calay's hand in her own and squeezed.

"It's a date, then," Calay said.

"It's a date."

"Can't wait." Briar squeezed back before turning to the door. She chanced a glance back, winked.

A kaleidoscope of emotion rushed through Calay. She resisted the urge to run after Briar. Everything was going to be okay, Calay told herself.

The door clicked shut, leaving her alone.

Well, almost alone.

She could feel Jacob lurking behind her. Their worlds had existed for centuries without ever coming into contact, without affecting one another. Calay found it impossible to imagine a world now that didn't have him in it. And yet, that was exactly what she was working toward.

The Atrium was where it would all take place. In only a few short days, the spot where Calay was standing would cease to exist as it was now. Pressure built behind her eyes at the acknowledgement of all that hinged on this decision. Her new friends. The Resistance. The planet. She'd only just found this place—these people—and she was going to have to risk it all if they wanted a chance at survival.

She allowed a whimper to slip past her lips when she sank to the first platform. Bathed in golden light, she exhaled, wrapped her hands over the back of her neck and draped her head on her lap. Tears pinched at the corners of her vision and she blinked them back.

She would cry, but not now. Not until all of this was finished.

Jacob's warmth pressed against her legs when he dropped to his knee at her side. One broad hand rested on her thigh. The dark, rich scent of cinnamon and leather flooded her senses.

"Thank you," Calay whispered, not looking up from her self-made burrow.

"I haven't done anything yet," Jacob whispered back.

"No, but you will, or all of these people die." Calay shuddered. "I die."

"I won't let that happen." Jacob steeled his jaw. "You still didn't tell them everything."

"They can't know. The full plan stays between us until it can't any longer. They deserve that."

"That's kind of you."

"It's the humane thing to do, Jacob."

"Like leaving me trussed up like a Thanksgiving turkey in your camp?"

Calay's lip curled, she balled her fists at her sides. "You gave me no choice."

"I shouldn't have walked into your camp like that, that's for sure." Jacob's laugh was rough around the edges. "That time feels like a lifetime ago."

"It was." Calay almost grinned back in response, but her smile fell flat. "I did the right thing then. I'm doing the right thing now."

"I know it." Bitterness—disappointment, maybe—rested on his words. His face. Calay's heart ached as she brought her gaze to his. She almost collapsed into his arms. It would be so easy, she thought. So simple. Only, nothing about what was to come was simple. "I wouldn't change a thing. Not a single moment."

"That makes one of us." Calay frowned. "Jacob, what if they're right? What if I'm wrong and this doesn't work?"

"It'll work." Jacob's fingers wrapped around her own and squeezed. Calay's entire body grew warm under the weight of them. She pulled her hand to her chest, out of his reach.

"I wish Tess was still here." Her voice was hoarse, her heart too.

"Do you?" Jacob pushed himself from his knees and sat beside Calay, his brows pulled together. She wasn't sure if he was asking out of curiosity or contrition.

She mulled his question over. Beads of sweat pooled on her back despite the lingering chill in the air. She gazed at the lush foliage around them. The twinkle lights. The tiny reflection of herself in the domed glass ceiling.

She felt so small. So insignificant. So powerless.

Tess had been Calay's strength. Her safety net. The light when everything else felt dark. Until she wasn't. Calay didn't fault Tess for what had happened, though she couldn't help but lament the way things worked out. Tess had chosen a path Calay could never have been a part of. The same was true of Jacob. She turned her gaze toward him, his crystal blue eyes earnest and clouded with pain. Knowing what was to come, Calay understood that now.

They simply were never meant to be.

"No," she admitted. "I don't."

"I know you don't think you're special, but if anyone can do this Calay, it's you."

"I feel like if I fail, I'll scream until whatever it is that's been clinging inside me rips itself from my body."

"Or Ash does."

A sick feeling swam through Calay's belly. It slithered into her chest, spread through her limbs. Somehow she'd almost forgotten Ash was out there. Somewhere. Waiting. For what?

She sucked in a breath, envisioning the intensity of Ash's black-rimmed eyes. The way she'd drunk Calay in—in more ways than one. Calay hadn't trusted her, exactly, but she'd recklessly let her inside. Now she couldn't get her out. Calay hadn't known what Ash was capable of then. She imagined she only had an approximate idea now.

She tamped down the growing anxiety riddling through her with each passing moment.

"What happened earlier? Before the Council announced their decision?" Jacob's voice quivered as if mirroring her concern. Calay didn't know how he did that. If the next few days went according to plan, she probably never would.

"I don't know."

"You don't have to tell them." Jacob tilted his head toward the back door. "But you can't hide it from me. Please, Calay. Maybe I can help."

"I don't know, okay?" Calay's teeth clipped at her bottom lip to stop it from shaking. "It felt like every atom in the universe was pulling on my mind. My body. It was like this rush of energy and I couldn't control it."

"Sounds like you're more connected to the hive than you know."

"Is that what that was? It felt different than before."

"Different worse?"

"Different like instead of controlling it, it was controlling me." Calay's eyes glazed over as she recalled the swell of emotion that had almost overtaken her.

"You know what they say about control?" Jacob's voice dropped an octave.

Calay felt his gaze examining her, the space between them.

She turned and watched his mouth smirk at the distance that they'd never close.

He leaned forward with both hands on the platform, inching his face closer to hers. Calay ignored the heat from his skin, the deep ferocity of his stare. She silently commanded herself to stay put. She wasn't about to run away from the Resistance, and she certainly wasn't going to submit to Jacob any longer.

Her heartbeat quickened, despite her resolve. Her body ached to feel his touch. The soft warmth of his lips. The gentle kindness in his embrace. She hated he still had this effect on her.

He crawled forward until she was backed onto her elbows, her shoulders bumped up against the next platform. Caged between the short wall and his strong arms, Calay's lips parted as she watched his gaze trace the crown of her head. It rolled over her lashes and paused on her mouth before trailing the length of her body all the way down to her toes. Back up again.

Her breath shallowed, she blinked as she looked up at him, dizzy with want.

A deep inhale later and his mouth was inches from hers. His eyes bore into hers, her mind swam. She hadn't been this close to him in a long time. It felt like a lifetime ago. In a way, it was. Calay managed to raise her eyebrows in question, daring him to try something. Anything.

He might inspire desire, but she had no interest in pursuing it. Not with him. Not anymore.

"What's that?" She exhaled.

"You can't control how people—or aliens—treat you. You only have control over how you respond."

Jacob's face shuttered as he pulled back with a sharp inhale. He pushed himself up onto his feet and extended his arm.

Calay's cheeks reddened, her mind cleared. The scent of jasmine and dirt replaced the thick aroma of his skin.

He was right, of course. She didn't need the Council's blessing to execute her plan, but a lot fewer people would die if they agreed to work together. People she cared about. Like Briar and Holden. Salem. Adam and Callum. Ryland. And all the other members of the Resistance. She even thought Ezra might come around if they had the chance to get to know each other. That, or one of them would kill the other one in due time. Either way, they deserved the chance to live their lives. To die on their terms. Calay couldn't control what the Council did at the end, but they'd agreed to her proposal tonight. She couldn't—wouldn't—believe she'd failed before she'd even gotten started.

She braced herself and took Jacob's hand in hers, allowing him to pull her to stand.

"It ends here."

CHAPTER SEVENTEEN

THE RESISTANCE barely slept for the next two days, Calay least of all. Her eyes were dry and itchy, the weight of her limbs, heavy. They were out of time and out of options. It had taken a fair amount of effort and trust, but they were finally getting it done. Fortifying the fences. Setting ground traps and attaching pressure washers to power generators. Creating a path of least resistance to the tunnels with the hopes the Others would spot the weakness and head straight for it. Assuming everything went according to plan, of course.

Things had changed though. Without warning or provocation, the attacks had suddenly ceased after the night the Council agreed to move forward. The Others seemingly vanished. The screeches of the Faceless hushed. Even the snow had stopped falling, though the frozen ground was unyielding beneath Calay's steps. Ice clung to the gutters and window ledges. It nestled damp and heavy on the trees. When she'd asked Jacob about it, he was unable to give her an answer—or unwilling, she thought. She hoped for all their sakes that wasn't the case. The stillness chilled Calay to the bone, and yet, sweat beaded on the small of her back. It seemed they'd been gifted with a calm before the storm. She didn't want it.

Dragging her feet, her legs grumbled in protest. Her stomach too. In addition to not sleeping, she hadn't eaten nearly enough. It seemed that was becoming de rigueur. As she scanned the grey sky, her gaze fell to the perimeter. She watched people reinforcing the compound security and realized they were probably struggling too—running on fumes. They weren't going to win this war if everyone was weak from hunger and exhausted. She needed rest. They all did.

Calay squeezed the bridge of her nose, clenched her eyes shut while she exhaled. As if she could shut out the truth. The danger. The questions she couldn't answer. When she opened them again, the sound of a sputtering engine pulled her attention. Callum had braved returning to the valley via the low road for the garden plow, despite Adam's protests. Now he was spearheading the task of filling the Atrium with snow, one rusted bucket at a time. It had sped up their progress exponentially. Without it, Calay wasn't sure they'd get it done in time. She knew how hard that had been for Callum—to not only disobey an order from their leader, but a heart-breaking plea from the man he loved most in the world. She envied their connection, their trust. They needed each other, and Callum taking the risk he did proved to Calay the Resistance had really committed. She made a mental note to make sure she expressed her gratitude to them when this was over.

Assuming she got the chance.

She bit back a sigh and turned her attention back to the fence. She frowned, watching the people she'd grown to care about out in the open. If the Others attacked now, it'd be a bloody massacre. But she understood their risk was prudent. Necessary. She should be out there with them, she thought. They needed all the help they could get. It wasn't fair that she was shielded inside while they risked their lives to execute her plan. Then again, as Adam had promised, her time would come. Until then, they needed to keep her safe. After all, without her, there was no plan.

Adam caught her gaze. The gravity of it could almost strip the flesh from her bones. His sharp features stern and his stance rigid, he looked every part the commanding officer. But Calay knew better. She saw the uncertainty in his green eyes. The people he loved—the home they'd built together—were depending on this. Their lives were riding on it.

On her. Adam nodded as he handed a dwindling spool of barbed wire to Salem, who knelt on the snow-covered ground. She attached it along the base of the fence with a patchwork of staples and zap-straps. It wasn't perfect, but they didn't need it to last forever.

Just long enough to get the Others inside.

The idea sent a wave of dread through Calay. Unable to meet Adam's stare any longer, she peeled herself away toward the unavoidable pull of Jacob. She didn't know if it was a heat signature thing or a star-crossed thing, but even with fifty feet between them, she could sense his presence.

He was near the tunnels, helping Briar, Holden, and Ezra (of all people) secure a funnel of chain-link over the tunnel entrance.

From here, Calay couldn't hear much of what they were saying, but their body language was clear as crystal. With his shoulders tight and jaw firm, Jacob's whole body looked ready to spring into action while he yanked the fencing over the hole. Ezra swung a sledgehammer against a peg of rebar to secure it. Everything about his expression sizzled, like a fire was lit somewhere inside him, waiting to explode. Somehow, Briar placed herself in the middle, her stance turned outward and focused on making sure it all held. Like the sooner they got this done, the sooner she didn't have to be there.

Calay could feel the tension pulsing from all the way across the yard. That meant others could too, and that wouldn't do.

As if in response to her thoughts, Ezra hauled the hammer above his head and swung wide beyond the proximity of the rebar. Calay's breath hitched in her throat, her stomach lurched. Jacob stumbled backward a fraction of a second before the blunt end struck him square in the temple.

Before she could move, Jacob was on his feet. He grabbed Ezra by the throat, threw him onto the hard, frozen ground.

Briar dropped her grip on the tunnel cover and dove between them, placing herself in the apex of Jacob's fury.

Calay ignored the nagging voice in the back of her mind telling her to stay put. Instead, she steeled herself and broke for the fence. Her feet skidding on patches of ice, she didn't slow down until she slammed

THE STARS INSIDE US   201

against it. She gripped the metal between her fingers, her eyes wide. She pried the cut end of the chain-link and squeezed through.

"Stop it!" Calay shouted.

The trio turned their attention to her. Ezra's face had gone white, Briar's fingers were purple where she gripped Jacob's forearm. Jacob's eyes bore into Calay like he could see down to her bones. For a breath no one moved. Then Jacob grunted, pushed himself off Ezra's chest.

"He started it," Jacob muttered.

Ezra pulled free the snow that had lodged in his beard. "Only proving a point."

Jacob blinked. "Which is what exactly?"

"You're dangerous."

"I'd be dangerous too if you swung a giant hunk of metal at my head." Briar's eyes narrowed. "You screwed up, Ezra."

"Again. Can you, for a few days, stop trying to fucking murder people?" Calay huffed, turning from Ezra to Jacob. "And you, I need you on my team."

Jacob lifted the sledgehammer from a nearby snowbank and heaved it onto his shoulder. "He's lucky I don't smash him into pieces right now."

"Yes, he is." Calay eyed Ezra brooding on the ground. She offered him her hand. "You two can tear each other apart after this is finished. But until then, you'll have to keep your differences to yourselves, or I go to Adam. You're part of the Council for fuck's sake, Ezra. People are looking to you. To us. They need us to remain calm. Understand?"

The obvious solution would be to separate this particular group. Calay didn't know how they ended up paired together—she figured they probably wanted to each keep an eye on each other, what little good may it do them. The three were a tinder box waiting to ignite.

"Yes, ma'am." Ezra shoved his hand into Calay's and allowed himself to be pulled to his feet. He almost pulled Calay over in the process. Standing, he had nearly a foot and a half on her. He cleared his throat, ran a hand over his face. "Let's get this over with then."

Calay nodded and inched her way back toward the fence-line, content the threesome could wait another few days to kill each other.

Briar turned her head toward Calay. Briar's eyes brightened as she pushed her fur-lined hood back onto her strong shoulders. The edges of her mouth lifted. She shrugged as if to say, "What can you do?"

Calay flashed her a smile in return, but her amusement was short lived. Her muscles tensed while Jacob straightened, his gaze draped over her, coating her in a heat she now knew she'd never escape.

He and Briar stood side by side. Calay's past and her future. She studied them for a long moment. As long as she dared. In a way, having Jacob back was an answer to everything she'd ever hoped for. Someone strong, beautiful, and comforting. He'd given her a gift—the truth of who she was. Her shoulders sank as she acknowledged that his version of her was a fantasy, though. Everything about him—everything he offered her—was contingent on her trusting him and abandoning herself. Briar, on the other hand, had never asked Calay to be anything but who—and what—she was. Briar trusted her to do what was right for her, and more importantly, Calay had begun to truly trust herself. Finally.

She released a slow, deep breath through her clenched teeth. Despite what she'd been through, she refused to let the pain of what had been infect what was to be. It'd done enough damage already.

Now it was time to give hope a turn.

Despite the lightness in her chest, Calay almost couldn't believe this was happening. The Resistance weren't fighting to keep the Others out anymore, they were inviting them in. Not only that, but they were collaborating with them, letting them walk free amongst them. They really were all working together.

Calay wouldn't have believed it if she hadn't seen it with her own eyes. Adam had been right the night of the big decision; Jacob didn't belong here. Though Calay had decided that she did. Assuming they survived, she didn't know what would happen when all of this was done, but she couldn't help but hope maybe there was a way for them to live together—humans and hybrids.

Somewhere deep inside she knew Tess would have never approved, but Calay wasn't her. She intended to carry out Tess's work and make up for her mistakes, but she was still her own person. She would adapt. She'd have to. They all would. The Others had to go, but if someone had even an ounce of humanity in them, didn't they have a right to live too?

A violent shiver raced down Calay's spine, all pleasant dreams for their future forgotten. The tattoo on her wrist burned. Not just tingled or itched—it outright felt like it was searing a hole in her flesh. She pulled back the sleeve of her parka to find it was coated in dark black lines. Just like the marks that had covered the Others' skin when they'd begun to transform. Every hair on her body stood at attention. Her mouth filled with bile. She doubled over as she lost the little contents of her stomach.

"Calay?" Briar's voice floated toward Calay, but she barely heard her. She suddenly felt as though she were falling again, even though her feet were planted firmly on the frozen earth. She struggled for breath before it halted in her throat.

The sound of Ash's voice echoed somewhere in the distance. Then it shrieked through the very fiber of Calay's cells.

Her hands flew to cover her ears, though it did nothing to stop the sound.

It was coming from inside her mind.

Holy. Shit.

Calay dropped to her knees. She'd made a horrible mistake coming out here.

"Run," she whispered between gasps.

"What's wrong Calay?" Briar kneeled next to Calay, wrapped her arm around her shoulder.

"Get everyone inside." Jacob's voice grew deep.

Ezra backed toward the fence. "What's going on?"

"Run!" Calay's voice cracked as she screamed.

The voice gave way, only to be replaced by something even worse. Calay could hear it before she saw it. A gust of wind swept through the forest, upturning ground cover and ferns. Fallen logs flipped over like they were twigs. In the distance, Calay could hear the snapping of pine trees as they arched under the wave of air and snapped in two.

Her eyes grew wide with panic, surveying the tree line. Searching the shadows huddling one on top of the other.

A dark silhouette appeared.

Tall and curvy, the shape emerged from behind a wide tree. One strong leg, then another. Her full hips sashayed as she drew closer. Calay blinked in disbelief, she couldn't look away. The creature advanced until it finally came into focus. Into the light. The strands of her wild, strawberry blonde hair curled at the edges, framing her perfect features. Between thick black liner, her eyes glowed an unnatural green. A feral grin spread across Ash's full pink lips, the ring in her nose twinkled when she crinkled her button nose.

Calay's heart skipped. "You found me,"

"I promised I'd come for you," Ash purred, taking another step forward into the open.

"You shouldn't be here." Jacob's voice quivered in warning. He moved to block Ash's path, but she simply pushed past him as if he weighed nothing. Like his wide frame was nothing but an inconvenience. She wafted her hand in the air and shrugged.

Calay's gaze darted from Ash to Jacob and back again. She couldn't help but notice, despite the cold weather, Ash wore very little compared to the rest of them. She slinked toward Calay, the black steam-punk style corset low on her waist. Calay didn't need to see the back—the lace she'd trailed her fingers over and the ribbon securing it in place. The tattoos on Ash's hips winked from the waistband of her flowing pants with each deliberate step. Calay swallowed, forcing herself not to cringe at the memory of her mouth on those tattoos. On a lot more.

"How are you here?" Calay managed despite her fear.

Ash blinked innocently. "Aren't you happy to see me?"

"Of course not." Calay's heart was pounding in her chest. She steadied her legs and faced the alien who had once been her lover. She felt the warmth of Briar moving beside her. Calay wasn't sure if she was closing the distance between them to protect Calay, or herself. Maybe it was instinct. Calay understood how Briar must have felt. She hadn't noticed it before, on the starship, but something about Ash felt dangerous and predatory now. She was an impossible monster that survived by sucking the lifeblood out of planets—of people—and she liked it.

"That's too bad." Ash exhaled, surveyed the compound. "Because I'm very happy to see you."

Calay swallowed. "Why me?"

"You know why." Ash squared her gaze.

"You can't have her." Ezra saddled on the other side of Calay, the sledgehammer positioned heavily between his hands.

Calay gaped, heat crept up the back of her neck. First he tried to kill her and now he was trying to save her? Her mind spiraled.

Out of the corner of his mouth he muttered, "You might be part alien, but this demon bitch is the full thing."

Ash inclined her head. "That's sweet, you've made friends. Too bad they're all going to die because of you. Just like your mom. Your dad. Your girlfriend."

A flash of pain rippled through Calay. She pulled her shoulders back. "They won't if I have anything to say about it."

Ash shrugged. "Tit for tat."

"Ash, come on." Jacob's hand wrapped around Ash's chiseled bicep, his voice softened. "They're gone. It's over."

A ribbon of unease wrapped its way around Calay's throat. Obviously she knew Jacob was alien, but hearing him refer to the Others she'd killed on their starship like he knew them almost made her double over again. She wouldn't give Ash the satisfaction.

A low hissing sound rattled up the back of Ash's throat, her eyes dipped to where Jacob's hand rested. "I think we're just getting started."

"Go now and we'll let you live," Briar spat.

Calay wanted to tell her to shut the fuck up. To run. Hide. That it was for her own good because there was literally nothing they could do to Ash that she couldn't do to them first. They all knew as well as she did what the Others were capable of, though she could see how easy it would be to forget when they looked so human. Calay shuddered. She almost wished Ash had come in her true form—the outside to match the inside. Almost.

"Get back," Calay whispered to both Briar and Ezra.

"Not a chance," Briar said, her eyes trained on Ash.

"Ash, it doesn't have to be this way," Calay croaked, desperate to save her friends.

"There isn't a universe where this doesn't have to be this way," Ash growled.

"I won't let you hurt them." Calay braced herself and moved forward. She willed her hands to stop shaking and inhaled slowly. She took stock of her options. It didn't take long—there weren't many. There was nowhere she could run. Not with Ash already this close. The best thing she could do right now was give her friends a chance to survive.

She squeezed her eyes shut, tensing for the impact she was sure would come.

When it didn't, she pried her them open again.

From a limb overhead, a bird released a violent chirp.

Calay's gaze met Ash's.

"Sweetheart, I think you're misunderstanding. I'm not locked out here with you." A low rumble reverberated from somewhere deep in Ash's throat. "You're locked out here with me."

Jacob's eyes flew to Calay's at the exact moment that Ash twisted out of Jacob's grip and began to change shape in mid-air.

The world bled black as Calay recoiled in horror.

The color of Ash's lips tinged grey, they cracked down the middle. Her eyes sagged, hollowing into wide, dark circles. Her back tore through the lace on her corset when she doubled in size. Her skin transformed from silky smooth amber into throbbing grey pustules. Giant, razor-sharp spines broke through her ribcage, shredding bones and flesh in the process. Black tar-like ooze dripped from each gaping hole and between the rows and rows of serrated teeth that tore into her tongue and lips.

Terror flowed through Calay's veins, it bubbled out of her mouth.

Someone screamed.

Calay thought it might be her.

In one swift motion, Ash's joints snapped backward and elongated into long spines. She swung with serrated, malformed claws, slicing the air.

Calay gasped and threw herself sideways. She winced as her head connected with the frozen ground. She didn't know what she'd been thinking coming out into the open. She'd believed she was beyond her impulsive nature. That she'd outgrown her selfishness. She should have trusted Briar the way Briar trusted her, and done what she was fucking told.

The world dimmed, Calay's vision swam. It seemed growth wasn't linear, and neither was time, because her past had somehow caught up with her present.

An ear-splitting screech cut the air. Ash crouched and leapt for Calay. Missed. She didn't stop coming.

Calay dodged and weaved each slash, her heart racing with fear and adrenaline. It took every trick she remembered from the starship to avoid getting pinned, which admittedly, was mostly duck and run. Her joints ached for rest, her limbs burned with exhaustion.

Whether Calay wanted to admit it or not, her energy was fading. She wasn't sure how long she could keep this up. She just hoped it was enough time for the others to get away. After all, Ash had come here for her, she was unlikely to go after them if she didn't need to. The Others would come for them later.

Calay squirrelled backward, her back pressed against the fence. Ash —or the creature that was Ash—reared back. She stank of death and sweet decay. The aroma overwhelmed Calay's senses. Her vision grew dark, her mind dizzy. She tried to launch herself away, but this time the ice and snow proved too much. Her legs slipped from beneath her and she landed hard on her belly. She peered up and braced for the bite of Ash's claws.

Just as Ash was about to strike, a figure barreled into her, knocking her off course.

Through the haze, Calay couldn't tell what it was. If it was another alien or something else. Something worse. Her pulse thudded in her head as she fought to catch her breath.

As her mind cleared, somewhere beyond her immediate awareness, she thought she saw Jacob splayed in the snow a few feet away. His jacket was torn and his hair matted against his head. She heard shouts.

The sound of boots on the ground. Out of the corner of her eye she spied Adam and Salem running toward them with weapons.

Calay shook her head, thrust out her hand. Their mouths set firm, they kept coming. No, she thought, Ash would kill them all.

Then something special happened.

Something new.

Calay's friends were suddenly crowded around her, and they were fighting with everything they had.

In coordinated formation, the group positioned themselves as if aligned on star points around Ash, surrounding her.

Briar looped the barbed wire into a makeshift lasso and was whipping Ash with the sharp barbs. Ezra swung the sledgehammer at Ash's spindly legs. Once, twice, three times—keeping her off balance. Salem and Callum had aimed their guns and were taking shots at the alien's head. Even Holden was there, bracing their shoulder against a machine gun, firing rounds into Ash's throbbing hump.

The only person unaccounted for was Adam.

Calay dared to peer beyond the scene, hopeful he'd retreated to the safety of the main building, getting everyone else inside. She spotted footprints in the snow, leading into the forest. Jacob's, likely. Calay couldn't explain why he wouldn't have stayed to fight for her, but then again, he'd broken a lot of promises over the time they'd known each other. It was possible Ash held too much sway over him; maybe he was afraid of her taking over his mind again. It didn't matter, not anymore. She shook off the thought and continued searching for Adam.

Her blood stilled in her veins when she looked up. He'd climbed the fragile branches of the nearest tree and was positioning himself above the scene. Hanging awkward in his hands was the long, rusty blade of a machete.

Calay'd seen that machete before.

Her heart plummeted. A squeak left her lips.

This was a mistake. The same mistake Adam had made in the hallway. It was happening all over again. Calay doubted he'd be as lucky this time around.

Ash was too strong, too fast.

Calay bit down on her lip and forced herself to stand just in time to watch Ash send Briar flying through the air with a swift yank on the barbed wire. Briar screamed before her voice was cut short with a hard landing.

Ash spun and ripped the sledgehammer out of Ezra's grip with her bloody, black mouth, then swung back to smash one of his knees. He squealed in pain as the head of the tool connected with its intended target.

Satisfied, Ash surged forward, plucking the gun out of Holden's grasp before turning it on Calay's friends.

Calay's eyes filled with tears and she nearly fell over when Ash pulled the trigger and it jammed. Ash tossed it aside, then tossed Holden too. They wheezed for air and clutched their chest.

Ash turned then, her attention focused on Salem and Callum. She seemed to double in size as she crept forward, savoring the moments before she finished them all.

This was wrong. It wasn't supposed to happen like this. Not now, not ever.

A blind rage overcame Calay. She swallowed her fear and screamed in fury as she charged, but not before Adam dropped down from the tree and onto Ash's back. He raised the weapon above his head and brought it down with one swift chop. It lodged into one of the gashes in Ash's side. She howled, lashing out by bending her long pointed limbs backward. They clawed at Adam, shredding not only his jacket, but his skin, too. It clung to the ends of her claws like ribbon. As her claws dug deeper, tearing at his flesh and severing his spinal cord, Adam's arms loosened and he fell off Ash's bloody side with enough force to knock the wind out of him. He stared skyward, his eyes wide with shock.

Calay watched in horror as Ash ripped the machete from her side and flung it into the forest. Calay barely registered the dull sound of it thumping beneath the snow when Ash lunged at what was left of Adam.

Her rows of serrated teeth bared, she sank them into his neck down to her weeping gums. Blood spurted across his chest. He screamed in agony. It gushed around his fallen body, turning the snow a sickening shade of red. Streams of his flesh and sinew pulled apart like Silly Putty.

The others stilled, frozen in place.

Calay was filled with a cold, burning rage that spurred her to action. She had to stop Ash, no matter what. With a burst of energy, Calay launched herself, catching Ash off guard and sending both of them tumbling into the trees. Calay could feel Ash's hot, putrid breath on her face as they struggled. She threw one punch. Then a kick. Ash didn't even flinch. It was like fighting a brick wall.

This was it, Calay thought. The end. After they'd come so far. So close.

The pressure on Calay's chest suddenly lifted when Ash pushed off and scrambled backward into the forest. She turned and ran, half-transformed, Adam's blood trailing behind her, until she disappeared into the darkness.

Calay frowned, confused. She didn't know what had stopped Ash, or why she herself was still alive.

She inhaled a long, slow shaky breath. Exhaled. She didn't need to understand. Her friends had rallied, the Resistance had won the battle. It didn't matter what the reason was. Everything that mattered was right here.

She pushed herself to her elbows, panting and bleeding. She looked around. All of her friends were gaping at the horrific mess on the ground.

Oh no.

Tears stung Calay's eyes as the truth fully sank in.

Adam was dead, his body mangled and lying limp on the ground.

And it was all her fault.

CHAPTER EIGHTEEN

THE REAL BATTLE hadn't even begun and already Calay had failed.

The primitive part of her brain pleaded with her to get up and run as far away from this place—these people—as possible, as fast as she could. Before she hurt anyone else. She hadn't torn Adam's throat out, but she was responsible. She'd been the one to leave the confines of the fence. It had been her decision. It was because of her that Ash had come. Calay shuddered. It was too much. Everything. It was all too much.

The metallic aroma of blood rose in the air, mingling with the fresh scent of pine and dirt.

Her heart cracked in her chest. Bile forced its way up her throat, but she couldn't bring herself to look away from what remained of Adam.

Her leader. Her co-conspirator. Her friend.

Terror condensed to a sharp point in Calay's veins. Her gaze darted to the surviving members of the Resistance, her eyes wide. The few people left in the world who seemed to give a shit about her. The people who loved Adam the most.

Briar and Holden leaned against each other near the fence, as if propping each other up. Briar's chest heaved while a thick trail of blood reached from beneath Holden's palm, pressed to her temple.

Ezra was across from them, on the other side of Adam. His eyes glassy but alert, his teeth clenched together as he wrapped both hands around his knee, which was clearly broken, if not shattered.

Jacob lay on the ground nearby, his clothes singed and his hair pasted against his head. In the brazen fury of the fight, Calay hadn't fully seen what had happened to him. One moment he was there, another not. Now, as his chest rose shakily, Calay willed herself to crawl to him and find out. Her legs refused to move. She watched his back rise and fall, sputtering with each inhale. Satisfied he was alive, Calay finally allowed herself to turn and look in the opposite direction.

To Callum.

He hung between Salem's long arms, his features mangled and his jaw agape. His normally immaculately styled hair hung into his eyes, which were unblinking and marred in disbelief. Salem pressed her red lips together and hitched him upright, trying to maintain her balance. Even with twenty feet between them, Calay could hear his breath, ragged and uneven.

A nightmarish howl whistled through the air; an Earth-splitting shriek fell on its heels.

For a split second, no one moved.

Then Callum wrestled himself from Salem's embrace, staggered forward until he reached Adam's side. He collapsed to his knees, his hands hovered over Adam's mutilated body as though trying to heal him through the air between them. Like touching him might make it real. Finally, Callum's hands came to rest on Adam's heart space. They didn't rise or fall with gentle breaths.

There was no healing this. No coming back from it.

Adam was human. He didn't have the gift of regeneration like the Others did.

Calay held her breath, watching Callum as he sank against where his hands were, weeping. His eyes still open wide with shock, his lower lip trembled. Calay's did too.

"My love," Callum whispered so quietly Calay almost didn't hear it.

She clenched her eyes shut, her heart breaking. Tears snuck past her lids and ran down her cheeks. She knew how Callum was feeling— intimately. A sob broke past her lips, she tried to stuff it back in. Failed.

She sniffed back a second one. This was all their loss, but it wasn't her turn to show it. She had to be strong. They needed her now more than ever.

The sound of movement pried Calay's eyes open. The others were converging on Callum. Moving quicker than she would have thought possible, given the gravity of their injuries.

Another screech.

"We have to get back inside," Ezra warned from his place on the ground.

"Working on it." Salem wrapped her hands around Callum's shoulders.

Callum clung to Adam's lifeless body. "No! Leave me."

"Don't do this," Salem said.

"Don't make me leave him."

"We'll come back for him once we get everyone else inside."

"No!" Callum said between heaving breaths. "I can't, Salem. I can't."

"You have to." Holden paused, limped to Callum's side. "So you're still alive to kill that thing when the right moment comes."

Callum jerked away, gripping Adam, his eyes frenetic. "What if they take him while we're gone?"

Ezra clenched through the pain. "Then we'll have even more reason to knock that bitch's head off."

"We have no reason to believe they'd do that. They've never taken the dead before." Holden nodded and turned back to Callum. "Come on, buddy."

"Callum." Calay shook her head, finally spurred into action by her friend's pleas. She glanced back the way Ash had disappeared and saw nothing but stillness. Whatever was making that noise didn't seem to be coming for them, but she couldn't be sure. The others were right—they had to move and get everybody inside. "I'm so sorry."

"We know you are." Briar glanced over her shoulder as she helped Salem ease Callum to standing. "It's not your fault."

Calay nodded sharply, wanting to believe Briar. Unsure if she ever would. Calay's entire plan hinged on luring the Others to them. If they didn't have the means or ability to fight them, Adam was just the first casualty of many. They were all going to die. She couldn't let that happen.

Calay moved forward. "Let me help you."

"You!" Callum spun to face her, his voice thunderous. Calay stumbled back. Callum advanced, pinning her against the nearest tree. Everyone fell to a stunned silence. "This is because of you!"

Calay blanched. Her world twisted. The gentle relief Briar's words offered melted away like tar in the sweltering summer heat. "I didn't mean for this to happen."

"You never mean for things to happen, but they still do!"

"I—"

"Callum, we know you're upset, but that's not fair." Briar pinched her eyebrows together and reached for his shoulder.

"Fair? You want to talk about fair?" Callum turned to Briar, his shoulders heaving. "My boyfriend is dead and it's *her* fault!"

"I'm sorry," Calay protested through the tears falling down her cheeks.

"Tell him that!" Callum's arm shot toward Adam. "He knew full well what was about to happen and he did it anyway. Not for you, but for us. Because he promised he'd always keep us safe."

"Callum," Holden started, their voice uneven. "He wouldn't have deliberately sacrificed himself. He wouldn't have done that to us. To you."

"Of course he would! He wasn't green, Holden. He knew he could never just stab one of those things to death. He gave himself up so we had a chance to get away, because that was the kind of man he is...was." The light in Callum's eyes flicked. He cleared his throat. "He never would have had to make that choice if she had just done what the fuck she was told."

Calay's stomach turned again. Her vision darkened. Callum was right, of course. She felt herself sway backward and didn't try to catch herself—but someone did. An arm wrapped tight around her shoulders. She found herself staring into Jacob's icy blue eyes. His dark curls tumbled over his forehead. Something wasn't right about the color in his cheeks, the temperature of his body. She could feel heat radiating off him through their winter coats.

"Where were you? Where did you go?" she managed to say through the haze. "I thought you left us."

"I'll never leave you."

"I thought... I thought you were dead."

"More or less." Jacob grinned but faltered. His full lips grimaced with strain.

"What happened to you?" she asked as he swept her upright.

"He became one of them." Holden fumbled with the broken arm of their glasses and spared a glance toward Calay.

"If it wasn't for him, we'd all be dead." Briar winced, squatting beside Ezra. She pressed a hand to her head. Calay's heart lurched. Briar waved her off and then signaled to Callum and Salem. "I'm fine. You two, get over here. I can't lift him on my own. Doc, get your med bay ready."

"You turned?" Calay's eyes grew wide.

"Only a little."

Her blood ran cold. "I know you can transform, but I've never seen you actually do it."

"You still haven't, and I hope you never will." Jacob exhaled a low shaky breath. "I did what I needed to do to keep you all alive, but she'll be back. With more."

Absolute silence. Nobody moved. Even the trees stilled.

Calay imagined her friend's thoughts turned to the same place hers did: the violent moments before Adam leapt from that branch. Ash's horrific form. Jacob's.

After what she saw on the starship, Calay was already uncomfortably familiar with the idea of a horde. For the people here, that was going to be something entirely different. A whole new inspiration for their nightmares. Calay imagined waves of them, one piling on top of the one before it. Hungry.

Her friends may have lost their leader, but they were still here. That had to count for something, and she wasn't about to let their victory slip away now. Too much depended on their success.

"The sooner we get Ezra inside, the safer we'll all be," Calay offered, her voice quiet and breathy.

"No, fuck that. You stay out here." Callum's cheeks flushed. "Both of you. Adam should have never let you in."

"Adam knew the risks." Holden shook their head. "We all knew the risks."

"We need them, Callum. We can't do this without them," Briar said.

Callum's lips quivered, he released an uneven exhale. His gaze darted between Calay and Jacob, finally settling on Salem, who simply shrugged. Her brows lifted behind her thick bangs. "They're right."

Callum's head hung between his shoulders. "I don't know."

"I do." Calay refused to let go of them—of this—now. This was her home as much as it was theirs. At least, it would be. After a long, measuring look at Callum, she continued, "We can still win this."

"We'll be ready next time." Briar sighed, tilting her head toward Calay and Jacob.

"Will we?" Callum huffed.

A heartbeat passed. Two. Then another.

Salem crossed her arms over her chest. "Unhinged aliens on our turf? No question."

"Different ballgame," Briar agreed.

"Fuck, it's an entirely different world," Salem said.

"We can make Adam's death mean something." Calay's voice trembled. She prayed she could make good on that promise. That this wasn't all for nothing.

"How?" Callum refused to meet Calay's gaze.

"Together."

"Consider me an ally." Ezra's eyes were filled with scorn. "To the cause."

"In that case, I'll carry this one." Jacob strode forward and hefted Ezra up and over his shoulder with one arm. "The rest of you do what you need to do."

A pained scream released from Ezra's mouth. "Easy!"

"Consider it penance," Jacob growled.

"I'll take you to the lab. Follow me." Holden turned to make for the gate.

Jacob followed close on their heels, his eyes grew dark. "I remember where it is."

Calay swallowed at the memory of what she'd seen there only a few days ago, and the way she'd fled from it months before. Her face grave, she turned toward Callum. "See?"

Callum's jaw tightened. She couldn't blame him. He'd been apprehensive about this plan from the get-go, but he'd backed Adam. Supported him. The way one did when one was truly in love. Calay knew from experience that only meant he blamed himself for Adam's death as much as she did. The odds hadn't been in their favor and they weren't about to get better.

It was only going to get worse.

AN HOUR LATER, CALAY PROPPED HERSELF AGAINST THE Atrium's back door. The blanket Briar had fetched from the treehouse lookout did little to keep out the cold. It crept through the soles of her boots, up her legs, through her chest, and down her back. She pulled the blanket tighter around her shoulders, the chilly air froze the tip of her nose. She let it. If only she could numb the truth that was hollowing her out. She refused to retreat inside; she wanted to watch what was about to happen. It had been her fault, after all. It was the least she could do while she was stuck inside.

Her carelessness had brought Ash upon them. Callum was right about that, though Calay wished he didn't have to say it so loud. Or at all. It was too painful. Too true.

Across the yard and beyond the chain-link fence, Callum and Salem built a pyre. Calay watched them track back and forth from the forest, stacking stick after stick until it was just larger than Adam's six-foot frame. When it was three feet high, Callum dropped to his knees next to Adam's stiff body on the ground. He cradled his dead lover's head in his lap before gripping his shoulders. Salem grabbed hold of Adam's feet. In a joint effort, they lifted Adam from the snow. Calay squinted between the rungs of fortified barbed wire. The crust of ice that formed on Adam's pooled blood cracked and fell from his shoulders in sharp crystals between their staggered footsteps. They paused before the bed they'd made, and it seemed with great effort hoisted Adam on top. To his final resting place.

Calay shivered. She'd asked them to bring Adam inside. Give him a proper burial. Callum, of all people, was the one to point out they'd never be able to dig deep enough in the frozen ground. So he'd done the next logical thing. Calay had offered to help. She'd practically begged. After a smattering of protests, she'd reluctantly agreed to stay put and not leave the compound again. It was too dangerous.

So now, painful as it was, she watched.

With her shattered heart hammering against her chest, Calay tried to fit the pieces of it back together again. After all, there was work to be done and people to lead. Until this was taken care of, however, those things were impossible.

Adam was dead. Callum, broken, and Salem always by his side. Holden was operating on Ezra, who would likely never walk again, and Briar was...off. Calay had sensed it the moment their eyes met after Ash retreated into the forest. Something shifted between them then. Between all of them. It was likely others would still die. It sucked. It seemed the only people truly on Calay's side now was the one person she wanted to count on least of all—Jacob.

He settled beside her. Salem finished pouring the limited generator fuel over Adam's body. tIt was the fuel they'd need to rely on in the coming days. Calay noticed Jacob's clothing had changed. Gone were the fitted vest and leather suspenders. Now he wore a simple button-down shirt and dark jeans. His boots bulged at the sides, and his shredded duster was replaced with a wool-lined jacket. They reminded her of the clothes he'd been wearing the first time she'd met him. All those months ago. Long before *this*.

She turned back to the yard, and together they watched Callum strike the match that would dispense Adam's fragile human form. Callum's shoulders shook violently, his sobs muffled by the ice-packed ground. They disappeared before they even reached the Atrium. He tossed the match on the pile and in mere moments, Adam's body disappeared in the raging inferno, as if he'd never ever existed at all.

A life cut short, Calay thought, a death, too.

Jacob's hand wrapped around Calay's shoulders and he sighed. She angled herself to look at him, her brows knitted together. After a moment, he zipped his lips closed again and squeezed. Calay paused, her breath short, before she eased out of the warmth of his embrace.

"Sorry." Jacob frowned, "I thought you were cold."

"I am." Calay turned her gaze back to the fire.

Callum and Salem stood side by side, their heads heavy. A mirror image of Calay and Jacob. Two friends bound by tragedy, two torn apart. The fire crackled and popped, hissing as if to punctuate the point. Flames snaked through the air, and Calay imagined the flesh wrapped inside them, melting. A wobbly smile crept across Calay's lips at the absurdity of it all. The horror.

"Callum's right. This isn't fair," she said.

"No it's not." Jacob nodded.

"Adam didn't deserve to die. He should still be here." Calay's voice hitched. She braced herself against the doorjamb. "That should've been me."

"I won't let that happen. I care too much about you."

"Now is hardly the time, Jacob."

"When is it the right time, Calay?"

Calay steeled herself. "Never."

"Yeah, you've made that abundantly clear." Jacob paused, rolled his eyes. "Look, I get it okay? We have bigger things to worry about than our relationship status."

"Then why do you keep bringing it up?"

"I don't know, okay?" Jacob's voice became uneven, his gaze wavered. "I guess I just find it a little hard to accept. That we're actually over."

"We hadn't even begun." Calay readjusted her stance, shifting her weight from one foot to the other.

"That's not fair either."

She knew it wasn't. They had meant something, once. Enough that they'd clung to each other when they had nothing else to hold onto. But he couldn't keep being her life raft, and she certainly couldn't keep being his. Not only was it unhealthy, it was wrong. The Others had destroyed her species. Her entire fucking planet. She was done with this, even if it meant she had to break their hearts in the process.

"You let me down." She shook her head, unable to keep the frustration out of her voice.

"You're not willing to give me another chance? I'm not going to keep asking forever, you know. I'm not a lost puppy."

"Then stop acting like one. You've had enough chances, Jacob."

"Is this because of her?" Jacob tilted his head behind them.

Calay turned to see Briar shuffling across the Atrium in their direction with two steaming mugs of tea, her dark eyes homed on Jacob. Her mouth turned down at the side, she hesitated as the steam wafted into the air.

A twinge of guilt shook Calay. She had to admit meeting Briar was something she hadn't planned on. In fact, after Téras, Calay had pretty much given up on the idea there might be someone out there for her.

The truth was more complicated than Jacob was giving it credit for. *She* was. This was just another example of how despite his charms, he didn't understand her at all.

Calay lifted a finger toward Briar and mouthed the word 'please.' Briar pressed her lips together and nodded, rerouting herself to the nearest platform to wait.

"No, but even if it was…" Calay looked at Jacob, sighed as if she was releasing the weight of the world in her breath. In a way, she thought maybe she was. "It's none of your business."

Jacob shuddered, his eyes grew dark. "I won't bring it up again."

"Thank you for hearing me, and for saving their lives out there. I know it had to be hard on you to…change shape." Calay nudged the snow with the toe of her boot. She knew her gratitude wasn't what Jacob wanted, but it was all she could give him now. After everything.

"Hm," he grunted, "I gave you my word."

"Does your word still stand if I don't give you what you want?" She lifted an eyebrow.

Jacob frowned at her, ran his tongue over his bottom lip as he thought. He reached for her chin and tipped her head to meet his gaze. "My word is not contingent on strings. It never has been, Calay. It never will be."

Her eyes searched his for something. Another lie. A condition. Anything. All she saw was him. Her heart ached with want. With regret.

She nodded. "Good."

Jacob nodded in return, turned, and left her standing in the doorway, alone.

He moved quickly. She watched as he passed Briar, his gaze focused on the door on the other side of the room. He pushed through it without slowing down. It banged on its hinges before closing slowly and with a loud click. Calay kept her eyes trained after him, as though he might change his mind and reappear at any moment. She stared through a wall of tears for what felt like forever, though it was probably only a few uncertain seconds.

Calay meant what she said. This mission was more important than Jacob ever could be, even if he hadn't betrayed her. It was more important than her. It was more important than all of them. Still, despite herself, Calay couldn't help but wonder if she'd just turned away the last person who was willing to stand by her side through this mess.

Would he stick to the plan? Would he be there when she needed him most? Would they survive the next forty-eight hours?

The questions rolled over in her mind like a turnstile, one after the other, making her dizzy—or maybe that was just the cinnamon and honey scented tea that aroused her senses when Briar handed her a warm mug filled to the brim.

CHAPTER NINETEEN

CALAY FORCED herself to peel her eyes from Briar's, accepting the offering.

She cupped the mug with both hands and let the warmth defrost the chill that buried itself in her fingers, but not the icy truth that hovered over their future.

Calay never meant to hurt anyone, but she couldn't deny the fact that everyone she'd ever loved was dead. She couldn't help but question whether or not the problem was her. Callum certainly seemed to think so. He'd said as much. To everyone. As Calay rolled his words over in her mind, she replayed the last moments of Adam's life, wishing she'd made different decisions.

Callum wasn't wrong—she should have stayed put, done what she was told. She should have come clean from the moment she arrived. Maybe she even should have died instead of him. Instead of Tess.

It didn't matter what Calay did—whether she was running or fighting or fucking or simply existing—she kept getting the same results. Failure. Over and over and over again.

She watched the steam rise heavily, inhaled the sweet cinnamon-honey aroma as if it could block out the smell of burnt moss and flesh that hung in the air.

"You look like you could use more than tea," Briar mumbled over the rim of her cup and took a long, drawn-out sip.

"You have no idea."

Briar's eyes flicked to Calay's. "I might have a small one."

"Oh Briar." Calay's heart lurched in her chest as she reached for her. "I didn't mean... I know he was your leader and your friend. I'm sorry."

Briar reached back and offered the slightest whisper of a smile. "I know you are, and I appreciate that, but you don't have to be. I meant what I said out there. Adam's death isn't your fault."

"Callum seems to think so." Calay dropped her gaze to the floor. "He'll never forgive me."

"He will when he gets a chance to process things. He just needs time."

Briar had a point, but Calay couldn't shake the feeling that it was still her fault. That one impulsive choice had led to another.

She sighed and gazed across the yard. Callum had sunk to the ground next to Salem, his eyes glazed and palm pressed over his mouth. Calay didn't think he was seeing what must have been happening between the flames. She hoped he didn't, anyhow. She didn't think he was seeing much beyond the impossible pain of losing the one person he loved more than anything.

She wished she could save him that, free him from it. But none of them were free anymore. She wondered if they ever truly would be again.

"I hope so."

"Honestly." Briar rested across from Calay against the doorframe. "It was only a matter of time before one of us made a mistake."

"You think Adam made a mistake?" Calay's mouth hung open.

"I don't want to point fingers, but I do think he made a rash decision and didn't think through the consequences. We still have to go through with your plan, and we could have used his leadership. Now it's all on us."

Calay considered this. Having made more than her share of risky choices, she understood Adam's need to act. To do something—

anything. It had been so unlike him, and too much like her. Too familiar. Maybe they really were more alike than she'd realized.

"We have to be smarter from now on. No more rushing into things and then thinking later."

"Adam would have approved."

"Callum's right about one thing, you know. This isn't fair. Adam didn't deserve this. He should have gotten to see us win when this is all over. Assuming we make it that far."

"Adam would have loved that, too." Briar nodded. "You really had an impact on him, you know. You changed him."

Calay winced, unable to stop herself from thinking of Adam's kind face, the grace and humility in which he carried himself. Then what was left in the end. Mangled and lifeless.

"Not like that." Briar's voice was gentle. Her lips turned downward and her brows knit together when she nudged Calay. "I mean you gave him hope for something better. Like we could build something bigger, the way it used to be. Before They came and ruined it."

"You're just trying to make me feel better." Calay shrugged.

"Is that so wrong?" Briar blinked from behind the curtain of her lashes.

Calay blinked back and shook her head. "Of course not. Just..."

"Just what?"

"Just promise me you won't lie to me to do it. Like, ever. I've had enough lies to last a lifetime. Probably several."

Briar's stare intensified, her jaw set. "I promise."

"Good. Now tell me the truth—do you think Adam's feeling was right? That we'll come out of this in a better position than when we started? That we might get it all back."

"Honestly?" Briar raised her eyebrows.

"Honestly."

"No, I don't." Briar turned her head to look across the yard. Calay shuddered. Briar exhaled and continued, "Adam's gone. The light he shined over this place is too. It'll never be the way he imagined it would be. It can't, but I think that's a good thing. The world was fucked long before the Others got here, you know? The system was violent and broken and I don't think we could have fixed it even if the people in charge wanted to."

The hissing and popping of the fire punctuated Briar's words.

A memory flickered through Calay's mind. The clinic. The one where she'd pushed her way through the picket signs so she could help women choose what they wanted to do with their own bodies; the one Jacob had stocked with supplies for her before he made first contact. As a bisexual woman, Calay had been active in the community, participated in demonstrations. She'd stood up for women's rights. But as the shes, theys, and gays gained one step, in another area they were forced two back. She didn't want to admit it then, but it had been a losing battle. She prayed the one they were fighting now wasn't.

"I hope you're right." Calay closed her eyes and nodded.

When she opened them again, the fire was beginning to slow. Salem was pulling Callum to his feet and saying something gently in his ear. He'd never get to bury Adam or give him a proper goodbye. There wasn't space or time for that. He couldn't even mourn and scatter Adam's remains—the wind would do it. With Ash nearby and the danger outside the fence at an all-time high, they had to come back inside.

Calay's heart ached for Adam. For Callum. For everyone in the world who'd loved and had that love cut short.

A new question weighed on Calay. "Can I ask you something?"

"Always."

"I know you lost your sister, Jada. Have you ever lost someone you loved? In *that* way?"

Briar shifted uncomfortably. "Yes."

"Will you tell me about it?"

Neither woman spoke as they watched Salem guide Callum along the perimeter and through the gate. They disappeared around the front of the main building when Briar finally spoke.

"There was a girl, once." Briar ran a smooth hand over the sides of her shaved head, piling the curls at the top higher. "She went her way, I went mine."

Calay wrapped her hands tighter around her mug. "Was that before or after the Change?"

"In the middle of it, I guess. Those first few days were a mess. We weren't together when it began. I tried to find her, but she wasn't at her apartment. My family and I locked ourselves in our house after that for as long as we could. Then the rioting started. Like a lot of people, we decided to get out of the city. She finally showed up on my front porch just as we were leaving."

"That must have been a relief," Calay offered, recalling the brief reprieve she'd felt when she found Tess at the mountain. Before everything changed.

"It was until it wasn't. I begged her to come, but she refused. I didn't want to leave her, Calay. I really didn't." Briar's eyes glassed over. "But people were literally ransacking houses on my block as we stood there. They were running door to door with baseball bats. Some had fucking guns. They were stealing TVs and attacking anyone who got in their way. Smoke was everywhere. Then people started exploding. Just clouds of red—everywhere. It was terrifying, and everything got all confused. In the end, we left her. I left her. I never saw her again."

Calay's throat closed, nausea rolled in her stomach. She remembered the fear she'd felt after she and Tess's building had been destroyed. Calay nodded, wanting to comfort Briar and knowing too well there was nothing she could say that would erase those memories.

"I'm so sorry, Briar."

"Me too." Briar swiped away an errant tear from her chin. "I wish I'd done it differently, but I can't change the past."

"Wouldn't it be nice if we could?"

"I don't think so." Briar said, surprising Calay. "Things work out the way they're supposed to. Even if they hurt."

Calay's fingers loosened around the blanket, she blinked back a swell of regret. "I wish I had your optimism."

"It isn't optimism." Briar's stance hardened. "It's realism. We have literally zero control over anything. I couldn't have made Alyssa come with me any more than you can change who you are. And Adam decided his own fate. The only things we have agency over are how we respond to the current moment, and I'll be damned if I'm going to let the Others take that one thing away from me. This is literally all we get, Calay. Right now. I'm glad I get to spend it standing here in the freezing cold with you."

Butterflies rose in Calay's stomach. "I'm glad for that, too."

"Damn right." Briar took a drink. "My turn?"

"Shoot."

"What's the deal between you and Jacob?"

Calay suspected this was coming. She wasn't ready for the question when Jacob first arrived, and she wasn't ready for it now. She tightened her hold on the mug and held it close to her chest.

"How much time do you have?"

"For you? However long it takes."

Calay didn't want to drive this woman away. To scare her with the truth. But if Calay expected total honesty from Briar, total honesty was what she'd give in return. She gathered her courage and tried to do the impossible: sum up six months—a lifetime—in a few short sentences.

"Jacob saved my life." Calay inhaled a slow, deep breath. "More times than I can count. When I needed someone, he was there. He gave me exactly what I asked for and a lot of things I didn't. I relied on him, and I guess he relied on me. I'm not sure either one of us would have made it this far without the other."

"That sounds really nice." Briar shrugged. "So what went wrong?"

Calay didn't know where to start. As she searched for the words, her mouth fell open, she closed it. Briar waited, not pushing or prodding. She gave Calay the space she needed to gather her thoughts, to slow the tremor building in her limbs. This was something that had been missing in Calay's life, and something she'd only recently started granting herself. The chance to be who she was, without expectation or hurrying. Just, there.

"A lot of things," she admitted, "but I think the biggest was that I couldn't be myself with him. He always wanted me to be someone—or something—else. He went to some pretty terrible lengths to manipulate me into being who he wanted me to be. It was always on his terms. I wanted to trust him so badly, but I just couldn't get my footing. You know, I was horrible to him for a long time, and I didn't know why."

"Do you know why now?"

"Yes, actually. I think a big part of me was just broken. I'd spent too long hiding and afraid, and when he came into my life, I didn't know how to trust him. Or myself. I also think a bigger part knew all along he was wrong for me. That something wasn't right—intuitively. I'd just spent so long stuffing that inner voice down that she stopped trying."

"You didn't recognize her when she finally spoke," Briar offered.

Calay blinked, nodding. "You get it. Yes, exactly. It wasn't until I went to Téras and found out the truth about the Others and what they planned to do that I finally listened to myself. The reason I couldn't ever get comfortable with Jacob was because he'd been dishonest with me from the very beginning. One deceit stacked onto another until it finally all came crashing down."

Briar repositioned herself, shifting her weight from one foot to the other. "Do you love him?"

"Yes." Calay's features twisted as she frowned. "And no. It's hard to tell if my feelings were real or if he tricked me into thinking they were. I can honestly say I cared deeply for him, and I probably always will, but never in the way he wanted me to. Never in the way I did for Tess. Or the way I think I might for you."

"You have feelings for me?" Briar's lips curled, her eyes lightened.

"Just a little bit." Calay bit her lip. "It's weird saying it out loud. The truth about Jacob's relationship and mine, I mean."

"Why?"

"It makes it true."

"It wasn't true before?"

"No, it was, but now I'm not the only one who knows it. I guess that means it's not a secret anymore."

"If you need it to be, we can keep it between us."

"If he hadn't come into my life, so much would be different. Sometimes I think Tess might still be alive if I'd never found out I was part Other. Then again, maybe everything happened exactly the way it was meant to." Calay shuddered. "It can be pretty heavy sometimes"

"Hey—" Briar leaned forward, her voice barely above a whisper. "I'll help you carry it."

"I'd like that."

"So would I."

"Calay…" Briar glanced back the way Jacob had gone. "You know I'll never make you do anything you don't want to do, right?"

"I believe that." Calay nodded, surprised that she actually did. "You seem too good to be true, Briar."

"I have my flaws."

"Like what?"

"Well, if we're laying all our cards on the table," Briar paused, "I tend to hog the covers at night."

"Is that all?" Calay muffled a laugh. A ripple of guilt crept up her spine. It seemed wrong to be smiling so soon after Adam's death. Like they owed it to him to show the proper amount of grief. And they did. It felt crass, but Calay couldn't help that life was still flowing through her veins. Between her and Briar.

Like Briar said, this moment was all they had. She didn't want to miss out on it.

"That's one thing. I also have a bit of a temper when someone I care about is threatened, and I don't know if you've noticed, but I'm a little bit jealous of your connection with Jacob. I'll never ask you to not speak to him or anything if you want to, but I don't give a shit about what he wants. I know it bothers him that you and I are close. As far as I'm concerned, after what he did to you, he can get fucked."

"On this, we agree." This time Calay really did laugh. "But Briar, I don't get why me."

"What do you mean?"

"I'm broken. I have baggage. I'm not the easiest to be around. I'm part alien, even."

"Because you're the light, Calay." Briar smiled.

Calay's breath caught in her throat. Jacob had told her the same thing on the starship. She didn't believe it then, and she didn't believe it now. A deep sense of concern wound its way around her chest, squeezed. She wasn't the light, and if Briar couldn't see that, then maybe Calay had gotten it all wrong.

Briar caught Calay's gaze and held strong. "But you're the darkness too. And I don't want you to be anything but exactly what you are. Dark, twisty bits and all."

"Oh." A gentle softness melted through Calay. Her heart swelled. This, she thought—this was what she'd been missing. What she'd been looking for her whole life.

Kindness. Honesty. True acceptance.

Briar.

Calay raised the mug to her lips. The spicy warmth of the liquid eased its way down the back of her throat and coated her insides. She peered into the cup. "This tea is amazing. What's it made with?"

"Love?" Briar's voice was light but didn't waver. Her gaze fell over Calay like the coziest of blankets.

Neither one of them spoke, an unsaid understanding fell between them. Their cards were on the table. They were a pair now, if they hadn't been before. Calay didn't know where they were going to end up, or if either one of them would even survive the coming days, but they were in this together.

"My favorite." Calay almost grinned, if it weren't for the ache in her heart. Some of the tension in her shoulders relaxed.

"I hoped it would be." Briar said, hesitating.

Calay could feel her next words floating in the air between them.

"What?" Calay prodded.

"Are you sure you're ready for…this?"

Calay drew her shoulders back and let the blanket slide from her shoulders when she stepped forward, closing the distance between her and Briar to mere inches. Want brewed between them. "I've never been so sure of anything. Ever."

Briar's eyes smoldered. "I mean, things could get a little intense."

"Like camping."

"What?"

"Fucking in tents."

This time it was Briar's turn to laugh. "That's a terrible joke."

"It's my *one* flaw." Calay shrugged, rolled her eyes. "Are *you* sure you're ready for *this*?"

"I've been waiting my whole life."

Emotion surged through Calay. She stepped forward until Briar's back was pushed against the wall and there was no air between them at all. Their mugs smushed awkwardly against their chests, tea sloshing out the sides and splashing to the ground. It melted the snow at their feet.

Calay leaned closer, her mouth hovering over Briar's. Then Calay pressed them together.

Briar tasted like sweet honey lingering on her parted lips. The warmth of Briar's breath flooded Calay with desire. Her breath grew shallow.

A low, deep moan escaped Briar's throat.

Calay pressed harder, slowly easing her tongue against Briar's.

Briar dropped her mug to the floor, it clattered. She brought both hands to Calay's hips and pulled her closer.

Calay's free hand slid to the back of Briar's head while the other wrapped around her waist, arching her back. Calay knew this was special. It wasn't just a crush like it had been with Jacob, or an act of self-sabotage as it was with Ash. This was the real thing. The thing she'd waited so long for. For the first time in her life, Calay didn't need to belong to someone—she belonged to herself—but she sure wanted to. And the someone she hoped to find a home in was Briar.

Calay gasped, pulled back to catch her breath.

She didn't have the chance.

Instead, Briar pushed forward. Calay stumbled back against the doorframe and let the weight of Briar pin her there. Briar kissed her again. Their kiss deepened, grew more fervent. A soft warmth pooled between Calay's legs.

Calay couldn't get enough of Briar. Not nearly. Not ever.

When their mouths finally parted, Briar nestled against Calay's neck, her lips delivering gentle kisses as if plotting a map to her heart.

"Hey," Calay's voice rasped, her lips swollen.

"Yeah?" Briar pulled her gaze to meet Calay's.

The affection in Briar's eyes nearly knocked Calay over. It sent a shiver of warmth through every cell in her body. She cleared her throat and centered herself before speaking again.

"Wanna get out of here?"

"Absolutely I do."

CHAPTER TWENTY

THE TRUCK WAS EXACTLY where it should have been. With Calay's hand wrapped firmly around Briar's, the sober tone of the day trailed them across the yard. In the opposite direction, smoke still lingered over Adam's pyre.

Calay refused to let it drag her into the darkness. She didn't hesitate. Didn't notice the new layer of ice beneath the snow. Didn't even care that what they were about to do could get her in some seriously hot water with the Council. What were they going to do to her at this point? Between Tess, the revelations about what the Others intended to do, and Jacob's betrayal, Calay wasn't pulling any more punches. She wasn't making any more compromises or shrinking herself so someone else could get what they wanted. She'd lost enough.

It was time to get something back.

Adam's death had nailed their proverbial coffin—this was going to be their final stand. With him gone and the Others on their way, there was no turning around. No going back in time. No regrets.

"Get in." Calay released Briar's hand and made her way to the driver's side door.

"Where are we going?"

"Wouldn't you like to know?"

Briar braved a grin. "I would actually, that's why I'm asking."

"Get in and I'll show you." Calay opened the door and slid behind the wheel. She checked the ignition. The keys weren't in it. Then she flipped down the visor. They weren't there either. She pressed her lips together and scanned the dashboard. The glove compartment. The ashtray. Bingo. They jingled when she jammed them into the keyhole and cranked the ignition. The truck roared to life.

Briar opened the passenger side door and leaned against the frame. Her dark eyes twinkled as her gaze met Calay's. A ripple of warmth slid down Calay's thighs and it took everything she had not to crawl across the seat and kiss Briar again.

"When you asked me if I wanted to get out of here, I thought you meant to like, your bunk or something."

Calay raised an eyebrow. "That could be arranged."

"Hopefully sooner than later."

Calay exhaled and brushed her hair off her forehead, tucked it behind her ears. "It better be. If we wait until later we might not get the chance."

"That's morbid." Briar frowned.

"You like it." Calay teased.

A smirk wound its way across Briar's mouth. "Guilty."

"Okay, good. Established. We'll get it on sooner than later. Now will you get in the damn truck?"

"Calay, they need us. Especially with Adam—" Briar's voice cracked and lodged in her throat. She paused, averted her gaze to the worn leather mats on the floor. "We can't just leave everyone."

Any trace of joviality drained from Calay. A gaping wound settled in her chest. It ached for Adam. For Briar's sudden emotion. Nothing about this was fair or right, and Calay wasn't entirely sure anything they did now would make it better.

This time, she did slide across the seat until her hands could reach the pink flush in Briar's cheeks. Calay angled Briar's face up to meet her gaze. Both their eyes were lined with tears.

"Do you still trust me?" The words leaked out of Calay's mouth before she could stop them. Trust was a tricky concept these days. "I don't blame you if you don't."

Briar's brows furrowed. She closed her palms over Calay's. "Of course I do."

Calay held her stare, chewed on her bottom lip. "Then I need you to trust that this is something I have to do. While I still can."

"What is it you have to do?"

Calay turned her eyes toward the compound. She scanned the grounds. People were already getting back to work fortifying the fences. Preparing for the inevitable battle to come. She couldn't help but wonder where Callum was. Or Jacob. What they were doing that very moment, or if it even mattered. The person Callum loved most in the world was gone and Jacob, well... Jacob wasn't the person Calay thought he was. So he could do whatever the hell he wanted and she would do what she wanted, and she wasn't going to feel bad about that.

Calay released Briar and pushed herself to her knees on the seat, her stomach tied in knots. She steadied herself on the doorframe, took one long slow breath. "Something I should have done a long time ago."

"Are you sure you want me to come?"

"Only if you want to."

"I always want to be with you." Briar blinked at Calay from behind the curtain of her long lashes.

A warmness rose in Calay's cheeks. "Good. Me too."

"So are you going to make room for me in there or what?"

"Right." Calay almost laughed with relief. After all the lies and manipulation, a big part of her wondered if she could trust her own judgement. If she was making the right call. She shook her head as she scooted back across the cab. *No, fuck that.* She knew what she needed to do, and it didn't matter what anyone else thought. This was her life— what little time she had left of it. Her decisions. She was finally free of the influence of people who never really had her best interests at heart. They could keep their agendas because she had her own.

As she shifted the truck into drive, she turned to Briar, who was buckling her seatbelt. "I'm glad you're here. Like, really glad."

"I wouldn't want it any other way." Briar reached for Calay's thigh.

She slid her long fingers across the fabric of her jeans and squeezed. "Now let's do this. Whatever this is."

Calay nodded and hit the gas a little harder than she needed to. A jerrycan of fuel slid the length of the truck bed, banging against the tailgate. They churned up snow and gravel as they peeled out of the yard without a glance in the rearview mirror, into the forest.

"Whoa, Lead Foot. We're gonna lose our replen if you keep driving like that. Where's the fire?" Briar gripped the holy shit handle with one hand and Calay's thigh with the other, but her voice was light.

"Like you said." Calay sighed, dragged her tongue over her lower lip. "The sooner we get back, the sooner I can get you alone in my room."

OVER THE NEXT THREE HOURS, THE DIRT ROADS GAVE WAY to highways, the highways gave way to buildings. Silence bloomed between Calay and Briar. They rumbled past the Portland city limit sign. Spray painted over 'Welcome' were the words 'Stay out.' The population number was scratched off and in its place was a giant red zero

A shiver crawled across Calay's skin.

Anyone with good sense and a desire to live knew to stay out of the cities. They rolled past, Calay thinking she seemed to have neither.

As she eased the truck between abandoned vehicles, she pulled her gaze from the road and peered at Briar, who was staring out the passenger side window, her hands wound tight in her lap, her leg bouncing against the seat.

"Regretting your decision to tag along?" Calay asked, only half joking.

A moment hovered. Long and drawn out like the winding road leading into town. Heat washed over Calay, though she wasn't sure whether it was from the heaters or her own vulnerability. She unrolled the window a crack and let the cool air from outside blow against her face.

Finally, Briar's voice sliced through the silence. Her honesty, too. "I'm still deciding."

Calay's chest clenched. She nodded and mouthed a silent "okay" to herself. "Should I have told you where we were going? Would that have changed your mind?"

"Of course not. I told you—I wouldn't want to be anywhere else. But can we agree to err on the side of over-sharing versus under-sharing from now on?"

"Yes, we can do that." Guilt wrenched in Calay's stomach. "I'm sorry."

"I just think if we're going to agree to be honest with each other like you wanted, we need to be totally honest."

"I could have told you more, I just… I think I was just so focused on what I needed to do, I didn't consider how you'd feel about it."

"I get that. I do." Briar glanced out the window. Frozen farmland and low brush was giving way to concrete. "If I found my parents out here and they needed my help, I don't know if my first thought would be how you'd feel, either. I like to think it would be, but it's emotional, ya know?"

Calay blinked, startled by her own selfishness, absorbing Briar's words. "Briar, it never even occurred to me they might be in Portland. Do you really think they're out here?"

Briar shrugged, sniffed. "I have to."

Calay took a shaky breath. "I know the Resistance needs us back at the compound, but we can take our time. We can look for them. The thing I have to do won't take long, this doesn't have to be all about me."

"Yes it does. That's not a bad thing, though. This is something we're doing for you."

"But if you have the chance—"

"I don't have the chance, Calay. Like you said, the Resistance needs us. I can't risk bringing my family back together only to have them lose me in this fight. If we survive whatever is about to happen, and my parents and sister are out here, I'll find them after. When we actually have…something other than this."

"I'll help you, Briar. You don't have to do it alone."

"After I help you with your big thing? You're damn right you will." Briar winked. "How much further?"

"Just around this corner."

Calay guided the truck around the curve, low sprawling buildings on either side. She eased off the gas, practically crawling past the flipped school bus. She held her breath, remembering the last time she'd been here. The panic she'd felt, the desperation. It was right before the Faceless had cornered her in that theater. Before she knew what they were.

At the end of the road was the fifteen-story building she knew so well. The first six floors sprang from the snow in tall, climbing pillars. Above that was floor after floor of boarded up windows, the odd one splintered or missing. She combed them from the top to the bottom, searching for signs of movement or light. Any sign that her former home had found a new resident.

All was still.

If she looked closely, she could see the broad scaffolding staircase hidden by painted plywood and shrubbery. Calay used to think this place gave her a certain degree of safety. But that was before everything she'd seen since she agreed to leave this place. The exterior was as she remembered it, unchanged. Yet now, everything was different. Nothing would ever be the same again. Including her.

Maybe it was for the best. Maybe not.

Calay gripped the steering wheel. "There it is."

"The building?" Briar pointed beyond the windshield.

"That's the one."

"What is it?"

Calay pulled the truck along the northside, sheltering it from view. She turned off the engine and exhaled deeply, preparing herself. "We called it the Loft."

"Who did?"

"Jacob and I. When we lived here."

"You lived here?" Briar's eyes grew wide when she craned her neck to peer out the side window. "When?"

"Before the Others took me to their home planet. Their spaceship. Whatever. It was after Tess…"

"After she died?"

"After I killed her."

Briar's gaze turned from the building to Calay. They weighed on her like a weighted blanket and without judgement. "Did you and Tess live here too?"

Calay shook her head, her fingers still gripping the steering wheel hard enough they were turning white. "No, we never, uh. We never made it this far south."

Briar nodded, her eyes narrowed. "You came here after. To get away from what happened."

"Yeah. Something like that. It felt wrong leaving her up on that mountain and then coming here, but it was just too..." Calay fought to describe an indescribable feeling. She came up with naught.

"Excruciatingly painful?"

Calay's eyes darted to Briar's. "That's a start."

"You did what you needed to do to survive. That's all that matters."

"It isn't all that matters. That's why I risked coming back to the Resistance. I knew they were hunting me and that I was going to have to face the consequences of what I did to Tess. That they'd hold me accountable. But I've been given a gift—being able to carry on her work. To end all of this. Or at least start to. That's why we're here. I need all the help I can get."

"I'm right here."

"I'm grateful for that. For you." Calay reached across the seat and squeezed Briar's hand. "But I'm afraid of what's coming. I came here to get something that will help."

"Are you willing to tell me what that something is?"

"We agreed on truth, right?"

"The whole truth and nothing but the truth."

"Even if it hurts?" Calay's voice wavered.

"Calay, nothing you can say or do will hurt me."

"That's not true."

"You have a past. I have a past. We've all done things, and we'll still do things."

"It's unavoidable," Calay whispered.

"Hey, I trust that you'll never do anything to intentionally hurt me. You trust that I'll never do anything to intentionally hurt you. Right?"

"Right."

"It might not always be comfortable, but if we're honest with each other, we honor each other. The truth can never do anything but make us stronger."

This was a new philosophy for Calay. A new way of being with another person. She felt as though she were floating over thin ice, afraid to put her feet down for fear she'd crack through the top layer and disappear beneath the surface. She'd spent so long hiding from others. The idea of fully opening herself up to someone was almost scarier than what the Others had in store for them.

"I don't know how to do that," Calay admitted.

"Yes you do. I've seen it. You just have to trust yourself."

Wasn't that the whole reason Calay was here in the first place? She shivered, worrying she'd made a terrible mistake coming back to the Loft. It was dredging up old feelings. An old version of herself. But she wasn't that girl anymore. She hadn't been for a while. She was someone else now. Someone stronger. She'd trusted her gut, finally. And Calay was confident it was going to pay off.

"Thank you, Briar." Calay swallowed. "I needed the reminder."

"I'll always be happy to kick your ass." Briar flashed Calay a radiant smile. "Now, are you going to tell me what we're here to get?"

"A necklace. Two, actually." Calay averted her gaze, shook her head.

Briar's mouth fell open. "Necklaces?"

"This is the part that might hurt." Calay released a shaky exhale. "They were the first gift Tess ever gave me. I dropped them off the roof before I left for Téras, thinking it was time to finally let her go. But I was wrong. She'll forever be a part of me, and they're the last thing I have of her. If we're going to win this war, I need to be whole."

Briar squinted as if she was trying to make sense of Calay's explanation. "The necklaces make you feel closer to her. To yourself."

"I know it might seem silly to you, with the whole world hanging in the balance right now." Calay shrugged. "But they're important."

"It isn't silly." Briar released Calay's hand and tilted her chin up. "Things have a way of becoming part of us."

"You understand then?"

"Sure. Why do you think I make tea all the time? I don't love hot water that fucking much. It's something my mom always made when my sisters and me were upset or sick. I guess in a way the ritual of preparing a pot of tea helps bring me closer to her."

"That's it exactly." Calay nodded. "And you aren't jealous?"

"Jealous? Why would I be jealous?"

"Because it's a romantic gift. From another woman."

"Like I said, we both come with pasts. It's unrealistic, and frankly, unfair to pretend that we don't. Where we've come from has made us into who we are today. And I love who you are, Calay. I want to know everything about who you were and who you want to be."

Calay swooned, drunk on the idea that someone—no not someone, Briar—actually wanted her just as she was. Flaws and all.

"You sure about that? I'm kind of a mess."

"You're my kind of mess." Briar leaned across the seat until their noses touched, their foreheads met.

Calay closed her eyes and took a deep breath, inhaling the sweet smell of Briar's skin. Briar brought her lips to the tip of Calay's nose and gave it a gentle kiss. Something blossomed in Calay's chest. It wasn't quite desire, but it also wasn't love. She wasn't even sure if she knew what that was anymore. But it was a sense of safety and acceptance she hadn't felt in a very, very long time. Her fingers grazed the shaved sides of Briar's hair and wrapped around the back of her head, pulling her mouth to hers. They kissed slowly. Their lips parted just enough Calay could still taste the cinnamon Briar had added to her coffee that morning. She lingered over it, savored it. When they pulled apart, the warmth of their proximity faded quickly as Calay resigned herself to getting out of the cab and doing the thing she'd come here to do.

"Do you mind waiting here?" Calay cinched up the zipper on her coat and reached for the door handle.

"You don't want me to come?" Briar blinked.

"I'm glad you're here, but I have to do this part on my own. If that's okay?"

"It's more than okay." Briar pulled Calay by the neck of her coat and kissed her again. "That one was for luck."

A giggle bubbled its way up Calay's throat and through her lips. She was beginning to like the sound of it.

She shook her head and exited the cab, rolling up the window and closing the door as silently as she could behind her. Despite the blue sky above, the sun held no warmth. Her gaze shifted toward the back of the building. That was where she'd intended to go but now that she was here, she was surprised by how overwhelming the urge to go inside was. There wasn't anything left here for her. Jacob was gone. Max, gone. Everything she owned in the world had went with her to Téras. Still, something inside called to her. Something deeper.

She chanced a glance down the street they'd come from. A flicker of movement down the alley. Calay braced herself, reached for the truck's handle. There was no way to tell if it was an Other, a Faceless, or another person. Maybe it was just her imagination. A trick of the light. It wouldn't be the first time she'd jumped at shadows. She waited. When nothing moved, and before she could second guess herself, she quickly crossed behind the truck and made for the curtain of artificial greenery.

It fell behind her with a quiet swoosh as she moved forward, squatting before the sheet of plywood that marked the door to the scaffolding staircase. She shimmied her fingers underneath it, the pavement sparring with her knuckles. It lifted without too much effort and she slipped inside.

She climbed. Bypassing the warehouse full of creepy mannequins with their blacked-out eyes and broken limbs, she sidestepped the traps they'd set all those months ago. Calay's pulse quickened, her heart too. With each step, she glided past them, under them, over them. It was easy. Dare she say, effortless. As if she'd done it a hundred times before.

She had.

The room called to her. When she finally reached it, the sight of the vintage couch almost stole her breath away. It sprawled in the middle of the dim room, the black kerosine lantern tipped on its side. She could almost picture Jacob napping on the sofa, somehow finding space to stuff Max between his legs. Between streams of sunlight peeking through the opening in the half-boarded window, she spied something sticking out from beneath the couch.

Her feet suddenly seemed to weigh as much as a planet. She shuffled across the concrete toward it. When she got closer, she bent down to find it was one of Jacob's novels. Probably the one he'd been reading the night they'd left for his home planet.

Before everything changed.

She turned it's cracked spine and dusty cover over in her hands.

War of the Worlds.

Figures.

She leaned against the couch and sank to the floor, letting the cold hardness of it seep into the backs of her legs. How had she ever called this place home? She sighed, realizing she hadn't. Not really. It wasn't just hunger that kept her combing the streets day after day in search of supplies. It was also the fact that she'd never truly moved in, or moved on. She'd been stuck in some hellish purgatory of self-blame for Tess's death. That was why she'd spent every night on the freezing roof. Why she couldn't be there for Max, wherever he now was. A wave of guilt rose in Calay's throat. Nausea, too. She hoped he was okay.

The guilt gave way to grief, and she sealed her eyes shut, but tears broke through them anyway, running down her cheeks. They dripped with small plinks as they fell onto the cover of the book. She let it slip from her fingers, the sobs rolling one over the other. Her shoulders shaking, she pulled her knees up to her chest.

She stayed there, letting the emotions come. For a moment. An infinity.

She sniffed, wiped away the tears that clung to her eyelashes.

She wasn't sure how long she'd been parked there on the floor, but Briar was waiting. It was time to do the thing she'd actually come here to do.

She had to get the necklaces.

Calay left the book where she'd found it and made her way back down the dark, treacherous staircase, and exited the Loft for the final time. She gave Briar, who had her feet up on the dash, a nod and a short wave before disappearing behind the building.

Calay scanned the horizon for pods or the Faceless. She seemed to be alone.

She trudged to the far side of the building. Calay had been wrong about a lot of things in her life, but she knew she wasn't wrong about this. Sure, the necklaces wouldn't give her magic powers, and they weren't a weapon. By most people's accounts, they were a waste of valuable time and resources, and an unnecessary risk. But it didn't matter what other people thought. One thing Calay had learned over the last five years was it wasn't necessarily important to be strong, but to feel strong. That was what would carry them to victory. And to feel strong, she needed to feel closer to Tess.

Calay scanned the ground, but of course what she was looking for was buried somewhere underneath two feet or more of snow.

She was going to have to get dirty.

She dropped to her knees in the approximate location of where she suspected the necklaces landed. She started digging. Her fingers grew numb while she methodically sifted for the chains, one square foot at a time. She brought her hands to her lips, breathed on them. Tucked them in her pockets. It did little to take the sting out of what was sure to be frostbite later that night. Still, she kept searching. They had to be there somewhere. She thought briefly about enlisting Briar's help after all, but the idea of forcing Briar to help Calay fix her own mistakes—mistakes Briar was only beginning to learn about—was too much.

A new sob formed in her chest, but just before it rolled up her throat, her fingers wrapped around something. She gasped and clung to the familiar feeling of it in her hand. She raised it to eye level and the small gold crescent moon glinted in the sunlight.

A rush of gratitude filled Calay. Small spots were tarnished black with oxidation, but she had it. She quickly uncovered the second one.

The two moons clinked together.

Like they were meant to be together.

Forever.

This time when tears ran down her cheeks it wasn't for what she'd lost. It was for what she'd found.

She pushed herself to stand and gazed across the white cityscape. On one side were sprawling low-rise buildings. Behind her an open field of undeveloped land. People lost everything since the Change, but this planet was still theirs. They would win and they would rebuild. They had to. As long as they got the chance.

Calay made for the truck. Through the windshield she could see Briar sleeping, her head propped up against the window. Calay paused before opening the driver-side door, knowing it would wake her. She watched Briar's chest slowly rise and fall with the deep rhythm of her breath. With her life. After today, Calay knew she could finally leave the past where it belonged—behind her. She and Briar had a future to create.

She tried to open the door quietly but the loud groan of the hinges startled Briar awake.

"Sorry." Calay grimaced.

"I was keeping watch but I guess I fell asleep." Briar rubbed her eyes. "Did you get your necklaces?"

Calay held them up for Briar to see. Inside the truck, without the twinkle in the sunlight, they seemed dimmer. Less impressive.

Calay didn't care; they were hers.

"They're beautiful." Briar smiled.

Calay smiled back. "We said we weren't going to lie to each other."

"You're right, they're ugly as fuck." Briar laughed. "But it's nothing a little baking soda can't fix."

Calay brightened. "You think?"

"We'll figure it out." Briar nodded.

"Have I told you how glad I am you're here?"

"Not nearly enough."

"Give me time." Calay turned the key and started the engine.

"Back to the compound, then?" Briar pulled her feet from the dash and gazed at Calay.

Calay blew a long, slow breath between her teeth and clasped the necklaces around her throat. When one door closes, another opens.

Wasn't that what Tess used to say? Calay realized coming back to the Loft wasn't a mistake like she'd feared. It was closure. Of a time, a place, and a person.

She supposed the hard part of the past wasn't looking back, it was leaving it behind.

"Soon." Calay cleared her throat, adjusted the rearview mirror. "First, I have one more thing I need to do."

CHAPTER TWENTY-ONE

THIS TIME as Calay rounded the bend halfway up the mountain, she didn't pull off to the shoulder of the road to get a better look. She blew right past the now-abandoned checkpoint. It helped no one was guarding the entrance. She wasn't sure why not, but she assumed it was because the woman who'd spearheaded the operation was dead.

Calay gazed in the rearview mirror at the reflective barricades, knocked onto their sides like discarded toys. Empty bottles and discarded blankets littered the shoulder of the snow-packed road. A vision swept through her mind. A memory. The last time she was here she was running from the Resistance. She'd been so afraid. So alone. She lifted one hand from the wheel and clasped the two necklaces around her neck in her fist. Now, she had Briar by her side. Herself, too. United and almost whole. Calay never considered her journey would lead her back to the compound. Back up this mountain. To the one place she swore she'd never return.

Yet here she was.

She trained her attention on the next turn. She floored the gas. The engine in the old truck screamed as it fought to maintain speed as the S-curves climbed higher and higher. Her stomach did backflips when the backend fishtailed around one. She probably should have put sandbags in the box or chains on the tires, but now that she was on a roll, she didn't want to slow down. She only wanted to do the one thing she needed to, and then never look back again.

This place belonged to Tess now.

"You take these corners like you know them," Briar said.

"I do."

Briar shivered across the cab. "You know, I can't help thinking about the last time we were on a road like this."

Calay nodded. Evidently she wasn't the only one haunted by winding roads and forest horrors. "You're talking about the earthquake."

"Not just the earthquake, but how we haven't run into the Others the whole time we've been out here. No Faceless. It was the same at the farm. It's weird, isn't it?"

A tightness curled around Calay's shoulders as she made the next turn. "It's not that weird."

"What do you mean?"

"I don't think Ash attacking us at the compound was a random attack."

"You think she's controlling them?"

"Maybe." Calay paused, tried to ignore the image of a horde of Eloras boring down on her on the starship. "At the very least, she's coordinating with them."

Briar tilted her head, her gaze settled on Calay. "You think the war has already begun."

A loud bang shuddered through the truck when it dipped violently into a gaping pothole. Calay gasped, swallowed. Took a deep breath. She didn't want to admit that could be the case. That the end was already upon them.

"The Others aren't dumb animals. They don't make impulsive decisions like we do. They're strategic by nature. That's how they've survived, moving planet to planet, destroying one after the other."

"That's fucked up."

"Try watching one of their planets implode." Calay shook her head and blinked away the memory. "I'm not going to let them do that to Earth. To us."

"Where do you think they are?" Briar peered skyward through the dusty windshield. Calay dared to follow her gaze between corners. The blue sky had clouded over with thick dark clouds. The shadows between the reaching pine trees had grown heavy, blanketing the ground. They were already losing light.

"I don't know." Calay shrugged. "But I think we'll find out soon enough."

"That's terrifying."

"That's what we're fighting against." Calay pressed her lips together.

"It's what we'll win." A warmth illuminated Briar's eyes. "Besides, you still owe me some alone time in your bunk. Or mine. I'll happily take either."

Calay rolled her eyes, but she was grateful for Briar's humor. Another deep breath and her nerves almost settled.

One hairpin curve and a few seconds later, the end of the road swept into view. Calay let off the gas and the truck rolled to a gentle stop before a single row of trees.

A soupy mist settled around them, thick. Hovering. Waiting.

Calay turned off the engine before she gathered her courage to peer between the branches that seemed to be reaching to them through the fog. She dragged her gaze across the meadow unfurling beyond them under a blanket of deep, undisturbed snow. It rippled in tiny mounds formed by the wind. The same wind Calay so distinctly remembered whipping across the mountaintop and her skin before she'd finally found Tess. Beyond that, the caves.

Calay had returned.

Briar blinked against the stark whiteness of the landscape—cold and brutal. "What is this place?"

Calay crossed her arms and stared into the distance. "This is the last place I ever wanted to come back to."

Out of the corner of Calay's eye, Briar frowned and made a disapproving sound from the back of her throat. "And we're here why?"

"Because if we're going to do this, I need to focus on what's ahead. I can't do that if what's behind me is still pulling my heart backward." She turned to Briar then, her voice dipped low with reverence. "I don't just mean saving everyone, though that's obviously the most important thing. I mean saving myself, too. So I'm ready for us. Ready for you."

"You don't have to do this if you aren't ready. *Any* of it."

Calay reached for Briar and pulled her into an embrace. "I'm more than ready."

As if in response—or maybe in protest—a gust of wind shuddered the truck. The two women gripped each other's arms. The sky fell calm again.

Calay sighed. "No time like the present."

"No time *but* the present." Briar grinned.

"Dark." Calay grinned back, recalling Briar's comments earlier.

"You like it." Briar nodded, understanding. Her gaze fell to Calay's lips. Briar brought a single finger to them and traced the bottom one.

"You're damn right I do," Calay replied breathily.

"Do you want me to wait here again?" Briar pulled her shoulders back and released Calay from her arms.

Calay turned her attention beyond the windshield, aching to be pulled back into Briar's warmth. She didn't want to do this. Didn't want to get out of the truck, even. But the sooner this was finished, the sooner they could get back to the compound and end this.

Whatever that meant.

"You can come." Calay said, her voice fragile.

"Are you sure?"

Briar's question shook Calay more than the truth. Was she sure? It seemed to her she'd spent the better part of her life—and especially the last five months—second-guessing herself. Evidently, repeatedly being lied to, gaslighted, and manipulated would do that to a person. She hadn't been able to get her feet underneath her, never mind move forward and make a clear choice. She'd even fled the entire fucking planet trying to make sense of what was real.

It'd taken uncovering the darkest lies and visiting the deepest parts of herself to figure it out.

Calay knew she still had a long way to go in terms of trust and honesty, but she was sure of one thing—she'd only get there if she was honest with herself first.

"You know, if you'd asked me that a month ago, I don't know if I would have been able to answer you." Calay's gaze fell soft and drifted from the caves to Briar. She nodded. "Truth, right?"

Briar's gaze hardened. "Truth."

"I want you. With me."

"You got it." Briar zipped up the front of her coat and pulled her hood up. "Ready?"

Calay sucked her bottom lip between her teeth and nodded. "Let's do this."

They met at the front of the truck. The warm engine pinged, cooling in the brisk evening air.

Calay claimed three determined strides, then faltered. Emotion welled in her stomach. Her heart. To be able to trace all that had happened to her here was something she never could have fathomed. This was where her tragic adventure both ended and began.

Suddenly, she found it hard to breathe.

"Hey." Briar's voice floated to Calay from behind. Her arms wrapped around her waist. Suddenly Briar's warm breath was on the back of Calay's neck. She pulled Calay's hair to the side and kissed the delicate skin at the top of her spine. "You aren't alone. I'm right here with you."

Calay closed her eyes, furrowed her brow. Briar squeezed. Calay nodded and took a tentative step forward. Then a second. Then Briar's arms slid from their perch on Calay's belly.

Calay braced herself and increased the distance between them.

The snow stung their calves as they plunged across the meadow at what became a steady pace. Calay's thighs burned, the snow growing deeper, rising above their knees. Walking casually across a meadow rich with long grass and wildflowers was decidedly easier than chugging through heavy wet snow. In addition to chains and sandbags, Calay added snowshoes to her growing list of items she should have brought.

Despite the cold, a river of sweat ran down her back and pooled at the top of her jeans. She glanced behind her more than once to make sure Briar was still following. She appeared to be struggling as much as Calay was. Calay turned forward and forced herself to keep moving.

When they reached the entrance to the caves, Calay paused to catch her breath.

"That sucked," Briar gasped.

"The snow is deeper than I thought it'd be," Calay admitted.

"If the Others find us here..." Briar let her voice trail off before she finished that sentence.

"I know." Calay gulped a mouthful of air. "We'll make this quick."

Briar pointed at the opening of one of the caves. A dark, gaping chasm that for Calay held nothing but secrets and death. Briar swallowed, and her eyes flickered between Calay's expression and the opening. "Are we going in there?"

"No."

"Oh thank God." The tension in Briar's shoulders visibly relaxed.

"We're going in there." Calay pointed at the cave that branched to the right. The one lined with ice and uneven rock.

Briar's mouth fell open. "Are you serious?"

"You can go back to the truck if you want to. I don't want you to do anything you don't want to do."

"Is it safe?"

Calay frowned. "Is anything safe anymore?"

Briar shrugged. "Good point."

"You don't have to come with me, Briar. You didn't sign up for this."

Briar clasped Calay's face in her hands. "I signed up for you. When are you going to accept that?"

A gasp became trapped in Calay's throat. Tears welled in her eyes. Her heart swelled. She'd only begun to accept herself, it seemed almost too good to be true someone else would too. She wasn't about to make the same mistakes she'd made before. She wasn't going into this shiny and new, and she wasn't about to let a bit of sweet talk blind her to the truth. But the reality was, Briar had done nothing but give her the space to be who she was. If Briar was willing to work with that, Calay could too.

"Okay." Calay clasped Briar's hands in hers before pivoting to face the cavern.

She braced herself and moved forward, ignoring the thunderous banging in her chest. It pulsated in her ears. Her limbs. Her every thought, which she tried her flailing best to limit to the task at hand.

Again, snapshots of memories scrolled through her mind like a home movie. Another time. Another woman. Calay had changed so much since the last time she was here—and the nightmares that followed. Since it'd been a place of safety.

She hefted herself up the cold, hard rock, taking baby steps over the rigid ground, careful not to slip and fall. Somewhere to their right, water unexplainably dripped. An underground river, perhaps. Maybe a hot spring. The sound of it was unnerving, given the cold temperature, but it also buoyed Calay's mood. Even in the harsh weather of a dying planet, life was trying to find a way. Water moved. So did they. Together, she and Briar made their way through the dark tunnel until the mouth widened.

Calay whimpered, stumbling into the familiar underground room.

Her eyes fell to the emerald pond. Its surface was only partially frozen, snow piled at the center. Where the table had been was just an open space—the spilled papers and overturned chair, gone. Minerals still sparkled against the granite walls, despite the fading grey light. Her eyes scanned the speckled boulders lining the shore, which were covered in damp, and new tufts of moss peeked from underneath. Roots of evergreens and pine trees hung from the opening at the top, icicles formed on their edges before they disappeared into the frozen mud and rock. What were once cascading ferns and billowing goatsbeard now draped from the walls in an eerie state of greenery and death.

Briar eased herself toward the closest wall and ran her fingers over one of the ferns. "How is this possible?"

Calay couldn't look away. She opened her mouth to speak, then closed it when no sound made its way past her lips. She shook her head. "I don't know."

"What happened to them?" Briar's voice cracked.

Calay moved forward and mirrored Briar's movements. She had to feel them for herself. It'd been so long since she'd touched a living plant. One that wasn't frozen in the ground or ensconced in snow and ice. The soft leaves bent between her fingers. She leaned in. Inhaled. The smell of nature was overwhelming. She let her mind swim with it before turning back to Briar.

"It has to be a spring. Or a well. Something underground. It's keeping it warmer in here. The plants are alive and growing, and the water doesn't freeze." Calay turned her attention to the center of the room. The pond. The last place she'd touched Tess's living, breathing body. She swallowed, focused. "But it isn't totally sheltered—look."

Briar directed her attention to where Calay was pointing. "That big-ass mound of snow?"

"Yeah, it's like the ecosystem is trapped between what was and what is."

"Between life and death."

"Exactly, but it isn't giving up. The Others' infestation hasn't made it all the way down here. They're trying, but see the pond? The ice? That all used to be running water. This place was full of it."

"Water's toxic to Them."

"Yes! They've tried to infect it with whatever their presence is doing to Earth, but they haven't been able to because of the hot spring or whatever it is underground. The water saves it. Do you know what this means?"

Briar blinked. "You want to go swimming?"

"Ha-ha. It means the planet is trying to survive." Calay spun in a circle, gaping. She suspected Tess may have known this all along, which was why she'd set up the operation from here. "The Resistance has been trying to use water to keep the Others out of the compound, but what if that's the wrong strategy? What if we need to adapt?"

Briar's dark brows drew together as if trying to make sense of Calay's stammering. "You're saying you want to move us all underground?"

"I'm saying it's not the worst idea. We can't very well live under water, but if this place exists, there must be more like it." The ground gave way, soft beneath Calay's feet. The soil bounced with each step. She knelt down and scooped up a handful of warm earth. "Either way, the Earth will support us. We just have to adapt and live more naturally. Smaller. More sustainably."

"And just how long do you expect us to live like this?"

Calay shrugged. "As long as we need to. Until we reclaim our planet and things get back to normal. Don't you see? If the planet can survive the Others, so can we. We just have to work with it. What do you think?"

Briar shoved her hands in her pockets and gazed across the room. "I think your hope gives me hope. It sounds impossible, but so does taking on the Others. Everything up until this point has been impossible."

Calay's eyes were wide, pleading. "But it still happened."

"So why not live like hermits underground? At least down here we won't freeze to death in our sleep if the power fails."

"No power to fail." Calay grinned.

Briar laughed. "Sweet."

A momentary lightness buoyed Calay before seeping out of her like a deflating balloon. She'd been lost about their next steps if they were successful against the Others, but this could work. It could really work. As long as she did what she'd come here to do.

A stew of horror and resignation settled on Calay's face. Shadows haunted her vision. She blinked them away. It was time to say goodbye.

She shuffled to the far end of the pond. The spot where the sun had shone its brightest the last time she was here. A humble pile of five small stones, stacked one on top of the other, was the only spot marking the grave. They'd planted wildflowers after, but none had taken root.

It was the place she and Jacob had buried Tess.

At the time, Calay had been wrought with anger and regret. She'd thought about leaving Tess's lifeless body for the animals. The elements. Whatever fury and damnation the mountain could throw at it. Because fuck her. In the end, Calay's humanity—her decency—had won out. Things may have gone sideways, and Tess had betrayed her horribly, but Calay couldn't let go of the woman she'd thought Tess was. The years they'd spent together. The truth that while Tess may have done some terrible things, she was still a person.

After everything the Others had done to them, people deserved better.

Calay leaned against the nearest boulder, her chest heaving. A sob she'd been holding back since they'd arrived finally escaped her lips. She sank to her knees, nestled into the sand. Her hands fumbled for the necklaces. She unclasped one, then the other.

"Hey. Um, what you did was wrong. It was fucked up," Calay whispered, her voice cracking. "But I understand now why you did it. I'm sorry I didn't understand then. I'm sorry for what I did to you. I'm sorry for so fucking much."

No words could describe the vast darkness that filled Calay as she lowered the chains and then draped them over the pile of stones. It bubbled in her veins, clouded her mind. It spilled out in the form of tears onto the ground. She collapsed onto her forearms, and she brought her mind's eye to the moon-shaped pendants. Pressed her forehead into them.

"I'm going to make it right. I promise."

Calay cried. Her shoulders shook with each inhale as her body sank lower and lower. She balled her fists, banged them against the damp ground. Her stomach roared with heat.

This was it.

Her final goodbye, and the start of something new.

A gentle warmth rippled over Calay's shoulders when Briar knelt beside her and wrapped her arm around her. Briar didn't shush her wails or tell her it was going to be okay. She didn't ask for an explanation or stomp off in jealously. She just held Calay. Allowed her to be.

Calay squeezed her eyes shut and leaned into Briar's chest. She gasped through breaths until her sobs slowed.

She hadn't planned on having someone there when she said her final goodbye, but she was grateful Briar was. A small part of Calay—an old part of her—worried Briar would turn and run when she saw her brokenness. A bigger part knew Briar understood the fractures. The pieces. Even more than that, Briar respected them.

They made a person whole.

A sudden movement out of the corner of Calay's eye caught her attention.

When she looked up and wiped the tears away, it was gone. She stilled under Briar's embrace. Strained her ears to make out the sound of something new and yet, something familiar. Something she'd heard before.

Yes, something was moving.

She could hear it coming from behind them, but when she turned her head, there was nothing there.

It happened again.

She spun, but save for Briar's arm falling from her shoulders, the landscape remained unchanged.

Briar rubbed her forearms, despite the humidity and warmth. "What is it?"

Calay shook her head, her eyes wide. "I heard something."

Briar bristled. "What kind of something?"

"Shhhh, listen."

They listened. Maybe Calay was hearing things, her mind playing tricks on her. That was a side effect of intense emotional breaks, wasn't it? Or was it? The facts jumbled together in her mind. She was having trouble keeping them straight.

Then she placed it. It was the soft whisper of feet scampering. She held her breath, her gaze darting across the cave.

It grew louder.

Closer.

Suddenly, Calay's breath came in short pants. They echoed across the expanse. No, she thought, they weren't echoing. They were being repeated. Something was breathing heavily and quickly.

Labored breaths carried across the wind and settled in Calay's bones.

"Calay," Briar hissed.

"You hear it right? You hear the sound of someone breathing?"

The breathing stopped, replaced by the deep purr of a low growl.

Briar gripped Calay's forearm, her nails digging into the skin of Calay's arm even through the thick fabric of her coat. "Turn around."

Calay spun, her eyes settled on the spot where the sound was coming from.

"No." She inhaled sharply. "It can't be."

CHAPTER TWENTY-TWO

CALAY BRACED herself on Briar's arm. Her eyes welled with tears. Her heart was pounding for too many reasons to count. In the falling daylight, she scanned Max's body for some sign he recognized her.

His golden eyes raged like fire. His floppy grey ears—the ones, she remembered fondly, that smelled like freshly popped popcorn—were pulled back, tight against the sides of his head. His tail was tucked firmly between his legs, framed by strong muscles that were poised for attack.

He growled, sharp fangs bared and dark lips twisted into an angry snarl.

A river of guilt twisted in Calay's stomach when she saw the newly healed scar across his left cheek. That hadn't been there before she'd left for Téras. Before she'd abandoned him.

The world hadn't been easy on him since she'd gone, but he'd survived. Somehow.

"Hey boy," she whispered.

A deep, throaty sound from Max sent a shiver down Calay's spine.

"We should back away slowly," Briar managed. Calay could feel her shaking with fear.

Calay shook her head and reaffirmed her stance. "Not yet."

"We have to go."

"Not without him."

Briar blinked and pulled her fearful stare from the dog to Calay. "You want to bring this wild animal with us?"

Calay licked her lips, released Briar's arm. "He's not a wild animal."

"It sure looks wild to me."

"He's my dog." Calay stretched out her free hand, her palm upturned.

Max growled again. His jaws chattered with the vibration.

"Your dog?" Briar gaped. "Since when do you have a dog?"

"Since before I found Tess. Before I met Jacob. Before any of it." Calay's heart lurched at the memory; she tucked the pain it radiated safely away. She squatted in the sand, dropped her gaze to the empty space between her and Max. From the corner of her eye she could see him pull back on his haunches and then lower his head. "I found him in my camp. I guess maybe he found me? We're a pack."

"Right now the only pack he sees is a couple of value-size New York strips."

Calay sighed, lowering her knees to the ground. She refused to see what Briar saw. Briar didn't know Max like Calay did. The unconditional love he'd given her, despite the many, many times she'd fallen short of what he deserved. Especially now. She had no idea what he'd been through over the last few weeks. All he'd ever wanted from her was love and attention, and she'd denied him that and turned him out into the cold.

Fine grains of sand embedded themselves in the fabric of Calay's jeans and the palms of her hands, and she found herself thanking the stars for their warmth. It was because of this place Max had survived. She was sure of it. Where else would he have found water? A warm place to sleep? It'd shielded him from the elements and saved him. Just like it would save them all.

Yes, he was due an emotional response. She'd left him, after all.

Calay clamped her eyes shut and swallowed. Stubborn tears leaked out the corners of her lids. When she opened them again, Max was practically nose to nose with her. His eyes held hers.

"Please don't be mad at me." Calay's voice shook with remorse.

Another rumble vibrated across her skin when he growled.

"Calay," Briar whimpered.

Calay chewed on her cheek, crawled forward, and dared to press the tip of her nose against the cool wetness of Max's. "I'm sorry I left you, my boy. I'm so sorry."

A moment passed. Then a second. Calay chanced a quick glance over her shoulder to see Briar's wide eyes watching their exchange, her arms pulled tight to her chest. Calay turned back and wrinkled her nose from the heat of Max's breath on her skin every time he exhaled. He breathed heavily and in short bursts. She couldn't tell if he could actually understand her or feel her pain, or if he was simply sizing her up and deciding how big a chunk he should take out of her face.

He wouldn't do that, though. Would he?

Then Max pressed back.

A high-pitched yelp rolled across Calay's skin. Suddenly, his face was buried against her neck. His tongue was wet on her cheek. His wiggly body leapt with each step, trying to get closer.

A secret smile peeled its way up Calay's lips in relief, but remained unripened and laced with regret. She never should have left him, but she couldn't have taken him with her. Not to that place. He surely would have died. The Elora army would have torn him apart. While it broke her heart to walk away from Max, she'd done the right thing. Because even though it hurt them both, they'd found each other in the end.

She wrapped her arms around the muscles in his back and pulled him against her. His tail flung side to side, striking her cheeks.

"Ow, whippy tail, whippy tail!" She laughed. She released him, and he ran circles around the two women before springing himself at Briar.

"Whoa!" Briar recoiled, her body tense.

"See? He's okay. He just needed some time to express himself." Calay grinned. "He's entitled to his feelings as much as we are."

"Lucky for us he's processed them." Briar's eyes narrowed as she tentatively reached a hand to Max. He seemed to mirror Briar's expression before rolling onto his belly at her feet. Briar laughed and bent down to give him a thorough rub. "He doesn't seem so dangerous now."

"He's not." Calay remembered the way he'd attacked Smith's men when she'd fled from the Resistance. The way he lunged and tore at their throats. It felt like a lifetime ago. "Not to us, anyhow."

Briar stood and laced her fingers around Calay's. "Thank you for bringing me here. I'm glad I got to be here for this. For you."

"Me too." Calay smiled, more tears pooled in her eyes. She didn't know where they all came from; surely she must be dehydrated by now. "I'm grateful I got to share this part of my life with you. Even if it is kind of weird."

"It isn't weird. It's what makes you who you are, Calay." Briar's voice dipped, her eyes darkened. "I never knew Tess, but I've heard the stories. She was a brave leader, even if her methods were flawed."

Calay turned and angled herself to face Briar. "Her methods weren't flawed. They were fucked up. She chose herself over everything, including me. When I found out, I'd never felt so alone. It was the worst moment of my life until that point."

"You have every right to feel that way."

"I know, but I...I resented her. For not choosing me. That's how it felt. It all seems so ridiculous now."

"Your feelings are valid."

"I know." Calay nodded, frowning. Something solid nestled in her heart space. "I finally do. I spent so long wanting to feel needed. To be wanted. To have somewhere to belong. And now she's dead."

"You couldn't have stopped her, Calay. You couldn't have saved her."

"I know that. And you know what the worst part of it is?" Calay blinked, sniffed. "I'm glad she's gone. After everything, I can forgive her for what she did, but I'll never forget. Does that make me a horrible person?"

"It doesn't make you horrible at all. It makes you human." Briar shrugged. "A better human than most."

"I just wish I understood all of this better. You know, before she tried to kill me. Twice."

Briar released a long, slow breath. "I'm glad she failed. Twice."

"Oh yeah?" Calay swallowed the sadness pooling in her throat. Tried not to choke on it. She pictured Tess's face. Her smile. It was hard. Like trying to remember a dream in the middle of the night that had long since faded. She knew the pain Tess put her through would take time to heal. Calay would honor those feelings. Take part in the process. But not today. Today wasn't about Tess. Or Jacob. Or even Briar. It was about putting the things to bed she needed to in order to move forward with her life. Her mission. Herself.

"Otherwise I'd never have found you." Briar's eyes slipped from Calay's and settled on her mouth.

Calay's breath hitched. Would she ever get used to the way Briar's saw her? Despite the lingering sadness, Calay couldn't stop the corners of her lips from turning up. She reached for Briar and pulled her into a long, slow, deep kiss. They melted into each other, and Calay sank into the strong, reassuring embrace of Briar's arms.

From somewhere in her periphery Calay could hear Max sniffing. The jingle of his collar. She'd missed those sounds. Missed him. More than she'd even given herself permission to realize.

Something adjacent to happiness spread through her chest as she inhaled Briar's signature rose and nutmeg scent. Briar pressed her tongue past Calay's lips, her teeth, and into her mouth. Calay trailed her fingers across the soft skin of Briar's neck, enfolding them around the back of her head. Calay kissed her harder. A low moan rumbled between them. Calay wasn't sure from which one of them it came. Then Max pressed his big thick head between her legs, forcing them apart. Calay laughed. She scratched the super soft part behind his ears with one hand, squeezed Briar's with the other.

She peeked skyward. The first glimmer of stars had started to wink above them in the darkening midnight-blue sky. Without cloud cover, it was going to be a cold night once they were out in the open again.

She shivered even though the cave was warm and muggy. "We should go."

Briar pulled the jerrycan of gasoline from the back of the truck and filled the tank before the three drove all night to make it back to the compound by dawn. By the time they were bouncing along the dirt road leading up to the main building, a new layer of frost had settled on the ground. The crunchy, frozen ferns. Even the branches of the trees were ensconced in ice. A sliver of golden sunlight cut across the landscape and through the forest. The undisturbed snow sparkled with it.

Nothing moved. No one in the guard towers. No animals. Even the wind seemed to have taken a rest day. The scene made Calay think of the portrayals of Christmas in the movies she'd loved so much as a child. Only in this winter wonderland, instead of twinkling lights and holiday carols, it was filled with the things of nightmares. Monsters that came for them in the night. Shadows brimming with danger. Everyone they ever loved, dead.

Calay shook her head. She didn't know where those dark thoughts came from. Everything about the last day and a half had been positive. A success, if she wanted to label it.

Afraid of jinxing their winning streak and breaking the cozy silence that had settled in the truck, she peeled her gaze from the approaching tree line and tried to communicate with her eyes to Briar that something felt off. The disturbed look on Briar's face conveyed she understood, and she wasn't happy about it.

"It's quiet." Briar's voice was low, her brow furrowed.

"Too quiet," Calay agreed.

"Where is everyone?"

Calay shrugged. "Something tells me we'll find out as soon as we make it over the hill."

They never got the chance. As they rounded the final corner, they noticed someone skidding across the snowscaped ground toward them, one arm over their head, the other clutching some kind of long stick.

No, not a stick. A crutch.

"Is that...?" Briar's eyes widened.

Calay's lids grew heavy, her voice hollow. She pulled the truck under the shade of the forest and eased on the brake. "Ezra."

Ezra slid up to the driver's side door, catching himself on the side mirror before his one good leg betrayed him entirely. The vehicle shook with the weight of him. Calay's eyes took him in, flitting rapidly across his body. His menacing blue eyes looked ashen, the hair on his normally manicured beard was wild. Something dark was smeared across the front of his grey hoodie, and he ignored the bomber jacket falling off his slumped shoulders. His bad leg was wrapped in white bandages and framed by a hard plastic brace. Suddenly the intimidation Calay always felt in his presence seemed insignificant. Right now he seemed less like a bull and more like a field mouse.

Ezra gasped for breath while frantically signaling Calay to roll down the window, which, she was already doing.

"Are you okay?" Briar leaned across the cab. "What are you doing out here?"

"Had. To. Warn. You," Ezra said between clenched teeth, clearly in pain.

Calay's eyes narrowed. "Warn us about what?"

"What's going on?" Briar said.

"Ezra." Calay cleared her throat. She reminded herself she was safe with Briar by her side. There was no way Ezra would try to hurt her again. Here. Now. Was there? Max tried to push his head into the front seat. Calay eased him back with the back of her arm. "What's up?"

Ezra gasped for breath. "Where the fuck have you been?"

"Went out for some pizza, caught a show, did a little dancing. You know, the usual." Calay rolled her eyes, despite the fear thudding in her veins. She knew something wasn't right, but she didn't like the guy.

"I'm serious."

Calay levelled her eyes at him. "So am I. It's none of your business where we were."

Ezra glared back. "Well, while you two were out on the town, we were attacked."

The color drained from Calay's face. Okay, she thought, now was not the time for being petty. Even if Ezra did bring that side out in her. "No! By who? What happened?"

Briar practically crawled into Calay's lap, eager for more information. "Was it the Others?"

"Of course it was the Others. The Faceless—whatever the fuck they are. They're all the same thing, right?"

A rush of coldness steeled itself inside Calay. "Oh my God."

"Is everyone okay?" Briar's voice raised several octaves.

"Now that I have your attention, no, everyone is not okay. Thanks for asking. We're screwed."

"Wait, start over." Calay blinked, her fingers gripped the steering wheel, her knuckles turning white as she angled herself to face Ezra. "Tell us everything. What happened?"

From the way Ezra's frightened gaze paused on Calay, she got the feeling she wasn't ready for the answer.

"I was on patrol. It was cold as hell last night so I shimmied myself into the tree-bunker to get one of the blankets. Thought I might be able to wait out the sunrise if I could just get some feeling back in my bones. Only when I got up there, something wasn't sitting right with me. The air had changed somehow. I can't quite say what it was."

"Like it was frozen, but alive. As if something was waiting." Calay stilled. "We felt it coming in."

"Like stasis," Briar agreed.

"I don't know what stasis is, but yeah, like *she* said." Ezra stared down the dark path they'd arrived on.

Calay followed his gaze in the rearview mirror and saw nothing but snirt and the growing light of the forest. That, and Max curled up on the backseat.

When she turned back, Ezra's eyes had glazed over as if he was seeing something else. Was somewhere else. She knew that unearthly look. She might have disliked Ezra, but she didn't think any person deserved to be haunted by their own memories. Not even the asshole ones.

"Hey." Calay laid a tentative hand on Ezra's forearm and coaxed him back. His gaze ripped to hers, slicing into her with the sharpness of a blade. She pulled her hand away and tucked it between her legs. "What happened after you were in the tower?"

"Nothing at first, but then I heard the screaming. That high-pitched wail they make. The clicking of their orbs, too. It sounded just like..." His voice drifted a little before he course-corrected. "I waited a long time, but no one came. I was about to drag my ass back inside and that's when I saw them. A swarm of Faceless hurling themselves through the trees. There were more than I could count. I've never seen so many."

"Did they attack you?"

"I...I couldn't run." Ezra let his shoulders slump. "So I hid."

Briar blinked. "You what?"

"With my leg, I couldn't run. So I made myself as small as I could and stayed where I was. I watched them." Ezra shuddered.

"Where are they now?" Calay forced the question from her mouth, refraining from calling him a coward. She tried to give him the benefit of the doubt, though she'd be lying if she said he deserved as much.

Ezra tilted his head toward the compound. "They're there."

"At the compound," Calay said.

"Have they hurt anyone?" Briar asked quick on Calay's heels.

Calay reached for Briar, wrapped her under the warmth of her arm. She understood Briar's concern. Calay had lost too many people not to. She knew the comfortable peace she and Briar had experienced wouldn't last. This had been coming. She just didn't realize it would come so fast.

"Not yet. We had a good head start to prepare and the fences are holding, but they won't last forever. The whole place is surrounded."

"Why now?" Briar balked and turned to Calay. "Please don't take this the wrong way, but I thought they were coming for you."

"I think they are." Calay shifted her weight, thinking. "They can track my heat signature which means they could have found us any time we were out here. I think Ash coordinated their attack on the compound specifically because I wasn't here."

Ezra frowned. "Why would she do that?"

"I don't know for sure, but I have a feeling it has something to do with Jacob."

Ezra snarled. "I knew we couldn't trust him."

"No, it's not like that." Calay blinked through the fog clouding her thoughts, fitting the pieces together. "They protect their own—

aggressively if needed. As far as Ash knows, he's being held against his will. They're all members of the hive, and it would never occur to them one might actually defect. That's not their way. Besides, those two have always had a strange connection. Something deeper than I understand."

"What does that mean?" Briar shifted, pulling back to meet Calay's gaze.

"I'll tell you about it later," Calay promised. "Plus, there's also the bonus that if they come for him and then have him on their side, I'll be alone."

"You'll never be alone." Briar shook her head.

"I appreciate that, but it'd just be me against Them—half other but mostly human. I have some of their abilities, but not all."

"And you're willing to sacrifice us to show off and make a point about how special you are?" Ezra raised an eyebrow.

Calay shook her head in disgust. "That's not true."

Ezra grit his teeth through the pain he was surely feeling. "It's all been about you since you got here. Guess what? Not everything is about you."

"Of course it's not about me, Ezra," Calay snapped. "This is about all of us. But you're lying to yourself if you think you'll survive any of this without me. I've seen what the Others are going to do to us. How they're going to eradicate the entire human race if we don't do something. I'm trying to save you, you dumb fuck. When are you going to get that through your thick skull?"

Ezra didn't miss a beat. "When you and everyone like you is dead."

"What happened to being an ally to the cause?"

"I'm loyal to the cause, not you. We'll all be better off when you're gone."

Briar narrowed her eyes and shushed them both. "Wait a second. You aren't on patrols. Not since you jumped Calay. Adam pulled you off duty."

The mention of Adam almost stole Calay's breath away faster than Ezra's news. She watched a blanket of grief wrap around each of them.

Ezra shook it off, his lips curled. "Thank you, Miss New Council. I know that, but I couldn't sleep last night. I couldn't stop thinking about her." He tilted his head toward Calay, his eyes hardened. "I needed some air, okay? I dragged myself, limping no less, through the freezing cold until I couldn't feel the pain radiating through my leg anymore. But you know, it didn't matter how I turned it over in my head, I realized something about Calay."

Calay swallowed. "Oh?"

"Yeah. I realized I wasn't just following orders when I tried to kill you. I did it because I hate you. Everything you are, I despise. The world would be better off without you in it." Ezra released an excruciatingly long breath. "But the thing is, there's still a war. And you better believe I mean it when I say this: we need you and your weirdo alien talents right now."

Calay suppressed the urge to smack Ezra. She didn't want to touch him at all, especially after what he'd done to her. She could still feel the force of him behind her, holding her face below the surface of the freezing water in the moat. But maybe a quick clip of her door on the way into the compound would suit her fine. She marked it as an item on her to-do list, pressed her lips together, and tried to ignore the prickling sensation of his eyes on her.

Calay sucked in her breath, shifted to their more immediate problem. "We knew this was coming. We know what to do."

"This wasn't how it was supposed to go. We aren't ready." Briar pulled herself upright and out of Calay's grasp.

"We have to be. Look, everyone is inside like we planned, right? The Others are out here. The Faceless. We can do this."

"We were supposed to be inside too."

"We're going to be."

"How?"

"I have an idea." Calay exhaled a deep sigh and gnawed on her bottom lip. "But you aren't going to like it."

Briar's charcoal eyes grew darker, her expression stern. "What are you planning to do?"

"Come on." Calay tuned off the truck's engine. She opened the door a little too swiftly, catching Ezra off guard. The frame smacked into his forehead and sent him stumbling backward against the nearest birch tree.

Calay smirked, slid out of the truck, satisfied. Ezra hissed in agony, swung himself upright as if to attack. Max bounded out the window and pounced in front of Calay, his teeth bared, his haunches raised. Ezra hesitated, his face drained of color.

Calay raised an eyebrow in his general direction. "You have something you want to say, Ezra?"

Tension wound in the air between them. Predator and prey. Only now, Calay wasn't sure who was playing which role. She kind of liked it.

Ezra shook his head. Then he sighed, seemingly resigned. He tucked the crutch into the crook of his arm and shrugged. "No."

"Good." Calay stepped around him and met Briar at the front of the truck. "You still have your supply pack?"

Briar's mouth was tight. "Always."

Calay held out her hand. "May I have the knife please?"

"What are you...?" Briar faltered, opened her mouth to speak, but then seemed to think better of it. Instead, she reached into the bag she carted on all the off-site trips. She pulled out a pocket-knife with a long leather handle. She unsheathed it from its matching case and handed it, handle first, to Calay.

Calay wrapped her hand around the hilt, eyed the blade. "It's not for me."

"What?"

"I need you to do it."

Briar gaped. "Do what?"

Calay dropped the knife on the truck's hood. She tugged her parka off one shoulder and hiked up her sweater, exposing the stitches. Goosebumps rose on her skin as the cold, early morning sunlight winked through the trees. "Cut out the thread."

"What? No."

"I can't do it myself. I can't see it."

"Tell me why you want to re-open your wound exactly?"

"The hive mind uses heat signatures to track me. That means they already know I'm here. But the Faceless might not, right? They're stuck somewhere between alien and human."

"Like you," Ezra muttered.

Calay ignored him, but the truth was, she wasn't so dissimilar from these monsters. The difference was she was willing to do what was right.

"They're animals. That means they might be able to smell fear. Or blood."

Briar thrust her hands on her hips in protest. "You want to draw them to you?"

"I want to draw their attention." Calay glanced at the truck. "We know they respond to movement at least. If we smear some blood inside the cab, open the windows, send it down the hill, maybe that will be enough."

"Enough what?" Briar said.

"Time. We just need an opening big enough to get to the tunnels. If we can make it there, we can execute the plan as we talked about."

"Calay, no."

"What do you mean no?"

"It's too dangerous. There's too much at risk."

"Don't you trust me?"

"Yes, I trust you, but this is different."

"How is it different?"

Briar stared at Calay, her eyes pleading. "We're too late. There's nothing we can do now."

Calay's expression turned pained. "This doesn't sound like you."

"I can't lose you too." Briar's voice cracked at the edges.

Calay's heart did, too. "Briar—"

"And I'm not going to cut a big hole in your body, Calay."

"I will," Ezra growled, catching Max's attention. He eyed the dog and put a few extra paces between himself and Calay before continuing. "No sense in ruining the doctor's good work, after all."

Briar scowled and stepped forward. "Don't you touch her."

"Briar, hey, listen to me." Calay pulled Briar's hands into hers. "It's just you and me now, okay? Wasn't it you who said we'd survive this together?"

"Yeah, but I didn't know what the hell I was talking about. I'm full of shit."

"After everything that's happened to me, everything I've done to make it this far, I can say with certainty that you are not full of shit, Briar. You are the furthest thing from full of shit I've ever met. You're kind, and loyal, and real. I've never met anybody like you. There is positively no shit inside you, okay?"

Briar weakly nodded. "Now you're full of shit."

"Probably, yep. I'm brimming with shit all the time. I'm an expert at shit, okay? Which makes me even more sure you are not full of shit."

"This is gross," Ezra mumbled, his wary gaze still trained on Max. "Can you two, ugh, wrap it up? We're kind of tight on time."

Calay didn't spare him a glance. She kept her eyes trained on Briar's. "I hate to admit it, but Ezra's right. I'm not leaving until I complete what we came here to do. We don't have the time we thought we did, and it isn't what we expected, or how we expected, but this is our opportunity to end this thing. To start to, at least."

Briar paled. "What if we fail?"

"We won't. Not if we stick together."

"What if people die?"

"If we tuck tail and leave them now, that's not even a question. They will die. All of us will. At least if we stick to the plan they have a chance to live."

Briar frowned, sighed. She pulled back her shoulders. "You're right. Let's do this."

The distant howl of the Faceless echoed across the hill. Calay could feel herself shaking with fear and anticipation. This was it. For real this time. No turning back.

"Yes!" Calay pounced forward and kissed Briar. Then reached for the knife. "I'm sorry I asked you to do this. I'll use the side-mirror or something."

"No, I can do it. I want to." Briar's hand closed over the handle before Calay's. Her eyes slid from Calay, to Ezra, and back again. She stepped forward and gathered Calay's hair over the opposite shoulder. She released a slow, unsteady exhale. "Together, right?"

"Right." Calay turned her back to Briar, readjusted her sweater to expose the stitches.

"You sure about this?"

"Absolutely."

A sharp sting crawled across Calay's skin when Briar slid the pointy end of the knife beneath the first stitch and pulled. Calay clenched her jaw, forced herself to breathe though each twinge of pain. A warm sticky wetness dripped down her back. The metallic smell of blood filled the air.

"If we can smell it, they must too." Calay glowered.

When Briar finished, Calay stalked to the driver's side of the truck and opened the door. It creaked unbearably loud on its hinges. She dragged her hand across the now-open wound on her back, wriggling her fingers inside, and quickly smeared the inside of the cab with as much blood as the opening would allow.

It was on the seat. The dash. The steering wheel. The windshield. It even pooled in the ashtray and in the grooves of the floor mats.

With each swipe and flick she grimaced as sharp bolts of searing heat rippled through her body. She shuddered, knowing if she'd been only human, she wouldn't be able to lose this much blood without passing out. She hoped this would be enough to keep the Faceless off their scent for the time they needed to get inside.

Calay allowed Briar to secure a scarf tightly around the wound to staunch the bleeding. She exhaled and started the engine.

"Ready?" she asked in a low voice she barely recognized.

Ezra shifted the truck into neutral and together, they pushed it down the hill toward the compound.

Max whined as they watched it gain speed in one direction; Calay gripped Briar's hand firmly in her own and spun the other.

Then, Calay ran.

Heavy on her feet, she implored their legs to move faster.

She didn't turn back to see where the truck had surely collided with the fence. She didn't need to. She could hear the shifting wails of the Faceless below, swelling like a wave as they chased after it.

CHAPTER TWENTY-THREE

THE WHOLE TRUCK-THING didn't work for long. Then again, Calay hadn't expected it to.

She just needed to buy them enough time to get past the Faceless's defenses and make it to the relative safety of the tunnels to carry out the next part of their plan. Besides, the Faceless were connected to the Others, who were connected to her. They were all one in the hive mind.

As though in reply, a vibrational clicking and whirring rumbled through the air. A throng of blue light cut through the trees in the distance.

The pods had arrived.

Calay knew it was only a matter of time. She may have destroyed most of them on the starship, but as Ash and Jacob had promised, there were others. She'd hoped her friends wouldn't be out in the open when they showed up. The idea of them exploding into clouds of red mist was almost more than Calay could bear. There was nothing she could do about it now.

She and Briar hefted their arms around Ezra and dragged him along as fast as their legs would allow.

"They're coming!" Briar shouted.

Calay strained forward, not bothering to look back. "We're close!"

"Not close enough," Ezra sputtered, wincing through each step.

Calay could already hear the screeching wails of the Faceless realizing they'd been duped. Before she could reply, out of the corner of her eye she spied the swell of pale bodies arching over the crest where they'd abandoned the truck only moments before. Fear gripped at her. Tore at her footing. She stumbled over Max as he wove across her path, growling at the throng.

Calay didn't want to admit Ezra might be right. That she'd risked not only her own life, but Ezra's and Briar's, too. Holden's. Salem's. Callum's. Ryland's. Adam had already lost his. And for what? The asinine idea that she could somehow save humanity? Doubt trickled into her thoughts like mud, coating her from the inside. Their plan was far-fetched. No, it was crazy. She couldn't believe the Resistance had gone along with it. Then again, they hadn't had much of a choice. She hadn't given it to them.

She never should have come to this place. Put these people in danger.

Oh my gods, what have I done?

Her thighs burned; her lungs ached. She pumped her arms, bracing herself as the steepness of the hill sloped sharply downward. She hissed through her teeth, clutching at the round of Ezra's shoulder to keep him upright. She could hear Briar and Ezra panting beside her. Good, Calay thought, they were still with her. For now.

She ran faster.

The dense forest stalked her as she slipped and skidded. She wound her way between trees. Each step a promise—or regret—she'd have to reckon with later. A chill wound its way around her insides.

"Something's not right," she called over her shoulder.

"You think?" Ezra laughed, his voice on the edge of losing it.

"No, Calay's right. Something's wrong with the ground. It feels like it's hollow."

"That's impossible." Ezra's eyes grew wide. "Maybe it's thawing?"

"I don't think that's it." Calay wrapped her arms around the trunk of a large Sequoia and tucked herself out of sight of the Faceless. Blue beams of light dotted the horizon, growing larger, searching. She clamped her eyes shut and knelt down to feel the snow. Max's cold nose pressed against her cheek. The other two huddled together. They only paused for a few seconds, but it was long enough to confirm Calay's worst fears.

The chill hadn't only climbed inside her. It hovered between them. A gripping cold that refused to let go. The undisturbed snow cracked beneath their feet. Spidering underneath their boots in jarring directions before disappearing beneath the nearby brush.

A deep rumble echoed through the trees.

"Oh my god," Briar gasped, covering her mouth with her hands. "Not again."

"What?" Ezra gaped.

Calay's mouth dropped open. "Avalanche."

Ezra sneered. "You got to be kidding me."

"As if aliens and mutants weren't enough." Calay chewed on her lip and glimpsed back the way they'd come. The Faceless even seemed to slow, but not enough. They were still coming. Calay and her friends couldn't hide here for long. "We don't have a choice, we have to keep going."

Briar's eyes turned skyward, scanning the hills and forest that surrounded them. "We could run right into it. I don't know where it's coming from."

"I do." Calay pointed beyond the trees and up the mountainside. Her arm shook with the effort. Her whole body, too.

A plume of white rose high against the grey sky and above the compound. A trickle of snow dusted their boots. Max whined, his sweet ears tucking firm against his head.

"Well shit," Ezra whispered.

Briar shook her head. "It's going to crush us. We'll never make it in time."

"Not with that attitude we won't. Come!" Calay commanded as she stood—whether she was calling her friends or the dog, it didn't matter. Maybe it was both. The trickle had already become a small river. She didn't wait for them to arrive at a consensus this time. They were just going to have to trust her.

Calay peeled away from the tree and broke for the tunnels.

The rushing snow nipped at her heels. It reached for her. She wasn't ready. It didn't matter. The ferns and overturned logs slid beneath the growing roar of the mountain. Never turning her head from the short, though seemingly never-ending goal ahead, flashes of her surroundings winked in and out. Glimpses of the compound down the hill on her right. The heaving shadows in the trees to her left. Briar and Ezra close behind her. Everything crashed together, forcing the white snowy ground to meet the impenetrable grey sky. Or maybe it was the other way around?

Putting one leg in front of the other, Calay couldn't help but feel the weight of the world upon her. The entire fucking universe. The harder she ran, the heavier it became. Pressing her into the frozen earth. Attaching itself to her ankles. Begging her to stop.

She wouldn't.

She couldn't.

Despite the cloying urge to chance a glance back and make sure her friends were okay, Calay couldn't risk falling. Not now. She clenched her jaw. The cold of the forest threatened to take hold of her lungs as she gasped for frigid air. It was smothering her from the inside out. An uncanny familiarity wound its way like barbs against her limbs. Her veins. There was no going back. There never had been.

At least this time she was the one calling the shots. Finally. It was time to put an end to all this.

Whether the planet was willing to cooperate or not.

She reached the tunnels and dropped to her knees. She swiped at brambles and overgrowth, exposing the metal grate covering. Her fingers ached with cold, and with the gash in her shoulder. It radiated down her arm in pulsing waves, blossoming in a pool of red beside her. Calay winced. She may have been part other, but she was human too. Her vision grew spotty, her mind swam.

She wrenched on the grate. It didn't budge. Not one generous inch.

She bit her cheek and tried again. And again. No matter how hard she pulled or twisted, regardless of how much she urged it with her mind, she just wasn't strong enough to get the damn thing out of their way.

"It's not working." Calay choked back a sob.

"Wouldn't be much of a security tunnel if it was easy to remove, now would it?" Ezra skidded and awkwardly lowered himself to one knee beside Calay before making room for Briar. He lifted an eyebrow as if to mock Calay, but she imagined he was simply masking his fear. "Together, right?"

"On the count of three." Briar's eyes were wide with fear.

Ezra's jaw grew slack at the oncoming assault from all directions. Calay couldn't blame him. It was entirely likely they were about to be ripped limb from limb, dissolved into a plume of plasma and ash, or suffocated and crushed to death.

"Fuck three." Calay sucked in a sharp breath. "Now!"

They heaved on the metal. It groaned beneath their palms, the sharp edges dug into their skin. But it moved. Just a little.

"Again!" Ezra roared.

They pulled again. This time it moved a little more, inching over the frozen ground and revealing the crack of the opening beneath.

"Almost," Briar whispered.

Calay didn't know if she was referring to the Faceless, the Others, or the avalanche. She hoped it was the progress they'd made. Just one more pull. The hair on Max's back bristled, his teeth bared. The ground shook, the long branches of the trees swayed and cracked. Calay was careful not to look too far up the mountain for fear of the wall of white bodies and snow headed their way. She focused on what was in front of her.

"Move!" Ezra shouted, though his voice was lost amongst the roar of snow and ice particles about to bury them.

Briar and Calay's eyes met, each one urging the other to go first. They didn't have time for this. Calay leaned forward and grabbed Briar by the collar before shoving her face first into the darkness.

"You next!" Ezra gestured.

"Not a chance."

Ezra's eyes darkened. "Calay—for fuck's sake, do you have any idea how much I want to leave you out here?"

"You wouldn't dare."

"Wouldn't I?"

Calay's mind recoiled at the memory of Ezra's stare on the top of that warehouse all those months ago. More recently, his hands on her neck and his thighs on her back. The bracing cold water that had filled her lungs.

She braced herself on the opening. "You wanted me dead, so why are you helping me now?

"We don't have time for this shit. Let's just agree there's more than meets the eye to both of us, hm? Now get in the fucking hole before I change my mind."

"Fuck you, Ezra." Calay pressed her lips together. She wrapped her arms around Max and guided his near-eighty-pound body into Briar's outstretched, waiting arms. Calay dropped through the hole after him. She collided with the hard, damp ground with her wounded shoulder first. A blinding hot pain radiated through her limbs. It stung behind her eyes. It begged her to give into the darkness and give up. But when she pried her eyes open and peered through the curtain of her lashes, gazing back up the way she'd come, she saw Ezra's boots coming in fast beneath a crest of white. Calay rolled out of the way just before he grunted and crashed to the floor.

A roaring tidal wave of snow followed.

It slammed through the opening with the force of a thousand planets. The very foundation of the tunnel shook.

The whole thing plummeted into darkness as the snow filled the entrance, arching all the way from the floor to the ceiling. Calay held her breath, her eyes nearly fell out of her head as she struggled to adjust to the lack of light. She watched—her gaze a mix of awe, fury, and terror. The snow piled inside. It grew higher. Denser. She worried she'd led all of them straight to their grave.

Then, everything went still. Silent, save for the group's gasping breaths. The sound of Max's tippy-taps on the floor. The aching creak of the walls.

Calay thought she could feel Briar's hands grip her shoulders as she scurried backward out of the snow's reach. Ezra leaned against her side, his breath ragged, whimpering. They braced themselves on each other. Waited. Nothing moved. Nothing sagged or crumbled or tried to rip them apart.

They were alive and in one piece.

It was almost a dream come true, if they weren't already living a waking nightmare.

"Everyone okay?" Calay finally exhaled. Finally able to see by the dim overhead lighting, she looked down at Max and scratched behind his ears—grateful they'd made it this far.

"Define okay." Briar shuddered.

Calay stiffened. "Not dead."

"I think we're good there."

Ezra chipped at the snow with the heel of his good leg. "The snow's blocked the entrance. They can't get in."

"Thank the gods." Briar's shoulders sagged but her voice was light.

"It also means we can't get out." Calay bristled. "This isn't good."

"Wasn't this the plan?" Ezra pressed himself to stand, wobbled on his good leg.

Briar reached to help him. "Yeah, but they were supposed to follow us down here. If they can't get in, what do we do now?"

They stared at the snow blockage. A silence fell over them. An awareness bloomed inside of Calay. One she didn't want to admit, but she also didn't have time to talk herself out of it either. When no one moved after several long, spine-tingling moments, she forced herself to say the thing she didn't want to say.

Calay rose, her legs shaking from fear and exhaustion. "I'll dig us out."

Briar blinked. Her mouth curled upward before falling. "The hell you will."

"Someone has to. I got us into this mess. Might as well be me."

"We need you, Calay." Briar's voice grew louder. "I need you."

"Okay, we're not going through this again." Ezra cleared his throat. "I'll do it, okay?"

Calay took a huge breath and it came out shuddering. "I can't let you do that."

"Why not?" Briar shrugged at Ezra when he frowned.

"I don't know if he'll do it." Calay pulled her shoulders back, hoping she sounded stronger than she felt.

Briar's gaze flickered between Calay and Ezra. "Maybe not, but sometimes you have to trust anyway. Calay, you've come so far. Don't give up now."

Ezra leaned hard against the nearest wall, obviously in a not much better physical condition than the rest of them. "I just saved your life, you ungrateful bitch. You think I'm going to throw everyone else's away? Why would I do that, Calay? Think."

A red-hot rage rose in Calay's blood. "All I'm doing is thinking, Ezra. Whoever stays behind to dig us out of this is going to die. The Faceless will rip them apart. The Others. The planet is trying to kill us. Who knows what else might be out there now? Don't you get it? I'm thinking this is all my fault. They're here for me. I can stop it."

"No, Calay." Briar weakly threw her hands in the air. "They're here for all of us. You said it yourself. They won't be satisfied until we're all dead. We have to find another way."

"There is no other way, Briar. It's all been leading to this." Calay punctuated her words by striking the tunnel with her palm.

She'd changed since she'd come back to the Resistance. Since she'd been to Téras. Since Tess had betrayed her, the Others had arrived, and her parents had abandoned her. With every hardship came a reinvention. A renewal. A rebirth. Something lived within Calay now. It watched this world through her eyes, but it existed somewhere else. Somewhere darker. Deeper. Somewhere only she could go.

The lights flashed. A steady vibration tingled across Calay's skin. When she gazed down the long, dank tunnel, motes of glittery energy floated beyond the darkness. As if guiding her forward.

Then, she screamed.

Through the darkness, the emergence of a figure. It appeared in the shadows, barely taking shape. It fluttered as if a mirage. A ghost. Then became more solid. Shapely. Large.

It loomed in the shadows, just beyond Calay's field of vision. She blinked, struggled to focus her eyes as she sensed the other two gathering behind her.

Then she felt it. The nervous energy shivering above them. Between them. Through them. It was everywhere. The collective of the hive mind. She didn't feel separate from it, nor did she feel at one. It threaded through her cells, fluid like water. And it was growing. Spreading like a disease. Like wildfire.

It seared Calay's veins, drove her forward.

She thought she could hear Briar warning her to come back. Ezra too. Calay continued. Something was drawing her deeper into the tunnel. A force she couldn't control. One she didn't want to.

The tears came quickly. For once, Calay didn't want to hide them. Didn't need to.

Suddenly the distance between them was gone. The illusion of some terrifying monster shrouded in a dark button-up shirt and fitted jeans. His dark curls hung over his forehead, his ice-blue eyes cut her to her core. She reached and took his hand in hers. The tremor of emotion passed through her and into him. She knew it was impossible for him to cry, but she watched the regret and fear she felt cloud his eyes.

"Took you long enough," Calay whispered.

"You told me to leave you alone." Jacob shrugged.

"Since when do you do what I tell you to do?"

"I was helping them get ready inside. I would have come sooner if I didn't think you could handle that on your own." Jacob tilted his head forward, as if nodding beyond the tunnels. The freckles under his eyes wrinkled.

A weariness washed over Calay; there was a time she would have kissed each one. Not anymore. Never again. Whatever was between them was over.

"We had it covered."

Calay turned to see Briar squat down and wrap her arms wrapped around Max's neck. Ezra looked tense, ready to spring into action if needed. A warmth crawled down Calay's spine. She exhaled. She didn't know when it had happened, but she'd grown to love these people. Even

Ezra, despite his hard edges, or maybe because of them. Somewhere in the faint recesses of her heart, Calay saw pieces of herself in Ezra. The fear. The stubbornness and bravado. The need to protect and hide. Sure, he'd tried to kill her, but hadn't she murdered her own mother? Her girlfriend? Her father? How was she really any different than he was?

Like Adam had said, no one was clean anymore. Maybe the difference between what made you good was how much bad you were willing to shoulder for those you loved.

It was what made you human.

Calay sighed, knowing they deserved better than this, and she was going to make damn sure they got it.

Jacob's wide hand rested heavy on her elbow, pulling her attention back to him. "I sensed you through the hive mind. You had time."

"So it would seem." Calay shrugged.

"I have no ill will toward you or your kind, Calay."

A roughness prickled across Calay's skin. A truth that until now, had gone unspoken between them. She'd known she wasn't one of Them, but hearing it from Jacob's mouth was like cementing it in stone. Like they could finally lay it to rest and move on. The both of them.

Calay released his hand. "You sure about that?"

"Of course I am. I'm on your side. I've been thinking about everything you've said. You were right. These last weeks. Months? However long it's been. I'm sorry I pushed you to be something you're not. You're perfect as you are. As is."

"Thank you." Her voice cracked, barely above a whisper.

"It's been hard to let you go, but you were never mine to begin with."

"It's nice to hear you say that."

A grin peeled itself across Jacob's full lips. "Don't get me wrong, I wanted you to be, and if you change your mind..."

Calay frowned, his words hovered between them. A shadow settled on her. *His.* Possibly for the last time, she realized. "I guess none of us understand until we're ready to. We only know once we know."

Jacob cleared his throat. "Let's end this. For good."

A brief moment of relief rolled over Calay, but it didn't last long. It was replaced with a loud banging against the hull of the tunnel. Tiny ripples of snow slid down the pile. Something scratched beyond it.

An icy knowing pinned Calay where she stood. "They're digging."

Ezra straightened. "Turns out we don't need anyone to stay behind after all."

Jacob flexed his fists. "It's the hive mind. They know we're down here."

Ezra glowered as Jacob spoke, but he didn't press further. Calay gave silent thanks for small miracles.

Briar released Max and stood. She shifted her weight from foot to foot, as if her legs were begging her to flee. "So what do we do now?"

"The same thing we were going to do." Calay pulled her shoulders back. "We stick to the plan."

"You still think it'll work? Even after this?" Ezra jabbed a thumb toward the snow.

"I think especially after this. I don't think Earth was trying to kill us with that avalanche. It was trying to buy us time and save us."

"How do you know that?" Ezra frowned.

"I don't." Calay's gaze flickered to Briar. A ghost of a smile crept across her lips. "But sometimes you have to trust anyway."

The sound of their footfalls on the hard floor of the tunnel did little to muffle the pounding of Calay's heart. They moved as fast as they could underground, leading the Others to the one place they shouldn't be able to gain access. The compound. They climbed one by one up the rickety iron stairs, popping up and out through the tiled floor of a distant hallway in the main building.

Calay allowed herself to be pulled up the final rung of the ladder. Finally back above ground, she peered over the edge, back the way they'd come. Below was an inky blackness and certain death. In response, a loud metal crashing echoed through the darkness, followed by the screeches of Faceless monsters.

Ezra slumped against the nearest nondescript concrete wall. "They're inside."

"Then we'll have to move fast." Calay nodded and pulled Briar into her arms, inhaled. "You and Ezra go on ahead. Make sure everyone is where they're supposed to be. Jacob and I will lure them and give you the time you need. Once this starts, there'll be no stopping it."

"Okay, I will." Briar's gaze was hard and pleading. "Just make sure you meet us."

"If you stop holding me up, I will." Calay grinned, but the smile didn't reach her eyes. "You have to go now."

Ezra scowled and grabbed Briar by the arm to lead her away. "This could kill us, you know. All of us."

"I know." Calay released a long, slow exhale. "I'm going to do everything I can to make sure that doesn't happen."

"I'm not going anywhere without giving her a kiss goodbye first." Briar snapped her arm away from Ezra.

She pressed her face against Calay's and wrapped her arms in her long dark hair. Calay grabbed Briar's hood and brought their lips together. She pulled her closer, harder. Calay thought she could feel Briar's heart through the thickness of their jackets, but that was impossible, wasn't it? Their lips parted and a gentle warmth flowed through Calay's heart, her arms, her mind.

Another screech, closer this time.

The two pulled apart. The air suddenly colder. More hostile

Briar's fingers lingered on the back of Calay's neck. "Don't die, okay?"

"I won't if you won't." Calay released her grip on Briar's jacket.

"I'm holding you to that."

"Deal."

Calay held Briar's gaze. Briar pulled Calay's hand to her mouth. From the curve of her brow, Briar grinned. It warmed Calay in a way that for a brief moment, hummed through her veins.

She hadn't expected to find Briar here. She hadn't needed to. But holy hell, Calay was grateful she did. Briar backed away slowly. It was still far too fast. Calay tried to lock in the memory.

Just in case it might be her last.

CHAPTER TWENTY-FOUR

BRIAR AND EZRA disappeared around the next corner. Calay and Jacob were alone.

It wouldn't be long. The Faceless were inside the tunnel. Calay could hear them pounding against the main doors, too. The Others were hovering above in pods, daring anyone to leave the confines of the building. And the tattoo on Calay's wrist hummed with energy. With their presence. Somehow it had become a homing beacon. A signal they were near. As if she'd unlocked something inside when she'd branded herself with Tess's locket insignia—an innate knowing.

Calay did her best to still her nerves and the climbing nausea in her stomach.

This was her plan, built on the idea she could exist as both—neither one nor the other. It was her super power and her greatest asset. It was about time she'd realized it.

The screeches were deafening. They were overwhelming, filling the room.

Jacob leaned against the wall and reached for Calay. She took his hand, nodded while she tried to find a moment of peace. Some semblance of a reason not to go through with this.

They were in too deep now.

If Calay failed them, everyone in the Resistance would die. Her new friends, even her enemies. They were all counting on her—and Jacob—to do the right thing. She shook her head and almost laughed. She'd been adamant about surviving together, but she never really imagined it would be possible. Either people or the Others would have—probably should have—ended things before now. Calay couldn't help but wonder if Tess had actually succeeded in killing her, if the people here would be in this position now? Not the position of possibly dying—that would always be a threat; Calay had seen the genocidal plans of the Others with her own eyes. Heard them from the cracked and oozing lips of her mother. From Ash. But rather, the position of potentially defeating the Others. After watching Them destroy civilization and pit human being against human being, the idea they could not only win, but survive—thrive and rebuild—was unbelievable.

And yet, here they were.

Hovering over the precipice of victory.

That, and a very dark, very loud hole in the ground.

"You ready?" Jacob interrupted her thoughts. He raised one brow as if he couldn't muster the strength or will to lift the other.

Calay replied by raising one of her own. "Let's get this over with."

Jacob's hand was warm and heavy around hers. He squeezed. "Deep breaths."

Calay nodded and tried to calm her mind. She gripped his hand in hers, and she inched closer until she could feel his warm breath on the top of her hair. She breathed in and out, her chest rising and falling with his. She stiffened, resisting for a moment. This was too familiar. Too comfortable. Too late. But when her heart pounded against her chest, his answered. Call and response. As it always had been between them. As it always would be.

It was destined in the stars.

"Just be calm," Jacob whispered.

"Don't tell me to be calm." Calay prickled, then released a slow, steady exhale. "I'm trying, okay?"

Some of the strain left her shoulders. She breathed in his leather and cinnamon scent. Not because she loved him, but because being closer to him helped her feel closer to the hive. To carry out the next and final phase of their plan, she could use all the help she could get.

"Better." Jacob smiled down at Calay.

Then it began.

Everything stilled.

The moment felt like theirs.

Secret. Final. Magic.

Butterflies swarmed in Calay's stomach, then her mind. She clenched her eyes shut, sparks of energy dotted her vision. Golden and purple. Then wound around it. It curled like luminous, glowing ribbon around her toes, up her legs, and over her torso before plunging into her mind. Her heart. Her soul. She shivered with the warmth of it. Embraced it. She whimpered with the welcome release of feeling everything and nothing all in one moment. The lightness of being, the heaviness of all-knowing. Even the pain seemed to be gone from her shoulder.

She gasped, full of light radiating from somewhere deep inside.

When she finally caught her breath, she opened her eyes to find Jacob gazing down at her, the stars in his eyes aglow with that same purple light.

"Winner winner chicken dinner." Jacob smirked.

Calay groaned. "I can't think of anything cheesier you could have said in this moment. And don't say dinner."

"Why not? That's what we'll be if they catch us."

"That's exactly my point."

Jacob winked. "You love the chase."

"Not this kind of chase." Calay shuddered.

The ladder leading below the tile floor convulsed. They were only a few feet away now. In the darkness. Calay didn't want to wait around for them to make their way into the light.

"Time to go."

Together, Calay and Jacob spun and made for the next corner.

Calay focused her gaze ahead, ignoring the tearing sounds of the floor being pulled apart. The sputtering of the Other's inky drool splashing onto the cracked tile. The sickening sweet smell of rot and decay in the air. She didn't need to look back to know the Faceless and the Others in their natural forms were close behind.

So she didn't.

She just kept running.

She'd spent weeks training for this without realizing it. The nights she couldn't sleep. The days that dragged hour after hour. Even the time she'd spent in the compound as a prisoner before she'd discovered the truth about Tess all those months ago. It had prepared her for this. Calay knew the layout of this place better than anybody.

As she zipped around one corner, then zagged around another, time seemed to accelerate. Maybe it stopped. She couldn't be sure. Her lungs begged for rest, the aching muscles in her thighs, too. She put one foot in front of the other, gulped another mouthful of air.

Keep going.

Jacob was faster than she was. They both knew it. Yet he always kept a couple paces behind. Calay didn't bother to question why. She didn't need to. After everything, she understood he had her back, even if his hold was secured by the blades of several knives still sticking out of it. Not that it mattered anymore. All that mattered now was that she had to keep moving long enough for the rest of the Resistance to gather everyone in the Atrium.

Then she'd do something none of them expected. Instead of leading the aliens to their last stand against the Resistance—and risking her friend's lives in the process—Calay would barricade them in Holden's laboratory. There, she planned to dispose of them the same way she did in deep space—she'd burn them alive. She'd intended to stock it with some of the generator fuel, but there hadn't been time. She was going to have to figure out "the how" as she went. For once, maybe her half-baked, spontaneous nature was going to pay off. For all of them.

She and Jacob burst from the main building and dashed for the low-rise one across the yard. The one containing the lab. Despite the fresh, cold air inflating her lungs, the smell of death was trapped in Calay's nose. Her hair. Her thoughts.

It was all that ever was. All that ev…

No, she thought, that was the past. This was going to be the start of something new. Something better.

She could feel it.

They rounded the exterior wall. It was the last corner they had to wrangle on the slippery pavement. Calay's eyes widened in horror. Blocking their entrance to the lab was an impenetrable mountain of sloping, dense snow.

"It must have come down in the avalanche," Calay stammered through panting breaths, her stomach twisting as she craned her neck side to side. "We can't make it through."

Jacob ran a hand over his strong jaw. "This way."

Jacob grasped Calay's hand in his and pivoted between the two buildings. The thought crossed her mind she should be the one leading; it was her plan, after all. She almost said as much, but then the sound of something scurrying behind them forced a gasp up her throat.

She pressed her lips together and ran harder.

Jacob led her through the maze of low-rise brick buildings, winding their way deeper through the compound. They crouched as low as they dared, watchful of the roofs. The last thing they needed now was to be ambushed from above.

Calay swallowed, spurred forward by the need to get somewhere more open. Less cagey.

Especially since the Others were undoubtably reading their heat signatures.

"We're leading them right to us," Calay hissed.

Jacob growled, clearly frustrated with being stuck between a rock and a hard place. Or in this case, humanity and his own kind. "Wasn't that kind of the point? Use our heat signatures and connection to the hive mind to drive them away from everyone else?"

Calay huffed and let loose a long breath. "It sounds better when you say it out loud than it does on actual paper."

They burst from between the buildings. Above them the grey sky had begun to part. Patches of blue winked across the frozen plain. Calay couldn't help but wonder if it the universe was promising a better future, or mocking them.

She blinked, redirected her attention forward, and was surprised to find they'd made it all the way to the back of the property. On one side was the uneven concrete and exposed black brick walls of the courtyard —where she'd reunited with Jacob and exposed the truth about who she was—and beyond that, the fortified chain-link fence. On the other, the Atrium.

It was the one place Calay didn't want to be.

If Briar and Ezra had done their jobs properly, literally everyone Calay cared about in the world now was in that glass dome. A veritable, human buffet, and she'd led the Others straight to them.

She slid to a stop, bracing herself against Jacob's arm to keep from slipping. Her heart thundered in her ears. She scanned back the way they'd come. Nothing had followed them out of the building corridor.

Yet.

But Calay could feel them. They itched underneath her skin like a bad rash, shallow and incessant. They'd been so close, she could taste their putrid stench in the back of her throat. Now, what? They just disappeared? This could only mean one thing and Calay didn't want to give it—Her—a name.

"Oh my god, we're trapped." Calay gaped, trying to catch her breath.

Jacob sighed heavily. "Shit."

"Do you think we could run around the perimeter? Make it to the other side?"

"Unlikely." Jacob frowned, slowly turning in a circle, scanning the grounds. "They know exactly where we are. They're probably getting into position."

"Getting into position for what?" Calay shivered, like she even needed to ask.

"To claim us."

Any remaining warmth drained from Calay. "Excuse me? I thought they just wanted to kill us."

"They want to kill humans, and I'd be lying if I tried to make either of us believe Ash doesn't have a personal debt to settle with you. You did murder most of our family, after all."

"And I'd do it again." Calay squared her shoulders. "You got something you want to say about it?"

Jacob smirked, despite the serious tone of his voice. "Hey, you don't have to convince me that we deserved what we got. I'm just saying Ash promised she'd come for you, and she has. Whatever that means. But they'll want to take me back alive."

"You're still going to go back to Them? Knowing they'll destroy planet after planet?"

"Did you think I wouldn't?"

"I thought..." Calay's brows drew together as Ezra's warning about allegiances rang through her mind. She let her head fall between her shoulders. "I guess I thought because you were helping people—helping me—you might stay with them. Protect them. On the starship you said you'd changed your mind about humanity. That we deserved to live."

"I did." Jacob nodded and shoved his hands in his pockets. "I do. That's why I'm here."

"What then? Why would you help us but return to them?" Frustration replaced the fear reverberating through Calay. "Is it fucking atonement? Help me understand, Jacob."

"What's fair is fair. We destroyed your civilization, you destroyed ours. We should call it even, but that's not our way. And I hate to say it, but *those aliens*, the Others as you call them, are my home."

Somehow, Jacob's revelation startled Calay even more than the impending threat of death. She'd accepted Jacob's betrayals and the fact that she couldn't trust him on a personal level. They were from different worlds that could never coexist. Still, she'd managed to talk herself into believing his help was for the good of humanity. That it wasn't just lip-service to win points with her. That his commitment was real.

A sadness settled somewhere deep inside Calay in that moment. She shook her head. She should have known that, as usual, his motives were self-serving. "So this is it then? Herd us like cattle and then kill us off?"

"Give me some credit, Cay."

"Don't call me that."

Jacob's crystal blue eyes darkened, he fixed them on Calay. "I'd never do that to you."

"But you would to humanity? And what about the next planet? The next civilization?"

"Don't you get it? I meant everything I said before. You deserve to live. Why do you think I risked my position in the hive to save you from Ash in the forest? You deserve to live Calay, but so do I. And while I'm willing to do what it takes to keep you and your kind safe, I'm also going back with Them when this is over."

"If there's anything to go back to." Calay simmered.

Jacob tilted his head and shrugged. "There will be."

Calay scanned Jacob's features, searching for what lay behind his stoic, if not arrogant, mask. Even now, with everything on the line, he was trying to get his way. Calay should have known better. Maybe she did. That's why she was fighting so hard to save the people of the Resistance.

She had her home, and he had his.

Calay strode forward, standing toe to toe with Jacob. She stared defiantly into his eyes. "The attack in the forest. When you changed shape. Why don't you want me to see you transform?"

"I didn't want you to see me like that." Jacob's shoulders turned inward. He scratched the five o-clock shadow that settled on his jaw.

"Why not? You've seen me at my worst."

"Mine is decidedly way, way worse."

Calay nodded, but resigned herself to the fact that Jacob would always need to manipulate the situation. Be in charge. In control. She stilled the anger thrumming through her veins. The ground shook with her emotion. No, she thought—an earthquake. Aftershocks, maybe. Whatever had triggered the avalanche wasn't done with them yet. The ground rumbled below their feet.

The sun broke through the clouds, sparkling across the mounds of snow.

It was beautiful. It was awful. It was so messed up.

A feral screech split the air. The sound of razor-sharp, serrated legs on the ice. Then the distinct whisper of Ash's voice calling Calay's name.

Calay startled. It felt like Ash's hand had reached inside her and just...pulled. A coldness poured through Calay's body. The overwhelming scent of roses filled her nose and mouth. Calay gagged on it, gripped her arms close to her chest, and instinctively backed against the nearest wall.

"She's here."

Jacob's head swiveled between the buildings. "We have to get inside."

"Where? There is no inside from back here."

An unease rose in Calay's stomach when Jacob twisted his gaze toward the Atrium. "There's one place."

"No. Not happening. We can't."

"What other option do we have, Calay?"

Jacob's question wasn't unreasonable, but his idea was. Calay clenched her eyes shut. "That's where everyone is hiding. Jacob. I won't lead the Others in there. People will die."

Jacob took a deep breath, though his stance remained tense. His blue eyes blazed. Even his clothes seemed extra taught, like they were prepared to tear free from their stitches.

Calay's eyes widened as she realized he was probably balancing on the edge of transforming again.

Calay scrunched her face, frustrated by their lack of options. "This is a terrible plan."

"It's your plan."

"Yeah, well you know me. Little Miss Impulsive. I'm a terrible fucking planner."

"If it weren't for you, all those people in there would already be dead."

Calay's arm thrust forward, the momentum almost knocking her off balance. "What do you think is going to happen to them if we lead Ash and the Others through those doors?"

Jacob's arms hung by his sides. "What do you think will happen if we don't?"

For not the first time that day, Calay's intentions were being derailed by forces she couldn't control. She chewed on her cheek, parsed through their very limited options. After discovering Jacob was returning to the Others after this was done made her uneasy. For all she knew, he really was rounding them up on a big shiny platter. She wondered if Ezra had been right not to trust an Other all along. Tess certainly wouldn't have.

Calay reminded herself she was half Other, too. She wanted to finish Tess's work and honor her legacy, but Calay wasn't Tess and she refused to lead like her.

A long pause rooted between Calay and Jacob. Longer than they probably had to spare.

Finally, Calay sighed, raked her fingers through her hair, and stared up at the blue sky. As she opened her mouth to speak, the distinct sound of rock music floated through the air.

"What the hell is that?" Calay gaped.

Jacob shrugged, his face somber. "Doesn't sound like we're the ones leading the Others after all."

They followed the melody and approached the vast dome of green and blue glass that rose from the cement like it was something not of this world. Except, it very much was. In that moment, it was the most naturally, surreal thing in the universe. A lush, verdant oasis in a desert of ice and snow. Alive and blooming. It was nature as Earth intended. Before the Others arrived and began sucking the lifeforce out of the planet.

The heavy fire door was cold beneath Calay's hand when she reached for the handle. It creaked open. Calay stepped through with Max and Jacob short behind her, and gasped.

Huddled on the far side of the dome was the Resistance. Dozens of them. Not as many as she'd hoped. But they were there. They'd made it. Some of them, anyhow. Between the unknowns, Calay spied Holden visibly breathing in long slow mouthfuls, Callum whose eyes remained puffy but his jaw set, with Ryland nearby. Briar and Ezra brought up the rear, making sure no one strayed too far from the group.

A mixture of relief and regret nestled in Calay's bones.

Max curled himself between her legs while she scanned everyone's terrified faces. She noted the big fucking guns in their arms. Those who didn't have automatic weapons had homemade ones, crafted from jagged pillars of metal and barbed wire. Others held fire hoses, presumably hooked up to generators near the moat.

In the center was Salem, her long dark hair pouring over the front of her midnight-blue electric mandolin. The sound of the instrument reverberated up and out the main doors, across the yard, and into the dense forest beyond. Sweat dripped from her forehead and over her stained red lips as she riffed on a ribbon of notes, climbing ever higher.

A thrill rolled across Calay's skin. These weren't people who needed saving. These were people who wanted to survive, or go down trying.

A curl tugged at the corner of Calay's lips.

That suited her just fine.

With a flick of her wrist, Salem cut the music and locked eyes with Calay. Salem nodded, raising her hand with the pick still between her fingers.

Salem smiled. "Sup."

Calay almost smiled back. "What are you doing?"

"Yes." Holden cleared their throat and inched forward. "Your plan had some flaws so we improved upon it."

Calay's mouth fell open. "You improved upon it?"

"It sucked," Salem offered.

"What are you all talking about? What's with the music? Do you realize the Others are out there right now? With Ash, and the Faceless, and God knows what else?"

Holden took gentle hold of Calay's elbow and she allowed her stunned self to be steered to the far side of the room. Several Resistance members rushed forward to secure the doors. Holden grasped Calay in their arms and pulled her close.

Calay found herself in tears, wrapping her arms around them in return, and inhaling the moth-eaten softness of their cardigan sweater.

"I was so afraid." She sniffed. "I am so afraid."

Holden pushed their glasses up with one hand while balancing their weight against Calay with the other. "We are too."

"So what the hell are you doing?"

Briar slid beside Calay. Her eyes were red, as though she'd been crying. "I'm glad you made it."

Calay squeezed Briar's shoulder. "Me too."

Callum stepped forward and extended his palm. "We owe you a thank you."

Calay stared at it. "A thank you? For what?"

"We weren't ready when they came. I don't think we ever would have been. But we were more ready because of you," Callum said.

Calay pressed her lips together and took Callum's hand in both of hers. "I just wanted to help."

"You have." Callum took a deep breath. "I'm sorry I didn't see it sooner."

"You're grieving."

"We'd be grieving a lot more if you hadn't come along."

The gentle grace in Callum's words grabbed Calay by the throat. She took a deep breath, grateful but unsure of what to do next. It'd been a long time since she received a compliment without something else lurking behind it.

She pulled her shoulders back and turned to the group. "Speaking of which, there are fewer than I thought there'd be."

Holden nodded. "We lost quite a few in the initial moments of the attack. Mostly in the dorms."

"They got inside." Calay's gaze dropped to the cement floor covered in dirt and melted snow.

"We couldn't stop them. Not with all our resources piled here."

"They're going to get through those doors, too." Jacob pointed toward the double doors that were now held together by plywood and sheet metal.

Ezra crossed his arms over his chest. "We're counting on it."

Calay pressed her hands to her cheeks. "Will someone please tell me what the fuck is going on?"

Briar fidgeted under Calay's confused gaze. "Your idea was good—to fight and blow this place up. But Ezra's was better."

Calay turned. "Ezra?"

"I'm more than a pretty face." Ezra sneered.

"We used most of your plan, Calay. We just tweaked a few elements."

"And you're just telling me this now? Which elements?"

"Earth. Water. Air. Fire." Ezra lifted his chin. "Four elements. Four phases."

Holden swallowed hard, then explained. "The first is to get them to come for us. That's earth. Phase Two is the initial assault. That's what the firehoses are for. Phase Three, air, is escape. Then Phase Four: death by fire."

"You wanted them to burn, but Ezra had the idea to use all of Earth's elements against them. They aren't from here, after all. Wouldn't the power of four elements be stronger than one?" Briar said.

"We're using our strengths while exploiting their weaknesses." Callum clenched his fists and then released them. There was tension in his body. Pain. It was flexing to get out.

Calay's jaw dropped. "What strengths would those be exactly?"

"Like you said, we survive together. Earth is our planet."

"And their weaknesses?"

Callum's lips pulled into a tight line, his eyes narrowed. "It isn't theirs."

"But my plan had the element of surprise—the Others would have been exposed. You've announced your location with Salem's little performance. If this doesn't work, we're all dead!"

Ezra's eyes flashed in anger. "It will work."

"When those animals come in the front door, we're going out the back. They'll have to cross the threshold to come after us." Briar scooted to the middle of the room where fuel barrels were lined up, her eyes wide. "This is your part of the plan. We'll blow them to Hell, right where they belong. The intense heat will melt the snow and the sprinkler system will activate. We're going to flood them out. Those who don't burn to death, will die in the water, or they'll be so mangled, we should be able to even the playing field and make it a fair fight."

A twisted smile curled across Salem's mouth. "Hence the weapons."

Jacob peered upward. "What's to stop them from blasting you with phasers through the ceiling?"

"Like Calay pointed out when she presented her proposal to the Council, the glass is protective. The Others can't see us through it. Can't shoot what you can't see," Callum said.

Holden's brows knit together over their round blue eyes. They handed Calay a utility lighter. "All you have to do is torch the place."

"Me?"

Holden exchanged an uncomfortable glance between Calay and the others in the room. "It was your strategy to begin with. Figured you'd like the honors. After that, boom. We've rigged this place to kill them every way we know how."

Ezra cleared his throat. "Including setting the bait. They might want us dead, but they want you more. So we used you and that one to buy us time to make sure we were set."

Calay slipped the lighter in her back pocket. "Should I be offended that you used me?"

"No more than I'm offended that after all this, you still don't trust me." Ezra shrugged. "I told you I was committed to the cause."

Calay swallowed an unexpected lump. Her gaze darted between Jacob and the group. "Well, what do you think about all this?"

Jacob regarded her closely. "I think it's as good a shot as any."

"That's not convincing."

Jacob puffed his chest. "We're stronger than humans in every way. It's one of the reasons we chose this planet. You aren't meant to survive us."

Briar frowned. "Well...fuck."

Calay's eyelids fluttered while she wrapped her mind around their approach. She searched for holes. For gaps. For impossibilities. She found more than she cared to count. If they didn't time it just right, the explosion would be wasted. The sprinklers might fail to come on. Another earthquake or avalanche could bring the protective roof down on their heads and crush them before the Faceless even got their chance. For all Calay knew, the Others could block the back exit and make it impossible for the Resistance to escape.

All of this could go terribly, horribly, irreparably sideways for a million different reasons.

But then again, what else was new?

In the moment of that realization, Calay turned to the people before her. Her friends. The home she'd just begun to call her own. Whether she liked it or not, they were a team now. A family. *A pack.* A brisk wind howled against the glass above, rattling up one side of the building and down the other.

An omen of horrors to come.

Calay secured her hair back with the elastic she kept on her wrist, letting her fingers linger on the tattoo that pretty much never stopped burning now.

"Care to kick us off, Salem?"

CHAPTER TWENTY-FIVE

THEIR SIGNAL WORKED LIKE A CHARM.

Between Salem's rough strumming, Calay's and Jacob's heat signatures, and their combined connection with the hive mind, Ash and her army of aliens couldn't have missed it.

Barricaded inside the Atrium, Calay threw her hand up to cut the music. Salem stopped mid-bridge, out of breath, and her fingers raw and red.

They looked the way Calay felt.

Something was whining on the other side of the door. It was ear splitting and high pitched. A series of clicks and whirrs followed.

"You write that yourself?" Calay breathed heavily, never turning her stare from the barrels between them and the Atrium's doors.

"I wish." Salem panted, threw her hair back over her shoulders. "White Stripes."

"Huh. What's it called?"

"'Seven Nation Army.'"

"I think I remember that one." Calay took a step backward, her heels meeting the toes of the people behind her.

A silence fell over the room. They waited a lifetime. Mere moments.

It didn't really matter. Calay knew they were on one side of the wall and the aliens were on the other.

Beside her, Ezra huffed. "What's going on?"

"Calm before the storm," Briar whispered.

Ezra cut her a sharp glare. "Well? What are they waiting for? A goddamn dinner bell?"

Calay gnawed on her bottom lip and sucked in a mouthful of air. "You said we're using their weaknesses against them, right? We're using their strengths, too. The one thing we have going for us is the hive mind."

"That, and the power of friendship," Salem chirped as she secured the mandolin to her back.

Ezra scowled, but Calay nodded. Salem was right. Calay didn't want to admit that the more she thought about Ezra's plan, the more it made sense. She'd wanted to separate them, take all the risk herself. But they were stronger together. Putting them in one room as a united force was their best fighting chance at winning this battle and gaining the upper hand in this war.

It was their best shot at survival.

Calay's breathing grew shallow. "Remember they flow together as one, usually under a central directive. With the home colony dead a few million lightyears from here, I'd be willing to bet my own ass their commands will be coming straight from Ash. Keep that in mind when they come through that door."

"All eyes on Ash. Got it." Callum nodded with certainty, though his voice trembled.

The noises stopped. The connection to the hive mind stilled. In its sudden absence, Calay felt alone and cold. Quiet, but not peaceful. A chill ran the length of her spine, even with dozens of people on either side.

Her head jerked up.

Something was coming.

The door banged open without so much as a crack or splinter.

Fury and panic rushed through Calay's blood, she hesitated, unsure which emotion she should act on.

At the precipice, hanging between life and death, was Ash.

With half-transformed arms braced against the frame of the door, her green eyes sagged in the corners. Her back bulged with oozing pustules. The black crevices between her teeth grew longer even as Calay stared. The smell of decay was overwhelming.

Calay retched, forced her eyes open despite the sting inching across them.

Behind Ash, a wave of Faceless bodies crested, almost defying gravity. The dark holes in their faces gaped, yawning. A horrible screaming sound erupted from one, then from all of them.

Beyond, an ocean of white pods lay discarded in the snow. Calay could hear the clickety-clackety legs on the concrete. They threw themselves against the glass, long legs and bulbous bodies pinging off the outside like enormous bugs on a car's windshield.

Calay winced and held her breath. She watched in agony and prayed to the god she now knew never existed, it would hold.

A hunger vibrated in the air.

It shook Calay's bones. Her resolve, too. She'd barely escaped the starship before, she was a fool to think things would be any better here. Her legs begged her to turn. Flee. Run. But the warmth of Holden's and Briar's hands on her back kept her in place. The feel of Jacob's gaze, too. Calay peeled her eyes toward him. He was only a few feet away, but it could have been a mile.

Jacob nodded ever so subtly to let her know he was there.

She wasn't alone this time, she reminded herself. And if they could stop the Others, she never would be again.

As if responding to Calay's thoughts, Ash's face twisted into a strange mix of sorrow and pride. She tilted her head. The skin hung from pointed, broken edges. It looked twitchy and wrong.

Inhuman.

Unnatural.

Watching.

Unable to stand it any longer, Calay exhaled. "Well then?"

"Silly human girl." Ash's gravelly voice floated to Calay without Ash moving her lips.

Calay blinked and shook her head, sure she was mistaken. But the glare in Ash's eyes told her otherwise. Ash was playing with her.

No one else could hear her. She was communicating through the hive mind. Through *Calay's* mind.

The last thing Calay wanted was Ash inside her head. She refused to give Ash the pleasure. Calay enunciated. "The only thing silly in this room is you thinking this planet is yours. It's over Ash."

Ash smirked and something putrid leaked out the lower side of her lips. She seemed to laugh, but the movement was irregular and convulsive.

"Is that what you think?" Ash mentally projected to Calay.

"Speak plainly. Out loud."

Ash's eyes narrowed, the projection of her voice unchanged. "Or you'll what?"

Calay didn't have time to play nice, nor the patience. Not anymore. This moment was fragile. A wrong word or movement could send the Others down upon them at any second.

"Come on," Calay goaded. "You came all this way to find me and you don't even want to talk about it?"

Ash seemed to shrink before them. Suddenly the long spiney legs jutting out the side of her corset were tucked neatly away, packaged behind soft, smooth skin. Her black eyeliner was expertly applied in sharp upright swooshes. The tattoos at the top of her pants proportionate and peeking as her hips rose and fell with each step.

"You can talk from there." Calay stretched her arms from side to side, as if she alone could protect her people.

They grasped back and squeezed.

"Fine." This time, Ash used her outside voice. It melted like crushed velvet in Calay's brain.

Ash shrugged, her full pink lips curling at the edges.

"What do you want?" Calay asked.

"What do you think I want?" Ash purred.

"I don't think you want to kill me."

"Oh?"

"You just wanted to beat me. To beat Elora. To beat Jacob. You want to rule us all."

"What makes you think that?"

"If you wanted me dead, I'd be dead already. You've had plenty of chances. This was always about control for you, wasn't it?"

"Oh, you'll be dead soon enough." Ash's eyes slid to Jacob, her lips finally parted. "Unlike some, I keep my promises. And what do you suggest we do with you, darling?"

Jacob's voice was low, he narrowed his eyes. "You already know I'm coming back with you."

"Is that so?"

Jacob side-eyed Calay. "They don't mean anything to us anyway."

"Well, we both know that's not true, don't we lover?" Ash growled.

"Leave them be. There'll be other planets. Let's just go."

Ash ticked her finger back and forth in front of her face. She arched it, pointing to the crowd Calay now called family. "They might have had more time if you two had left them alone."

A rush of frustration stabbed at Calay. "Not enough."

"I'm surprised they took you in, to be honest." Ash gave a half shrug. "You're one of us. You prey on people. Suck them dry. Then dispose of them. Come on Calay, you're one of us."

"I might be one of you, but I'll never be like you." Calay's breath quickened.

"Keep telling yourself that, sweetie."

Calay's stomach turned, bile rose in her throat. The sharp feeling of her nails dug into her palms. She hadn't even realized she'd been clenching her fists. Ash knew all the right strings to tug on to make Calay second-guess herself. To twist her reality into something unrecognizable.

She breathed slowly, releasing the urge to lunge forward and scratch Ash's eyes out. Calay unraveled her rage until it thundered through her veins like fuel in an engine. She allowed it to consume her. Hot and scorching, it nestled inside her skin, under her nails, down her throat. She let it spread through her mind—passing Jacob's lies, Tess's betrayal, her parent's desertion, her *self*-abandonment—and soak into her flesh.

Revenge. Retaliation. Fucking justice. But even those words didn't feel big enough. The Others had done horrible things to humanity. Invaded their planet. Destroyed their civilization. Turned human against human. She wanted to do the same thing to them. But something small whispered somewhere deep inside Calay. More than that, she wanted to *live*.

That started with love.

She imagined her walls crumbling, one painful brick at a time, and on the other side, her chosen family.

The Resistance.

Adam. Briar. Holden. Salem. Callum. Ryland. Even Ezra.

Ash waltzed back to the throng of alien creatures in the doorway, now frothing from their distended, grotesque mouths. "This is just nature. We all do what we have to do to survive."

"If that's what it takes to survive, then you don't deserve to."

"Maybe not. It's too bad, you know. I liked you." Ash sighed and positioned herself in front of the heaving horde. "But you're the one who has to die."

A cloud of darkness boiled at the Atrium's precipice, obscuring Ash from view. It rushed forward in a whipping cold wind. The sound of Others swarming grew louder. A buzzing Calay normally only heard in her mind when she was connected to the hive. She gasped, realizing this was what she'd been shown. The journey through the forest before finding Tess, when Elora had urged her to come home. The naked embrace of the pods when she'd traveled to the starship. This was that place. Only instead of that lovely balanced, ethereal feeling Calay had always felt, this was something different. Something sinister. Something worse.

Someone screamed to the left. A loud thump and wet tearing sound echoed to the right.

This was it.

"Now!" Calay yelled.

With a single click, the firehoses gushed on, sending a barrage of water into the sticky, grey murkiness clouding the air. Calay almost wished it hadn't.

To her horror, she saw it'd saved the lives of those closest together as the creatures dove away from the stream, but put those on the edges at risk. The alien hell-creatures wasted no time scurrying up the platforms, using the jungle greenery as cover. The glass ceiling shook with their screams. They snapped at people with their barbed-covered legs, tearing at their flesh before ripping them limb from limb. Weapons tumbled down the stairs, followed by entrails or discarded corpses.

The Faceless made quick work of what was left.

Ash was nowhere to be seen.

Callum scrambled across the nearest platform. "Back! Everybody back!"

"Phase Two!" Holden had propped open the back door and was reaching for people, helping them get outside as the Others clawed and maimed their way further in. Several Resistance soldiers were holding the Others off, hacking at them with machetes and makeshift axes.

Something wrenched Calay sideways. It all happened so fast. She was standing, and then she wasn't. She didn't even get the chance to scream. She choked on her own breath, grasping for anything to protect herself.

"Hey, stop! It's me. Calay!" Briar's charcoal eyes were pried wide with fear. "It's me. Are you alright?"

Calay froze, relief flooded her mind. She nodded, unable to speak.

Something visceral and wet slopped overhead.

Briar pulled Calay to her feet. "Come on!"

The floor was slick with dark red blood. Mostly human, Calay thought. Black drops peppered throughout. A little alien, too.

Her mind reeled. She had to do something. But what?

Somewhere in the distance she heard someone shouting, "Phase Four. Fire!" It seemed Calay had missed the call for Phase Three; maybe escape was no longer an option.

Calay grasped for the lighter in her back pocket, but it wasn't there. She checked the other. Her heart plummeted. It was gone. Her one job, and she'd fucked it up.

This was her plan. Her responsibility. Most of the people had made it out, but without the big bang, life wasn't going to be possible. The Others would simply follow them out the back door and kill them all.

Everyone was going to die because of her.

Just as Ash predicted.

And Ezra.

And Tess.

Calay had failed them. She shuddered and dropped to her knees in the chaos, tears surging down her cheeks.

Max curled under her arm, baring his teeth, ready to attack the nearest threats.

Briar fell beside Calay, pulled her face into her palms.

"Go!" Calay wailed. She thrust Max's collar into Briar's hands. "Go now!"

Briar's frantic tears mirrored her own. "Not without you!"

"If I stay you'll have more of a chance."

"Our chances are up, Calay."

"Not quite." A deep voice resounded from above. Jacob's wide hands grabbed Calay by the forearms and he heaved her to her feet. "One more."

"What are you talking about?" Calay cried.

"I've bought you some time, but it won't take Ash long to repair herself. You have to go now."

"I can't go."

"Yes you can," Briar sobbed.

Calay's gaze darted between Briar and Jacob. "They'll be on us in... seconds. Minutes? Hours? We'll never know how much time we have left and the Resistance—all of you—will have a lot more if I'm not with you."

"Not if I can help it." Jacob produced the missing lighter.

Calay's eyes grew wide, her mouth, dry. "You took it?"

"I knew you'd sacrifice yourself for them, and I couldn't let you do that."

Calay reeled that they were still going through this. After all these months. "You don't get to decide that for me, Jacob!"

"You're right. I don't." Jacob levelled his gaze at Calay and released her arms. "You do."

"What? You want me to choose you to die? Like, actually?" Calay's heart cracked in two.

Jacob grinned. "Not like you haven't already done it before."

"That was different!" Calay shrieked and grabbed Jacob by the lapels on his shirt. "I was angry with you. I wanted you to pay for what you did to me. The pain you caused me. But I had no right to ask that of you. Of anybody."

"Yes you did." Jacob grasped her hands in his. "This is my fault. All of it. The lies. The half-truths. The invasion, for fuck's sake. I'll never regret having met you, Calay. Our time together was the best months of my life. Without you, my universe is darkness and death. You were my light, and I have a brief window to offer you the same gift. A renewal."

"This is an impossible decision." Calay shattered into a million tiny pieces with each syllable. "You've put me in an impossible place."

"I know, and I'm sorry. I see now we should never have come here. My species is parasitic. All we do is consume and destroy. You were right—we don't deserve to live."

Calay swiped at the tears clinging to her chin. "I can't have another death on my hands."

"You won't. In a few minutes, you'll have dozens of lives. A planet of living, breathing, thriving creatures. I can end this and you'll be able to rebuild."

Calay's shoulders shuddered under her sobs. The growing tremors in the Earth's crust. Another earthquake was rumbling beneath them, but the very fabric of her universe was shaking so hard she barely noticed.

Jacob pressed his lips together and wrapped his strong arms around her. She didn't stop him. His breath was familiar and warm against her hair.

"I just wanted somewhere to belong. To call home," she said.

"You've found it." Jacob squeezed her one final time. "You have to be willing to let go of the old to let in the new. This is the cost, Calay. It's always been the cost."

Calay pulled out of Jacob's arms. Her gaze met his. There was no deception in Jacob's face. Not a hint of manipulation. Calay swallowed, realizing he meant it. She could resist and say no. She could turn him away if she wanted. Or she could finally take control of her future and let her past end here.

"Thank you," she whispered.

Jacob winked, but the humor didn't reach his eyes. "I started this by coming here. I'm going to end it now. This never should have been your fight. Get your people to safety."

A dark buzzing filled Calay's brain. She winced at the sharp pain of it. The aching lust. The sound of Ash's voice, tucked between the folds of her mind.

Jacob's head whipped the opposite direction, back toward the double front doors that now barely hung by their hinges. "I'll hold her off. If there's one thing that gets under Ash's skin more than you, it's me."

"Jacob…" Calay's voice broke. Fear poured into her heart like a sieve.

Jacob flicked the lighter to Calay and nodded. "Go."

The warmth of Briar's arm fell across Calay's shoulders as they retreated into the haze. They'd reached the back door. The one she'd run through only days before when she found out Jacob had let himself be caught. She couldn't help but wonder if he'd known then that this day was coming. He'd said this had always been the cost, so maybe, somewhere deep down, he had. The fear that death was always looming, thirsty and waiting, was no way to live. Calay didn't think it was a good way to die, either. But he'd made his choice, and she'd made hers.

She squatted against the frame and brought the tip of the lighter down to the gasoline soaked concrete. Max sniffed it and whined. Once she clicked the little red button, there'd be no going back. There wouldn't even be anything to go back to. She and Briar would have a few moments to get clear of the building and then it would all be over.

Gone.

A tension knotted deep inside Calay unraveled.

This was hers. It was all of theirs.

The end of something terrible and beginning of…something else.

A rush of freedom wound its way through Calay's fingers, and she realized with one single motion she could relieve herself of the weight of this burden.

She held her breath. Closed her eyes. Clicked the switch on the lighter.

In a sudden and furious woosh, flames licked the floor. The platforms rising inside the Atrium, blocking the exits. The palm trees and twinkle lights. It swirled around the barrels at the center, the power within begging to be released.

Between them, stood Jacob and Ash, monstrous and half-transformed.

Lurking beyond the flames, dodging the growing fire, were the shapes of more Others than she could count. Dozens of them, if not hundreds.

The plan was working.

Calay refused to look away. In the end, Jacob had honored the truth of who she was. She wanted to do the same. She lingered a moment, but only one. There wasn't time for longer. She, Briar, and Max turned and stumbled across the frozen ground, making a line for the makeshift hole the Resistance had cut in the fence.

All around them, bodies littered the yard. Some human, some not. So it hadn't been an outright slaughter after all. Some of her people had survived long enough to take a lot of the Others out.

Calay searched their faces as she ran and tried to commit them to memory. They'd all lost people along the way. Many of them were no different from her—they had no one left to miss them once they were gone. The least she could do was remember them in her dreams.

They reached the tree line as Ash's mangled screams echoed behind them. Calay allowed Salem and Callum to pull her into the shaded cover of the forest. A dozen or so people were huddled together, gasping. When Calay turned, she dropped to her knees and stared in horror at the reflection of flames against the dome, and monstrous shadows fighting against the snow packed ground.

It took barely a blink for her to see Jacob was outnumbered.

It didn't matter, Calay thought, because any second now...

A sudden boom sent Calay flying backward. She landed several feet away and without breath. Stars danced across her eyes from the impact. She thought they looked familiar, like she'd seen them before. But they floated away before she could be sure. Her vision swam. Then it became light again. Blindingly so. She fell into a state somewhere between consciousness and not.

When she finally came to, the first twinkling stars were winking down at her from a darkening blue sky. Her back ached, and the snow had melted and her clothes had grown cold and wet, but she was alive.

At least, she thought she was alive.

Someone was shouting.

With each echo, the residual pounding in her head thumped like a drum.

Yes, she was definitely alive.

She ignored the stiffness in her joints as best she could and rolled forward, forcing herself to sit. Curled beside her were Briar and Max, the weight of them comforting and warm against her legs.

It would have been cozy if it they hadn't almost just died.

Calay's heart thudded against her chest. She whipped her head up and peered across the wintery landscape.

Part of her didn't want to see what was left. Like it might make it real. There was no way he would have survived that blast. Even if he did, the water backups would have finished him off. Calay had to admit that was probably overkill in the grand scheme of things, but she'd rather the Others be extra dead than under.

She squinted, trying to make sense of what she was seeing. She rubbed her eyes, tried again. When it finally came into focus, something snapped inside her. Sweat broke out over her skin, despite the cold.

She'd wanted the Others gone, and she'd gotten it.

It wasn't just the Atrium that had been destroyed. It was the other buildings too. The explosion must have blasted a hole in the nearest one —maybe a few—and the fire spread from there. Everywhere she looked, Calay counted one gutted building after another.

Resistance soldiers were scouring for supplies, trying to pull what they could from the wreckage. It didn't look like much. If it hadn't been for the enormous field between them and what had effectively been an IED, she and the other survivors would have been dead, too.

"Oh my god," she coughed.

"Hey." Briar stirred. "What's going on?"

"We made it." Calay swallowed, her throat swollen and sore.

Briar grasped at her ribs. "Ouch."

Calay eased Briar to sit. "Careful."

Briar winced. "Feels like I broke something."

Calay cupped her hands over her knees and bowed her head between her legs, staunching a wave of nausea. "A few broken bones looks like the least of our worries."

"Holy shit." Briar gaped. "What happened?"

"I think we might have overshot the landing."

"Worth it, as long as those things are dead."

"Right." Calay nodded, her eyes ached for tears that wouldn't come.

"Calay." Briar waited for Calay to look at her. When Calay finally did, Briar held her gaze strong. "You did the right thing."

"He died because of me."

"And a whole planet was destroyed because of him. Millions of people."

Calay's fists clenched at the memory of her conversation with Jacob in the holding cell. "I said something similar to him not too long ago."

"So you see? You know it. You just don't know you know it. Not in here." Briar exhaled and leaned close, resting her hand over Calay's thumping heart. "But you will. This is what you wanted, wasn't it? What Tess wanted?"

Calay opened her mouth to agree, but then thought better of it. That might have been what started this journey, but it wasn't what ended it. What Calay wanted was more complicated than that. She wasn't ready to explain, though. Wasn't even sure she fully understood it. Instead, she gripped the bark of a nearby birch tree with both hands and pulled herself to stand.

In the distance, Callum was prying open one of the kitchen fridges with an piece of rebar. Salem seemed to be helping, rather ineffectually. She waved. Calay smiled broadly, even though she didn't feel it, and waved back.

"She's awoken." Holden hobbled through the cut in the fence toward the two women. They raised their hand to Calay's forehead. "Glad to see you decided to finally join us."

"How long have I been out?"

"Not long enough to worry too much." Holden sighed. "Long enough to get out of clean up duty for the day."

Briar peered skyward. "It'll be dark soon."

Holden followed her gaze. "It will, and we don't have a proper place to shelter for the night. It's going to get cold if it stays clear like this."

"Maybe we can wish ourselves somewhere warm." Calay exhaled. Her breath pooled in a brief cloud.

"I've had enough stars for one lifetime." Briar shivered. "They can keep their damn wishes."

"It's a good thing we have a lot of shit to burn," Ezra muttered, approaching. Max stretched and wagged his tail, trotting over to meet him.

"Is that such a good idea out in the open like this?" Calay wrapped her arms around herself. "What if the Others come?"

Ezra scoffed. "What Others? There hasn't been an orb flyby in hours. Don't you think if they were coming, they'd be here already?"

"Can you...feel any of them? Like you did before?" Briar asked.

"I dunno," Calay said. "If I try to connect, it might send a signal."

"After all we've been through, it'd be a pity to be ambushed by something we could have prevented. I think it's worth the risk," Holden said softly.

Calay remained silent. She closed her eyes. Stilled what she could of her already fried nerves. She tried to focus her attention inward, as Jacob had taught her. She breathed slowly, one long breath in, one long breath out. She opened her mind to the buzzing of the hive mind. The energetic vibration. The strings of the whole universe.

Calay shook her head. "I have nothing."

"Calay." Briar rested a hand on her shoulder. "That's a good thing."

It took Calay a moment to realize Briar was right. Still, she'd seen enough to know this wasn't over. Not by a mile. "There'll be more. Eventually. There's no way we got them all."

"Even after your deep space pyrotechnics?" Ezra smirked.

Calay couldn't tell if he was showing appreciation or contempt. She shrugged. "We've lost everything. We have nothing. We're in more danger than ever."

"Maybe so." Briar blinked at Calay from behind her long, dark lashes. "But I heard someone very brilliant once say we could survive as long as we were together."

Calay grinned, despite the fear thrumming through her veins. She laced their fingers together.

Ezra ran a hand over his beard. "Look, we've always known water was useful for our protection. We can continue to use the natural elements of our planet to our advantage. Only now, with you, we'll have like an advanced warning system."

"You're saying I can stay?"

"I'm saying I'm willing to consider it."

"That's progress." Calay nodded, her mind already circulating on the possibilities for their future. She shifted her weight to the other foot and thrust her hands on her hips. "You know, there are others like me. We can find them. Grow our numbers."

"Don't get ahead of yourself," Ezra muttered, but the glimmer of a smile crept onto his lips.

"We'll need people. Their help." Calay gestured to the compound remains. "We can't just go around blowing up the entire planet every time the Others come for us."

"Why not?"

"I don't think we'll have to." Briar pointed, her attention pulled toward deeper into the tree line. "At least not for long."

Calay squinted over her shoulder and almost gasped.

Beneath the branches of a fragrant evergreen was a small patch of mushrooms.

One that hadn't been singed by fire. Or frozen in the harsh cold. The snow around it had melted.

Calay rushed to it. She dropped to her knees. She brought the tips of her fingers to the dirt. Her mouth fell slack, and she shook her head in disbelief. She dragged her thumb against the soft earth again for good measure, before settling on the heart tattoo on her wrist. It had finally stopped hurting. Maybe in time, her actual heart would, too.

"Impossible." Ezra mouth-breathed over their shoulders.

"It's not impossible." Calay pulled herself up and turned to him. "Don't you see?"

Ezra frowned, his eyes darkened. He shook his head and crossed his arms.

Calay brightened. "It was only a couple hours ago we thought we were going to starve to death. We thought everything was frozen and dead."

"What does that have to do with us not blowing up the Others?"

"Well..." Briar slid her arm through Ezra's and smiled in reassurance. "Maybe nothing. But maybe everything."

Ezra cleared his throat but didn't shake Briar off. "Clear as mud, thanks."

"The Others are parasites, and we just killed a fuck ton of them. I think we're already making a difference."

Ezra gaped. "I don't buy that."

Holden laughed. "Aliens from another galaxy invaded our planet and destroyed everything we ever built, mutated into weird zombie things—Calay's half-alien for Christ sake—and you find the hardest part of all of that to believe is the Earth wants to regrow?"

Ezra scuffed his boot against the snow. "I'm just saying it's a little fast."

"It is fast, and I believe that's how badly the Earth wants this. We all do. You guys, I know it sounds crazy, but Briar's right, what part of the last five years hasn't been insane? Maybe it's our collective energy or just a normal biological process, but the planet is already healing." Calay let her gaze linger on the small patch of green. "She's on our side."

"If we just give her a chance," Briar said.

"I still don't get it." Ezra's mouth turned down at the sides.

A rush of warmth filled Calay from somewhere deep inside. An awareness she was only beginning to understand. She let the gentle feeling rush across her limbs, hold her. Max pressed himself against her side, sniffing the damp pine needles where the snow once was. His cold snoot nosed her cheek. She nosed him back.

"She will provide everything we need if we just work with her. With each other. If we can pull ourselves together, we won't need to cause her any more damage to beat the Others. We'll have the full power of Mother Nature behind us."

"And maybe a few weapons." A glint twinkled behind Briar's eyes as she nudged Ezra.

Ezra mulled over their words, a low grumble unfurling from his throat. "I'm not saying that's not a nice idea…"

For once, the fear in Calay's mind relented. While she knew they had a long road ahead of them, she allowed a small feeling of peace to nestle somewhere inside her. One that would later take root and grow.

The corner of her mouth curved up.

"No, it's life."

Ezra pouted, sucked in a deep breath. "Whatever, sounds a little preachy to me."

"Maybe it is." Calay pressed herself to stand and met his gaze. "But maybe that's what we need right now."

Holden adjusted the bent frame of their glasses, the one lens cracked. "A little hope never hurt anybody,"

"Just what the doctor ordered." Briar pulled herself taller.

They all laughed. All of them except Calay. Her attention had drifted back to where the Atrium used to be. The feel of a hand on her shoulder startled her.

Briar's eyes were gentle. "Hey, we're going to be alright."

"I know. I just don't know *how* we're going to be alright." Calay pressed her lips together. "Guess we're just going to have to trust that things will work out."

"That's what I've been sayin'."

Calay wanted to believe. She really did.

"I need a minute." Calay lifted Briar's soot-marred hand to her lips and kissed it. "Do you mind?"

Heat flared in Briar's eyes. "Only if you promise there's more where that came from."

"I swear."

Calay trudged across the yard. She passed Salem and Callum, hugging them both before moving on. Drawn to the last place she'd seen him, like a wildflower to sunshine.

Black scorch lines marked where the barricade of barrels exploded. The snow was gone. The glass ceiling of the dome, too. Melted, most likely. There was no sign of Jacob.

There was nothing left but scraps of metal. Shards of her heart. And a wide open future, ripe with possibilities.

Five years ago the Others stole everything from her. Levelled her, ripped her apart, and smashed her to bits. That was then. This was now. She'd changed. Never in a million years could she have seen this evolution coming. The Others' invasion, Tess's betrayal, and Jacob's dishonesty and manipulations were the catalyst for Calay's transformation, but they didn't get all the credit. Those events broke Calay; they destroyed her. But she was the one who'd gathered the scraps, and piece by fragile piece, built herself back up.

That woman she was when everything began wasn't here anymore.

She was dead.

In her place, someone stronger. Someone who trusted the stars—the light—inside herself. Someone who knew the only real thing was survival.

And love.

Unable to resist, Calay sank to her knees. She pressed her palms against the cold concrete and let it seep into them. She listened.

The buzzing was gone. The hum of the hive mind all but erased from her memory. It was silent.

A screech cut through the air.

Calay stiffened, her heart quickened. She turned slowly around and froze, wishing she'd thought to bring a pistol with her.

"Easy!" someone called from beyond the blast zone.

Calay exhaled, realizing it was the community coming together. Prying apart layers of debris. Salvaging what they could.

Her hands were empty, but her heart was somehow, slowly, being filled back up. Something about the scene reminded Calay of that first day. The one when the Others arrived and she and Tess's world—their apartment—was turned upside down. The difference then was they'd been grieving their loss. The people here now, they were preparing to move on—reimagining what they might gain.

If only she could do the same.

She shuddered, knowing her journey had only begun. She allowed herself to sit in Jacob's absence. To feel the clarity of mind that came without his and the Others' presence. Calay couldn't help but wonder if this lightness would remain in the days to come. The nights. The many, many months of fighting that lay ahead of them. She was going to have to tap into the hive mind sooner or later. To alert the Resistance to an imminent attack, and to find others like her.

They were intertwined in ways she was only beginning to understand and was wholly unprepared for the relief she felt now that they were gone. The despair too. It was a breath of fresh air and suffocation all in the same moment.

For the first time in a long time—maybe for the first time ever in her life—she was free.

Thank you for reading! Did you enjoy? Please add your review because nothing helps an author more and encourages readers to take a chance on a book than a review.

And don't miss more from Kristy Gardner coming soon! Until then read LOVE AT 20,000 LEAGUES by City Owl Author, Lizzy Gayle. Turn the page for a sneak peek!

Also be sure to sign up for the City Owl Press newsletter to receive notice of all book releases!

SNEAK PEEK OF LOVE AT 20,000 LEAGUES

BY LIZZY GAYLE

I'd never felt so vulnerable. The ocean closed above me, swallowing the shuttle into a suffocating vastness that made me itch to claw at the 360-degree windows. Obviously, that would have been useless, but it was hard to turn away from the unending view. So I hugged myself in an attempt to stifle my panicked urges and found a seat in the circular back-to-back rows of the luxury pod.

Not only were there thousands upon thousands of tons of water pressing in on us, but now that it was too late to change my mind, a million reasons not to go raced through my brain. The faster we accelerated toward the bottom, the less convincing my reasons for coming felt. The engineer in me studied every rivet, weld, and seal and found them flawless—beautifully designed actually—but that did little to sooth my near-panicked emotional state.

The other fifty people onboard crowded close to the impossibly thin AC glass, gawking and chattering like they were viewing the Grand Canyon for the first time and not an endless darkness illuminated by the blue glow that caught the occasional school of silver herring. The new technology that allowed such a thin barrier had been thoroughly tested over the years, but that didn't mean I had to like it. Proven or not, I couldn't help but long for the days when glass for underwater vessels had been four to six inches thick. My father and Jackson stood front and center with the other sheeple, smiling like they hadn't a care in the world, like we didn't just leave Mom, weak and battered by chemo, all alone on the surface.

Her unnaturally thin face was all I saw behind her smile, the smooth skin of her scalp visible through the woven texture of her large brimmed hat.

"I need you to go," she'd said for the fourteenth time, framed by the sun like an angel with a halo.

She'd finally convinced me with her crazy, characteristically unselfish wish that I play nice with Dad and the woman he'd cheated on her with.

"Excuse me, Miss Meadows, but you look a bit peaked."

I stared up into the plastic face of Dr. Candice Lawry, chief operating officer and artificial intelligence guru of Bennet Systems. *Wonderful.*

Candice always looked like she swallowed something horrible but was trying to smile through it and not let on. I suspected it had something to do with being as high ranking as one can get inside Bennet Systems, yet not being a complete insider, aka literal part of the disfunction that was the Bennet family.

"Thanks," I said, taking the hydropod she held out to me in the hopes it would be enough to send her on her way.

"Your profile shows you are at an increased risk for DSI," she said, sitting on the edge of the seat beside me and crossing her long legs.

"Depth sensitivity illness is a made-up term to excuse the psychological effects of being crushed beneath a million tons of ocean water," I said, taking a sip from the malleable pod she'd handed me. A genius invention, the bubble-shaped object held the perfect amount of electrolyte-enhanced water, and when it was finished the thin skin remaining could be swallowed as well.

She smirked. "I'll let that comment go, considering the symptoms include lowered inhibitions and heightened anger."

I took another swig, not wanting to feed into it. She leaned in, elbows perched on knees, glassy green eyes unnervingly close as she tapped her thumb and finger together like she had an invisible castanet.

"Let's not have any issues that might spoil this demo trip for anyone. If you feel like you can't control yourself, there's always the option of stasis until it's time to leave."

Did she just threaten to put me to sleep for a month in a box if I didn't behave?

She rose while I remained speechless and cleared her throat to get the attention of the fourteen other families. Bennet Systems, or BS as I lovingly referred to them, was all about family. Frankly, to me, it was more like a cult that kept everyone close enough to monitor. As Candice warned, those who misbehaved were dealt with.

"Welcome!" she chirped in a fake voice that sounded like an animatronic gone wild. "And congratulations on reaching this milestone. You will be the first people to enjoy the new luxury resort, Paradise Atlantis."

She paused for applause.

"We at Bennet Systems are thrilled to be able to offer our very own employees and their families this opportunity before opening our doors to the public. You've worked hard to make this happen, and we extend all the finest luxury to each of you in thanks. You will experience AI like never before as all of your needs are met, and hopefully exceeded, by our artificial staff members. If there's anything you need, just press one of the silver call buttons located throughout the grounds and buildings, and you will be showered with assistance. Enjoy the ride, we should be docking in less than an hour."

Everyone erupted into more applause and chatter as Candice waited, clearly not finished.

"One last surprise. We are not the only ones spending a month on Paradise Atlantis."

A hush fell over the shuttle as people began to pay attention.

"The Bennets have decided to join us. Mrs. Bennet wants you to know that you are all part of her extended family."

With this information, Miss COO disappeared into the crowd, which seemed to swallow her whole.

The entire Bennet clan? For a month? Trapped down beneath the waves with us? My mind immediately went to the only Bennet I'd ever been interested in meeting, Mason. My mouth dried up despite my hydropod. I'd never been able to string two words together around him. One look at his sparkling eyes or glorious physique, and I was destined to become a tongue-tied adolescent all over again.

Pull it together, Sam, I told myself, tightening my ponytail. I needed to focus, for shit's sake. I was twenty-six years old and had a master's of engineering in Artificial Intelligence from MIT. I'd be starting work on my doctorate once Mom was healthy again. Not only did I not have time for a man, Adonis-like or not, but I did not have time for frivolities while Mom suffered.

I would simply tour the gallery as often as possible, inspect what I could about the engineering while avoiding certain people, and stay in my room the rest of the time. I closed my eyes and leaned my head back, seeing no reason to keep them open and stare at the dark beyond. Planning would keep me focused on the right things.

"At least somebody here isn't ogling a window with a view of nothing," said a deep voice to my right.

My eyes popped open and took in the face of the dark, handsome stranger. His deep brown eyes reminded me of the woods above land. Thick hair framed his face and carefully trimmed beard.

"Travis Gould." He held out a large hand to shake.

It was warm, but calloused, and he didn't hold back on the strength of the welcome.

"Samantha Meadows," I said. "What department are you in?"

He scoffed. "None. I refused the work study. My parents, unfortunately, did not. My dad is head of Interior Design, and my mom is the main vital-systems engineer."

I nodded. Bennet Systems notoriously hired females for lead science roles. With the exclusion of my father of course, since he and my mother met Mrs. Bennet back in college. He'd been a fixture since the start, which meant the rest of us were as well.

"Why'd you refuse the work study?" I asked, curiosity getting the better of me.

"I will never work for those assholes."

I smiled despite myself. Maybe we had something in common.

"I don't work for them either," I said. "Dragged here with family, same as you."

The shuttle lurched like it'd been hit by a torpedo, and I froze, clutching the armrests of the seat. My head pounded as my blood pressure skyrocketed.

"You okay?" Travis asked, his thick eyebrows furrowing into one as he stared at my white knuckles.

"What was that?" I breathed.

He grinned and pointed toward a giggling group of girls by the glass. They waved and made silly faces at a dolphin that hovered on the other side. The creature appeared to be smiling ear to ear. I was confused for another moment until one girl put her hand on the glass and the dolphin headbutted it, making the whole vessel seesaw.

"What if it breaks the AC glass? Or it knocks us off course?" I asked, staring at the horrible sight. The engineer in me knew it was a ridiculous fear, but the terrified woman in me disagreed.

Travis laughed, bringing my attention back to him. The rest of my blood rushed to my face and down between my legs when he set his hand on mine. I guess not getting laid in over a year had unfortunate effects on my body.

"It's a dolphin, not an enemy submarine. I'm pretty sure even the assholes could've predicted that. In all seriousness though, are you sure you're okay? If you're afraid of the ocean, this is not going to be a pleasant trip."

"Thanks, Captain Obvious. I'm good." I stood up on shaky legs and strode as confidently as possible over to join my father and Jackson. Alyssa was off chatting with Candice, so it was as good a time as any to make a half-assed effort.

"Sammie." Dad held out a hand for me and I took it, forcing a smile. I promised I'd try after all. "Enjoying the view?"

"Jackson sure is," I said, noting my brother's wandering eyes, which were locked onto his newest target, a young woman with the body of a super model, too much of which showed beneath her tangerine romper.

My six-foot-two brother bumped me with his hip, making me stagger.

"Are you eight or twenty-eight?" I asked, downing the remainder of my water and popping the rest in my mouth.

My father's smile was worth it though. The way his eyes crinkled when it was genuine always warmed my heart. If only he'd reserved it for our family and not shared it, first with BS and then Alyssa.

"Stand over here, Little Dragon," Dad said, repositioning me with a clear view of the glass. My heartrate sped up, but he held me tightly from behind, grasping my arms for security.

"Dad, I'm not twelve anymore," I said, making light of his pet name, given because of the way my nostrils flared when I was super angry, like I was about to spit fire.

"You'll always be my baby. Now if you look a bit down and to the left, you'll be able to get a first glimpse. It should come into view any minute, and this is the prime spot. That's why I've been staking it out."

I bit my lip so as not to make a snarky comment. I promised Mom I'd try. I should at least do so for the first day, I supposed.

Within the next thirty seconds or so, a glowing light appeared in the dark waters. As we swooped toward it, the shining bubble seemed to rise from the depths of the Atlantic, revealing a ten-mile-wide snow globe of something out of a 50's futuristic B movie. Emerald green pastures dotted with bright red and yellow blooms punctuated the circular space. In the center of the maze-like perimeter stood a speckled white statue of some sort. Around it, gleaming silver buildings of rounded glass and metal shone beneath what appeared to be...sunlight.

"How?" I asked, unable to take my eyes off the scene. The cheesy brochure I threw in the recycling can upon receipt didn't do it justice.

"They're called nanosuns," Dad said, reading my thoughts. "I developed them myself. They even dim and wane into a moonlight effect at night that follows the actual cycle of the moon."

It was amazing. But I was not admitting that to him. If that's what started his years of absence from our home—from Mom, then I refused to compliment it.

"Please prepare for docking," Candice chirped.

"Prepare?" I said, unable to control the high-pitched way it came out. "Is it dangerous?"

Jackson laughed, no doubt enjoying torturing his sister. It was like we'd gone back in time to elementary school. I shouldn't have been surprised. We hadn't spoken much since he took the job at BS in our father's department, working under him. Better that than in AI with Alyssa. Truthfully speaking, she was closer in age to him than our father.

Youngest woman to ever earn a PhD in Artificial Intelligence from Bennet University, she was the logical choice to take over the position from Candice when she was promoted to the equivalent of second in command four years earlier. That's when the affair started and when Mom's first bout of cancer was diagnosed, which made it that much worse. Before that, we'd all gotten quite good at pretending it was normal for Dad to never be around—always working.

I wondered where Alyssa was. It was entirely possible she was avoiding me. That thought brought a big smile to my face.

"You have nothing to worry about, Little Dragon. Just a formality to announce the docking procedure."

I nodded and leaned back into Dad's chest, allowing myself to feel safe for once. It was almost perfect until I heard Alyssa's voice.

"Oh, I'm so glad you two are getting along!"

I pulled away from my dad and hugged myself, stepping far enough away to make a point without saying it. She didn't seem to notice, though, as she cozied up to him, taking my place in his arms. Her perfect face with her perfect, smooth, dark skin and perfect long lashes, and perfect straight smile lit up as though from within as he rocked her slowly side to side, wrapping his arms around her.

My stomach swam as if the angelfish outside the closest window had crawled inside it.

"Have you enjoyed the ride, Samantha?" she asked, continuing to beam like a bunch of nanosuns.

"Not really," I said. Dad's crinkle smile faded behind her, and I almost regretted speaking the truth.

Before anyone could say anything else, the shuttle lurched slightly. To calm down, I tried to convince myself it was another dolphin. But I soon realized it was the ship slowing for the docking procedure Candice mentioned.

It looked like we were about to smash straight into the giant glass bubble when we came to a full stop and dropped downward like an elevator until the view was replaced by a bright green door that slid open to admit us. Smooth as silk, the shuttle slipped inside and the door closed. The water around us drained through the grated floor and a second door opened, offering an upward slope festooned with marble mermaid and merman statues lining the glowing path.

"Impressed yet, sis?" Jackson asked as the oohing and ahhing crowd around us pushed their way outside.

"Too gaudy for me," I said, feet stuck to the ground.

Jackson narrowed his hazel eyes at me and drew a hand back through his tawny hair as understanding lit his face.

"Come on. I'll help you."

Heat rushed to my pale cheeks. I'd never been able to hide a blush, so instead of arguing I accepted his offered hand. It was better than being stuck in the shuttle for a month. I scanned ahead and caught sight of Travis at the top of the incline. His sharp gaze bored into me, causing a tingle of anticipation to spread throughout my body. And together with my somewhat estranged brother, I moved forward, focused on possibilities I hadn't originally considered, as opposed to the oppressive view.

Don't stop now. Keep reading with your copy of LOVE AT 20,000 LEAGUES by City Owl Author, Lizzy Gayle!

And sign up for the latest news, giveaways, and more from Kristy Gardner here.

Don't miss more from Kristy Gardner coming soon and discover all about her work at kristygardner.com

Until then, discover LOVE AT 20,000 LEAGUES by City Owl Author, Lizzy Gayle!

Paradise Atlantis: The underwater, high tech vacation destination where utopia awaits.

Not for Sam. Not only is she deathly afraid of being submerged under millions of tons of ocean water, she's stuck for an entire month with the people she blames for her family falling apart. Even with the unexpected attention of two sexy men, including her longtime celebrity infatuation, Sam is sure the trip will be a nightmare.

She's both right and wrong. A type of pressure sickness she was unprepared for hits Sam hard, causing both lowered inhibitions and blackouts. When she gives in to her desires, a passionate romance blossoms.

Unfortunately, even this steamy new relationship can't salvage the trip when a saboteur uses the AI to commit murder – murder timed perfectly with Sam's mysterious blackouts. Now Sam must clear her conscience by finding the truth. But is she prepared for what she'll find? Because either she's a killer or she's setting herself up to be next on the growing list of victims.

Please sign up for the City Owl Press newsletter for chances to win

special subscriber-only contests and giveaways as well as receiving information on upcoming releases and special excerpts.

All reviews are **welcome** and **appreciated**. Please consider leaving one on your favorite social media and book buying sites.

For books in the world of romance and speculative fiction that embody Innovation, Creativity, and Affordability, check out City Owl Press at www.cityowlpress.com.

ACKNOWLEDGMENTS

The Broken Stars trilogy began out of unexpressed sadness and suppressed rage. It was written by a woman who'd barely escaped the pits of self-abandonment and narcissistic abuse. These books took root in that pain, and with time and enough sunlight (hot girl hike, anyone?), grew beyond it. I am forever grateful to those who gave *The Stars Inside Us* the time Calay (and I) needed–and the ending she deserved–to make it this far, nine years later. I couldn't have done this without a single one of you.

I'd like to thank my editor, Danielle DeVor, for understanding the darkness in this story and also the light. To my copy editor, Marianne Hull, for making my words make sense and putting up with my relentless use of em dashes and sentence fragments. And to Tina Moss, Yelena Casale, and the teams at City Owl Press and MiblArt for making this book more than the sum of its parts.

To my husband for allowing me to curl inside his ear and relentlessly whisper sweet nothings about monsters and mayhem at the end of the world. Thank you for your patience.

Huge gratitude to my friends, family, beta readers, street team, and fellow authors–the ones who intimately know my deepest, darkest, most embarrassing secrets–that is, I am eternally unable to decipher the difference between past and passed.

To anyone who recommends this book, posts it on social media, stocks it in their bookstore or library, or leaves a rating and review on Goodreads and/or Amazon. Thank you for joining me on this journey. I hope you enjoyed it as much as I have.

To you: Dear Reader...You are the reason I write. I hope this story was worthy of your time, attention, and love. As always, if the stars should align and we're fortunate enough to find ourselves in the same room, please say hello.

ABOUT THE AUTHOR

KRISTY GARDNER is a queer sci-fi, fantasy, and horror writer. She is the author of the *The Broken Stars* series and the award-winning cookbook, *Cooking with Cocktails*. Furnished with degrees in Gender Studies & Sociology, she crafts complex characters who adventure through space, time, and emotional maelstroms questioning what identity – and home – really mean.

When she's not jet-setting words on her laptop, she's chasing stars, mountain adventures, belly laughs, curating playlists for her books, and packing her carry-on for another escape to SE Asia. She resides in Vancouver B.C. with her partner.

kristygardner.com

instagram.com/kristy_gardner
tiktok.com/@kristy_gardner
goodreads.com/kristy_gardner
threads.net/@kristy_gardner

ABOUT THE PUBLISHER

City Owl Press is a cutting edge indie publishing company, bringing the world of romance and speculative fiction to discerning readers.

Escape Your World. Get Lost in Ours!

www.cityowlpress.com

facebook.com/YourCityOwlPress
x.com/cityowlpress
instagram.com/cityowlbooks
pinterest.com/cityowlpress